I0691813

LIGHT up the NIGHT

THREE RIVERS BOOK THREE

New York Times and *USA Today* Bestselling Author

Jasinda Wilder

LIGHT *up the* NIGHT

THREE RIVERS BOOK THREE

THREE RIVERS

LAKE MICHIGAN

MAIN STREET

FIRST STREET

CINEMA

BOOKSTORE

GROCERY

The Cellar

COOPER'S HOLLOW

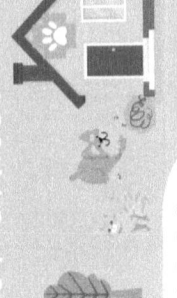

N
W — E
S

1

Cadence

THE DECIDEDLY STRANGE, UNEXPECTEDLY KIND, and improbably handsome stranger, Riley Crowe, fills the cab of his enormous silver pickup truck with his presence. By which I mean his scent—cedar and a spicy-sweet cologne. In addition to his scent overwhelming me, the sheer size of the man intimidates me. As does the fact that he is, very literally, the most attractive human being I have ever laid eyes upon.

He puts me in mind of Superman. Or, perhaps more accurately, Clark Kent without his spectacles.

His jawline rivals the White Cliffs of Dover for sheer rugged, craggy perfection. One could easily imagine God sculpting Riley's jawline out of Carrara marble, tapping away with a chisel and mallet. His eyes are blue, but to stop describing them as merely "blue" is to do them a deep injustice. They are ice chips—in shade, rather than warmth; they are electric blue, the precise shade of a lightning bolt. And, disconcertingly, when he fixes them upon me, I find myself as paralyzed as if I had seized a downed power line with my bare hands.

His hair is black. Jet—obsidian. Glossy. Neatly cut in a classic side-part, short on the sides, and with just enough length on top to allow for volume and style, it reminds me of Cary Grant or Rock Hudson. His is messy at the moment, however, as if he has run his hands through it repeatedly.

The suit he is wearing is at odds with the old but well-cared-for automobile we are riding in—the suit is well-cut, with trim, modern lines, while the truck is aging, battered, and dirty. The faux leather of the dashboard is peeling, the analog gauges are filthy with dust, and the cloth seats are stained and ripped. The radio is on with the volume low enough that I can barely hear it over the engine and the hum of the tires—alternative rock from the late nineties and early two-thousands, based on the recognizable strains of "Glycerine" by Bush. The truck's manual transmission shifter has been replaced by a gigantic silver wrench, the rounded head of which is larger than my fist; the area just beneath the wrench-head is tarnished to a dull grayish color from the oils of his hand and long, repeated use.

The song on the radio fades, and the DJ's voice is a low, inaudible murmur, and then "Like a Stone" by Audioslave comes on.

"Riley?" My voice emerges soft and faint and hesitant: making any kind of request is difficult for me.

He shoots me a look. "Cadence?"

I blink as I process the discrepancy between what he said, how my brain interprets it, and how my study of the nuances of human social behavior interprets it. I arrive at the conclusion that the returned stating of my name as an interrogative; he is asking me what I would like to say.

"May I please adjust the volume of your radio a few degrees louder? I enjoy this song."

He laughs; it is what an author of fiction might term "an amused chuckle." I cannot find an answer to the question of what Riley is laughing about.

He reaches out with his right hand and turns the volume knob three clicks clockwise, and the song becomes fully audible. I feel a smile find its way across my face. "Thank you," I say.

Once he has adjusted the volume, his hand comes to rest on the top of the shifter-wrench, and I cannot help but perform a visual inspection of his hand. Out of curiosity, of course—nothing more. It is a very large hand, with a dusting of black hair across the back. It is a weathered hand, a hard, rough hand. Scars crisscross the knuckles and the backs of the fingers. The nail of his index finger has a black spot near the cuticle—a bruise that will take approximately four to six months to fully grow out and vanish.

Once again, despite the suit, his hands provide evidence that he is a laborer, a wearer of the metaphorical blue collar, rather than white.

The song ends, the DJ performs his obligatory station identification and introduces the next song—"How's It Going To Be" by Third Eye Blind. Frowning, I return the radio to its original volume, sighing in relief.

"Not a fan of that one, huh?" Riley says, grinning at me.

My goodness, that smile is dazzling. White, even, perfect teeth; Dr. Edmondson, my dentist back in Chicago, would be quite impressed.

I shake my head at his question. "No, not at all. I very strongly dislike that song."

He laughs again. "Yeah, I'm with it until he starts that weird, stupid, shouting part." His incredible, Photoshop-blue eyes turn to mine. "You like this kinda music, huh?"

"Yes." I clear my throat, risking another look at him; he is so unbelievably handsome that I can only view him directly for a few moments at a time. Rather like how one cannot look at the sun directly. "I have quite an eclectic taste in music. The alternative rock of the nineties and early two-thousands are a favorite genre. It is what I listen to when performing menial, repetitive, physical tasks, such as cleaning."

He performs a right-hand turn off of the main thoroughfare onto a side street. The street is narrow, with cars parked on our right side. Enormous, spreading oak trees line both sides, the branches forming an arch over the street. The houses are small, mostly one-story ranches from the forties and fifties; most feature detached garages, small front yards, and even smaller porches. It is a cute, quaint neighborhood. The homes, while small, are well-kept, with neat landscaping indicating residents who take pride in their homes and their neighborhood.

Riley makes a left turn onto another street, and then slows to turn left again onto a driveway that leads past the house to the rear of the property and a detached garage.

The house is clad in vertical white siding, which appears new, and a hunter green metal roof, also new in appearance; the garage matches the house. Box shrubs precisely trimmed into neat rectangles line the front of the home beneath the picture window, and a row of bright coneflowers in an array of hues runs the front edge of the landscaping bed. The walkway leading from the sidewalk to the porch is stamped concrete; once upon a time, I believe it would have been ruler-straight, but is now a graceful, serpentine S-shape, the verdant grass carefully edged. The metal roof extends past the home's front wall to create an overhang—another update to the original design—and three new wooden steps lead up the porch. Small pots of daisies frame the steps, and a bench swing made of the same stained wood as the steps hangs from the underside of the porch's roof.

It is a lovely, welcoming home.

Riley presses a button on a remote clipped to his sun visor, and the garage door slides upward, revealing a one-and-a-half-car bay, the ceiling low enough that the truck fits by a margin of less than half an inch. A workbench littered with tools runs the right side of the garage, and the left wall bears racks of tools and implements for yard work, with a battery-operated push mower and a gasoline snowblower in the back left corner. A mountain bike hangs by a hook from its front tire, flat against the rear wall near the mower and snowblower. Other than the workbench, which is messy and disorganized, everything in the garage is neat and orderly.

A bright green-yellow tennis ball hangs by fishing line from the ceiling, and Riley pulls into the garage until the tennis ball bumps against the windshield—putting the nose of the truck a precise distance of six inches from the rear wall. Shutting off the motor, Riley climbs down from the cab, pausing by the rear corner to wait for me.

He is forced to wait because I am moving slowly—I am filled with trepidation. I have never entered the home of an unknown male before, and I do not know what to expect. He claimed that he only wishes to be of assistance, but I am aware of the propensity of males of our species towards dishonesty, especially where their intentions regarding women are concerned. I must be on my guard.

My feet throb, and I most definitely have significant blisters on the heels of both feet from my shoes—white wedge heels to match my dress. I never wear fancy shoes if I can help it, but my visit to the Crenshaws was meant to be a formal visit, and it would have been unseemly to arrive wearing sneakers with this dress. The pain in my feet is another reason for moving so slowly, and I feel even more awkward, uncomfortable, and uncertain than usual.

Riley does not appear to lack patience, however; he smiles kindly as I reach the rear of the truck and pause, waiting for him to lead the way. Halfway from the garage to the house, I trip on a crack in the driveway, and Riley's large, rough, strong hand shoots out, wraps around my bicep, and keeps me on my feet.

Flushed with mortification at my clumsiness, I find it hard to breathe. More so than ever because he once again does not let go of me; instead, his hand slides down my arm and his fingers wrap around mine.

He is holding my hand.

Again.

My pulse slams in my chest and in my ears. My skin burns and tingles.

Yet, I find myself unable to open my hand and release his. This is an extreme oddity. Physical contact—with men in particular—is something I fastidiously avoid.

Riley glares at the crack that tripped me. "Been meanin' to fix that fuckin' crack for months, I just never seem to find the time. Sorry about that. You good?"

I nod once. "Yes. I am unharmed. Only embarrassed."

He gives another of those soft laughs; I wish I could be sure whether he is laughing at me. "Don't be embarrassed, Gorgeous. If anyone should be, it's me. You tripped on *my* crack."

I cannot find a suitable answer for this, so I say nothing.

We reach the side door; a glass storm door rattles as he opens it and props it open with his backside while entering the code into a digital keypad set into the main door. A deadbolt hums as it withdraws, and Riley pushes the door open. We enter a dark kitchen: white cabinets, dark, wide-plank floors, quartz counters, and white-and-gold high-end appliances.

"Your home is lovely," I say, as he flicks on a light switch.

The side door opens to a small landing; to the right is a large laundry room—more white with black and gold accents—and a mudroom, the appliances on the left and a bank of floor-to-ceiling cubbies with built-in seats on the right, and a door to the backyard at the rear. Straight ahead from the side entrance takes you down to the basement—pitch black, so I cannot see whether it is finished or not. Left takes you to the kitchen.

He gives me another dazzling smile. "Thanks. It's been a labor of love, but she's almost done."

I absorb his statement and examine the various possible interpretations. "By labor of love, do you mean that you have performed the labor yourself, out of love? And by she, you refer to the home?"

He looks at me for a moment; likely, he is attempting to figure out why I am so strange. "Yeah, yeah. I'm not as good at this shit as my brother Felix, but I do okay. I think it's turned out alright."

"I do not follow your meaning."

This causes him to frown. "I...um. What?"

"You claim to not be as good at this...stuff...as your brother, but I do not know what stuff you are referring to."

"Oh, uhhh, this." He waves a hand at the kitchen. "Home renovations. Building. My brother Felix is the master at this shit. Walk into one of his houses and you'll get your hair knocked back, they're that fuckin' pimp. Like, just sleek and..." he waves a hand, shaking his head. "All professional and shit."

There is much to his statement I do not quite follow, but I can piece his intent through the utilization of context clues. "If your brother is better than you at home building and renovation, then he must be quite talented indeed. You have done a wonderful job, if you did all the work and design yourself."

He grins—I could be mistaken, and probably am, but it seems like an embarrassed grin. "Eh, it's alright. Thanks, though. It's nice to hear."

I shift my weight from one foot to the other, and cannot hide the wince of pain as I do so. Riley is observant and notices my discomfort. "Your feet hurt like a bitch, huh?" He presses his big, hot hand to the small of my back and nudges me out of the kitchen and into the living room, around the corner; there is a small, round, oak dining table with four chairs in the corner between the kitchen and the living room. "C'mon, sweetheart. Sit. Relax. Lemme see what I've got as far as grub goes."

I frown. "I...I do not wish to seem ungrateful, but I do not think grubs would sit well at the moment. They are rather dense, and far too rich for my system to process on an empty stomach."

Riley stops mid-step, partway back into the kitchen, pivots slowly, and stares at me. "Huh? No, Cadence, not— not *actual* grubs. Grub. Like food?" He blinks rapidly a few times. "And...have you...have you actually *eaten* grubs?"

"Of course I have," I say. "I spent several months providing medical care to tribes in central Africa, where bugs, including grubs, are a staple."

"No shit? What do they taste like?" he asks.

I tilt my head and look up and away, recalling. "Well, it depends on a variety of factors, including but not limited to the type of grub, how it's prepared, and what one pairs it with. My favorite ones are baked on hot stones and have a nutty flavor."

He laughs—amazement, perhaps? Or amusement, or bemusement; I am uncertain. "Well, I ain't got any grubs. One sec while I see what I *do* have."

He leaves me standing in the middle of the living room and returns to the kitchen; I hear the refrigerator opening and closing, cabinets rattling closed. I look around the living room and find it as pleasing as the rest of the home. The same dark, wide-plank floors carry throughout, with white drywall everywhere except a single accent wall behind the large black leather couch—the accent wall features narrow, horizontal shiplap painted a bold French blue. The ceiling is vaulted and trimmed with dark wood to match the floors. There is no television, only a large framed black-and-white photograph of cherry trees in full bloom opposite the accent wall over a long, thin table littered with decorative knick-knacks and a few framed photos of what I assume to be Riley's family and/or friends—the same handful of men are featured in most of the photographs: a large, muscular man with blond hair and facial features which strongly resemble Riley's—most noticeably the intensely pale blue eyes; another blond man, also very attractive, wearing the uniform of a law enforcement officer; there is another attractive man, this one with wild, shaggy, curly black hair, heavy, dark stubble, and dark eyes; last is a giant of a man with bright red hair and a beard so long it's braided, the end of the braid capped with a silver cuff.

"You were supposed to sit down," Riley says behind me, startling me so badly I jump, gasping. Laughing, Riley settles his hands on my shoulders, once again making my pulse hammer crazily. "Whoa, whoa. Sorry, sweetness, didn't mean to scare you. C'mon, take a seat." He guides me to the couch, turns me around, and gently but firmly forces me to sit. He presses a button on the outside of the armrest, and a foot support extends and lifts up under my feet. "Better?"

I close my eyes in relief, sighing. "Yes, thank you." I open my eyes and look at him. "Would you be offended if I remove my shoes?"

"I'll do you one better." He drops to a knee at my feet and slides my shoes off of my feet; he hisses. "Jesus fucks a monkey, Cadence. What the hell is *this* shit?" He shows me my shoe, the inside of which is stained with blood from my blisters.

I blink at him. "That is an offensive statement."

He blinks back. "What is?"

"Your reference to Jesus…erm…fornicating…with a primate."

"You're a church-girl, huh?" he grimaces. "My bad, sorry." He shows my shoe again. "But for real, Cadence. You've just been standing around with your feet in this state? How are you functioning?" With strong but gentle fingers, he lifts my bare foot and examines my heel. "I mean, *damn*, girl. Your feet are shredded to hell. Wait here."

Not wishing to get blood on his nice leather couch, I place my bare feet on the cold wood of the floor and wait as instructed. He returns from the hallway, which I assume leads to the bedrooms and bathrooms, a white metal tin bearing a red cross logo in his hands; he also has a packet of unscented baby wipes, strangely enough.

He perches on the edge of the couch beside me, turns to face me, and pats his knee. "Foot."

I take that to mean he wishes me to put my foot on his leg, and I, shaking with nerves and fear and confusion, do as I am instructed. When he takes my foot in his hand, I jerk at his touch, inhaling sharply.

"Hey, hey," he murmurs, his tone soothing. "I'll be gentle, I promise."

I do not know how to begin explaining my sensory issues, let alone my aversion to being touched, and he is overwhelming me with his enormous size, his intense attractiveness, and his mere proximity. I force myself to breathe and to hold absolutely still, fixing my gaze resolutely on the couch between us so he cannot see—hopefully—that I am fighting an anxiety attack.

He does not seem to notice. He tugs a wipe free of the

package, bringing several with it; he uses the baby wipe to clean the old, dried blood off my heel, and then wipes at my Achilles tendon and the bottom of my foot. His touch is exquisitely gentle, despite the strength and roughness of his hands.

"It has never occurred to me to use baby wipes in this fashion," I say.

He rolls a shoulder. "Use 'em for everything. They're super versatile."

Once both of my feet are cleaned of blood, he opens the first aid kit, hunts for and finds Neosporin, and applies it liberally to my open blisters. Next, he expertly applies large square bandages to the back of each foot, adhered with medical tape.

"There," he says, gently settling my foot on the foot-rest. "Not as good as new, but hopefully a bit better. Best leave those shoes off, though."

I scrutinize his work with a professional eye. "You appear to have experience with minor injuries."

He chuckles. "Doin' the work I do, cuts and shit like that are par for the course. I always end up being the nurse on the job-site." He glances at me, eyes widening. "Oh, shit, you're, like, an actual doctor, aren't you?" He dips his chin at me, which I, perhaps erroneously, interpret as a gesture at my foot, and his work. "I do okay for you, Doc? You can be critical. I won't cry."

"You did quite well. I cannot find anything to criticize." I frown. "If I were to criticize your performance, however, I would like to think I would be kind enough that you would not need to cry."

He shakes his head, snorting quietly in a way that

seems to be laughter. "You're a literal sorta gal, ain'tcha, Cadence?"

I nod. "Yes, quite so."

He laughs yet again—he laughs rather frequently, I am noticing. "You must watch a lot of Downton Abbey or somethin.'"

I frown. "I do not watch television."

"Whaddya know? Me either. Too ADHD to sit around staring at a damn screen."

I feel a frisson of excitement. "You have ADHD?"

He shrugs. "Undiagnosed but pretty sure." He laughs, waves a hand. "I mean, can't sit still for more than a minute or two, can't focus on books or shit like that. I was always in trouble at school for daydreaming and goofin' off." His next laugh is a snort and a head shake that feels self-derogatory. "Good thing for me, I never had to finish school, huh?"

"University degrees are not necessary in order to be successful," I say, intending to be encouraging.

He tips his head to one side. "Yeah, that too."

I frown. "I do not understand what that means."

"Oh, well. I don't have a university degree. But I meant *school*…as in high school." He pats my knee. "I came out here to see how you felt about dino nugs and mozzarella sticks."

I hesitate. "How do I feel about them?"

"Yeah, like, do you like them? Ain't been shoppin' in a while, so I don't have much by way of fresh food, which means frozen bachelor shit is all I got."

I think it through. He obviously cannot mean literal nuggets of dinosaur meat, which is patently impossible— my brain tries to spin me off down a rabbit-trail of wondering what dinosaur meat would taste like. Therefore, he must be referring to chicken nuggets in the shape of dinosaurs.

"I enjoy both chicken nuggets and mozzarella sticks," I tell him. "Thank you."

"Cool. Comin' right up." He does not rise to his feet immediately, however. "You are one tough cookie, Cadence. I've had some gnarly fuckin' blisters, but those were the worst I've ever seen." He returns to the kitchen without waiting for my reply—not that I had one.

Gnarly—a fun, enjoyable word that puts me in mind of a California surfer with dried brine in his hair.

Gnarly.

I have gnarly blisters.

I wait for Riley to return and spend the time letting my mind wander from the word "gnarly" to dinosaur meat, to my bizarrely intense response to physical contact with Riley. With other people—men in particular— who have made contact with me, my response is to recoil, sometimes rather violently. Yet with Riley, I do not recoil. I am uncertain if this means I enjoy the contact or not, but it is certainly unusual.

Before I can wander too far down that rabbit hole of thought, Riley enters the living room with a single red, square ceramic plate piled high with chicken nuggets and mozzarella sticks. He also has two small bowls, one filled with ketchup, the other with ranch.

"Here we go," he says, setting the plate and bowls on the low wood coffee table. "Now, drinks. I've got Diet Coke, beer, water, and a bottle of Crown Royal."

"I believe ice water would suffice, thank you, Riley."

"Boring! Two beers, you say? Comin' up."

"No, I said—"

He's gone already, though. I hear the fridge open and close, and then the crack-hiss of beer tops being wrenched off. He appears with two green bottles and hands me one. "Here you go."

I stare at the proffered bottle. "I…I have never had alcohol."

"Uh, is that, like, a religious thing?"

I shake my head. "Not exactly. It is a personal choice influenced both by my spiritual upbringing and by my own convictions."

He pulls the bottle away, clutching them both in his hand. "My bad. Hope I didn't offend you." He tugs a bottle of Spring Mountain from his back pocket, flips it dexterously, and catches it, offering it to me. "Water it is."

I do not take the bottle, however. "I do admit to a certain curiosity regarding the popularity of alcoholic beverages. Beer in particular has existed in the historical record since the days of Ur."

"Er? Er what?"

I giggle at his misunderstanding. "Ur. The Mesopotamian city, one of the first, if not *the* first cities in human record. Jericho and Gobileki Tepe are also contenders for that particular crown."

"Oh." He makes a face—impressed? "Beer is that old, huh?"

"Oh yes. Some of the oldest writings are recipes and invoices for beer."

"No shit?" He extends the beer to me. "Well, try it. I won't tell no one. 'Sides, one beer ain't gonna get you drunk."

Hesitantly, I take the sweating glass bottle. Sniff the opening—yeast, malt, and the sourness of fermentation.

I take a sip. Shock rockets through me at the assault of flavors and textures, and I cough. "My goodness." I cover my mouth with the back of my wrist and cough again. "I am unsure how I feel about that."

He laughs. "Well, like my dad told me when I tried it for the first time, it's an acquired taste. Don't like it, don't feel obligated to finish it." He places the water bottle on the table beside my beer bottle.

"One must always give new experiences a minimum of three attempts," I say. "I shall try a few more sips." I gesture at the plate of food. "I have two questions."

I wait for him to reply, and he just frowns at me after a moment. When I continue to wait for his reply, he frowns at me. "Cadence?"

"You are supposed to ask me what the questions are before I ask them."

He seems puzzled by this. "Oh, uh, yeah. Right. What are the questions?"

"One, is someone else joining us?"

He shakes his head slowly. "No. Why?"

"Because that is far too much food for two people. In case you had not noticed, I am a rather small woman. I do not eat very much."

He chuckles. "I ain't one to assume things, generally speaking. I've known some pretty tiny chicks who can put away a shit-ton of food." He means human females, not actual chicks, I assume. "And two?"

"We are eating here? Not at the dining room table?"

He looks at the table, which is littered with mail, stacks of papers, a mug of pens, and an open laptop. "I eat my meals on the couch, usually. The table is my home office." He turns his gaze on me, then. "You, uh...you prefer a more formal dining situation? I could clean it off, if you like."

"Um, no. Thank you. That will not be necessary. I have never eaten dinner on a couch before."

He laughs. "God, you're weird."

I place the nugget I just picked up back on the plate, heart plummeting into my stomach, or so it feels. "I...yes, I suppose I am." I am always aware of how strange I seem to neurotypicals.

He must hear something in my tone, because he looks at me rather sharply. "Cadence, that wasn't an insult. In case you hadn't noticed, I'm kind of an odd guy myself."

"Your version of weird and my version of weird are entirely dissimilar."

He peers at me, his eyes searching my face. "I upset you, huh?"

"I am well aware that I am very unusual. People have taken great pains throughout my life to point it out to me, as if I am unaware of my own oddity."

"So...yes." He ducks his head, trying to make eye contact with me. For his sake, I force myself to endure approximately ten seconds of eye contact. "I apologize, Cadence. I really didn't mean to hurt your feelings."

I cannot help a smile—he sounds genuinely remorseful. "You are forgiven."

"So...we cool?"

I nod. "Yes. We are quite cool."

He cackles. "Quite cool, she says. You're a fuckin' hoot, girl. Never met anyone like you."

"A hoot?" I shake my head. "I am not an owl."

This produces another bemused, amused look from Riley. "No, I...interesting. Funny. Entertaining."

"Oh. I see."

"Quite cool." He holds his fist toward me; uncertain as to what to do, I grab his fist in my hand and shake it up and down.

For reasons which leave me utterly mystified, this causes Riley to break down in gales of laughter so uproarious he falls backward against the couch.

"Jesus…oh god. Jesus, Cadence. Oh boy." Wiping tears of hilarity from the corners of his eyes, he holds out his fist again. "Gimme your hand—make a fist." I do, and he takes me by the wrist and guides my hand against his so our knuckles tap together. "Like that."

"Oh." I frown at him. "Are you laughing at me?"

"No, god no. Not in a mocking sense, at least. You just…were you raised in a commune or something?"

There is simply no easy or quick way to explain my upbringing. "No."

He seems to be waiting for further explanation, which is not forthcoming. "No. Just no?"

"It is a difficult thing to explain, and I am not at all certain you will understand if I try."

"I see." He lets out a breath. "Well, maybe you can try me, someday. If you wanted to. I've been told I'm actually a pretty good listener."

A sharp note in his tone alerts me to the possibility that I may have offended him. "I did not intend offense."

He grins, waves a hand, "Nah, it's good. I get it. There's a lot I don't understand. One of the super fun perks of never finishing high school."

It takes me a moment to connect his previous statement regarding not finishing school to my insinuation that he would not understand my upbringing. "Oh. Riley, no. I did not mean it in that sense. It is not a matter of you not being able to comprehend it, as if it were too complex a concept. I only meant that my upbringing was rather unusual in a variety of ways."

"Oh."

"May I ask why you did not attend high school?"

He sighs, eating several nuggets in a row before answering. "I, uh…I attended. I just…didn't get to finish."

My sessions with Dr. Murthy provide me with enough understanding of body language that I realize I should not press the line of questioning. He appears physically uncomfortable, which tells me he does not want to discuss this any further.

"I see." It is all I say.

I attend the food, then; I eat triple what I would normally. He and I eat in silence, which is not entirely uncomfortable. There is one mozzarella stick remaining, and he and I both reach for it at the same time. Our fingers brush, and a spark of something intense bolts through me at the contact—so intense is it that I wonder if there was not an actual, literal spark of static electricity.

I jerk my hand away violently and shove it under my thigh. "You may have the last one," I whisper, turning my head away so he cannot see the furious blush on my cheeks; being of pale complexion, blushes show readily, and given my state of extreme innocence and naïveté, I blush easily.

"Hey." His voice is gentle. "Cadence?"

I turn to look at him. "Yes?"

"Open your mouth."

My jaw hinges open before I register the fact that my body obeyed his command automatically. He places the deep-fried cheese stick into my mouth, and I bite down through it. He pulls it away so the cheese stretches out like the wires of a suspension bridge….and then eats the other half. While it is still connected to me.

I freeze, eyes going wide, lungs shuttering closed, as he uses his lips and tongue to draw the string of cheese connecting us to into his mouth—which means his face grows closer and closer, until he is mere inches away, pale eyes wide and big and searching my face. A small, private smile curves the corners of his lips up.

For a wild, terrifying instant, I think he is going to kiss me. Instead, he bites through the cheese and then taps the tip of his nose to mine. "Boop." He says the sound-word in a falsetto voice.

"Boop?" I echo in a normal tone.

He grins. "Yup. Booped your nose."

"I…but…why?"

He shrugs. "Fuck if I know. To be cute?" He grins at me again. "Dunno if you've noticed, but I'm kind of a goofball."

"It has not escaped my notice."

"You don't know what to do with it, do ya?"

I shake my head solemnly. "No. I do not."

"That's cool. No one really does." He removes the plate and heads into the kitchen; I hear the fridge open and close and then the crack-hiss of another bottle opening.

I have only tried the one sip of mine, and take another. Just as shocking, but not…bad. I pause to let my taste buds settle, and then try again. Better. Still a jarring barrage of flavors and textures—the bubbles tickle my mouth and throat, which is why I rarely drink carbonated beverages. But this is different. Soda is too sweet, and I dislike the artificial flavors of canned, flavored, carbonated water. This, however, has promise.

Riley sits beside me once more. "Whoa, hey, guess you like beer after all, huh?"

"What?" I ask.

He points the mouth of his bottle at mine. "Drank half of it while I was in there."

I realize with no little astonishment that he's right. "Oh. I suppose I am discovering a taste for it, yes." I make eye contact with him. "Thank you for your hospitality, Riley. I should not take up any more of your time."

He does not respond immediately. "I mean, I wasn't doin' much anyway. You're cool."

Cool. Like the F-word he uses with such variance and frequency, "cool" seems to have many meanings to him. This usage seems to indicate that I am welcome to stay.

I think.

"I would not like to be an imposition."

"You're not. Promise." He takes a sip from his bottle, the liquid glugging quietly. "Honestly, it's nice having the company."

Curiosity burns. "May I ask you a question?"

"Sure. Shoot."

"What is your job?"

"I was expecting something more personal," he says. "I do demolitions."

"As in with explosives? Implosions and things of that nature?" I ask, a conversational tangent already taking over my brain.

"No, I wish. Boring demolitions, unfortunately. Nothing that cool. I told you my brother Felix builds and renovates houses, right?"

I nod. "Yes, you did."

"Well, with the renovations, we buy an old house that needs to be fixed up. I rip out the interior and clean it up so he can do the updates."

"Oh!" I say. "You flip houses." I sip my beer, finding a certain pleasure in the sourness, now, and the way it commingles with the carbonation and the yeast and the malt. "My former roommate at Harvard flipped houses with her cousin to pay for her degree. Or, rather, to help defray the costs."

Riley coughs, choking. Once he has regained his breath, he gives me a wide-eyed stare, clearing his throat obsessively. "Harvard? You went to *Harvard*?"

I nod. "Yes. Why?"

"Well…I…" he clears his throat again. "Choking on beer sucks, fuck me. Um, so, you graduated high school at fifteen and got your MD from fucking *Harvard*? At *twenty-two*?"

"I am uncertain as to the reason for your shock."

"Because that's fucking *insane*. You're, like, wicked smart, huh?"

"I…" I consider carefully how to phrase this so as to not seem braggadocious. "I have always been…academically advanced, yes."

Riley shakes his head. "So let me get this straight, Cadence. You're crazy smart, you're a freaking certified medical doctor at twenty-four, went to Harvard, did medical missions in Africa…*and* you're a fuckin' smokeshow?" Another head shake. "Man, I am way the hell outta my league with you, Gorgeous."

"I do not know what a smokeshow is, but the rest is accurate, yes. I also do not know what you mean about being out of your league. I do not play sports." I feel my breath catch in my lungs, as it has every time he refers to me as *gorgeous*. "Why do you keep calling me that?"

He arches an eyebrow at me. "Calling you what? Gorgeous?"

"Yes."

A laugh—dry, perhaps sarcastic, although sarcasm is often lost on me. "Um, because you are?" He sips. "Smokeshow is just another way of saying you're fine as hell."

"Fine as hell" is not much clearer to me, but I understand his meaning.

I just do not believe him.

I cock my head and look in his direction. "What do you hope to gain from flattery?"

He laughs again—this time it seems laden with discomfort. "Gain? Jesus, babe, it's not flattery. Well, I mean—I guess it is, but not in the sense of buttering you up for a selfish reason. You're beautiful." He shrugs, makes a face. "Just callin' it like I see it."

He says this utterly shocking, devastating statement with such ease, so offhandedly casual, as if it were the most obvious thing in the world.

"I know a good optometrist," I tell him. "I will provide you with his number."

Silence follows this.

And then Riley cackles, laughing as if I had told some great joke. "Aw, man, Cadence. You're funny. I have perfect vision, I'll have you know. I also happen to be a connoisseur of beautiful women, so my opinion should hold weight." He looks at me expectantly, perhaps waiting for me to join him in laughter. "Whoa, hold up. You *were* joking, weren't you? About the optometrist?"

"I am not well-known for my sense of humor."

His entire demeanor changes, then. He seems to soften. To become warm. He leans toward me. "Good fuckin' god, woman, do you really not know how beautiful you are? How on God's green earth is that even possible?"

"I do not know," I whisper. "Perhaps you are mistaken."

"Not a fuckin' chance."

I look at him, searching the planes and angles of his handsome face. I note the way his eyes seem fixed on my mouth, and I wish I were brave enough to ask what that means.

Alas, I am not, so I languish in humiliating ignorance.

He abruptly shoots to his feet, and his hand scrapes through his hair, messing it up even more. For reasons I cannot begin to fathom, the messier his hair gets, the more attractive I find him. Some silly, immature, irrational part of my brain wants to bury my hands in his hair and make it messier and messier, just to see if there is a direct, linear relationship between the messiness of his hair and the degree of his attractiveness.

It is the thought of an irrational mind, and I push it away.

It is impossible.

He yanks at the knot of his tie, ripping it off and hurling it onto the couch violently, and then unbuttons his shirt with a deep gasp, as if he has been asphyxiating.

"Fuck," he mutters—I get the impression I am not supposed to hear this. "Get a goddamn grip, asshole."

When he turns back to me, even I, with my limited understanding of how the emotions of others show on their faces, can tell he is…distraught. Perhaps "haunted" is the better word. "Let's get you home, huh?"

I swallow hard. "Well, Chicago is home. I am not sure that it is feasible or responsible to leave for Chicago at this time of night."

"Shit, you said that, didn't you? Um, just out of curiosity, what was your plan? If your friends or whoever, the Crenshaws, did pony up the cash for your trip? Where were you going to go?"

"They are friends of my parents. My original plan was to spend the night in their guest room. It was arranged. But, as I said, I very foolishly allowed my emotions to overrule my better sense, and I walked away."

"Those assholes shouldn't have let you. No way in fuck you shoulda been wandering down the highway alone at night like that."

"It was not night when I left, it was late evening."

"Point stands." He remains some distance away from me, as if suddenly unable to handle being in proximity to me, for reasons which are quite murky, as with everything else to do with this utterly perplexing man. "So, look. This time of year, the hotels and motels in town are all booked. I ain't lettin' you wander around by yourself, either. Three Rivers is safe, but crime happens everywhere. You're staying here. I'll take the couch—I've passed out on it many a time. You'll take my bed. Just gimme a minute to change the sheets for you. Sit tight, okay?"

"I am assuredly overstaying my welcome. You have been most hospitable, Riley, but I cannot take your bed."

He comes over to me, drops to his knees in front of me. Rests his hands on my legs, as if he has all the right in the world to touch me, which he does not. Yet, I let him. I cannot breathe when he touches me, yet I let him.

I do not know why.

"Cadence. You assuredly *can* take my bed. You can lock the door—the lock ain't the kind that can be popped easily, either. It's late. You've had what sounds like a hell of a fuckin' day. You'd be doin' me a favor."

I shake my head. "That is irrational. *My* staying with *you* cannot be considered a favor to *you*."

"Sure, it can. If you left, I'd be up all night worrying about you." He squeezes my knees, and I struggle to draw a breath as a chaos of sensations and emotions boils inside me, overwhelming me. "Please stay? You're safe here, I promise."

I examine myself: worn out and exhausted. Aching, agony-riddled feet. Emotionally depleted. Mentally drained.

"There really isn't anywhere else to go?"

He shakes his head. "Not really. Not close, and not at this time of night."

"Very well. I accept your invitation, Riley. Thank you. You are much too kind."

His smile is dazzling. "Baller. Let me get the bed changed for you."

Baller? What on earth does *that* mean?

I have no chance to ask, however, as he disappears down the hallway, leaving me alone with my thoughts.

Which are chaotic, tumultuous, and confused.

2

Riley

I HAVE *GOT* TO BE THE WORLD'S MOST ASTOUNDING dumbfuck.

What could possibly have possessed me to bring this girl back to my house, I can't imagine. Like most dudes, crying chicks short circuit my brain. Turn me into a panicking fucknut.

Like, *Oh god, she's crying! What do I do? Bring her to my house, obviously.*

Raina all but threw herself at me, and I turned her down because I am—say it with me, now—THE WORLD'S MOST ASTOUNDING DUMBFUCK. And then, mere hours later, I bring home a girl who is even more sweet and clean and innocent. I mean, no, I didn't bring her home in *that* sense. For one thing, my home is my haven. My safe space. I don't bring chicks back here. Ever. That's a hard-and-fast rule, one I am even more obsessive about keeping than putting a hat on my bishop before hooking up.

For another, this girl, Cadence, is absolutely, unequivocally untouchable. By me, I mean. She doesn't curse. Has never, until she met my sinful ass, even touched alcohol. She doesn't watch TV. She goes on medical missionary trips to fucking *Africa*. She's devastated because no one will fund her intent to go to South motherfucking Sudan, where a vicious, dangerous civil war is raging. She graduated high school at fifteen and got her MD from goddamned Harvard at twenty-two. Doogie Howser, who?

Yeah, she's…strange. Talks like a Victorian age robot or some shit, and seems to be a walking encyclopedia of literally everything.

But *fuck me,* she's breathtaking.

Her hair is a wild explosion of strawberry blond ringlets that's always in her eyes, though she never seems to notice, never brushes it away, never tosses her head. She has literally picture-perfect posture—ramrod spine, shoulders back, chin up. Even sitting, you could balance a glass of water on her head. She's around five-six or seven. She's delicate, with silky, creamy skin, tiny, clever, restless hands, and the biggest, deepest, greenest eyes I've ever seen.

Her beauty transcends—and yes, I know what the fuck "transcend" means, shut up—her individual features. I can't explain it. There's just this…light, to her. An internal brilliance that takes the angles and curves of her face and transforms them into something wholly angelic.

This is what's going through my brain as I strip my bed of the sheets, wad them up in the fitted sheet, and toss the giant ball of sheets toward the door. After struggling with the fitted sheet for a moment, I finally get the fucking thing on the bed, after which the rest is easy. Fuck fitted sheets. You'd think by this point in our race's technological advancements, we'd have come up with a better alternative to fitted sheets. I settle the giant king-size-plus blanket over the bed, and then fold my grandmother's quilt in half and drape it over the bottom third. I do my best to arrange the pillows into some semblance of order, but I honestly don't make my bed too frequently. Cole, the type-A goody-goody fruitcake, swears by making your bed every morning; he says even if your whole day is one big fuckup, if you made your bed, you've accomplished one thing, and then you get to go home to a neat, made bed. Fuck that. When I crash at the end of a long, frustrating day, I like to wrap up in the blankets like a fluffy mouse's nest. When the bed is made, getting the blankets into the right nest shape takes longer.

I scan my room, making sure there's nothing embarrassing left out. Dirty clothes are in the hamper, and clean clothes are put away. Check the bathroom—fortunately, I just had Mrs. Henshaw over to do a deep clean of the kitchen and bathroom earlier in the week, so it's decently clean.

Satisfied that I've made things as female-palatable as possible, I head back out to the living room. And there's Cadence, perched on the couch like a mannequin in that picture-perfect posture, staring straight ahead with her hands folded demurely on her lap. If I couldn't see her chest rising and falling ever so gently, I'd wonder if she was some sort of super-advanced android from a hundred years in the future.

She doesn't notice me enter; I'm not sure she's even blinking.

"Cadence?" I keep my voice low and quiet, not wanting to stare at her. She doesn't register any reaction, so I approach closer. "Cadence?"

Nothing.

I have to be inside her field of peripheral vision, but still, not a sign that she knows I'm here. I touch her shoulder as softly as I can, keeping my voice quiet. "Cadence?"

She jumps six inches, gasping, clapping a hand to her chest. "Oh! Goodness gracious, Riley. You startled me."

"Goodness gracious, huh?" I echo, laughing and shaking my head. "My grandma used to say that all the time."

"I have a propensity for anachronistic speech patterns and syntax," she says.

"Yeah, no clue what that means," I say. "I did say your name like three times."

"My apologies. I tend to become too lost in my thoughts to the exclusion of all else."

"So, how do I not startle you when you're thinkin' deep thoughts?" I ask.

"With great caution. Approach from the front. Try to catch my gaze." She blushes furiously. "If you have ever attempted to approach a skittish horse, you might understand."

"My buddy Nyx grew up on a farm not far outside town, and they had horses." I don't know why I'm telling her this. "They had this horse, Spook. Nyx's older sister was the type who was always bringin' home birds with broken wings, stray cats with injured legs, malnourished dogs. Well, she found Spook being neglected, bullied the owners into selling him, and brought him home. Only, Spook

was called Spook because he could be spooked by literally anything. And for some reason, that weird-ass fuckin'
horse took a liking to me."

She smiles. "So you have an affinity for weird, easily
spooked creatures."

"Nah, just that one horse."

"And me, it would seem." She yawns, then, a huge,
jaw-cracker of a yawn, stretching her arms overhead and
arching her back.

My eyes, the dirty fucks, fix like laser beams on her
chest as her stretch presses her tits against the neckline of
her dress. Yeah, I'm getting the impression that she's hiding
a pretty damn killer body under that loose, modest, flowy
dress. I drag my eyes away before she ends the yawn, not
wanting to be caught ogling her.

Her moss-and-pine eyes find mine. "I am extraordinarily tired. That walk was woefully ill-advised. I feel stupid for subjecting myself to it so unnecessarily. I should
not have allowed myself to behave so rashly."

"Well, I've got the bed all made up for you. So, you
know, you can crash now."

She smiles at me tiredly. "That would be wonderful.
I have not looked forward to sleeping this much in a very
long time."

I stand up and hold out my hand. "C'mon, I'll show
you."

She just stares at my hand for a moment, and then
tentatively fits her tiny, delicate hand into mine. Allows
me to help her to her feet—I don't miss the wince she
tries to hide, or the way she limps and hobbles a few steps
before willing herself to walk normally. God, she's tough.
Her feet were *destroyed*. If you've never walked that far,

you don't understand what it's like, or the toll it can take on your body.

I lead her by the hand to my room at the end of the hall. She stops just inside and takes it in, studying her surroundings. I try to see it from the perspective of someone who didn't put the floors down and paint the walls: I picked a soothing pale blue for the walls, and instead of harsh can lights in the ceiling, I picked wall-mounted light fixtures in a warm bronze with Edison bulbs. Same floors as throughout, obviously, but I put a big, thick-pile rug under the bed to soften the room a bit. My bed is a sleigh bed, a handmade antique that I restored myself.

"This is very much not what I expected from the bedroom of a single adult male," she says. "It is…cozy. Inviting. And…clean."

"Used to be a slob, growing up," I hear myself say. "Dad and Fee were always on my ass about picking up after myself. My car was a science experiment, and I'm pretty sure there were entire ecologies growing in my bedroom."

"You clearly learned the value of cleanliness at some point," she says.

"Sure did. I spent a few years in a place where there wasn't much of a choice about keeping your shit neat." My gut burns—the last fucking thing I want is to tell this girl—the poster-child for "good girl"—that I'm an ex-con who did a nickel in a state pen.

She doesn't reply to my statement—no follow-up questions, no leading statements, trying to dig deeper. She just turns those virulently green eyes on me, her expression unreadable.

I can't take it. "Not gonna ask what that means?"

"No." She resumes her examination of my room,

wandering over to the bed, where she trails her fingers over the quilt.

"Just no?"

"If you wished to elucidate, you would have done so. Curiosity does not excuse nosiness." She traces her fingertip around the perimeter of a quilt square made out of my grandfather's flannel shirt. "This quilt is quite old, is it not?"

"Yeah," I answer. "My grandma made it...ah, shit, when? Fifty years ago? Sixty? If there was ever a house fire, god forbid, and I could only save one thing, it'd be that quilt. Loved the shit outta my grandparents."

"It is lovely. One can sense the love that went into its creation."

I nod. "Right? After my folks split up, Grandma and Grandpa were what kept me anything like sane. Second-worst day of my life was the day Grandma passed. Grandpa went less than a week after her." My throat is hot and tight and thick. "Not bein' there for the funeral is somethin' I doubt I'll ever get over."

Fuck, fuck, fuck—what the actual shit is happening to my stupid mouth? I keep saying shit I never, ever bring up, even with Fee or the boys who have known me my whole-ass life and know what happened.

"You *did* not attend, or *could* not attend?" Cadence asks.

"Couldn't."

No follow-up, but she does turn to look at me, searching me. Her expressions are hard—if not impossible—to read, but this look seems speculative, thoughtful. Like she's putting pieces together.

"So, uh. You don't have a bag or anything?" I ask. "No, like a purse, or a change of clothes?"

I watch her face go through a series of expressions I *can* read: confusion, a dawning realization, and then horror. "Oh no. Oh no, no, no. Oh dear. Oh dear, oh dear, oh dear." She covers her face with both hands. "Darn this impossible brain of mine!"

I shift closer to her. "Ah, shit, you forget it somewhere?"

"At the Crenshaws! It has my phone in it, in my wallet, my laptop, *everything*." She lets out a frustrated growl. "Stupid, Cadie. You're stupid. Stupid. *Stupid*." She repeatedly smacks herself in the forehead with a closed fist.

I seize her wrist and prevent her from hitting herself. "Hey, whoa, whoa. Easy, Cadence. None'a that."

She's panting raggedly, whimpering in her throat—nearly hyperventilating. "I forgot it! I forgot my bag. I forgot my bag."

She's still trying to hit herself, and my god, she's stronger than she looks. I end up holding both of her wrists and pulling her against my chest, pinning her hands between our bodies in a bear hug.

"Cadence, hey—hey. It's okay. It's alright."

She writhes in my grip, strong and wiry and soft and exploding with panic. "No! No! No! It's-not-it's-not-it's-not. I forgot my bag. I have to have my bag. I have to have my bag."

Fuck. What do I do? I've seen and had plenty of panic attacks and anxiety attacks in my life. My first cellmate in prison, Rick, had them all the time, and I learned by necessity how to help him through them.

But this?

I don't know what this is.

"Hey, Cadence?" I keep my voice low and soft,

holding her flailing, thrashing form—which is sort of like trying to hold onto a mid-death-roll alligator…if alligators could be soft and sexy. "Try to breathe for me. Take one deep breath, please."

"No, no, no, no, no, no…" she whimpers, and then launches into a refrain of "I lost my bag, I need my bag."

Shit. I really wish to fuck I knew how to help her calm her down. It's fuckin'…what? One-thirty in the morning? But it doesn't seem like there's much that's gonna calm her down except getting that damn bag from Grand fucking Lafayette.

She's rocking back and forth, or trying to, in my arms, chanting about her bag. I'm not even sure how aware of me she even is, except as a vague feature of the world beyond her panic, or whatever this is. I just know I'll do any-fucking-thing to stop it.

"How about we go get your bag?" I say.

She stops rocking instantly. "Get it?" She turns tear-wet eyes up to mine, and fuck my entire world, but the look on her angelic face guts me to the core: it's look of pure, raw, ragged hope shining through tears of despair.

I am so, so, so fucked.

"Yeah," I whisper. "You need your bag, so let's go get it."

"It is far away."

"That's okay. I don't mind. You know the way?"

"Yes," she whispers.

I slide my hand palm-to-palm with hers, thread my fingers through hers. Pull away and step carefully backward through the door into the hallway, tugging her after me. "C'mon, then, Gorgeous. Let's go get your bag."

"I am not gorgeous."

"Hell, yes you are." She's following me easily, now, sniffling and shuddering, eyes semi-vacant—this is a look I recognize.

It's the post-panic empty, shell-shocked lethargy.

I stop backing up and let her step closer, into my space. I try to find her eyes, but hers keep slipping away from mine like same-polarity magnets. I brush my thumbs under her eyes, swiping away her tears. "You with me, Cadence?"

Her gaze finds mine for a few seconds, and then she squeezes her eyes shut, and lets outa breath. "Yes. I am with you."

"Cool. C'mon, then. I like a nice late-night cruise." Good thing I didn't start drinking that second beer, I guess.

I lead her through the house, out the side door, and to the garage. Help her up into my truck. She still seems shell-shocked, making no move to buckle up, so I lean across her and click the seatbelt in place. When I take my seat behind the wheel, she's in that position again—knees together directly over her feet, hands on her lap, back perfectly straight, eyes fixed sightlessly forward.

It takes ten minutes or so to get out of town, and then I can open her up a bit. It's a beautiful night, warm and clear, so I lower my window to let some air circulate in the cabin.

I notice Cadence turns her face toward the open window, eyes closing as the wind buffets her. "Want yours down?"

"Yes, please."

I roll all the windows down, and now her already-wild hair is fluttering and whipping like streamers. Her eyes close, and she leans toward her open window; the tension on her face fades. Tentatively, as if unsure whether she's allowed to, she lifts her right hand and drapes it out the window. Gradually, as the miles pass, the lean of her head angles toward the B-pillar beside her seat, rests against it.

Twenty-five minutes later, I'm rolling through the darkened, quaint downtown area of Grand Lafayette. The stores are dark and shuttered, and the diagonal, on-street parking spots are all vacant. As much as I don't want to, I have to rouse Cadence so I can ask her where to go.

We come to the stoplight at the north edge of town, and I stop for the red. Rub her shoulder gently. "Cadence?"

This time, she responds immediately; with a soft snort, her eyes flick open and find mine. "Riley." She looks around, confused. "Oh. We are here."

"Yeah, this is Grand Lafayette. Can you tell me where to go from here?"

"Yes." She sits up, scans the intersection, and then points left. "That way."

Turns out the Crenshaws live on the west side of town in one of the wealthier neighborhoods, where all the houses are waterfront properties worth half a mil minimum for the dumpiest piece of shit on the street.

The Crenshaws' house is stunning, a mid-century modern masterpiece, all dramatic angles and acres of glass letting in natural light.

Now, obviously, it's dark. I pull into the driveway, shove the shifter into neutral, and yank the parking brake, leaving the engine idling. "You wanna go up, or you want me to?"

"I do not know if I can." She stares out her window, looking at nothing. "It is enough that you have driven me all the way here, but I simply cannot make myself go back there. Not after my behavior. And now this."

I pat her hand. "I got it. No worries. Back in a sec."

I trot up to the front door, hesitate, and then ring the doorbell. A good thirty seconds pass, and then a light blinks on. Locks thunk open, and then the door swings open inward. A grumpy, sleepy old man stands hunched before me in baggy blue-and-white-striped boxers, calf-high black socks, and a thin white terry cloth robe, open and unbelted. "May I help you, young man? Do you know what time it is?"

"Yes, sir, and I apologize for showin' up like this at this hour. I'm a friend of Cadence's, and she believes she forgot her bag here. If I could just grab that from you, I'll be outta your hair."

He frowns at me. "A friend of Cadence's?" His brow scrunches, the frown deepening. "That seems unlikely. Forgive me, young man, but you do not seem like the type of person Cadie would be friends with."

"That's fair enough," I say with a laugh, pivoting out of the way so he can see my truck with Cadence in the front seat. When Mr. Crenshaw and she make eye contact, she drops her gaze immediately and covers her face with both hands. "See? She's kind of embarrassed about the whole thing. But she's pretty upset about the bag, y'know?"

He stares me down, blatantly assessing me. "Young man, Cadence is not like other girls. I—"

I cut in. "Sir, I mean no disrespect. But really, I just want to get her the bag, okay? I know you probably know her way better than I do. I'm just a friend trying to help her out. That's it."

He harrumphs, staring me down another moment, and then nods. "I'll need to speak with her first."

He bends down, somewhat laboriously, and picks up a bag—it's an ancient, battered satchel made of olive-drab canvas and supple, well-worn leather straps. An antique, I think. Ex-military, maybe. It's a cool piece, whatever it is.

I let him precede me to the truck; he approaches the passenger side and gives Cadence her satchel, which is bulging with her belongings. "Cadie, my dear?"

Cadence won't look at him. "Mr. Crenshaw. I beg your forgiveness for my behavior this evening. It was inexcusable."

He reaches in and pats her shoulder affectionately. "Nonsense, dear. I'm sorry we couldn't help. It's just that Mary and I would never forgive ourselves if something happened to you over there and we'd helped facilitate it. If you change your plans for somewhere more safe, we'll gladly help you with any amount of money you need. But there? I'm so sorry, I know how much it means to you, but we just can't. It wouldn't be right."

She nods, gaze on her lap. "I understand. You must follow your conscience. As I must follow mine."

"This friend of yours...." he glances at me—I'm leaning my ass against the hood, waiting. "Do you feel safe with him?"

She nods. "Oh, yes. Quite." Her eyes lift and meet mine through the windshield—briefly, as ever. "He has been very kind to me. You need not worry for my safety."

He sighs. "Well, if you're sure." His voice drops to a murmur meant only for her, but he's obviously got hearing loss and doesn't realize how loud he is. "I just want you to be sure. He seems a bit...rough around the edges."

I turn my face away and suppress a laugh. He's not wrong.

He pats her shoulder again. "It was good to see you, Cadie. I'm sorry to have let you down."

She just nods, pauses. "I understand your position, Mr. Crenshaw. Give it no more thought. I shall find a path forward."

"I know you will, dear. When you set your mind to something, nothing can stop you. And if it's meant to be, God will provide."

"So He will. Goodnight, Mr. Crenshaw."

"Goodnight, Cadie." He pats the lip of the open window, turns away, nodding at me as he passes. "Young man."

"Sir." I nod back and wait until he's inside before hopping behind the wheel.

Cadence is rifling through her bag, taking inventory, muttering to herself. "Laptop, check; phone, check; composition book and pens, check; my book, check; wallet, check…"

I wait until she seems finished with her inventory. "Got everything?"

She nods once. "Yes, everything is present. Not that Mr. or Mrs. Crenshaw would take any of belongings, mind you."

"Of course not." I put the truck in reverse, back out, and head for the highway and home.

For a good fifteen minutes, Cadence alternates between hugging the bag to her chest and flipping obsessively through the items inside.

Eventually, she seems to sort of…tune back in to the world around her, and me. "Riley?"

I glance at her. "'Sup?"

She frowns. "Sup? We just ate."

I laugh. "Just ate? No, I—I meant 'sup', like what's up?"

She blinks a few times. "Oh. I see." A long pause, and then she turns her attention to me once more. "Thank you. You cannot know what this bag means to me. I am honestly flabbergasted that I left it there in the first place. I was immensely distraught, however."

"It's a cool bag, that's for sure. It's vintage?"

"Yes, it is. My great-grandfather fought for Britain in the Great War. He kept this as a souvenir. It is a French military issue field knapsack, model M-1893, originally manufactured in 1914. Light green canvas body, brown leather straps, black buckles, and a wood frame. The design itself dates back to the Napoleonic Wars." A brief pause. "My grandfather bequeathed it to me as a graduation gift from Harvard. It has traveled with me throughout Africa on my previous missions."

"Well damn," I say, genuinely impressed. "That's cool as fuck, babe. No wonder you were crashing out about it."

She blinks at me. "Translate, please."

"Uhhh…" I give an awkward laugh. "I just…I mean, it's a really cool bag, and I can understand why something with so much sentimental value would be so important, why you'd have a panic attack about forgetting it, especially after the day you've had."

She nods, once. "Indeed. Like your grandmother's quilt, this is the one item I would attempt to save, in your hypothetical fire situation."

She fiddles with the straps and then turns her gaze out the window once more. I drive in silence for a while.

After a few minutes, she opens the bag yet again, rummaging; this time, she withdraws a headlamp and a battered paperback novel—*Pride and Prejudice* by Jane Austen. She puts the headlamp on, clicks the light on to the lowest setting, adjusts the angle, and then begins reading.

This chick, man. Fascinating. Unpredictable. Weird. I've never met anyone like her, and I doubt I ever will.

⟳

We pull back into the garage at just past three in the morning. Cadence, absorbed in her book, doesn't realize we've arrived and that I've shut off the engine.

"Cadence?"

She startles a little, shaking her head as if surfacing from the depths of a pool. "Oh. we have returned."

"Yeah, sure have." I hop out, round the tailgate, and open her door. "Step on down, there you go." I hold her hand as she slides to the ground.

She stands in front of me, looking up at me, searching my face without ever meeting my gaze directly. "You are a kind man, Riley Crowe."

I grin. "Hey, now. Keep it down. I've got a reputation to protect." She gives me that look which I'm starting to recognize: she has no clue what I mean. "Just joking, babe. A lot of what I say is jokes. I just mean." I shake my head. "You know what? Never mind. It's stupid and not important. Let's go in, yeah?"

Inside, Cadence pauses in the hallway, looking at the couch and then the doorway to my room. "Are you *quite* certain you will not allow me to rest on the couch? After all the kind and generous things you have done for me this day, it seems ungrateful to put you out of your bed as well."

I cup her cheek; she tenses, eyes flying open wide, and

she swallows hard. I drop my hand, seeing that reaction. "Yeah, babe, I'm sure. I paid a fuck-ton of money for that couch. I've got a tendency to crash on the couch when I'm too tired to make it to my room, so I wanted to make sure my couch is comfy enough to sleep on."

Her fingers touch her cheek where my hand was, absently, in a way that makes me think she's not aware of it. "A most logical decision."

I grin at her, amused at her formal turn of phrase. "So, you got any jammies that bag?"

"Jammies?" She frowns, perplexed, as if having never heard the term.

"Yeah, you know…pajamas? PJs? Something to sleep in aside from the dress."

She looks down at herself, at the bag in her arms— carried like a baby or an armload of books rather than by the straps—and then at me. "No, I do not. I do not wear… jammies."

"Oh, okay. What do you sleep in, then?"

She blushes, cheeks flaming damn near scarlet. "Well, if you must know, I sleep in the nude. It is scientifically proven to improve sleep quality, digestion, circulation, speeds the metabolism, enhances fertility in males, and improves vaginal health in women."

"No shit?" I say, trying like hell not to think about this chick naked in my bed.

She shakes her head. "No. No…crap. I can provide study abstracts and meta-analyses, if you like."

"Oh no, I believe you." I'm frantically trying to prevent my idiot, caveman, horndog brain from going anywhere inappropriate. "Uh, yeah, well…okay. You do you, boo." I point at the room. "I'm just gonna grab some shorts to sleep in." I grab what I need and pause in the hallway. "So, um, you need anything?"

She shakes her head, standing in the middle of my room, clutching her bag. "I do not believe so."

"Cool." God, why is this awkward? "I'm gonna go grab some sleep. You need anything, I'll be on the couch."

"Sleep well, Riley. Thank you again for everything you have done for me tonight. I shall not soon forget your kindness."

I can't help grinning—the way she talks is just so damn cool. Weird, maybe, but cool. She just doesn't give a fuck, and I like that.

I like it a lot.

Too much, maybe.

I leave her there and head for the living room. I hear the door shut and lock, and the creak of the floorboards as she moves around. Seconds later, the light shuts off, the crack beneath the door going dark.

I grab a fleece throw and a pillow from the hall closet, make myself comfortable on the couch...

And completely fail to fall asleep.

There's a beautiful naked woman in my bed.

Fuck.

Keeping my thoughts from going anywhere inappropriate is a constant effort that eventually sends me to sleep.

3

Cadence

A S IS USUAL, I FALL ASLEEP EASILY; THIS DAY, more so due to extreme physical exhaustion and severe mental and emotional fatigue.

I have barely begun to enter true sleep when a deafening digital clamor arises from somewhere in the room, startling me out of my slumber. Bolting upright with a gasp, I blink in the darkness, disoriented and confused. I search the room, hoping the noise will cease on its own and allow me to reenter sleep.

It does not.

Red numerals to my right read 5:30.

An alarm.

I do not own an alarm clock.

Where am I?

A new sound strikes my awareness—the rattle of a doorknob; a widening crease of light from a hallway beyond the door appears. In that opening looms a massive masculine figure, backlit into a brawny silhouette.

I hear myself cry out in alarm—the clanging clamor of the alarm slices through my brain, pounds violently upon my psyche like fists on soft flesh.

A male is approaching.

Danger! Danger!

Where am I?

The figure is a shadowy shape moving toward me, and I scrabble across the bed, reach the edge of it, and topple off onto the hardwood floor, which is cold beneath me. I watch the large figure—now partially illuminated by the light from the hallway. Bare male flesh wraps around hard, rippling muscle. The male is intensely fit, with low body fat and high muscle mass.

He does something to the alarm clock, and the awful noise is mercifully silenced. "Cadence?"

He knows my name?

I cannot move. Anxiety has my higher faculties short-circuited—I recognize my state, but I cannot do anything about it.

He rounds the foot of the bed, pauses, staring at me. "Hey, hey, hey. Cadence, try to breathe for me. Yeah? It was just my alarm going off. I forgot about it. I'm sorry. Are you okay?"

My head shakes—I am not okay. "Wh—wh—where—?"

The male approaches another three steps closer to me, and my body tightens into an even smaller ball. He reaches for something at the end of the bed—a quilt. He allows it to unfold, holding it up as he shifts closer to me. "I'm just gonna cover you, okay?" His voice is low and calm.

Soothing, somehow. My anxiety recedes a tiny amount.

Creeping cautiously closer, the man's eyes remain fixed with laser focus on mine, neither blinking nor wavering. The warm weight of the blanket settles on my shoulders.

"There," he murmurs, crouching before me. "I need you to breathe for me, Cadence. Take a breath in, like me. Ready?" He inhales sharply through his nose for four seconds. "Hold it and count to seven with me. One…two… three…" After seven, he murmurs again. "Now let it out slowly for eight. One…two…three…"

His eyes are such a pale shade of blue, they are nearly white, and shocking in their intensity. They mesmerize. Hypnotize. I breathe with him for three cycles; the breathing slows my panic, and his deep, strong, soothing voice calms my raging tumult of overwhelm.

I return to coherence gradually, and then all at once, Riley is sitting cross-legged on the floor before me, between the bed and the wall. The hardwood floor is cold beneath me, and I'm covered in the quilt.

I am naked beneath it.

"You…" I swallow, finding words difficult to summon, these words in particular. "You saw me. Nude."

"It was dark, and you were in a ball. I didn't see anything. I did my best to not look, Cadence. I swear." He rests a hand on my bent knee; my breath catches sharply at the contact, and he removes it instantly. "I'm so sorry about my alarm. Are you okay?"

One of the many curses of my mind is my memory. Even in the grip of panic, I forget nothing; I cannot. I remember the way he approached, carefully and cautiously.

His eyes did not seek or search or scan, but remained locked on mine, and he shielded me from his sight with the blanket.

"I will be well," I manage. "Thank you for your assistance." A pause. "And your…consideration for my modesty."

"Can I help you up?" he asks.

My muscles have not yet received the internally circulated memo that the time for anxiety has passed.

"I…I cannot seem to move," I say. "I would be grateful for your further assistance."

He rises to a crouch, gathers the extra material of the quilt around me, and scoops me up in his arms—without touching my skin. He stands easily, lifting me as if I weigh nothing at all. He moves around the foot end and sets me on the bed where I had been sleeping. He covers me with the comforter, holds it up near my chin, and deftly removes the quilt, draping it over top.

It is apparent that he is taking great pains to neither touch me inappropriately nor accidentally look at me in my nude state.

The care he is taking to show respect is touching. More so, perhaps, is the calm, compassionate, patient way he nurtured me through the anxiety attack.

I look at him—bearing, for his sake, direct eye contact for as long as possible. "I thank you, Riley."

He shakes his head, sighing. "That shouldn't have happened. I'm so sorry. Are you okay?"

"I am alright now. I was…discombobulated, which triggered an anxiety attack due to unusual surroundings and an unexpected noise during the initial stages of REM sleep."

"Yeah, that'd do it. Well, again, I apologize. Think you'll be able to get back to sleep?"

I nod. "Yes. I believe so."

"I'll leave you to it, then." He smiles at me, and my goodness, the man is just so handsome.

The smile makes my stomach do flips, or so it feels. One's stomach cannot actually flip, nor can one's heart flutter—if it does, one should seek immediate medical attention. In this case, the flip of my stomach indicates a specific emotional response: I am attracted to Riley Crowe.

This is concerning.

My heroine, Elizabeth Bennet, would say that Riley and I are of vastly different stations, and thus eminently unsuitably matched.

It simply will not do to waste any further time or effort considering any manner of attachment between Riley and myself, as such is patently impossible.

He is debonaire, wildly, ruggedly handsome, confident, charming, a homeowner, and a man with useful skills.

Men such as he do not enter romantic entanglements with women such as me.

I shall simply have to recognize my attraction and endeavor to move beyond it without allowing hope to enter the equation.

But my gosh, that smile.

I hear myself sigh as I look in his direction once more, performing a smile in return. "Riley?"

He stops in the open doorway, partially turning back to me. In the light of the hallway, his bare torso is displayed and illuminated to wondrous effect. His abdomen is magnificently developed, with eight large, blocky rectus abdominis muscles which draw my gaze. Most beguiling of all are his iliac furrows—those deep, sharp grooves running beneath the rectus abdominis and the internal and external oblique muscles, vanishing in a V beneath the waistband of his shorts.

Which are…well…quite short, and quite tight. They cling to the enormous girth of his quadriceps, hamstrings, and gluteus muscles, to the degree that little is left to the imagination.

To one with such vast and intimate knowledge of human anatomy such as I, little imagination is required to form a rather accurate visual understanding of his appearance, *sans culottes*, as the French would say.

I am being disrespectful. It is shameful, and I feel my cheeks burn with the flush of blood as a physiological response to mortification.

I force my gaze away, eyes shutting. I had been about to say something to him, but the thought has fled in the wake of my spinning thoughts.

"Cadence?" He leans against the doorframe. "Was there something else?"

I shake my head. "No. Only…no. Nothing else."

He slaps the frame lightly. "Cool. So, yeah. You need anything, I'm right out there."

"Yes. Thank you."

He closes the door, returning me to darkness.

This time, my sleep is uninhibited.

C∘

When I wake again, sunlight is a hot yellow lance bathing me in light and warmth. I am sweating beneath the blankets, and toss them away.

A glance at the cursed alarm clock informs me that I have, most unusually, slept until eleven. I feel refreshed,

although the specter of my failed fundraising attempt oc-
cupies a large portion of my attention. But once one has
rested sufficiently, one can reassess the situation and formulate a new plan.

First, however, I must see to my bodily needs. Once
I have finished in the restroom, I return to the bedroom. I
dress in the change of clothing from my rucksack—a pale
blue ankle-length dress made from loose, breathable cotton
with cap sleeves and a square neck- and back-line. Clean
undergarments, of course. My worn clothing I roll into a
tight cylinder and slot into place with the rest of my things.

Dressed, I withdraw my small satchel of toiletries and
brush my teeth and attempt a futile detangling of my hair;
without a shower and my curly-hair regimen supplies, however, there is little I can do about the state of my hair.

I leave Riley's bedroom and find the living room
empty, and any trace that he slept there has long since
been put away. I do not find him in the kitchen, either.

I do find, however, a pale yellow sticky note adhered
to the cabinet above a coffeemaker, the carafe for which
holds hot coffee. "*Help yourself to coffee,*" the note reads.
"*Cream in the fridge, mugs, and sugar packets in this cabinet.
I'm down in the basement.*"

The note is unsigned, but I suppose it cannot be anything other than obvious who left it. I am not an avid coffee drinker, but as a doctor, it is a necessary part of life, at
times, despite my natural preference for a nice cup of green
tea. I fix myself a mug of coffee with a splash of cream,
no sugar. I carry the mug with me down the steps to the
basement.

Fluorescent bulbs shine a harsh, unkind, and vi-
sually offensive white light on bare concrete floor and

white-washed cinderblock walls; the ceiling is no more than the underside of the floor above, with exposed wiring and pipes. Several metal poles support the load, dividing the space in half. Plastic bins and cardboard boxes line a section of wall to my right, stacked three high. Further along that same wall, a washtub stands beside an old, white metal washing machine and matching dryer, both of which are operating rather noisily.

The wall opposite the stairs is broken up by a doorway, which is partly open to reveal the unfinished guts of a bathroom; outside the doorway are stacked boxes of supplies of unknown provenance and purpose, and tools.

To the left is an extensive home gym setup—a large red metal cage with black pegs and evenly spaced holes, a rack of dumbbells, another rack akin to a bicycle stand containing black bumper plates, a cluster of kettlebells of varying sizes, an air assault bike, a rowing machine, and a treadmill.

Riley is standing inside the red cage, a barbell across his broad, wide, thick, hard shoulders, three plates on each side of the bar, which bends slightly downward under the weight of the plates. He takes a shuffling, straining step backward and then a second, the bar and plates wobbling precariously; his back muscles tense and ripple as he shifts his grip, packs his shoulders down and back. He begins descending into a squat, and his immense leg muscles flex into sharp relief. His gluteus muscles go hard as iron as he drops into the bottom of the squat, pauses for a two-count, and then I hear him grunt through gritted teeth, straining mightily under the weight. If each of those plates is forty-five pounds, as is customary, with a standard bar weight of an additional forty-five pounds, then he is lifting 315 pounds. An impressive feat, I believe, though I know next to nothing of such things.

At the top of the movement, he lets out several harsh, gasping breaths, his whole frame swelling with each breath. He inhales again, prodigiously, and drops down slowly into another repetition, grunting on the ascent. A third repetition. A fourth, which is wobbly, slow, and incredibly strained. It does not seem likely that he will achieve a fifth repetition.

And, indeed, he manages the descent well enough, but strains and grunts as he tries to ascend—every muscle seems about to burst through his skin from the effort, and his grunt of exertion becomes a veritable shout of primal rage.

And then, improbably, through sheer force of will, I believe, he ascends. Only an inch at first. Then two. Shaking, snarling with exertion, he rises…rises…and against anything I'd have believed possible, reaches full vertical lockout. Gasping raggedly, he staggers forward, dips to allow the barbell to rest on the hooks, and moves out from beneath the bar, still gripping it with his hands. Sweat streams down his body in rivulets, following the grooves and concavities and convexities of his impressive musculature.

I have forgotten my coffee. I have forgotten everything but the sight of Riley—he is a sweaty, shirtless Adonis.

After panting for a few moments, bent over with his head hanging between his arms as he grips the bar, Riley steps back out of the cage and turns, scraping the tattered black ballcap, worn backward, off his head so he can rake his hands through his sweaty black hair.

"Fuck me!" he says, clapping a hand to his glistening, heaving chest. "Scared the shit outta me, girl."

"I apologize," I say. "It was not my intention to startle you, nor to interrupt your exercising."

"Nah," he says, panting. "All good. Sleep well, after that whole stupid fucking alarm clock fiasco?"

I nod. "Yes, I did. Thank you. And you? Did you find any rest on the couch?"

He grins, nodding. "Oh yeah, no problems." He juts his chin at me. "See you found coffee. Hope it's okay. I tend to brew it so thick you can chew it."

I take a sip and cough. "My goodness, you are not exaggerating very much, are you?" I cannot stop myself from grimacing at the monstrously bitter taste.

He chuckles. "You don't have to drink it. Not a coffee person?"

"I prefer green tea under most circumstances. Of course, I have learned to tolerate coffee as the only option during long shifts, particularly during midnights in the ER."

"The ER, huh?"

"Yes. I specialize in emergency medicine and mass casualty events. I perform best under high stress situations."

He blinks at me. "Huh. No shit?"

"Please correct me if I am mistaken, but I seem to note an element of surprise at this information," I say. "Why?"

"Uh, I mean, you just…" he trails off. "Well, if I'm honest, you seem kinda anxious, sometimes, is all."

"Ah, yes. I see your confusion." I consider what to say, how much to explain to this relative stranger.

On one hand, he has done me many kindnesses and deserves an explanation for…well…me. But then, on the other hand, he is just being kind. This does not mean I owe him any personal information or answers, and I certainly do not feel any obligation to explain myself to him.

"I…" I trail off and start over. "There are two distinct aspects to me—personal and professional. I am a doctor. Furthermore, I have studied, prepared, practised, and trained for emergency medicine since I was five years old. Medicine is not merely a job for me, or even a passion. It is an integral part of my personality. It is a calling. As such, when I enter a working environment, I am in control. I am aware of every aspect of my job, and I am intimately familiar with every possible risk. Control puts me at ease. My training, knowledge, and experience mean I understand my environment. In a professional setting, I am in control of my world." I pause, sighing. "Outside of the narrow scope of my profession, I do not have such granular control, and that lack frequently produces anxiety. Which means in my personal life, I am a much more anxious person."

He absorbs this in silence, then nods. "That makes sense."

I wait for the questions, but they do not come. "Are you not going to inquire further?"

He swaggers over to me, gleaming and glistening and distractingly attractive, even under the awful, garish fluorescent lights. "Nope." His eyes scan my face, although I couldn't guess what he hopes to see there. "Do you want me to inquire further?"

I shake my head. "Not at this juncture, no."

"Yeah, I can tell." He uses his index finger to brush an unruly lock of hair away from my eye, and where he touches, my skin tingles. "I'd love to know more about you, Cadence Creswell, but only if you wanna tell me."

I hardly know what to say—a dozen lines of thought

run through my brain concurrently, and he is so darned distractingly beautiful that I find it hard to seize on any of them.

"I…" I take a sip of coffee, but it's so thick and bitter, even with cream, that I cannot swallow it. "Mmmm!"

I stagger up the stairs and spit the coffee out into the sink, find a glass, fill it with water, and then rinse out my mouth.

I hear him on the stairs, and then I become aware of his presence in the kitchen with me—he fills it, exuding dominance and heat and masculinity.

"You need not interrupt your workout," I say.

"Eh, I was done. That was my last set."

"I see." My stomach gurgles noisily, alerting me—and Riley—to my hunger.

He grins at me. "Gimme a minute to clean up and then I'll take you to get some tea and something to eat."

"Very well," I answer. "That sounds lovely. Thank you. I shall wait."

He snorts softly, smiling at me in a way that I cannot quite translate. Is he laughing at me? I am used to being laughed at, but from him, for some reason, it would hurt more than from others. I do not care to examine why this might be, as I do not think the answer will do me any favors.

Curiosity, however, overwhelms even embarrassment. "Why do you laugh at me?" I ask the question while unable to bring my gaze up even near his.

He steps closer to me, and I catch the scent of his sweat, which I would normally find unfavourable and off-putting, but from him, for further reasons I shall not be examining, I do not find at all distasteful. "Hey, I'm not laughing at you."

I frown. "You need not lie, Riley. I am aware that I am strange to you. I have been laughed at all my life."

His index finger, loosely curled around an invisible trigger, meets the underside of my chin and brings my head up. "Cadence. Hey."

I shake my head. "Mmm-mmm." I turn away. "Do not, please. I understand."

He ducks until he is within my line of sight, and then straightens, that finger still tugging my chin up. "I *wasn't* laughing at you, Cadence. That's not what that was. I promise you it wasn't. You're the last person on earth I'd ever make fun of."

Discomfort wriggles in my belly like a worm on a hook. "Riley. I know what laughter is, and I most certainly know what it looks like when it is directed at you."

"There's a lot in what you just said that I'd like to get into, but not right now." The pad of his thumb snags at my lower lip, tugs it ever so slightly, and then drifts down my chin, hesitates, and then slides ghostly soft over my lower lip. I cannot breathe when he touches me. My heart pounds frantically. "I did laugh, yes. But Cadence, it wasn't…" He shakes his head, and while I am far from anything like an expert on facial expressions, his seems to express genuine dismay, as if he is troubled by something. "I wasn't laughing *at* you in the sense of mockery. Swear to fuckin' god, I wasn't."

"Then I do not understand why you laughed."

"Because you're so fuckin' adorable!" he says, the words seeming to explode from him, sudden and intense.

"Adorable?" I echo. "Please elucidate."

He snorts again, this one openly derisive. "Yeah, no clue what that word means. I'm an uneducated bumble-fuck, sweetheart. Gotta use small words with me."

"A bumble…what?"

He laughs, shakes his head. "Just a dumb word I made up to be funny."

"Oh. I see. Well, elucidate means to explain. To make clear."

"Got it." His thumb seems curious, drifting across my upper lip; I dart a glance at his eyes, and they follow the path of his thumb, as if there is something fascinating about my lips. "Not sure what there is to *elucidate*, Cadence. You're adorable. Cute. Fascinating. Funny."

"I did not tell a joke."

He shakes his head. "No, you didn't. But there's lots'a ways to be funny."

"Nor was I attempting to be funny."

"I know, sweetheart."

"So if I did not tell a joke and was not attempting to be funny, how was your laughter not directed at me?"

"It *was* directed at you, but not with a mean spirit. It was…fuck, I don't know how else to put it. The way you said that—'very well, I shall wait,'" and here he chuckles again, grinning and shaking his head. "So fuckin' cute. Just makes me laugh. "I just think you're so goddamned cute I have to laugh."

"Ah," I say. "I begin to comprehend. You find me entertaining in the way one finds babies funny when they do something that is inadvertently comical."

"Yeah," he murmurs, tracing his thumb over the seam where my lips meet. "Except you sure as hell ain't a baby."

"No, I am not. I am a fully grown woman of twenty-four years."

"And a really, really beautiful one," he says. Before I can process this, he steps back and turns away. "Lemme get changed real fast. Just hang tight and I'll get you fed."

"Riley," I call, and he stops, turns, and glances at me. "You need not make haste on my account. I shall not perish of hunger if you wish to shower as well as change."

"You sayin' I stink?" His expression communicates merriment, I believe—he is teasing me.

"No!" I protest. "You do possess a…erm…musk following your exercising, but I…I confess I do not find it altogether unpleasant. I merely wished you to know that I am content to wait, should you desire to take longer to prepare for departure than a swift changing of your clothes."

He grins, turning back and stepping closer to me than before—so close all I can see is him, all I can smell is him. And his scent is…problematic. Before I can ruminate further on this, he sidles even closer, and now he is no longer grinning. He is searching me intently, his expression serious.

"'A certain not altogether unpleasant musk," he murmurs to me, repeating my words. "Meanin', you *like* how I smell."

"I…um." *Warning, warning, warning!* Pheromone levels are peaking. "My subconscious is reacting to the androstadienone in your sweat, creating a pheromonal response over which I have no control."

"No clue what an andro-what-the-fuck even is, Gorgeous, but I know what a pheromone is." He's close—so close. So big. So…muscles. And…skin. And heat.

Everything is upside down in my brain and body. "But what I hear you saying is...you like how I smell."

"No, I...yes. Sort of." In refusing to look at his eyes—because I cannot—I find myself staring at his chest.

Beads of sweat drip and trickle, and a shaft of sunlight streams through the window to turn the beads of sweat into glittering diamond drops. I want to touch one. I want to touch *him*.

"Go for it," he murmurs. "I don't bite."

"*Eeeep*!" I squeak. "I said that out loud?"

"Eeep?" He echoes. "Did you just say...*eeep*?"

"No. I did not *say* anything. It was an involuntary ejaculation."

His head drops and his shoulders shake. "Ah shit. Don't say it, Rye. Do *not* fucking say it."

"Are you speaking to me?" I ask, absolutely baffled.

"No, to myself, " he whispers. "I'm tryin' so fuckin' hard to be a good boy, Cadence. I really fuckin' am."

"I do not understand."

His eyes, twinkling with mirth, search my face, a soft, kind, amused smile on his face. "Yeah, I'm startin' to get that. You're all kinds'a innocent, aren'tcha?"

He closes his eyes and lets out a slow sigh, a mannerism which I take to mean he is exercising extreme self-control; over what, I cannot say. He circles my wrist with his fingers, holding gently, carefully, as if I am made of the most delicate porcelain, and lifts my hand to his chest.

I gasp at the contact—his skin is sweat-damp, soft to the touch yet hard as iron, and so warm. I press my palm into the firm, springy muscle, and then dimple my fingers into it, and then slide my fingertips over the slick, soft surface, marveling internally at the way it feels…the way *he* feels under my hand.

Watching his expression carefully for signs that he wishes me to stop touching him, I allow myself to explore the hard expanse of his chest until my hand covers his heart. I feel his pulse thudding rhythmically under my palm. It is a hypnotic tattoo under my hand, and I find myself wishing desperately that I could put my ear to his chest and listen to it.

It is a dangerous thought, however. For one thing, I would never want to stop listening to it. And for another, I am acutely aware that a man like Riley Crowe is simply never going to want such intimacy with me. It is a fate to which I have long since resigned myself.

That final thought is sobering enough that I drop my hand and my eyes, stepping back. "I thank you for that, Riley."

Another of those soft snorts which I am beginning to realize can mean a wide variety of things. When I bring my eyes up to his face, his expression is too complicated for me to fathom.

"What does that laugh mean, please?" I ask.

"You. You are just too fuckin' much, girl. I can't with you."

It feels as if a rush of acid has filled my stomach. "I am aware that I am too much for most people. You needn't point it out."

Strong, rough, gentle hands frame my face. "Cadence, again, that is *not* what I was saying."

I am frozen in place, unable to move, to breathe, to do anything with the feel of his hands on my face—they have the texture of a cinderblock against my cheeks, and despite the gentility of his touch, I sense the incredible strength in them.

It is terrifying, overwhelming, mystifying, and deeply troubling how my body responds to his touch. My lungs are blocks of ice. My stomach is a lepidopterarium. My hands clench into fists at my sides, and my eyes are wide and fixed on his too-handsome face, as if I could read there the answer to my question: *Why is this impossibly handsome and utterly confusing man touching me this way?*

Why do my mammary glands feel so tight, so hard, so wickedly sensitive inside the dratted, awful, constrictive prison of my brassiere?

Why, above all, does my female sexual organ feel so... uncomfortably hot and damp?

Before my brain can supply the medical answer, which I am quite certain I do not wish to know, as it will do me no good, I retreat from him, taking two decisive steps backward, out of his reach. "You should have your shower, Riley."

He glances at his hands, for some reason, and then nods. "Yeah. Yeah, I'm going. Be out in a minute."

I am obviously mistaken, but it almost seems as if he is disappointed that I took those steps out of his reach. But that is patently ridiculous. I am not now and have never been and likely never will be the object of *anyone's* physical desire, least of all a man like Riley.

No, it simply would not do to allow myself to germinate the seed of hope his innocently-meant touch inadvertently planted.

Instead of allowing my imagination to wander to the illicit, inappropriate, and sinful place of Riley in the shower,

I turn my mental faculties to the much more important—
and solvable—problem of my trip to Sudan.

Yet instead of considering solutions, my attention
continually and frustratingly wanders back to his chest
under my hand, and the searing bolt of electricity I felt
shock my entire system when I touched him.

I simply *must* leave this place—this town, this home,
and this man. I must. Before I become attached to someone who will not, cannot return that attachment.

Again.

Before I am heartbroken.

Again.

4

Riley

I ABSOLUTELY DO *NOT* UNDERSTAND CADENCE Creswell at fucking all.

She's gorgeous and doesn't seem to have the first fucking clue that she is. And unless she's lying—which I'm 99.99% sure she isn't—she's crazy, crazy smart, accomplished, and talented. But she misunderstands the simplest things, misinterprets the most obvious statements or gestures. She uses words I've never heard—not that that in itself is hard, considering my formal education stopped at seventeen and I didn't exactly spend my time in prison reading. She acts so shy, so unsure of herself, and seems unable to recognize and/or believe my attraction to her, even when plainly stated.

I brush my teeth While the water is getting

hot—replacing the twenty-year old water heater with a tankless one is high on my to-do list. I consider shaving, but I hate shaving and decide against it. Once in the shower, I rush through getting clean. Mainly because if I let myself linger, my attention will wander to Cadence.

To the brief, tantalizing glimpse of her naked body when I first opened the door. Any enjoyment of that quick look was eradicated when I saw her sheer terror as she huddled on the floor between my bed and the wall, shaking, hyperventilating.

But now, my idiot caveman brain keeps summoning that fragment of wonder—pale, creamy skin, the long curve of spine to buttock to thigh. The plump curve of her breast, mostly hidden by her arm.

Fuck.

I twist the knob until the water runs cold, spluttering and gasping as I race through washing and conditioning my hair and scrubbing my body clean.

Shocked out of lust, I rinse off and get out, towel off, run some gel through my hair and give it a quick brush, and then dress in my usual jeans, gray tee, and work boots.

I find Cadence still in the kitchen, leaning a hip against the sink as she stares vacantly out of the window above the sink.

God, she's so fucking beautiful.

Look, I'm a player, okay? I don't use women, don't get me wrong. I just don't try to make things last beyond a few nights, maybe a few weeks at most. It's always consensual, from the sex to the casual, limited-time-only nature of things.

Point being, I've been lucky enough to be with some seriously hot chicks.

Cadence is not hot.

She's truly, exquisitely, classically beautiful. Megan Fox was *hot* in the first *Transformers* movie; Marilyn Monroe was *beautiful* in *Seven Year Itch*. See the difference?

I hang back and just look at her. Her dress today is ankle-length, plunging in a straight line from bust to hem, white cotton that floats loosely around her figure. I can't say for sure from two outfits, but my guess is she dresses for comfort rather than looks. But yet, the dress flatters without being provocative or revealing. Her hair is loose and as wild as ever, a chaotic profusion of strawberries-and-cream curls that in this light looks more strawberries than cream.

I have a brief but powerful mental image of my hands snarled in those curls as I kiss her senseless. The image, however, quickly shifts from an innocent but passionate kiss to something altogether more potent: my hands buried in those curls as she wraps her lips around my cock...

FUCK.

I savagely suppress that image, forcing myself to think of that time I accidentally walked in on Grandma fresh outta the shower. As much as I loved my Grandma, that's a real boner-killer. I go through the latest Lions stats. I think about being in the prison shower full of naked dudes.

When none of that works and the image of Cadence doing gloriously sinful things to me while I hold on to that glorious mass of curls remains burned indelibly on my mind, I pull out the biggest guns of all.

The wreck.

The day that ruined my life.

Those images will haunt me the rest of my life—

The world spins and wobbles. It's dark. Late. My stomach is sour and full of pressure. I know I should have listened to Cole, but I didn't. Oh well. Almost home. That godawful Uncle Kracker song I hate so much starts playing, so I glance down and turn the knob to find a different station. When I look up, the world freezes. A tiny red Kia is turning in front of me. I've drifted across the centerline while fucking with the radio.

I hit the brakes and jerk the wheel, but it's too late.

The impact is abrupt and violent, a deafening, jarring, jolt of smashing glass and crumpling metal.

In reality, that's when I blacked out. I have no memory of anything past the impact.

Turns out being "black-out drunk" isn't a valid excuse for murdering a 76-year-old widow with your car.

The nausea, guilt, shame, and self-loathing does the trick, dousing my horniness more effectively than any cold shower or visions of naked grandmothers ever could.

I step into the kitchen, clearing my throat. "Hey, you ready?"

She's utterly motionless except for the slight rise and fall of her breathing, and shows no sign of having heard me.

I move closer and put myself in her line of sight. "Hey, you. Ready?"

She doesn't startle this time, but seems to…turn back on, almost, blinking her eyes and shaking her head. "Riley. Hello. Yes, I am ready."

"Where do you go when you're like that?" I ask.

She frowns, a cute little furrowing of her brow. "I went nowhere. I am here."

I suppress the laugh—she's misconstrued it every time, thus far. "No, I mean mentally. I'm asking what you were thinking about."

"Oh. Of course. I am thinking about South Sudan. More

to the point, I am trying to come up with an alternative solution to the problem of attaining the requisite funds."

I hold out my hand. "Well, let's talk about it over brunch, yeah?"

She frowns at my hand as if unsure what she's supposed to do with it, and then looks at me as if trying to determine why I would be holding out my hand like that. And then, finally, after several long, weird, silent seconds, she fits her small, soft, slender hand into mine. I lead her outside through the side door—the only door I ever use—lock it behind me, and then pull her across the driveway to my garage. I enter the code one-handed, and the garage door rolls up with a loud squeal.

I open the passenger door for her and hand her up and in, lean in and buckle her up.

"Riley, I have a question to ask." She says this once I've clicked the buckle into the receiver.

"Okay."

"Do you think I am going to become lost on the way from your house to the garage?"

"Um, no."

"A follow-up question, then. Do you think me incapable of operating a seatbelt?"

"No."

"Then why insist on holding my hand, and why insist on buckling me in like a helpless child?"

"I…" I clear my throat while processing this interaction. "Are you offended?"

"Yes. I am an adult." She looks at me intently, her expression one of perplexed offense. "I do not need a hand to hold. I do not need assistance buckling myself into an automobile."

"I'm sorry I offended you, Cadence," I say, half-in the cab, still. "I held your hand because I like holding your hand. That's it."

She blinks at me without otherwise changing her expression. "And the seatbelt?"

I grin at her—the smirk that others have called the panty-melter. Not my words, ya'll. "That was just because I wanted an excuse to be closer to you."

"Oh." Another flat, expressionless, slow blink. "How strange. Why?"

Again, I have to choke back a laugh at her ridiculous question. "In the kitchen, earlier. You touched my chest. Why?"

She blushes furiously. "I do not know. It was a strange impulse which I cannot explain."

I think you can, Cadence Creswell. But I won't press the issue…yet.

Bad Riley—bad. You won't press the issue *ever*. This girl is as pure as the driven snow, and you've got no business even *looking* at her.

"Well, never mind then. I buckled you in because it's something I like doing. But if it bothers you, I won't do it again. I certainly didn't mean it as an insult, and I truly am sorry if it came across that way."

She nods. "Very well."

I step down and close the door, laughing to myself as I round the bed. She's just so…regal…when she says shit like that. *Very well.*

Alright, Queen Elizabeth.

I know it's not that. She's the least arrogant, entitled, or grasping person I've ever met. It's just how she talks. It's adorable, bizarre, confusing, frequently makes me feel dumber than a bag of broken hammers, and is inexplicably hot.

I have issues—I am aware, thanks.

She's still lost in thought, so I leave the radio down low and leave her to her thoughts as I drive us to The Alt, the vegan, gluten-free, vegetarian, and other kinds of weird-food cafe owned by the Cartwright sisters.

She doesn't stir from her position—elbow on the armrest built into the door, chin on her hand, gaze out the window—even after I've shut off the motor and opened my door.

"We're here," I say.

No answer. My god, when this chick gets lost in her thoughts, she *really* gets lost in them.

"Cadence?"

Nothing.

I don't want to startle her or scare her, which seems to happen when I touch her when she's like this, but it also seems to be the only way of getting her attention, other than putting myself in her line of sight.

I get out of the cab and go around, open her door. This finally gets her attention.

"Oh! We have arrived, I see." She sighs, sounding annoyed. "My apologies, Riley. I am not very good company at the moment, I fear."

"Sure you are," I say, holding out my hand as she unbuckles.

"I am easily absorbed in my thoughts, to the exclusion of all else," she says.

"Yeah, I'm getting that. It's all good. Doesn't bother me."

"I am not ignoring you on purpose—I hope you are aware."

I smile at her. "Yeah, I got that. Just thinkin' deep thoughts. I told you—it's all good. No worries."

I release her hand once she's on the ground, but she pauses, staring down at my hand. Then at me. "You may hold my hand, if you wish." She's blushing like crazy, not looking at me. "I misunderstood your intent earlier."

I wrap my hand around hers—I doubt she's ready for intertwined fingers just yet. "There."

She looks at our hands, then at the restaurant. "But… will the staff and patrons not form incorrect notions regarding our relationship, should we be holding hands when we enter?"

"That's long for 'get the wrong impression,' yeah?"

"Correct."

"Fuck 'em. Let 'em get the wrong impression." I frown, then. "Well, on second thought, you may have a point. It won't do your reputation around here any good to be seen holding hands with me."

"Why would that be?"

"Because I don't have the best reputation."

She hesitates, looks at our hands again, and then at me. "If I allowed myself to care what other people thought about me, Riley Crowe, I would never leave my bedroom at my parents' house in Chicago." She tightens her grip on my hand and moves for the entrance. "But more to the point, I find I quite enjoy holding your hand."

This should not thrill me, but it does. I ignore that and just focus on enjoying the moment for what it is— innocent hand-holding totally free of any deeper meaning or significance.

We enter The Alt, and the bell above the door rings, announcing our entrance. It's pretty packed in here, so our only choice of seating is a two-top near the bathrooms. We stand in line to order, and Cadence never lets go of my hand as she studies the menu—hand-written in chalk by Lainey, with cute doodles here and there.

We're next in line when Cadence turns to me, looking worried. "It is our turn next, and I cannot decide what to get. Will you choose for me, please?"

"Sure. Any foods you can't eat or don't like?"

"Yes. I dislike onions and olives. And I am not a fan of spicy foods, although this does not appear to be the sort of establishment which serves such fare."

I grin. "You vegan, vegetarian, or gluten-free?"

"None of the above, although I limit my red meat intake, and prefer whole grains and simple, natural carbohydrates, and almost never indulge in fast carbohydrates or ultra-processed foods."

"Well, you're in the right place, in that case, 'cause Lainey and Layla don't serve any of that shit here. This is the healthiest place to eat in town. The food is damn good, too." I pick something at random from the menu. "How about the Upside Down Turkey Wonder?"

She reads the description—an open-face turkey sandwich with the fixings on the bottom, layered under turkey and melted brie. "That sounds excellent."

Layla is at the register and gives me a bright smile when she sees me. "Riley! I never see you in here." Her bright light brown eyes dancing merrily—and then fixing like lasers on Cadence's and my joined hands. "Who's your…friend?"

"Layla Cartwright, co-owner of this fine establishment, this is Cadence Creswell, MD."

Cadence lets go of my hand and extends hers to Layla. "It

is my pleasure to make your acquaintance, Layla Cartwright. Your cafe has a very welcoming ambience."

Layla blinks and then laughs. "Why, thank you! Are you new in town?"

Cadence frowns. "I suppose so."

"So then how did you and Riley meet?"

Cadence goes still, as if the question, innocently meant, has put her off balance. "I was sitting on a park bench crying, and he stopped to inquire as to how he could be of assistance."

I see Layla picking up on Cadence's unusual way of speaking. "That's Riley for you. Loves to be of assistance. Especially for pretty girls like you."

I glare at her. "Layla, c'mon. It wasn't like that."

She snickers. "I'm just teasing, Rye." She winks at Cadence. "Don't take me seriously. I just like to fuck with Riley."

Cadence nods sagely. "I see." She glances up at the menu and then at Layla. "May I have the Upside Down Turkey Wonder, please?"

"Anything to drink?"

She freezes, looks to me as if for some kind of reassurance and then clears her throat. "Um. Tea. Hot tea. Please. Oolong, if possible."

"Certainly." Layla offers her a warm smile. "For you, Rye?"

"I don't see it on the menu, but I'm hoping you can still do it," I say. "Last time I was here, you had this bowl that had diced chicken, hummus, spinach, Greek yogurt—all sorts of good shit."

Layla snorts a laugh, shaking her head. "That was a

weekly special, but since I'm so fabulous, I'll whip it up for you, seeing as we have all the ingredients on hand."

"You *are* fabulous, Layla." I hand her my card. "Iced tea with mine, please."

Layla runs my card, hands it back, and flicks her gaze one more time to our hands…which are still joined. "I'll bring it out to you. Sit wherever."

"Thanks."

By the time we've ordered, a table has opened up by the window, and we sit, finally releasing each other's hands. Cadence looks at Layla, who is preparing our drinks. "You and Layla seem to know each other quite well."

I shrug. "I guess. Three Rivers is a small town. Everyone knows everyone. The Cartwright twins were…a grade beneath me, I think? Hard to remember."

"She is extraordinarily pretty," Cadence says.

I nod. "Yup. Always has been."

"I wonder that you do not seek to court her."

"Court?" I can't help but laugh. "Like…date? Nah. I, uh…Layla and I…yeah, no."

She peers at me. "You are omitting something, I believe."

Fuck it. May as well make it perfectly clear to her what kind of guy I am, so she can make the only smart decision and get out of Three Rivers and away from me as fast as possible.

"I hooked up with her, few years back."

"Hooked up." It's a statement, not a question. "You mean you had consensual, extramarital sexual relations with her."

At that precise moment, Layla walks up to the table with Cadence's hot tea and my iced tea. "Yes," she says, placing the beverages on the table. "That's precisely what we did." She smiles at Cadence. "But don't worry, it was a long time ago, and it didn't mean much."

"That's…" my gut twists at the way she's presenting it. "Layla, hold on, now. That's not entirely fair."

She cackles. "Bro, you bounced literally fifteen minutes after we finished. My legs weren't even working, yet." She pats me on the shoulder. "It's okay. I knew who you were. I knew what I was doing. I wasn't mad then, and I'm not mad now."

Cadence looks from Layla to me. "Perhaps this is not the correct time or place for this conversation. Nor should it include me."

Layla inhales, holds it, and lets it out slowly. "Girl, you are all kinds of right. It's ancient history and not worth bringing up. Rye is a good guy, Cadence. He really is." She leans closer to Cadence, stage whispering. "He just doesn't realize it."

"Is that a secret?" Cadence says, puzzled. "Why did you whisper so loudly?"

Layla barks a laugh. "I…no, I was teasing."

"Oh. Of course."

Layla looks at me, and her expression communicates a whole lot of questions. Not that I have answers for any of them, and not that I'd give them to her, even if I did.

Layla forces a smile at us both. "Your food will be out shortly."

When she's gone, I lean toward Cadence. "Look, Cadence, I…"

"Please pardon the interruption, but I neither need nor desire explanations. Your life is your own."

"Yeah, but…" I scrub my hand through my hair. "Fact

is, babe, that's who I am. I've never been serious about anyone."

She nods but says nothing. "I believe it is time for me to admit defeat and return home. I have attempted to come up with a scheme which might allow me to raise the money I need, but nothing I can think of will have the desired effect in the time necessary."

"What's the urgency?" I ask.

"There are very few flights going anywhere near where I wish to go. I have managed to secure a seat on a flight into South Sudan, which I have already paid for and which is nonrefundable. That is not insurmountable, as I could deal with the loss of money if it were simply a matter of the airfare, but I have raised a rather large amount of funds for this mission. I have purchased supplies. I have arranged for security. I have secured lodging. I have arranged for personal protection. I have the necessary visa and vaccinations. I have a contact with a local organization that will place me where I am most needed. The money I am missing is vitally important, however. Without it, all of the preparations I have spent the last six months of my life working for will be for nothing."

"And you need eighty grand?"

"Yes."

"And that old man we visited, Mr. Crenshaw, was gonna give you *eighty* fucking grand?"

"The Crenshaws are very wealthy. Mr. Crenshaw invented a piece of technology that has something to do with commercial airplanes—I am afraid I could not say what, only that it made them very, very wealthy. They were patrons of my parents when they were missionaries. And now that I am carrying the torch of my family's medical missionary legacy, they seek to support me, as well. But as you heard, they do not feel it is responsible to encourage or support me in going to a war-torn country."

"I…maybe there's merit to that, though. Y'know? Like, I don't know shit about global politics or whatever, but I know that place is supposed to be pretty fuckin' dangerous."

"Indeed, it is. It is a level Four 'do not travel' advisory."

"So…why there? Surely there are people in other, less dangerous places who need help just as badly."

She nods. "Assuredly there are. There are people here in this country. But my mind is made up. I…" she looks away, thinking. "I met someone when I was in the Congo last year. A refugee from the war in Sudan. Her name was Atong, which means 'born in war.' She is—*was*, rather—a very beautiful, very kind young girl. She had suffered a great deal in her escape from Sudan. Her father was killed in front of her. Her mother was violated and killed in front of her. Her elder brother helped her escape, but he too was killed, although his death was a tragic accident rather than violence. But Atong was a precious child, so utterly innocent. She carried no hatred in her heart despite all that she had seen and suffered."

"What…um…what happened? To Atong?"

She drops her eyes, swallowing hard. "I could not save her. The Congo has seen more than its share of violence, of course. She stepped on an old unexploded landmine. I worked on her for hours. I stopped her from exsanguinating via severed femoral artery, but she developed a terrible infection that would not respond to antibiotics. I could do nothing."

"Fuck, man," I murmur. "That's brutal."

"Yes. It was quite brutal." She sighs. "In my profession,

one is going to lose patients. It is simply a reality of the world—people die, and even the miracles of modern medicine cannot save everyone. But Atong...she left an indelible imprint on my heart. When she passed away, I swore an oath that I would go to her country and do what I could to help. I understand the risks. I know very well that I could be killed, kidnapped, violated, or merely trapped by airport closures, among a myriad of other possible risks. But I swore an oath to Atong's memory." Her eyes fill with tears. "I *must* find a way. I simply *must*."

"Well, when you put it like that..." I say, trailing off.

She blinks at me. "When I put it that way, what?"

"Oh. I just mean, when you put it that way, I can see why you're so determined. It's personal. It's not just a... fuck, what's the word? Altruistic—it's not just an altruistic desire to help, or some kind of virtue signaling."

"Virtue signaling? I am virtuous, I think. I am flawed, of course, as are we all. But I...yes, I do not believe I would need to signal my virtue. Unless of course you mean virtue in the sense of..." she blushes. "The other sense."

I shake my head, laughing. "I don't know what the other sense is, babe."

"Virginity," she whispers.

"Oh." I laugh again. "No, definitely don't mean that. Virtue signaling is...ummm..."

Lainey arrives from the kitchen, then, with our food. "Lane, can you define virtue signaling? I can't spell that shit, let alone define it."

"Sure, um..." Lainey looks up and away, thinking. "Posting something on social media purely for the attention, so people look at you and go, 'wow, that person must be super duper...ummm...like, good. Morally good, I mean, because of this reason or that reason. You're not doing anything of any value, it's purely for the attention, so people around you or online think you're this moral paragon or whatever."

"Oh." Cadence blinks, tips her head to the side. "No. My mission to Sudan is not that."

Lainey makes a surprised face. "Girl, you're trying to go *where*?"

"South Sudan."

"Why?"

"I am a medical doctor. I wish to provide medical care to those suffering from the war."

"You've got *wayyyy* bigger balls than I do," Lainey says, laughing. "Shit, I get scared leaving Three Rivers."

"You refer to metaphorical testicles, I assume, as it does appear to me that you are transgender, and I certainly am not."

Lainey snickers. "Yeah, metaphorical testicles, for sure. All lady bits here. So, when do you leave?"

"That is the issue at hand," Cadence says, unwrapping her fork from the paper napkin and prodding at the sandwich with it. "I cannot go. I am short eighty thousand, four hundred and sixty-two dollars and forty-seven cents, and I am meant to depart in fifteen days and…" She looks at the analog Garfield clock on the wall behind the counter. "Twelve hours."

Lainey stares out the window. "Well, what was it…two years ago? Yeah, it was before Bear showed up, that winter before he got out. Callie Masters got sick. Remember, Rye?"

I nod, recalling. "God, yeah, how could I forget?" I address Cadence. "Callie was the type of girl everyone loved, y'know? Prom queen, but the type of girl who invited the kid with Down syndrome to go as her date. She didn't tell anyone, didn't record it or make a big deal about it, she just showed up on Barry's arm like a boss. Man, that kid was on cloud nine for *weeks*. She did fundraisers for underprivileged kids, and she...man, Callie was the *shit*."

"Oh dear," Cadence says. "I am not sure I like where this is going, based on your usage of past tense."

Lainey takes over. "It has a happy ending. She got treatment and beat the cancer. She's in school in Glasgow, now, I think. The reason I bring it up is that Callie's family was poor as hell, and they couldn't afford the treatments she needed. Insurance, obviously, wouldn't do dick, because why would they, the fuckers. Useless, piece of shit, motherfucking—" she trails off, muttering. "Sorry. I've just had my own issues with insurance. Anyway. Callie's family started a fundraiser here in town. And they needed *way* more than eighty grand."

"Cancer treatment is exorbitantly expensive," Cadence says. "I do not need to imagine the costs involved."

"Exactly. People around here are generous, that's the point. I bet you could probably put that much together."

Cadence sighs, frowning. "Perhaps. This Callie, however, was a known quantity. People in your town knew her. They cared for her. I am a stranger. An outsider. I have no claim to their heartstrings."

I grin. "Babe, you don't know Three Rivers. I can't make any promises, but it's worth a shot."

She peers at me steadily. "Please, Riley. Do not play upon my hopes."

I cover her hand. "I told you, I'm not promising anything. But Lainey is right—we know people. And we know people who know people. Make it an event, get the right folks to talk it up, get you up on stage telling your story, just how you told it to me, about Atong? I bet you'd clear eighty-grand easily."

"S-Stage?" She breathes, looking utterly petrified at the mere thought. "My goodness, absolutely not. I could not do that. Absolutely not."

Lainey claps me on the shoulder. "Well, good thing our buddy Riley Crowe can charm the panties off a nun."

Cadence rears back. "You...*what*?"

I laugh, playfully shoving Lainey. "Figure of speech, Cadence. I've never attempted to charm a nun's underwear off."

"Oh. I see. Meaning you are so charming you can convince anyone to do anything."

"I dunno about all *that*."

Lainey cackles, leaning toward her. "Junior year, he convinced Mrs. Murphy, the history teacher, that *Fast Times at Ridgemont High* was a historical film and the class should have to watch it."

"I do not watch television."

Lainey laughs. "Well, then the reference won't mean much. Point is, that movie *is not* suitable for viewing in a classroom."

"Lots and lots of awkward boners when Phoebe Cates walked outta that water, lemme tell ya. Mrs. Murphy was out of her seat so fast it's a wonder she didn't break the sound barrier."

"That is impossible," Cadence says.

I laugh. "No shit." I squeeze her hand. "What we're saying is, don't give up yet, Cadence. Three Rivers just might come through for you."

5

Cadence

RILEY IS GIVING ME A GUIDED TOUR OF THREE Rivers, but the tour is less about viewing local attractions than introducing me to certain personages known to Riley.

Our first stop after we leave the cafe is the local library, where he introduces me to a Mrs. Joanne Aldis, the librarian and, not incidentally, a key member of the Three Rivers Chamber of Commerce. Riley is not a subtle man. He clearly and explicitly lays out my mission and my need and asks Mrs. Aldis for her assistance in leading the fundraising.

Mrs. Aldis is a trim, short, severe-looking woman with silver hair in a tight chignon, wearing cat's-eye glasses and a sour expression. Yet, when she speaks, her voice is soft and kind.

"I am sympathetic to your cause, Ms. Creswell, but I cannot push a fundraiser on the townspeople without performing some due diligence, even on the word of a well-known and -respected citizen like Mr. Crowe."

"You require some manner of proof that I am who I say I am and that my mission truly is what I say it is." I nod, withdraw my laptop from my bag, open it, and glance at her. "May I show you some photographs?"

"Certainly," the librarian says.

I turn my back to her and Riley and pull up my folder of personal photographs from my most recent trip. "These are from last year and the year before. After I received my medical license, I took a position with an NGO and spent the better portion of the past two years performing medical work in the DRC, Ethiopia, the Central African Republic, and Mozambique. These are my personal photographs, therefore I will not appear in them."

I click slowly through the photographs—as a photographer, my eye focuses on humanity rather than the landscape, so the photographs are of the people of Africa. Little girls, little boys. Babies. Pregnant mothers. Emaciated fathers. Children in the throes of various illnesses. Packed and overflowing makeshift triage tents in conflict zones. Severed limbs. Mass graves. Mothers weeping over dead children. Not all of them are so morbid, however. There is joy, too, such as when our caravan arrives with food and supplies. A particular favorite photograph of mine is of a young girl embracing her very first actual toy doll, a look of supreme ecstasy and joy on her young, innocent face.

Mrs. Aldis has her face covered with one hand, her eyes moist with unshed tears. "How awful."

"Unless one sees this kind of suffering firsthand, one cannot imagine it to exist," I say. "It is easy, here in this land of peace and plenty, to ignore the realities of life elsewhere. I am the daughter of missionaries. I cannot ignore it." I clear my throat and close out the photographs, and open my slideshow. "This is the presentation I created to show my corporate sponsors."

Riley looks at me. "Corporate sponsors?"

I blink at him. "Well, yes. I have cordial and productive relationships with several medical supply companies, who have pledged financial support as well as supply donations. The scale of the funds I require for the mission I intend cannot be met entirely via private donations."

I flip quickly through the slides, which cover my credentials as a doctor, my experience in emergency medicine during rotations and then two years of residency, my background as a missionary with my parents, and the various letters of recommendation from professors, supervisors, fellow residents, and the head of my department at Harvard. It also goes into detail regarding the situation in South Sudan and my plan to provide aid while mitigating the risks.

Riley says little while I give a much-foreshortened version of the presentation, which I have long since memorized. When I have finished, he regards me with an expression I cannot parse.

"Why do you look at me that way, Riley?" I ask.

He shrugs, shakes his head. "Just…it's a lot, I guess. Seeing what it's like over there, what people are going through. Plus, it's one thing for you to say you're a doctor and what you're planning, but seeing the evidence of it is something else."

Mrs. Aldis turns away, pacing a few steps in thought. After a few moments, she comes back. "Can you give that same presentation on Monday, for the Chamber of Commerce?"

I nod. "Yes, of course."

"I am only one vote, understand, but I know the others well enough to know you will find support."

My heart palpitates madly. "You…you truly believe I might find enough support to finish my fundraising?"

Mrs. Aldis nods, smiling kindly. "I do, my dear." She addresses Riley, then. "I'll work on the Chamber. If you get your friend Sheriff Mannix involved, the rest of the first responders will follow."

Riley grins. "My thinking exactly, Mrs. Aldis. Noelle has a lot of reach, too, both in the church community and as a business owner."

I glance at him, somewhat sharply. "Church community?"

"Yeah, my friend Noelle grew up in the church. She's had her issues on the church front, which isn't my story to tell, but she still has friends and family who are involved. She's our next stop."

The stop turns out to be a hair salon on the main street. Noelle is a very beautiful young woman about my age and of a similar height, although where I am slender and slight of build, she is more of a Venusian beauty—and a heavily pregnant one. Riley leads the way into the salon, and the young woman sees him and lights up. "Rye-guy! Finally gonna let me at that hair of yours?" she says, grinning at him with a teasing twinkle in her green eyes as she clips with expert speed and precision at a teenage boy's hair.

Riley blows a raspberry. "Not even close, babe, not even close. You got a minute after you're done there?"

She glances at her client and then at the smart watch on her left wrist. "Yeah, like five minutes? What's up?" She turns her gaze to me. "And introduce me to your…friend?"

It only occurs to me when she hesitates on the word 'friend' that Riley and I are holding hands again.

I look up at him. "Riley, you are giving people an incorrect impression regarding the nature of our relationship."

"It bothers you if people think we're together?" he asks.

I frown, considering it. "Hmmm. No. You did say you have a reputation to consider, however."

"Yeah, that was out of concern for you, babe. I was sayin' you may not want to hitch yourself to my wagon."

I frown all the harder. "But…why? Mrs. Aldis said you are well-respected member of the community."

"By some. Not by everyone." He gestures at his friend. "Cadence Creswell, MD, this is my good friend Noelle."

Noelle smiles at me, but her attention seems to be more on Riley as she finishes with her client, takes his money, and cleans her station. "So, Riley. I take it this isn't a social call."

A door in the rear of the salon opens and closes, and then I hear a bizarre clicking sound. I have no time to prepare myself for what happens next.

That being the bounding, slobbery arrival of a canine roughly the size of a not very small horse. It is the most terrifying creature I have ever seen, and I have come face to face with wild lions—sleeping on a game preserve, but still.

I scream and shrink against Riley, all but climbing his body like a tree as the gigantic, slavering creature barks deafeningly, greeting Noelle with a wild, slapping tongue. It then spies me and trots over to me, tongue extended.

I leap fully into Riley's arms, shaking like a leaf. "Get that creature away from me!"

Riley is laughing. "Hey, hey, hey, easy, hon. That's Panzer." He turns, so I am forced to look at the beast, which has claws like sabers and teeth like daggers, and the most intimidating, terrifying visage one could imagine. The beast could devour a lion, I do believe. "He's big and scary looking, but he's a sweetheart. He's just saying hi."

"Panzer. *Platz*." The voice giving the command—in German—is monstrously deep, rough, and quiet. The dog immediately flops to his belly, panting without taking his eyes off me.

"Bear!" Riley says, his voice betraying his pleasure at the newcomer's arrival. "Come meet Cadence."

The owner of the voice is every bit as terrifying as the dog. Several inches taller than Riley and carrying a veritable mountain of muscle, he has bright red hair in a long, thick braid, with a beard also worn long and braided—the man from the photographs in Riley's home. His eyes are kind, however, and the way he embraces Noelle with gentle, loving affection puts me at ease.

He kisses Noelle and then releases her, approaching me. "We're scary dudes, Panzer and me." His smile is patient and warm. I wriggle, and Riley lets me find my feet. "I get it."

I stare at the canine, who is panting and drooling and watching me like I'm his next meal. His eyes, for a dog, don't seem aggressive, but I am unfamiliar with dogs.

"Dogs frighten me," I admit. "I was accosted by a dog when I was a child. It bit me and would not let go." I extend my left forearm to show the scars I still bear.

"I'm sorry that happened. Panzer is a highly trained dog, though. He won't move from that spot unless I tell him he can. You don't need to be afraid of him." He extends his hand to me. "I'm Bear."

I shake his hand—his is more of a paw than a hand, so big and powerful, I find it plausible that he could crush bricks into dust, if he so chose. Yet despite this, his grip is gentle. "I am Cadence Creswell." I eye the dog, Panzer, warily. "May I approach him?"

Bear crouches at his dog's side, gripping the beast's collar with one hand and wrapping his giant, burly arm around the dog's enormous neck. "Yeah, 'course. Let him sniff the back of your hand. He won't bite, you have my word."

I shift forward by inches, hand extended, teeth clenched, heart palpitating furiously. Once I am in range, the enormous beast sniffs my offered hand with surprising delicacy. His nose is wet and cold. His tongue, when it flips against my knuckles, is warm and wet, in contrast. One lick, and then the dog gives me what I can only describe as a big, eager, doggy grin.

"Oh." I clear my throat and force myself to let go of Riley's hand, shifting the last few inches toward the dog. "*Hallo, mein Hundefreund. Du bist sehr gross. Aber ich muss doch keine Angst vor dir haben, oder?*" The dog woofs at me, a quiet noise, a huff of hot breath.

I feel three pair of eyes on me. Riley palms the back of his neck. "You speak German?"

"Yes. I speak several languages in varying degrees of fluency."

"*Several*?" he repeats. "Such as?"

"Well, in addition to German, in which I am only relatively conversationally fluent, I am passable in Spanish and Portuguese. I am well-versed in French, as it is rather widely spoken in certain regions of Africa. I can make myself understood in Italian. I have a smattering of quite a few African dialects as well, but I do not consider myself fluent in any of them."

Riley laughs—it sounds startled, or perhaps shocked. "For real?"

"Um, well…yes. Why?"

He shakes his head. "You speak *five* languages other than English fluently?"

"Yes. And I know words and phrases in perhaps six more African dialects."

"Fuck me," he mutters. To me, then. "How do you know so many languages?"

"I am what you might consider a black hole when it comes to information. Languages in particular have always come easily to me. I first began learning Spanish as a young child, as one does. I then discovered the similarity of Portuguese to Spanish, which led to the understanding of the influence of Latin on Spanish, French, Portuguese, and Italian. Therefore, I taught myself to read and write in Latin—it is not a spoken language, so one cannot be considered fluent in it, per se, however. Once I understood the structure and syntax and such of Latin, it was a relatively easy matter to absorb the relatively minor differences in the romance languages. German is similar to English— or rather, English is similar to German, I should say, so that was not very difficult. My family and I spent a year in Germany when I was nine, while my parents attempted to gain entry to Rwanda, and that was when I became truly conversant. The African languages I picked up out of necessity, while living among the people who speak them."

"Jesus," Riley breathes. "Make me feel like a real dumbfuck. I barely speak English properly."

I shake my head. "No, please. Do not feel that way. My mind is, as you may have noticed, rather different. It seeks patterns above all else, and language is nothing *but* patterns for the most part. What is not a matter of patterns is a matter of memorization, and I happen to have an eidetic memory."

"A what memory?"

"Eidetic. It was once called a photographic memory, but recent advancements in understanding have rendered that term obsolete. It merely means I retain information with perfect recall."

"Yeah, I guess that tracks," he mutters.

Noelle, having finished cleaning her space, joins the conversation. "So, since this isn't a social call, to what do we owe the pleasure?"

Riley explains my mission, the need, and Mrs. Aldis's plan to bring the Chamber of Commerce on board.

Noelle listens politely. "So, what does this have to do with me?"

"Well," Riley says. "Cadence's whole thing is missions. And, well...look, I know you've had your issues with church folks, considering what happened with you and your ex, but I was hoping you still had some connections in the church community. I guess this just seems like the kind of thing church folks would get behind."

Noelle sighs. "You aren't wrong, there. It's just...I pretty much cut all ties with the church when everything happened." She looks at me, thinking. "My parents, however, are a different story. I'll talk to them." She looks at me again, frowning. "You're really going to go there? Isn't it pretty dangerous?"

"It is," I agree. "But I cannot allow that to deter me. I made a promise which I intend to keep. The people there deserve care, precisely because of the danger which they live with every day. When I have finished my mission, I will return here, where it is safe. They will not."

"You've got guts, I'll give you that," Noelle says. "I'd be too scared."

"Nah," Bear says, regarding her with affection. "You're way braver than you think."

She smiles at him. "I'm glad you think so, baby." To me, then. "I'll see what I can do."

"That is all one could hope for," I say. "And considering you do not know me at all, it is more than I could have asked."

The main salon door opens, and a woman enters.

"That's my next appointment," Noelle says. "I'll get ahold of you, Riley, once I've spoken to my parents."

"You're the best, No-No." Riley hugs her and then gives Bear an exuberant, back-slapping, hyper-masculine embrace. "See ya 'round, Bear."

"Yeah, man," Bear rumbles. "Nice to meet you, Cadence."

"You as well, both of you," I say, waving as Riley leads me outside.

He points down the street. "Next stop, the sheriff's office!"

"Why the sheriff?" I ask.

"Oh, well, because the sheriff happens to be my lifelong best friend. Well, one of two, not counting my brother." He grins. "You'll meet everyone, don't worry."

"My head is already spinning, Riley," I say.

He looks at me, concerned. "Oh, nope. It's okay. No spinning."

I frown at him. "Are you mocking my literal nature?"

"Mocking? Never. Teasing, affectionately? Yes."

"Oh. I see." We walk together in silence for several blocks. Finally, I can hold back the question no longer. "Why are you doing this?"

"Doing what?" he asks.

"Helping me. Any of it, but the fundraising in particular."

He does not answer immediately. "I want to. It's a noble cause, for one. And, honestly, I like you. I want to help." He says it so bluntly, casually, as if it wouldn't rock the foundations of my world.

"You like me." I register the words and their meaning—and the fact that he has said them more than once—but my heart cannot accept their veracity.

"Yep."

"Interesting." It emerges flatly, atonal.

He walks a few steps and then looks at me. "Wait, hold up." he stops, moves in front of me, and tries to catch my eyes. "Cadence…do you not believe me?"

"In all honesty, no. To be clear, I do not think you are lying. Rather, it is obvious you do not understand me, which makes me an interesting puzzle, at best. Experience informs me that you will lose interest once the novelty wears off."

"Nah." He waves a hand. "It ain't that."

His dismissal of my statement is breezy and casual. Utterly without value or merit, or so it seems.

"History would beg to differ," I say.

"Maybe." He frowns in my direction. "Meanin' you've been through that? People show interest, get bored, and move on?"

"To put it kindly, yes."

"What's the unkind version?" he asks.

I sigh. "People can be cruel, Riley." I swallow hard, look straight ahead, buttoning up the overwhelming barrage of emotions before they can spill out. "Especially to someone as…different…as I am."

"People can be real dicks," he says, and while I do not trust my translation of his expression, it appears he understands the sentiment from personal experience. He looks at me, searching my face—for what, I could not say. "I'm not helping you out of idle curiosity or boredom or whatever. And the truth is, I don't like all that many people. You, I do."

"When you say you like me, what does that mean?" I hate the way my heart clatters hopefully within the concrete prison I imagine it to be concealed within.

I know better. But one cannot help hoping, I suppose.

Futile as that hope may be.

A shrug. "You're different. You're interesting. I dunno. I just like you. That's what it means. I like who you seem to be, and the more I learn about you, the more I like you."

As friends? The question remains unasked, percolating in my metaphorical gut.

The inference which follows the unasked question

burns even hotter: or as more? But this I cannot allow to even form as a thought.

It simply would not do.

One can only hope and be disappointed so many times, after all.

Riley stops outside a small, one-story brick building, one foot on the bottom-most step; a sign painted on the glass announces that this is the county sheriff's office, and that Cole Mannix is the sheriff. "C'mon, let's go say hi to Cole."

"Riley, wait." I hesitate. "You have helped me more than anyone could expect. You have done enough. You need not waste any more of your time on this, or me. I am quite sure you have better things to do on a Saturday."

He frowns at me, perturbed. "Haven't wasted a damn thing, babe. I'm doing exactly what I want to be doing." He takes both of my hands. "C'mon. I want you to meet Cole. More to the point, I want Cole to meet you."

"I do not think it necessary to inflict my oddity upon anyone else, Riley," I murmur. "You will erode the good-will of your friends."

"The fuck are you talking about?" he demands, sounding genuinely disturbed. "No one is inflicting anything on anyone, and also I don't even know what you mean by the second part of that bullshit statement."

"Never mind. It was an obviously poor attempt at self-deprecating humor."

He stares at me, and I think he can detect the lie in my words. "More bullshit. I thought you didn't lie."

I blush. "Riley, I—"

He frames one side of my face with his palm. "Don't do that, Cadence."

"You engage in self-deprecating humor," I point out.

"Yeah, but I'm an ignorant shithead." He smiles at me, and my stomach seems to twist and to melt and to flip all at once. "You're a fuckin' genius and literal fuckin' saint. Ain't much of a comparison, sweetheart."

"I have yet to see any evidence that you are an igno-rant...what you said. Perhaps you are mistaken in your assessment of yourself."

He shakes his head, wrinkling his nose. "Nah. There's a few things you don't know about me." He grabs me around the waist, lifts me like an ice dancer prepar-ing to throw his partner into a triple axel, and deposits me on the step above him. "C'mon, Gorgeous. Best not keep Sheriff Mannix waiting."

He seems oblivious to the fact that I cannot breathe. He touched me—he had his hands around my waist. I know it meant nothing to him, but it does to me.

I am still regaining my mental and emotional equilibrium as we enter the police station. It is a calm, peaceful place. Uniformed deputies sit at desks doing paperwork and using computers and whatever else po-licemen do when they aren't on patrol. Riley greets them all by name, trading handshakes with them and ask-ing after wives and girlfriends and kids and pets—he is known and well-liked. He leads the way through the office, which is fluorescent-lit, with thin industrial blue carpet on the floor and a drop-tile ceiling, a mostly open space with desks facing each other in three rows of two abreast. Cole Mannix's office is at the rear of the build-ing, with a direct line of sight to the front door and the reception desk—the office is glassed off with built-in louvered blinds, the door propped open by a thick tome of Michigan's laws.

Cole is a large man, not as large as Bear but more heavily muscled than Riley. His golden hair is cut short and brushed to the side, a little messy from his hand passing through it, and a short, neat beard frames a strong jaw. He has blue-blocking glasses on his face as he stares at a large computer monitor, frowning in concentration as he shifts his attention from the monitor to a stapled stack of papers on the desk, a silver ballpoint pen moving from line to line.

Riley knocks on the doorframe.

"One sec," Sheriff Mannix mutters, not looking up. He finishes his line-item comparison and then looks up, a grin spreading across his face when he sees who it is. "Rye, what the fuck are you doing here, bro? Come to turn yourself in, finally?"

Riley goes tense, his shoulders hunching. He did not like that joke, for some reason. "Nah, man. You know me, I'm a good boy." He juts his chin at the desk. "That looks fun. Love the sexy specs, Manny."

Sheriff Mannix whips the glasses off and tosses them on the desk. "Ah, fuck you," he says, his tone implying affection and humor rather than offense. "Bein' the big boss means going over several hundred pages of expense reports, line by fucking line. Staring at that damn screen all day kills my fuckin' eyes. Some days, I'd rather go back to being a lowly deputy."

"Three Rivers wouldn't let that happen, " Riley says. "You're gonna be in that office till you retire, buddy."

Cole laughs. "Yeah, I know. I just hate paperwork, and I hate computers." He turns his gaze to me. "Who's your beautiful new friend?"

I feel my cheeks burn under the heat of his compliment and his curious eyes. "I am Cadence Creswell, Sheriff Mannix. It is a pleasure to make your acquaintance."

He half-rises from his desk to shake my hand, his grip firm but gentle. "Pleased to meet you, too, Cadence." He juts his chin at the two chairs facing the desk. "Have a seat."

"Cadence is in town raising funds for a medical mission trip to Sudan," Riley explains as we sit. "We're hoping you can help get the first responders of Three Rivers on board. We've got Mrs. Aldis working on the Chamber of Commerce, Noelle is going to her parents about the church folks, and now we're here hittin' you up."

"Fundraising, huh?" He looks from me to Riley, and then to our hands, which are—yet again—joined. I hadn't even noticed, so accustomed have I become to Riley's insistence on holding my hand wherever he takes me. "How much? I can pass a hat around the office."

Riley chuckles. "This ain't pass-the-hat shit, bro. We're putting together an event."

"Hmmm," Cole hums. "So, how much?"

"Eighty grand," Riley answers. "And change."

Cole snorts. "Yeah, passing the hat won't cut it." He glances at our hands again but doesn't comment on them. "So...what do you need from me?"

"Just spread the word about the cause. She's presenting to the Chamber on Monday. I'm thinking we pack out the town hall."

I squeak at this. "Riley! A memorized presentation of a PowerPoint to a handful of executives is one thing. Giving that presentation to a significant percentage of the town is a whole other proposition. I am not comfortable with the latter scenario."

"You'll be fine," he says. "I'll be with you every step of the way."

"I wish I shared your confidence," I say.

Cole rises from his desk and moves around to lean back against the front corner of it nearest to Riley; his gun and gear belt hang from the back of his chair. "So, Cadence. South Sudan, huh?" He stares away, thinking. "Riley wouldn't hitch his horse to your wagon if he didn't believe in you and your mission. If he's in, I'm in."

Sheriff Cole Mannix appears to be a competent, rational man, an authority figure, and Riley's best friend. Where Riley has the air of a court jester, Cole seems to be more serious. Therefore, his willingness to throw his weight behind my cause simply because Riley has done so speaks volumes as to Cole's opinion of Riley.

"You both used the same phrase," I say. "Regarding hitching one's horse to a wagon."

Riley chuckles. "Great minds, right, Manny?"

Cole just snorts. "Some kinda minds, at least." He pushes off the desk. "Much as I'd rather shoot the shit with you two, I'm gonna be at that expense report all damn day, so I gotta get back to it. I'll rally the troops, though, and put the word out about the cause. Soon as you have info on the event, let me know and I'll pass that along."

"Will do, buddy. Thanks for your time. Dinner and drinks with the gang, later?"

Cole frowns as he rounds his desk and sits down. "Is there a plan? Hadn't heard."

"There is now. I'm callin' it."

Cole nods. "I'm in. You seen Nyxie recently?"

"Not for a few days. He had a big-money frame-off

restoration he was doing for some rich cat up in Petosky. You know how he is when he's got a project on."

Cole nods, putting his glasses on. "Ah, yeah, that explains it. Assuming I get this done," he taps the paper on his desk, "I could meet up around six, six-thirty."

"We'll be at the Cellar. Usual table." Riley backs out of the office, both middle fingers raised. "Later, dickhead."

Cole returns a middle finger without looking. "Backatcha, fucknut. Don't let the door hit you on the way out." He looks up and smiles at me, and my goodness, his smile is nearly as dazzling as Riley's. "Cadence, it's wonderful to meet you. Keep our boy outta trouble, yeah?"

I frown. "Is he prone to run-ins with your department? He appears to be rather law-abiding, in my experience, limited though it is."

Cole laughs, believing me to be joking, I think. Which is when I realize my error—*he* was joking. Of course. "Nah, he got that out of his system a long time ago. We just like to give each other shit."

"Yes…obviously." Embarrassed, as usual, I turn on my heel and walk away before I can say anything else idiotic.

It's only when I'm outside that I realize my abrupt departure could be construed as rude. Riley emerges after me by a few moments, having hung back to finish his farewell to his friend. "Hey, you okay?"

I sigh. "Yes."

He frowns at me. "Bullshit. What's up?"

"It is difficult to explain." I turn away.

He moves around, staying in my line of sight. "Whoa, hey. Cadence, I'm lost. What are you upset about?"

"I am embarrassed. I embarrassed you. I was rude to your friend." The storm of feelings rages, perpetually, inside me, chaotic and confusing and impossible—overwhelming and disorienting.

"The fuck are you talking about? No one embarrassed anyone. You weren't rude. I'm so fuckin' lost, babe."

He tries to take my hand, but I am overwhelmed and cannot tolerate physical contact—I pull away and hold my palms out to keep him at arm's length. "Do not, please. I need a moment."

"Uh, sure. Sure. Okay." He backs away, hands up, palms out. "Sorry."

Inside, I am a hurricane of feelings and thoughts, paralyzing me. I cannot breathe. Cannot move. Cannot even blink. I suppose to Riley, I must look supremely strange, standing stock-still on the sidewalk like a statue.

I cannot seize upon a single thought or emotion. There are too many, and they move too fast, like bats trapped in a belfry.

"Cadence?" His voice is low and quiet, the calming, soothing, patient tone he used when I was turtling on his floor.

Something truly extraordinary happens, then.

"Hey, so…I'm gonna hug you." I hear him, but I cannot formulate a response.

Do not.

That is my response.

Touching me when I am functionally frozen like this is typically problematic. I have been known to melt down because of it. I have gotten better about managing myself, and I have not had a real meltdown in a long time. But so much has happened since yesterday that I simply do not know how to cope with—the walk to the Crenshaws, losing their support, the walk back, crying, meeting Riley, being attracted to him even though I know it is a hopeless case for me, forgetting my beloved rucksack and having to interact with Mr. Crenshaw again, the alarm situation, and now all of this? My social faux pas was the last straw.

Therefore, when Riley announces his intent to embrace me, I expect it to cause a full meltdown.

That is not what happens.

His arms circle me gently, and then he pulls me against his chest. I am as stiff as a board, arms at my sides.

Instead of the paralytic agony of sensory overload, I feel...

Comfort.

This is nearly as overwhelming.

It should not be. Yet, it is.

He smells divine—pine, cedar, soap, clean laundry. The fabric of his T-shirt is soft against my cheek, and I hear his heart beating under my ear. His arms encircle me, but rather than imprisoning me, they shelter me, they anchor me to the earth when the maelstrom within threatens to carry me away.

I cannot measure the time it takes for me to calm enough to emerge from the functional freeze, but past examples have lasted upward of ten minutes. Riley merely holds me through it.

He asks no questions.

Demands no answers.

He does not shift in discomfort or boredom.

He is a steadying, calming presence.

Warm.

Patient.

Kind.

When I am finally able to function again, I look up

into his eyes for as long as I can, still in the shelter of his embrace. "I believe I owe you an explanation."

"Don't owe me a goddamn thing, Cadence." He is serious, but despite the aggression of his cursing, he does not appear to be angry.

"Surely you must be wondering what is wrong with me," I say, my voice barely above a whisper.

"Nope."

I frown up at him. "How can that be? You obviously do not understand the way I function. I find it impossible to believe that you have not once wondered what is wrong with me."

"I'm curious about you. It's true, I don't always understand…well, a lotta shit. The things you say, the way you talk, why you're so literal about things, and why you don't pick up on certain things. But I've never once thought there's anything *wrong* with you." His eyes, so pale, so blue, so intense, so hypnotic, search my face. "Because there ain't. There's not a single goddamn thing wrong with you."

Tears spring into my eyes, and I hide them by burying my face in his shirt again.

He tucks his finger under my chin and lifts my face, passing a thumb under my eyes, one and then the other. "Hey, what's this?"

"You cannot…" I shake my head, hating the tears—the intensity of the emotion causing them as well as the physical discomfort of them, the salty burn, the tightness in my throat, the embarrassment of them. "You cannot understand."

"Maybe not," he whispers, "but I'd sure love a shot at trying."

"Can we return to your home, please?" I whisper,

fighting for composure. "I have had enough of being out in public for the moment."

He pulls away, and his next action nearly sends me into another tailspin.

He kisses my cheeks, under my eyes. "C'mon. Let's get you outta here."

Soft.

Sweet.

Gentle.

"Oh, do not give me hope, I pray," I breathe, but Riley is ahead of me, pressing the button on the light pole to engage the pedestrian crossing lights, and he cannot hear me. "Please, Riley Crowe of Three Rivers, do not give me hope. I cannot bear it."

Yet when he takes my hand to escort me across the street, his smile is so genuine, so bright, so dazzling that I cannot help but hope.

Risking death to aid others is frightening, yes. But I understand the risks. I have seen the worst that can happen, and I have to come to terms with the possibility of it happening to me.

What truly terrifies me into paralysis is the prospect of letting myself hope that this man, Riley Crowe of Three Rivers, could develop real feelings for me. That he could accept me as I am. That he could—

I cannot even think it. It is impossible.

There is no hope of that.

But for all that he has done for me, I owe him answers. I will tell him my truth, and I will accept the results, whatever that may be.

6

Riley

I GOTTA ADMIT, HER ABRUPT EXIT AND SUBSEQUENT statue act is a little freaky. Maybe *freaky* is the wrong word. Weird. I dunno. But her implication that I have to think something is wrong with her is a big, fat megaphone for her insecurities.

The drive back to my place is short and silent. I let her be, since it seems like when she's silent like this, it's best to just let her do what she needs to do.

The tears, though, man. Fuck, they kill me. When she looked up at me with those big green eyes all wet with tears, looking so lost and so hurt and so lonely, I just…

I wanted to kiss her. So motherfucking bad, I wanted to kiss her. I didn't, because she deserves better than my bitch ass. This girl is a legit, certified genius, more saintly

than Mother Theresa, and unless I'm way wrong, as innocent as I am the opposite.

I settled for kissing her tears away, which was a mistake. Just another nail in the coffin of my feelings, which
will be decimated when she busts the fuck outta here for
Africa, never to return.

We pull into the garage, and as seems to be the case
with her, she doesn't realize it. I don't mind. It gives me
an opportunity to look like I have manners when I open
the door for her. If nothing else, it puts her soft, warm little hand in mind, and fuck, I love that.

Walking around downtown Three Rivers with her,
holding her hand? Man, I felt about ten feet tall. That girl?
A 24-year-old Harvard-educated doctor, a missionary who
speaks like a dozen fucking languages, who's drop-dead
goddamned gorgeous to boot? She's so far outta my fuckin'
league it ain't even funny. I can't even *see* her league from
where I am.

Yet she doesn't seem to realize it.

Yet.

Once we're in the house, she beelines for the couch
and sits down, palms on her knees, back straight as a ruler,
and…does nothing.

She doesn't blink, barely breathes. Just sits there, staring at nothing.

But this seems to be how she thinks or copes or processes or whatever, so I leave her to it. I've got a handful
of emails to go through—bios from inmates hoping for a
slot in my program. I grab my laptop from the table and
sit near her, but not touching, and start reading.

This only lasts for a few minutes—enough time to
read through the first bio—and she…emerges, I suppose.

She blinks, looks around, sees me. "Riley."

"Cadence."

She clears her throat delicately. "I am sorry."

I close my laptop and set it aside. "For?"

"Embarrassing you in front of Sheriff Mannix. Freezing on the street. Zoning out just now."

"You didn't embarrass me, Cadence."

"But my faux pas—"

"What's a fo-paw?" God, I feel dumb around her.

"An embarrassing or tactless act or remark in a social situation."

"Oh. What faux pas would that be?"

She frowns at me. "My misunderstanding of his request to keep you out of trouble and my subsequent tasteless exit." She shakes her head. "Sheriff Mannix responded with grace, as you and all of your friends have. But it is mortifying nonetheless."

"It was a misunderstanding, Cadence. Not a big deal."

She shakes her head. "I do not mean to be rude, but are you being intentionally obtuse?"

"Obtuse? Like a triangle?" I hold up my hands before she can reply. "Kidding. I *do* know that word. Look, I…" I let out a long, slow breath. "I will admit to a certain amount of curiosity. But you don't owe me any explanations."

"I feel that I do," she says. "You have been so patient and kind with me, and despite how many questions you must have, you have not pressed when you would be well within your rights to do so."

"No one has any right to demand answers from anyone, Cadence." I tip my head to the side. "I mean, sure, there are circumstances where answers can be expected. But we just met. I'm helping you because I want to. I'm choosing to. That doesn't put any kind of burden or obligation on you. None whatsoever."

Cadence is quiet for a moment and then turns on the couch to angle toward me. "I am autistic."

"Okay." I'm not sure what to make of that.

She seems to be waiting for more. "Okay? That is your only response?"

I shrug. "I mean, yeah. I don't know much about it, to be honest. I've heard people talk about the spectrum or whatever, but the god's honest truth is I'm ignorant as fuck about what it really means. I don't know what autism is, and I don't understand how it can be a spectrum."

She considers her response for several silent moments. "Many things in this world exist on a spectrum. Physical things, like light and color. Human conditions, such as autism or addiction."

"Addiction is a spectrum?"

"Well, certainly," she responds, as if it's obvious. "It is obviously not merely binary, correct? Consider these differing hypothetical scenarios, if you will. There is a man, let us call him Roger. Roger has a normal life. He is married, he has children, and he has a job. He loves his wife and children and is content enough at his job. He has no obvious, major stressors beyond those of normal human existence—bills, traffic, family problems, marital disagreements. Roger, when he returns home from work, immediately opens a beer. A second. A third. Perhaps he drinks beer through dinner, and while watching a television program with his wife. He does this every night. He cannot fathom *not* doing so. But yet, he is never violent. He does not yell at or harm his wife or children. He arrives at work on time and is productive. But yet, every night, he drinks his beer, hour after hour, and if you told him he could not, can you imagine his response?"

I absorb this. "He'd flip his wig."

"By which I assume you mean he would be greatly displeased."

"Right."

"Is Roger addicted?" she asks. "Is he an alcoholic simply because his addiction is not problematic in the stereotypical sense?" She doesn't wait for an answer. "Now consider an alternative scenario. A woman named... Rachel. Rachel is unhappy. Rachel hates her job. She hates her husband. She does not hate her children, perhaps, but they stress her out—everything in her life stresses her out. Rachel drinks wine until she cannot function. But not every night. Not every day. Some days she only has a glass or two. But sometimes, it spirals out of control and becomes problematic. Is she more or less addicted than Roger? Roger drinks every single day, and he drinks quite a lot. Rachel only drinks sometimes." She displays her hands, like *see*? "Someone who goes to the bar every night but never gets drunk. Someone who binges, but only on Friday and Saturday nights. The person who drinks a whole bottle of vodka or whiskey every day. These are examples of the spectrum of alcohol addiction. They do not look the same on every person. Some have it more severely than others. That is a spectrum."

"Fuck, dude. I never thought about it like that."

She smiles. "This is something I have studied rather intensely. So now, autism."

"What is it? Like, pretend I don't know jack shit. Not that you have to pretend."

Once again, she speaks as if reciting a textbook

definition. "Autism Spectrum Disorder is a condition characterized by difficulties or differences in social communication and/or interaction, an intense need for predictability and routine, sensory processing difficulties, a tendency to hyperfixate on areas of personal interest, and repetitive behaviors."

I blink, processing. "Uhhh, you're gonna have to break all that down for me, sweetheart. That was a lot."

"Very well." She's sitting in perfect posture—back perfectly straight, chin high, hands folded on her lap, knees together; regal, that's the only word for it. "Let us go through the definition piece by piece, as it relates to me. First, difficulties or differences in social communication or interaction. This is the one that is most glaring, with me. ASD, Autism Spectrum Disorder, means that my brain is wired differently from yours. Very, *very* differently. I have a hard, if not impossible, time understanding the emotions of others. Not merely emotions—facial expressions. Nuances of verbal expression. When you look at your good friend, Sheriff Cole Mannix, for example. If he makes this face—" she scowls. "You would interpret that how?"

I shrug. "Depends."

"On what?"

"Context. He could be thinking. He could be mad. He could just be concentrating. He might be trying to fart."

"Precisely. A scowl can mean many things. My brain only sees it as anger. And a scowl is a fairly broad expression, correct? It is not subtle." She blinks. "Trying to fart?"

I laugh. "Caught that, huh?"

She shrugs, nodding. "It is a valid answer. Anyway, consider the infinite other facial expressions that you, a neurotypical person, easily and automatically interpret on a daily basis. If you say something inappropriate, you can tell that you have made someone uncomfortable simply by the way they look at you. I, on the other hand, will not be able to see that. I will miss the nuance of facial expression."

I hum thoughtfully. "I'm following you so far."

"Now consider verbal social expression. This is where, more than anything, I struggle the most."

"Verbal social expression," I say, "You mean... talking?"

"Yes. I realize that to you, it may seem redundant to differentiate between verbal and nonverbal social expression, but to me, they are vastly different things. Nonverbal expressions are largely lost on me, as I have said. Verbal expression, however, is far more nuanced. As you may have noticed, I am quite literal in my understanding of what is said to and around me."

I can't help a laugh. "Yeah, I did notice."

She smiles, but it's thin. "When your friend told me to keep you out of trouble, of course he was not being literal. You are not, so far as I have witnessed in the time we have been acquainted, prone to misbehavior, legal or otherwise. But my mind does not automatically process these facts. It ignores them. I hear Sheriff Mannix tell me to keep you out of trouble and my reaction is, 'Oh, alright. I shall keep him out of trouble. But...why, if he is not prone to troublemaking?'" She shrugs. "The idea that he could be jesting simply does not occur to me. It is the same with anything which may have more than one possible meaning. It is not that I do not enjoy laughter or that I do not have a sense of humor, but what registers as humor to my brain is broad, if you know what I mean by that. Slapstick, for example. Physical humor. Metaphorically speaking, in order to register something as humor, I need the broad wink to tell me so." She peers at me. "You have thoughts to share, I believe."

"Yeah, I…" I exhale, trying to figure out where to start and how to ask the questions that are bubbling up as she explains this shit.

Before I can go further, she rests her hand on my knee. "Before you say anything, Riley, please hear this. I wish you to be honest. Do not seek to preserve my feelings by tiptoeing around what you really wish to know. Whatever cruel, unkind, or mean-spirited thing could be said about me, know that I have heard it before, many, many times. Furthermore, I believe I know you well enough to know that you will not intend anything to be mocking or mean-spirited."

"I hate that," I say. "That people have been so fuckin' mean to you."

She shrugs. "People are frequently cruel, Riley. It is a fact of life. And people are never quite so cruel as to those whom they do not understand, and to many people, I am so different that I may as well be an alien." She huffs softly, a sort of sighing laugh. "Do you know what my nickname was, when I attended public high school?"

I groan. "Oh god, I'm scared. What?"

"Rosie."

I frown. "Um…I've gotta be missing something."

"Yes, most likely. Have you ever watched the old animated series, *The Jetsons?*"

The meaning of the nickname comes crashing down on me like a ton of bricks. "The robot maid."

"Correct. It began as Robot-Girl, along with a variety of infantile derivations, such as Robo-Cop, Robo-Bitch," she shakes her head, waves her hand. "I need not list them all, of which there were many. And then some humorous soul with too much time on his or her hands created a…a meme, I suppose, of me. The person must have stumbled across a clip of the show featuring Rosie the robot maid, thought of me, and used computer software to transpose my head onto Rosie's body, using a previously recorded video of me taken during a school function, in which I speak as I normally do. I do not remember what I said in the clip, and it does not matter. It went viral throughout the entire school. And from then on, I was never again addressed as Cadence or Cadie by anyone at the school—by students *or* faculty."

I gape at her. "The fucking *faculty* called you that?"

"Yes. I combated the efforts for some months by simply not responding to the name, but it became so widespread that by the end of the year, I simply had no other choice but to respond to it. To this day, if I run into someone in my hometown with whom I attended high school, they will address me as Rosie."

"Jesus fuck, that's evil."

She shakes her head. "No, it is not. It is completely understandable. Hurtful, perhaps, but understandable." She looks at me, hard and piercing. "Can you truthfully tell me you have not had a thought along those lines?"

I can't, so I don't answer.

"Precisely." She pauses, regarding me steadily. "What was the thought, please? I shall not be angry with you, I promise."

"Cadence—"

She squeezes my knee. "I am curious. I give you my word, I will not think less of you, and I will not be offended.

I like to think I have grown out of being offended by such things."

"Something like, you sound like a robot who learned English at Downton Abbey."

She blinks at me for a moment, and then...laughs, genuinely amused. "A Downton Abbey robot? My goodness, that is apropos, Riley. Very humorous." She pats my knee. "So. Questions. You may ask me anything and I will answer honestly and to the best of my knowledge."

"Why do you talk the way you do?"

"Well, first, you must know that I was nonverbal until I was five years of age. I understood what was said, I simply did not speak. I *could*, since I obviously have functional vocal chords. The second thing you must know in order to understand my speech patterns and syntax is that I have always been academically precocious. I was reading *Run Spot Run* type board books at eighteen months. By three years of age, I was reading at an adult level—by five, I was absorbing every book I could find. My parents are scholars and academics, so our house was and still is full of books on every subject one can think of, primarily nonfiction. We did not and do not own a television, I have never owned a smartphone, and rarely access the internet for any purpose other than research or other such utilitarian purposes, such as booking flights or lodgings. I read encyclopedias, histories, biographies, old textbooks, collections of essays by renowned thinkers from all ages. So, what you must understand from this is that the language to which I was exposed from birth was largely formal."

"Makes sense to me."

"Indeed. When I finally began speaking at age five, it was in complete sentences, using formal structure and syntax. Then, when I was eight, my private tutor assigned a novel for me to read. I had read fiction, of course, but unless assigned fiction for school, I only read nonfiction. The book Mr. Craig assigned me to read was *Pride and Prejudice*."

I nod. "Now that tracks. I watched the movie with Kiera Knightly in it a while back, me and the chick I was seeing at the time."

"So you are at least familiar."

"Yeah, for sure. I got the feeling that there was a lot going on, especially in the dialogue, that I was missing, though. Like, it just went way over my head."

She nods. "Oh, certainly. That is why I enjoyed the books so much. Because it was written, I could take my time with it as I attempted to understand the difference between what was being said and what was implied, inferred, or otherwise left unsaid. I suppose something in the way they spoke in the Regency Period resonated with me. I became fixated, and devoured everything that was written about and during that period." She taps her bag. "*Pride and Prejudice* is still my favorite novel, and I re-read it regularly."

"You mentioned fixation," I say. "What does that mean?"

"Hyperfixation is a hallmark of autism. Neurotypicals like yourself will discover something they are interested in—baseball, finance, chess, pornography, photography, automobile restoration, what have you. A neurotypical brain can balance that interest or hobby with other things—eating, drinking, social events, sleep, sex, television, reading. A neurodivergent brain, like mine, does not. The scope and severity of hyperfixation, like everything else, differs from person to person. My particular hyper-fixation is the absorption of information—the process-ing of data."

I frown. "Meaning?"

"I enjoy all topics. Science, mathematics, history, lan-guage, anthropology, sociology, philosophy, everything. But when I was five, around the same time as I began talking, I came across a somewhat dated copy of Pearson's *Human Anatomy and Physiology*, a standard university issue textbook. Why one becomes fixated on something is, so far as I am aware, inexplicable. For me, it is human anatomy. I read that book cover to cover multiple times, highlighted and annotated it to the point of absurdity. I memorized it, cover to cover, every word, diagram, and photograph."

I boggle at her. "You *memorized* an entire fucking anat-omy textbook at age five?"

She nods. "Yes. I told you—I possess an eidetic memory. I do not forget what I have seen, read, heard, or learned."

"Ever?"

She shrugs. "Not so far."

"So you still have that in your brain? The whole thing?"

"Yes."

I rock back. "Fuck me, that's incredible."

She shrugs again. "It is merely how I function." A wave of her hand. "That textbook was the beginning, for me. I moved on to everything medical. Textbooks on every subject—the nervous system, musculature, veins and ar-teries, the brain, sedation, everything I could find in the li-brary and everything I could beg my parents to order from Amazon. I subscribed to medical journals. I read study abstracts and meta-analyses. I became hyperfixated to the point of obsession with all things medical, but anatomy in particular. The human body is a fascinating machine. It is endlessly complex, and at once delicate and fragile yet remarkably resilient."

"So becoming a doctor was sort of a no-brainer, then," I say.

"Oh, yes. My father is a surgeon and my mother is a nurse. When I was six, we moved to Kenya to become missionaries. Being fascinated with all things medical already, I attended the clinic where my parents worked on a regular basis, and frequently watched my father perform surgeries while my mother assisted as his nurse. Many thought it wildly inappropriate, if not borderline abuse, to allow a six-year-old to watch her father reduce a leg fracture, or stitch up a laceration, or repair a severed artery. But my parents knew that I was different. It was not common back then to apply the ASD label to girls, as it presents much differently in females than it does in males, especially cases like mine."

"Cases like yours?"

"Yes. My presentation of autism is high-functioning with savant tendencies." She smiles, anticipating my questions. "It means I am capable of autonomy. I do not need constant care and supervision. I can function in society—feeding and clothing myself appropriately, navigating, learning, all the things that a neurotypical person takes for granted as everyday actions, things you don't think about doing—you just do them. Savant tendencies indicate the overlap of my eidetic memory and hyperfixation—meaning, my somewhat extraordinary capacity for informational intake and retention." She pauses, thinking. "For many with autism, savant tendencies or hyperfixation tends to focus on one thing, either to the exclusion of all else or nearly so."

"The kid in class who's obsessed with dinosaurs and can tell you everything about them," I say.

"Yes," she says. "Exactly. Or trains. Or space. Or World War Two, or any subject. I tend to focus on medicine, but not exclusively."

I think about what she's telling me, and a billion questions crop up, too fast to seize any of them. One in particular ends up floating to the top, and I address it to her. "You tend to refer to your brain almost as this…*other*, d'you know what I mean? Something that's not…*you*."

She nods. "Yes. An astute observation. In your experience, I believe, you are one cohesive whole. Your mind and your body are one entity. Not so for me. My brain operates…not independently, but it often seems that way. I cannot stop my brain from spinning out of control. If your brain is an engine, you have both brake and throttle controls. I do not. My brain is stuck revving at the redline at all times. Day and night, waking and sleeping, my mind races from topic to topic, usually on multiple tracks at once, as well."

I frown at this. "Dude, that sounds…exhausting."

"Yes, it is, rather. One adjusts, however, as one must. My point is that more often than not, I feel…" she sighs, looking away, thinking. "Like an observer of myself."

I shake my head. "Yeah, I have not a single fuckin' clue what that means, honey. How can you be an observer of yourself?"

"Most frequently, it means it feels to me that my body is merely a kind of…exoskeleton in which I am a passenger. My body operates to carry me through the world, but that is all. I feel disconnected from my physical self. In fact, dissociation from one's body is a common trait in the neurodivergent experience."

"Meaning?"

"Meaning I forget about my body. When I am studying or reading or am otherwise fixated on something, I forget to eat, to drink, to sleep. I do not feel tired, or hungry, or thirsty. I can go dangerously long periods without remembering that I have a body that has needs."

I shake my head. "I don't understand that *at all*."

She smiles. "How could you? It is beyond the understanding of a neurotypical mind. You *are* your body. *I* am my *mind*. But sometimes, when I am stimming, crashing, turtling, or experiencing a functional freeze, I am something else, something beyond my mind or body. I am just an awareness isolated within the chaos of my mind and the disconnection of my body."

"Stimming, crashing, turtling, or freezing?"

"Stimming is something you will have noticed, surely, though likely not in me, as I do not stim very often. It is a repetitive action or vocalization meant to calm and soothe, examples being tapping one's fingers together, flapping one's arms, rocking back and forth, humming, things like that."

I nod. "Ah, yeah. There was a kid in high school who did this whole thing where he tapped his middle finger to his thumb, like all the time."

"Walking on the toes is another common example. I imagine your schoolmate did that as well."

"Yeah, he did."

"You have witnessed me crashing, turtling, and freezing. When you first encountered me, I was crashing."

"Okay, but anyone would be crying in that situation," I say.

"Perhaps. The situation with the alarm clock is a better example. I had fallen asleep and was awoken abruptly and unexpectedly by a loud, jarring noise. As an aside, autism nearly always carries with it sensory issues, meaning sensitivity or hypersensitivity to sounds, lights, scents, and textures. I do not wear denim because it bothers me quite intensely. I do not watch television because the constant shifting of scenes and colors and the sounds…it is overwhelming. I do not wear tight or constrictive clothing—social norms mean I must wear undergarments, brassieres in particular, which is a form of torture for me."

I laugh at this. "Every woman I've ever known hates them."

"I, more than most. Anyway. When your alarm went off, I woke up disoriented, confused, and overwhelmed by the noise, in a strange bed and a strange room. It was frightening, and my automatic response was to protect myself."

"By curling up into a ball. Turtling in on yourself."

"Precisely. Many younger autistic children find comfort in small spaces, incidentally. They will hide in closets or under tables or beds—this is a form of turtling."

"And the functional freeze? That was what happened outside the station."

"Correct. My mortification at my faux pas with Sheriff Mannix triggered it. I am aware of how I am perceived, especially when I crash out in public. In order to prevent the embarrassment of crying or stimming in public, or simply to contain one's overwhelmedness, one enters a sort of physical paralysis known as a functional freeze."

"Is that different from when you're sitting here thinking and don't see or hear anything around you?"

"Similar but not the same. That is simply being completely absorbed in my thoughts to the point of tuning out the world around me." She watches me for a moment or two. "Any other questions?"

"I mean…" I look back at her, processing what she's told me. "I guess what I'm hearing is that you have, like, a super-powered brain. Like, super, super rocket-powered, mega-genius level shit goin' on."

Her answering smile is complicated—sweet, flattered, but with a sarcastic "oh, sweetie" undertone. "Yes, I suppose that is true, to a degree. But with that super-powered brain comes a host of attendant problems. As you have undoubtedly noted, I am the most socially awkward human being you will ever meet." She regards me blankly. "That is hyperbole."

"Hyperbole? Girl, you're takin' me back to ninth grade lit class—and spoiler alert, I didn't exactly excel at literature."

"Exaggeration for effect," she explains.

"I'm sure I'll have questions later, but I think I get the overall situation," I tell her. "I'm glad you shared that with me, Cadence. Thank you."

She shrugs, smiles, and gives a little bow at the waist. "And that concludes my TED talk."

This gets a laugh from me. "See? You *do* have a sense of humor!"

"Occasionally," she murmurs. She searches my face, then. "Riley, after all that, has your opinion of me… changed?"

"If anything, I'm even more amazed by you than ever.

It's gotta be tough, dealing with all that shit, day in and day out. Dealin' with assholes not understanding you and not even trying to. Feeling like…I dunno. Like things are going on in the world that you don't see or understand."

She swallows hard, nodding. "It is challenging, certainly. It is my lot in life—I cannot change it, even if I wished to."

"Do you? Want to…be different?"

She looks away. "At times, yes. Who does not, though? When the world is too much and I cannot breathe and my mind is flying a thousand miles per hour along a dozen different lines of thought at once, yes, I have wished I could just…silence my mind. Not be…this way. Even for a few minutes. But when I am working? *That* is when I truly come alive, Riley. When I enter an Emergency Room or a triage tent, something in me shifts. I become…almost a different person. My mind quiets. I am aware of nothing except the patient, assessing the problem, coming up with a solution, and ascertaining the swiftest and most effective means to that end. When I am in that world, I am in control."

"So what exactly is it you do? As a doctor. I mean, you've mentioned the ER, so is that your, what is it—specialty? Your area of focus?"

She nods. "Yes. I specialize in emergency medicine. I excel in high-pressure, chaotic situations."

"So when shit hits the fan, you're the lady to call."

"For medical attention, yes." She appears to be chewing on something, mentally. Considering what to ask, or whether to ask it. "You…you do not think I am…" she drops her voice to a whisper. "A freak?"

My heart cracks. "Ahhh, fuck, Cadence." I reach for

her, tug her toward me. She resists at first, but gradually allows me to bring her close enough that I can cup her cheek. I hold her eyes—something I've noticed she has a hard time with; after a moment, her gaze drifts away, dropping to my lips. "No."

"But I *am* weird. You said so yourself."

"Yeah, but babe, we're all weird."

"I have a monopoly on it, however."

Fuck, I want to kiss her. "So what? Makes you the most fascinating person I've ever met. I like your brand of weird a whole fuckin' lot." I frame her face in both hands, holding her attention even if her eyes won't stay on mine— that doesn't bother me. "You are *not* a freak. And if anyone ever calls you that again, you tell me, and I'll kick their fuckin' teeth in."

She frowns. "Absolutely not, Riley. Violence only begets violence and rarely solves problems, but rather engenders more." She swallows hard, her eyes darting this way and that over my features, stopping again and again at my lips. "Riley, I...I...."

"What, honey? Whatever it is, say it."

"You frighten me."

Gut punch, acid in my veins, cold water on my desire. "I know I'm rough around the edges, to say the fuckin' least, and I know I'm an ignorant, uneducated dumbfuck, especially compared to you. But I...Cadence, you gotta know I'd never hurt you."

"No!" She exclaims, as if shocked by what I said. "No, no, no. That is not *at all* what I meant." Her eyes close, as if it's easier to say some things without feeling my eyes on hers. "Emotions are difficult for me. Touch is difficult for me—for the same reason certain textures and sensations make me uncomfortable. My emotions are…chaotic, powerful, and confusing. I cannot control them. so I…I tend to ignore them. Block them off. Bury them. But with you, I…I cannot. And that frightens me. It frightens me greatly. Because I simply do not know what to do with how I feel." She presses her hand to the center of my chest, and I swear to god my fuckin' heart stops beating for a split second. "You are not ignorant. You are not dumb. You have had a different life experience than I have. You have not been exposed to the things I have. We could not be more different, you and I, but…" she drops her voice to a whisper. "You are *not* dumb."

Fucking eyes, man. Burning. "I didn't even graduate high school, Cadence."

There. That part is out in the open. It's a hard thing to admit to a girl you like, especially one who can speak a dozen languages, including fucking *Latin*, and went to goddamn *Harvard*, that you don't even have your fucking high school diploma. *Or* a GED. Or that even in high school, I was barely keeping my grades up enough to stay on the football team, and that was with a tutor and studying my dumbfuck ass off for twice as long as Fee, Cole, and Nyx did. Shit just didn't stay in my head. Letters swim around. Every little thing distracts me.

"But yet, even with that fact, Riley, you are successful and well-regarded."

I snort. "Successful. Okay, sure. I break shit for a living."

"You own the business, do you not?" she asks.

I shrug. "Sure—well, sort of. Our company is weirdly structured. Fee owns Crowe Construction, and I own Crowe Demolitions, and they're sort of separate entities, but then we co-own the umbrella corporation-thing, Crowe Construction, Demolitions, and Fine Homes." I grumble wordlessly. "I was against adding that third part, but Fee insisted, so what the-fuck-ever. It's a mouthful, but it works, I guess."

"So you own a business. That business has consistent clientele?"

I shrug. "Yeah. We stay busy."

"And you own your own home. You own a car."

I shift uncomfortably. "I mean, yeah."

"The community knows you. The chairwoman of the Chamber of Commerce indicated that you are well-liked and respected here."

"I've got my detractors, but yeah, I guess that's true."

"You have friends. You are close with your brother. I presume you have hobbies you enjoy."

"Yeah."

"Then, by every metric I am aware of, Riley, you are a successful man. Do you enjoy your work? Is it fulfilling?"

I nod. "Yeah, for sure. I mean, demolitions, the kind I do, it ain't exactly rocket science. You can't just go around blindly swingin' the sledgehammer around or you'll take out a load-bearing wall, but for the most part, it's simple but hard, honest work. I guess if we're talking fulfillment, though, I get that more from my program."

She blinks at me. "Which program is that?"

"Oh, uh. Well, it's a work-release program through the Michigan Department of Corrections."

"Department of Corrections?" she says, surprised. "You work in prisons?"

"No, I work with prisoners. There's a state pen not far from Three Rivers—Holbrook State Correctional Facility.

I work with the warden over there to find model inmates—the ones who show signs of genuinely working to be better, the ones who want to get out and be upstanding, contributing members of society. The ones we pick come work for me, doin' demo. They put in the time in my program, working for me, and I pay them fair, competitive wages. Part of that pay goes to pay off their fees with the prison, and the rest goes into an escrow account. There's a whole complicated equation that goes on, but the state, the judge on the case, the warden, the parole board, and I all coordinate so that time served plus good-time credits plus my reports on the inmate's behavior and work ethic is subtracted from their sentence, and they get out on parole earlier than they otherwise would be able to. Once out on parole, they keep working for me. They only have to report to their parole officer once a month, the rest of the time my reports serve as check-ins.

"When they get out on parole, they have money in the bank. They have a job. I have a deal with an apartment complex in town, and when I have an inmate about to get out, they make sure a unit is available—I help with paperwork, references, all that shit, so they have somewhere to live—somewhere safe, and away from temptations and distractions that might put them back on the inside. I help them find a car. They have friends from the jobsite—again, dudes who won't pull them back into the shit that put them in prison in the first place."

She's silent for a long time, thinking, processing. "Riley, I don't know what to say. That is…it is amazing. Inspiring. It is no wonder you are respected in this town."

I shake my head. "Not everyone likes having convicts with sledgehammers, shovels, and saws in their neighborhoods. I'm just tryin' to give these guys a half-way fair shot at life after prison. It's…It ain't easy."

Her thoughtful frown deepens. "Riley…did…did you go to prison?"

I close my eyes, sighing heavily. Restless, knowing she deserves this answer, I shoot to my feet away pace across the living room.

"Yeah, I did." I say it without looking at her, without turning around.

"What did you do? Or were you wrongfully convicted?"

"No, I…" I swallow. "Fuck. Fucking fuck me, I hate talking about this shit."

"Then do not."

"You oughta know. You deserve to know."

"Riley—"

I have to just put it out there—just say it. Get it over with. "I drove drunk and killed someone."

Her gasp of shock cuts like a knife. Of everyone in the world, it's her I want to impress the most, it's her attention I crave, and it's her respect I want.

That's fucked, now.

"Yeah," I bite out. "Exactly. Now you know."

7

Cadence

I REGRET MY AUDITORY REACTION—HIS shoulders hunched as if I had struck him a physical blow, and then his entire body language simply… deflated.

I am not a comforting, nurturing person. My bedside manner is brusque—some find it off-putting or abrasive. If I can even discern that a person is emotionally distraught in the first place, I rarely know how to comfort them. I am best with facts and logic rather than emotion.

But Riley—having divulged what is, obviously, even to me, a deeply painful subject—appears to be crushed by the admission. Flattened. I simply *must* comfort him.

How?

I rise from the couch and move to stand behind him. I reach a hand toward him, hesitate, and then place it on his shoulder. Once again, he flinches.

"Riley," I whisper. "Will you tell me what happened?"

"Why not?" He sighs deeply. "Spring of my senior year, there was a party. Big ol' kegger in a field on the far north side of Ernie Henstrom's property." He hesitates. "You know what a kegger is?"

"A party centered around the presence of a keg of beer," I answer.

"Yeah, but...they can get pretty crazy. This was all high school kids and college kids home for spring break. Couple hundred kids. Big fuckin' bonfire, several kegs, music, the whole thing."

"Who allows such things? That sounds incredibly irresponsible. And illegal," I say.

He chuckles. "Yeah, on both accounts. Story I'm telling is a case in point. So, we all went—me, Fee, Nyxie, and Cole."

"Fee and Nyxie are whom?" I ask.

"Fee is my brother, Felix. Nyxie is our other best friend—Cody Nyx. The four of us have been tight since we were snot-nosed brats."

He rakes his hand through his hair, messing it up even more; I have an inexplicable urge to neaten it, to smooth it down, to play with it. I clench my fingers into fists to keep from doing so.

"I got fuckin' wasted. I mean, it's what you do at a kegger—you get blasted with your friends. It was a fun party until someone got wind that the cops had been called, and everyone scattered. I'd driven separately from the others. Nyx and Fee took off in Fee's car, leaving me with Cole. And Cole, he's always been the good one. His dad was the sheriff before him, so he's always been the voice of reason for the three of us. Nyx and I…we're the crazy ones. Jumpin' off roofs into pools, swimming in the lake in winter, crazy stunts, stupid shit. Cole…he, uh… he begged me to let him drive. He was more sober than me. But I was young and wasted and stupid. So, *so* stupid. We argued about it until we heard sirens. And he…he told me to fuck off. Ruin your own life, then, asshole, he said. Hopped in with Ryan Tomlinson and Becca Shore. Left me there. Me, my keys, and my car."

He is silent for a while, and when he speaks again, his voice is and low and rough with emotion. "I drove away from that party. I couldn't even see straight. Fuck, I could barely *walk*. Fuckin' stupid thing is that if the cops hadn't been called, the party woulda gone till…shit, three, four in the morning? No one would've been on the road. I'd have made it home. None of it would have happened. Instead, someone called the cops, and the party broke up at, like, ten." He shakes his head, rakes his hand through his hair again, making it wild.

"And then?" I prompt.

"And then…I was close to home. Less'n a mile. About to turn onto the street that would take me home. I looked down to change the radio station. A song came on that I couldn't stand, so I went to change the station. When I looked up, a car was there. Ellen Johnson. Seventy-six years old. Grandmother. Widow. She…I found out later she was coming home from a prayer meeting that had gone late. I used to shovel her driveway for her. She'd pay me ten bucks and a mug of hot chocolate. Sweetest old woman you'd ever wanna meet. I changed the radio station, looked up, and there she was, turning onto the same street I was about to, coming from the opposite direction. If I'd been sober, I'd have just hit the brakes. There was time—I could have stopped or turned. Instead, because I was drunk, I just fucking plowed right into her front left quarter panel at thirty-five miles per hour. Knocked her off-course, and she smashed into a telephone pole head-on."

My heart constricts awfully at the brokenness in his voice. The guilt. The shame.

"She was driving this little Kia, tiny little thing made of fuckin' tin. And the—the pole was old and wooden and rotted to hell. So when she hit it head-on, the pole fell right onto her car. Crushed that poor old lady like a goddamned bug." His hands flex, tighten into fists, flex again, shaking with extreme, intense emotion. "I didn't know any of this at the time. I was obliterated. I was driving a big old F-150, and that thing barely dented. I remember the crash itself, but that's it. I blacked out. Apparently, I drove away. I don't remember. All I do remember is waking up confused. Hungover. Felt like shit. But I didn't have a fuckin' clue what happened. First indicator that somethin' wasn't right was my truck was gone—wasn't parked in the driveway where I usually put it.

"We had this old barn on the property. Falling down old thing that we stored junk in, basically. I had parked behind it. I could see the tail of it from my room. I knew I'd driven drunk, so I was already feeling guilty and stupid, but I was like, whatever, so what if I parked behind the barn? Right? Well, I vegged out and nursed my hangover until like three or four that afternoon. It was a

Saturday. Nothing going on. Everyone was hungover, I guess. So then Cole calls me. He's upset. Someone pulled a hit and run, killed sweet old Ellen Johnson."

His head hangs and his shoulders shake. I feel pulled to him—drawn by his guilt and sorrow and shame. I lean against his back. Rest my cheek between his shoulder blades and wrap my arms around his middle. I cannot think of anything to say, however.

He grips my hands in his, breathing hard. "When I heard Cole say that—when he told me Ellen Johnson was dead, it all came back to me. The radio. Looking up and seeing her little Kia in the middle of the turn. Smashing into her. Her car hitting the pole...the way that thing wobbled, tilted, and then...fuckin...I see it in slow-mo, *every—goddamn—night*. The pole falling. Crushing her car. The roof caving in right over the driver's side. I can— *fuck*. I can still see the driver's window all shattered and spiderwebbed. All...all fuckin' bloody." He groans as if sick, bent double. "Fuck—Jesus, *fuck*."

"Riley," I whisper, at a loss. "Breathe. It is okay. You are okay."

He shakes his head. "I drove away. Drove home. Left her there alone. Dead. I killed her, and I just fucking *left* her there." He straightens, turns to face me, and his eyes are red and wet. "Told you, Cadence, I'm a piece of shit."

"How did the authorities find out it was you?" I ask.

He shrugs. "I turned myself in. Walked to the station, sat down in front of Cole's dad, and told him it was me. He didn't have a choice but to lock me up. I pled guilty, got six years at Holbrook. Paroled out in four." He scrubs his face, groaning gruffly. "When I got out, everything was different. I was different. Prison changes you, man. No matter what, it changes you. And it changes how people see you. People I'd known my whole life wouldn't talk to me. Couldn't get a job. Felix was out on his own by then and was Dad's number two. He... Felix let me crash on his couch. Put me to work on his demo crew. He, Nyx, and Cole were the only ones who treated me like nothing had ever happened to me. I...the shit I went through trying to put my life back together after prison is what prompted me to put the program together, although that came years later, after Fee and I started flipping houses together and I had Crowe Demo up and running."

"What was your life trajectory before the accident?" I ask.

He laughs—a bitter, sarcastic sound. "Full-ride scholarship to Ohio State for football and hockey, which I only managed academically by seeing a shitload of tutors just to keep my GPA high enough to be eligible. I was damn good at hockey, but I was fuckin'...legit, I could've been All-state QB. Maybe even pro. Everyone says that, I know, but it's true for me. My plan was gonna be to focus on football. And then...one terrible decision fucked my whole life. I can live with that. I didn't go to college, so the fuck what? Killing Mrs. Johnson? It's *really* fuckin' hard to live with that."

"Riley, I..." I press my hand to his chest again, feeling the rhythm of his heart. "I am finding it hard to know what to say."

He shrugs. "What is there *to* say? Not a whole lot, honey. 'Oh, it's okay?' No the fuck it isn't. 'You did your time.' Yeah, and a woman's life is only worth four years behind bars? Her kids and grandkids have had to live without her, and I only did four piddly little years."

"You regret it," I say.

Another bitter laugh. "Yes, Cadence, I *fucking* regret it." He spits the F-U sound of the curse word, harsh, explosive. "Every day I regret it. I have nightmares about it. Been out for almost ten years, and still I see that car crumpled up like a tin can because of what I fucking did." He looks down at me, swallowing hard. "That's the story, babe. You...I'll understand if you need to bounce. I get it."

"Bounce?" I echo. "As in...*leave*?"

He lifts one shoulder, shoving his hands in his hip pockets. "Yeah. Ball's rolling for your fundraiser. Good girl like you, Cadence? You don't need my shit dragging you down."

"Do you..." I breathe out shakily and try again. "Do you *want* me to leave?" I look up at him, afraid of his answer.

"Fuck no," he whispers. He clears his throat. "No. I don't want you to leave. But I'd get it if you did."

"I will not. I do not want to. Why would I?"

"After what I just told you?" He snorts, shaking his head. "Anyone in their right mind would ghost me. I don't go around announcing that to everyone I hang out with, Cadence. Most of the girls I've hooked up with, when they find out? That's it. Done."

"I am not most people, Riley Crowe." I gaze up at him, noting the way his jaw moves, grinding his molars, the way his eyes search and scan my face. "You made a terrible, dangerous, irresponsible choice, Riley. That is a fact. It had a terrible, tragic result. That is also a fact. The time you served in prison cannot alter what occurred. Nor can it assuage your guilt. You took responsibility for your actions, Riley. And it seems to me that you have spent your life since then trying to be a better person. You give back to your community. You created a program to give to others what you lacked."

"It's not enough," he says, his voice so rough he may as well have swallowed gravel. "It'll never be enough."

"No, and nothing ever can be." I step closer to him, hyper-aware of my body, of his, of how close we are, of the fact that my chest is touching his. "The event in question is long past, Riley, as is your time in prison. I do not say that you have earned forgiveness—it is not my place to say such things, if only because I do not know anyone involved except you. Who *can* forgive you, Riley? Mrs. Johnson cannot. Her children? Her grandchildren?"

"I wrote letters to them from prison," he says, his voice hoarse and ragged. "Her son...her son didn't answer. Her daughter wrote back that while she was struggling with it, she knew her mother would have forgiven me and would have wanted her to, too. The grandkids..." he laughs, and it is a complicated sound—rueful, perhaps, or almost amused; the emotions layered in that laugh are myriad and too tangled for me to name. "They came to visit me, all four together. Good kids. Everybody makes mistakes, and they knew Gran-Ellen, as they called her, like it was all one word, Gran-Ellen...they knew she'd forgive me. They said she'd invite me over for a cup of hot chocolate, and she'd give me a hug, and..." He trails off, voice thick and damp, head shaking, eyes red. "She'd...they said that God loves me and so does she."

I let both of my hands rest on his shoulders. "Then Riley, take what they are offering." I look up at him, trying mightily to keep his gaze, no matter how uncomfortable it makes me. He needs it. "Despite the fact that a significant percentage of my life, both personally and professionally, has been spent in the pursuit of spiritually motivated missions, I am not a person who will ever tell you what you should believe. It is not my place. I know what I believe, but that is for me alone."

"I'd like to know," he whispers. "Please."

"If the family of the victim has forgiven you and believes that she would have as well, then who are you to cling to your guilt? Humans have a plethora of remarkable abilities, I have observed." I pause, considering my words carefully. "Some of them are good things—resiliency, adaptability, empathy, creativity, cooperation. But we have other abilities that are not so good. Humans are capable of astounding twists and leaps of logic in order to justify something we want, even and often especially if that thing we want is something we know is bad for us."

"What's that got to do with anything?" he asks.

"Just this, Riley: whom does your guilt serve? Why do you cling to it after so long, when those who have cause to despise you and cling to resentment do not? Because some part of you has decided that the guilt is your penance. You do not feel you have been punished enough, and so you clutch your guilt and shame and self-loathing to your chest like a starving child with a crust of bread. But again, I ask you: whom does your guilt serve?"

He blinks hard and then looks at me. "Am I supposed to answer?"

"If you would."

"Ahhhh…" he looks away, lifting his shoulders in a hint of a shrug. "No one, I guess."

"Will it bring Ellen Johnson back to life?"

"No."

"Will it assuage the pain her family surely feels at her absence?"

Miserably: "No."

"Is guilt the only thing preventing you from repeating the mistake?"

This causes him to think more carefully. "No. I mean, maybe in a way, yeah, a little bit. I still drink. I get wasted now and then—less and less frequently as I get older. But I never, *ever* drive if I've had anything more to drink than, like, a beer or two."

"So, then…of what value is guilt?"

"None."

"I believe in God, Riley. That much must be obvious, I hope. I believe that Mrs. Johnson's daughter and grandchildren would be…surprised, at best, that you still hate yourself for your mistake. It is not easy to forgive someone who has wronged you, Riley, and they have. Do not waste that. The God I believe in is one of forgiveness. He—or she, or they, if you prefer—has forgiven you. Mrs. Johnson's family has forgiven you. They have clearly communicated in one voice their belief that Ellen Johnson herself would forgive you. The only person who has not forgiven you is…*you*."

"How are you so wise, on top of everything else?" he asks.

"I am not wise," I answer. "But in my work, I have the opportunity to speak to many people from all walks

of life. I have held the hand of dying men as they confess their many sins, hoping to find absolution before
they pass beyond this life. I have heard people express regret for many things major and minor, awful and irrational. No one has ever regretted forgiving someone, so far
as I know. But I *have* heard regrets about living in guilt
and shame unnecessarily. Clinging to anger. Clinging
to self-loathing, and in so doing wasting one's life and
squandering one's joy."

"Jesus, Cadence."

"I think the topic of Jesus is one for another conversation." I clear my throat. "That was an attempt at humor.
I am aware you were cursing."

He huffs a laugh, shaking his head as he regards
me with an expression I cannot parse or translate. "My
god, Cadence. You're amazing." His wet, reddened, beautifully pale blue eyes search me. "Fuck me, I wish I was
good enough for you."

My heart stops beating—or so it seems. "*No one* is
good enough, Riley; *that* is the purpose of grace."

He frowns. "Grace?"

"Another topic for another time," I say, unwilling to
be distracted by points theological. "Why do you wish
you were good enough for me?"

"Don't you know?"

I shake my head, swallow hard—he is so close, ra-
diating heat and searching me with eyes fraught with
emotions I have no frame of reference to understand. I
only know that my heart is tripping over itself as it tries
to hammer wildly yet skip beats at the same time. I only
know that his eyes seem to snare, again and again, upon
my lips. My hands rest on his shoulders, and I slide them

down to his chest, and I feel his pulse under my right hand, rabbit-rapid, as frantic as mine feels. His hands, so large and so strong, grasp my waist between my hips and my latissimus dorsi muscles.

For a moment, I could almost believe myself to be Elizabeth Bennett, rain-soaked and eager, as Mr. Darcy prepares to kiss her.

Almost.

"Do not tease me so, Riley, I pray you." My voice is so quiet it is more of a breath than speech.

His eyes dance over my features, settling once again on my lips, and an amused smirk stains the corners of his mouth. "Tease you? How'm I teasing you?"

I lick my lips. "I cannot find the words."

"Try. Please? I don't wanna misunderstand the situation."

Bloodrush burns in my cheeks, and my eyes drop from his face, eyelids shuttering closed, pulse faster than the rat-a-tat-tat of a snare drum at a college football game. "The way you are looking at me...I...it makes me think you might wish to..." I squeeze my eyes shut more tightly, shaking my head.

His hands leave my waist—part of me regrets it, and I am startled to realize I not only *tolerate* his touch but... *crave* it. His palms cradle my cheeks, his touch so gentle it seems he considers me to be as delicate and easily shattered as the finest china.

"Riley," I breathe, daring to peek through slitted eyelids at him; his expression has not changed, and his eyes are fixed on my lips.

"God*dammit*," he hisses.

"What is wrong?" I ask, startled by the abrupt intensity of his curse.

"I just can't help myself."

My eyes meet his, then, just for an instant, as his face grows larger, nearer. He tilts his face to one side, and surely I must be dreaming—if so, let me not awaken.

This is a dream I would live in, always.

This moment, one I have dreamed of and wished for and despaired would ever happen...

Shock ripples through me when his lips brush mine, ghostly soft and hesitant. I gasp, and my pulse ramps to an impossible pace and my hands tremble and my breath is stuck, hot, in my throat, as he presses his mouth more firmly against mine. His lips are moist and warm and smooth on mine, and I can scarce believe this is reality.

He is kissing me.

It is over before it begins, however.

He pulls away only far enough to whisper. "I'm sorry."

Crushing disappointment shatters my brief joy. "Oh, Riley, please—please do not apologize. It would break my heart beyond repair if you were to regret my first kiss."

He rears away, shocked, almost distraught. "*First*...?" he breathes. "First kiss?"

"Yes, of course," I answer, hoping he cannot detect the tremor in my voice as I fight overwhelm—I'm feeling so many things. So many. Too many. "It certainly is not as if I have had suitors lined out the door, you know. I am no Penelope. Who would want to kiss a freak like me?"

"Hey," he growls, his voice gruff and angry. "Unh-uh. None'a that shit."

"None of what?" I ask. "It is true."

"That was your first kiss? Ever?"

"Yes," I whisper, feeling small and silly and childish. "I am quite certain it must have been a disappointment to one so experienced as you in the romantic arts."

"The romantic arts?" he echoes, amused.

"Do not laugh at me," I whisper. "I am confused and...and...frightened, and..."

"Not laughin' at you, sweetheart. Never that." He tucks flyaway curls behind my ears and brushes the pad of his thumb over my lips. "And sure as fuck not disappointed. Or regretting anything."

"Then why apologize?"

"Because..." he cups my face, shaking his head while dropping his gaze from mine. "My turn to not have the words."

"Then I shall return your words to you: Try. Please."

"I shouldn't have kissed you."

"Wh—why n-not?" I whisper, stammering as tears fill my eyes. "Am I not..."

"Oh god, fuck—no, no. Cadence, *no*." He kisses my eyes, and I must close them as his lips touch them, and I know he must taste tears. "You're *good*, Cadence–you're pure. So fucking smart. So accomplished. Wise. More beautiful than...than anyone I've ever met." He pauses, swallowing hard. "And I'm not. I'm not any of that."

"So you..." I put the pieces together. "You don't think you should have kissed me because you—" I pause. "I hesitate to put it into words. Because *you* do not feel worthy...of *me*?"

I am so stunned that he could think something so patently ridiculous that I could almost laugh. It is no laughing matter, however. And he does not answer, not in words, but his lack of denial is affirmation enough. The way his gaze skitters off of mine is answer enough.

How could I possibly make him understand how I am feeling? The mad spin-cycle of thoughts and feelings in my mind leaves me wobbly and uncertain, like a newborn colt.

"Yes, goddammit," he hisses. "Yes! That."

I bring my hand to his cheek, and the rough black stubble is like sandpaper, but the skin of his cheekbone is soft. "Do you know how often I have wondered what my first kiss would be like? Can you begin to fathom how desperately I have wished…" my eyes shut on their own, watery and hot. "I am twenty-four years old, Riley. I have all but lost hope that anyone could want…that…*any* of that, with me."

"I do," he murmurs, stroking my lips with his thumbs, my cheekbones as well, and each swipe of his thumbpad over my skin leaves scorched lines of tingling heat in its wake. "I don't regret kissing you. Direct opposite."

How do I tell him I want another kiss? My voice will not form the words, my lips will not shape them.

Where words fail, perhaps action might succeed.

I am not courageous enough nor bold enough to kiss him. Instead, I can only hope to communicate somehow that I would welcome another kiss. A longer one, even, maybe.

To that end, I draw together what little daring and resolve I possess, and shift my body closer to his. My breasts flatten between us, and I feel my nipples harden and tighten with anticipation and arousal. His hard belly rolls against mine as he breathes. I tilt my face up, find his eyes. Part my lips.

"So goddamned beautiful," he whispers, his eyes searching my face and lingering, lingering, lingering on my lips. "Tell me not to kiss you again."

"I will do no such thing," I answer. "Not when that is precisely what I am hoping for."

This time, I keep my eyes open. His hands cup my face, pulling me up to him as he lowers his mouth toward mine. A lifetime of fantasies and daydreams have not prepared me for this. My heart is wild behind the cage of my ribs, and I feel a delirious sort of wonder that I am here, that I am experiencing this, *finally*, that a man like Riley Crowe—rugged, rough, charming, debonair, impossibly handsome—is kissing me.

I gasp again when his mouth meets mine—shrill, breathless, shocked. Desperate for this kiss to last beyond an instant, I give in to impulse, sliding my hands around to his nape, diving my fingers into his cool, silky hair, trying to hold him here even for just a moment longer.

His lips are warm and soft and plump against mine, and I feel his breath, taste it. I clutch his nape and whimper when, instead of pulling away again, he tilts his face the other way and his mouth opens and his tongue intrudes into my mouth—which I seem to have opened instinctively.

I've always wondered what this would feel like—having a man's tongue in my mouth. Would I recoil? Would it feel…slimy? Why, I have always wondered, do humans kiss with open mouths, with tongues?

I have my answer.

As far as data points to answer the question, I am

disappointed: I cannot explain why we do it. But it is *maddeningly* wonderful. When his tongue sweeps over my lips and darts in to tease my tongue, I whimper and then gasp, and I grip his neck and cling hard, desperate for this kiss to continue. His hands leave my cheeks. One curls around the back of my head, holding me into the kiss, and I glory in the resurgence of hope—he wants to kiss me, still. He does not want this to end any more than I do.

His other hand slips down the side of my neck, briefly encircling my throat; instead of feeling choked, however, his touch there settles me. Soothes…yet maddens. And then his hand moves again, and he roams my shoulders, shoulder blades, travels down my spine.

Our mouths part, but he only draws fresh breath and then delves in again, tilted back the other way now, and kisses me again. This one is commanding. He steps into me, crushing his body against mine. My breasts are pancaked between our bodies, and his belt and zipper dig into my belly, and his thighs touch mine. I have never been so close to any man—I have never felt a body against mine like this.

I should be suffering an overload of sensory input, but the kiss consumes my entire mind, and his hands anchor my body to this plane, to this realm. Whatever thoughts and feelings blatter and blast in my mind, I cannot feel them or hear them—there is only Riley.

Only our kiss.

I hear myself emit a sound—a quiet groan, an expression of arousal and pleasure. I have never made such a sound. I marvel that it came from me.

He draws back at the sound. "Fuck." His brow is

furrowed; part of me reads it as anger, but his words put the lie to that. "Don't wanna stop. Don't know how."

"Nor I, on both accounts," I admit.

His eyes search my face as his hand drifts down my spine and comes to rest on my lower back, low—mere inches above my coccyx. "You have any fuckin' clue how you make me feel, Cadence?"

I can only shake my head. "No," I admit, after a moment of effort. "Not a one."

"Taste like honey," he whispers, and kisses me—softly, quickly. "So damn soft." His hands skate down my bare arms, leaving piloerection pebbling my flesh wherever he touches. "So…" a kiss, "fucking…" another kiss. "Beautiful."

I am overcome, then. All the blood in my body, it seems, has rushed, confused, to all the wrong parts of my body—my breasts feel engorged and heavy and my nipples ache; the sexual organ at the apex of my thighs feels swollen, yet also…slippery and…wet, in a way that is highly disconcerting and more than a little embarrassing, although I am perfectly aware of the medical symptoms of sexual arousal.

It just feels…*strange*.

My skin is pebbled all over—the piloerection response to his touch, and it feels too tight around my bones and muscles; were he to touch bare skin right now, I might erupt, I worry.

Erupt with what, I cannot say. This is utterly unexplored territory for me, and all of my medical knowledge has fled me, or, at very least, is of no use. Knowing what is happening to me is no preparation for the reality of experiencing it.

Overcome, flooded with sensation, shaking all over, my knees give out. I cling to him, and he catches me.

Yet, even in catching me, he manages to overload me all the more with a wild, new, maddening sensation:

His hands grip my bottom.

I sprawl against his chest, my weight mostly on him, supported only by his strong, powerful grip on my bottom. My eyes are wide with shock and fear and wonder, and my mind attempts to categorize the sensation.

It fails.

The sensation is too much to be neatly categorized and shelved.

My mouth hangs open and I stare up at him, wide-eyed, wondering, and breathless.

Riley lifts me to my feet…

But does not let go of my bottom.

I…I do not want him to.

I feel a thick, hard, bulging *thing* behind his zipper, pressing against my belly, and I shy away from thinking about that. It is too soon. Too much. Not yet.

A part of me, however—the part that knows exactly what that is—is gleeful. Swollen with pride: I, Cadence Creswell, have caused that reaction in him.

Watching me with hawk-like intensity, Riley gentles his grip on my backside, but instead of moving his hands up to my back or to my waist, he splays his hands wide, cupping my bottom…then smooths them down to where my backside meets my thighs, and then up to my back and then down, and around—caressing, exploring.

My lungs, aching from a lack of oxygen, scream, hot and empty. I suck in a gasp, finally, mouth trembling, hanging open, eyes on his rugged, handsome face.

My arms sling around his neck, and I lift on my tip-toes, panting. "Riley..." I breathe.

Now it is I who initiates the kiss. I lift higher on my toes and lean into him, trust him to take my weight, and I kiss him.

He makes a low, gruff sound when my lips slide against his and I open my mouth and—only panicking a little—offer my tongue to him.

It is a small, rough sound he makes, involuntary and surprised and greedy.

I did not know, until now, that one could be aroused by a sound. Yet I am.

Not merely the sound itself, however. By what it represents.

His desire.

For me.

And then I cannot kiss him anymore because I am weeping—embarrassed, aroused, amazed, over-whelmed, overcome, and a million, million other things besides.

8

Riley

CADENCE PULLS BACK, SOBBING.

Guilt craters the ecstasy of mere moments before. I see tears sliding down her cheeks, and hate myself for putting them there. "I'm so sorry, Cadence," I whisper, swiping tears with my thumbs. "I shouldn't have let things go so far."

Her head jerks up, and she looks at me, surprised through her tears. "No!" She covers my mouth with her palm. "Please do not say that." She rests her forehead against the back of her hand, which is over my mouth. "You keep apologizing for things that I...I..." she pauses. "The correct and appropriate word eludes me." She inhales, holds it, lets it out, rolling her head against her hand. "Crave. Enjoy—no, need. Things which I have dreamed about, the reality of which so greatly surpasses my dreams that I can scarce believe this is real."

I pull back a hint, slide her hand to my cheek. "I thought I'd pushed you into…" I shake my head. "I thought you were upset that I was touching you. Your first kiss, ever, and here I am groping you. I should know better."

Her cheeks flame. "I am not upset."

"You're cryin', though."

"I…ugh!" she groans, sniffling, and nuzzles her warm nose and hot, wet tears into my throat. "Sometimes, when I have so many thoughts and feelings that I do not know how to process them, the only way I am able to express it all is through crying." She pulls back, looking up at me with wet, deep, green eyes, and she trails the pads of her fingers over my cheekbones, down my nose, across my lips, almost how a blind person would. "In this case, there is an added emotion, or rather an added web of emotions, and very potent ones at that."

All I want to do is take her mouth again. Fuck, so damn sweet, the way she kisses. Tender, eager, hesitant, gentle, hungry. And the gasps and whimpers? Fucking hammer to the gut, takes my breath away, and leaves my cock hard enough to drive railroad stakes.

And then there's her ass. Fuck me. Underneath the loose, flowing cotton dress, the girl has the ass of a goddess.

"Riley?" She says my name like she'd already tried to get my attention.

I shake my head. "Sorry, sorry."

"Where was your mind, just now?"

I grin, shaking my head. "Not sure I should say."

"Well, now you simply must," she says, frowning up at me. "My curiosity demands it."

"Cadence, I don't wanna scare you or scandalize you."

Her eyebrows arch. "Scandalize me? Why, Riley Crowe, what were you thinking about so intently?"

I slip my hands around the small of her back and pull her flush against me. Instead of the truth, though, I chicken out. "I was thinkin' that I'm not sure I believe you've never been kissed before, 'cause you took my damn breath away, sweetheart. And all I can think about is kissing you again... and again...and again."

Her blushing cheeks are apple red. "Riley, I do not believe for an instant that *that* is all you were thinking."

"No," I admit. "But I *was* thinkin' it."

"Tell me the rest please." She gazes up at me, her expression pleading. "I must know."

I skim my hands through the wild strawberry mass of her curls, dip at the knees, and kiss the side of her throat.

She giggles, writhing away. "That tickles!"

I kiss her throat, her cheekbones, her eyes, the corner of her jaw, and she giggles, but the giggles turn breathy and aroused, and she tilts her face away, literally physically melting into me as I kiss her.

Finally, she pushes me away only to grab my shirtfront in her fists. "Riley, you cannot distract me with kisses."

I laugh and kiss her mouth until she gives me that whimper again. "Beg to differ, gorgeous."

"Diabolical, I tell you," she grumbles. "Riley. Please tell me what you were going to say. It will drive me mad if you do not."

I sigh. "Fine, fine. Don't say I didn't warn you." I tip her chin up so she has to look at me. "I was thinking that your ass is..." I trail off with a growl, shaking my head. "Goddamned epic."

She lets out a shrill whimper of dismay, clinging to my shoulders and slumping against me, burying her face in my chest. "Oh." Her voice is tiny. "Epic?"

"Epic."

"That is…good? Right?"

I burst out laughing. "Yes, Cadence. It means you have an absolutely magnificent ass, and I was thinking that I… *gah.*" I tip my head back and groan. "I'm gonna corrupt you, sweet girl."

"Riley."

"No."

"Riley." More insistent, now. "You *what*?"

"I'm just very, very attracted to you, that's all."

She swallows hard, looking at me as if summoning courage. "The feeling is mutual." Her eyes skim my face and catch at my mouth, and her hands grip my shoulders with surprising strength. "Thank you, Riley."

I let out a huff of shocked, confused laughter. "For what? Complimenting your ass?"

Her cheeks go so red it's a miracle they don't burst into flames. "I have never received a compliment on that portion of my anatomy before, so yes." She frowns. "I have never received a compliment on *any* portion of my anatomy, come to think of it."

"Well, that's a goddamn national tragedy," I quip.

She rolls her eyes at me. "That is a rather extreme exaggeration." Serious, once more. "That is not what I was thanking you for, however."

"Can't think of any reason for *you* to be thanking *me*," I say.

"My first kiss, Riley," she whispers. "I know I am not like other girls, but I…I have dreamed of my first kiss my whole life. I have waited and waited for the right person to come along. The right situation. I have…" she looks down, voice dropping. "I have been bitterly disappointed, more than once. Someone I thought…well, that does not bear repeating at this time. The point is that I have built up my first kiss in my mind until it became this mythical, fairytale thing. I was so certain that when…*if*…I ever did receive a kiss, it would not match my absurdist fantasy."

My heart pounds. My palms sweat. "Cadence, I…"

Her fingers, warm and dry and small and clever, touch my lips, silencing me. "Please. I…" she looks into my eyes for a moment. "Nothing could have prepared me for how it felt to be kissed by you, Riley Crowe. You surpassed anything I could have imagined. So…thank you. You have made this lonely, neurodivergent girl's heart very, very glad indeed."

My eyes burn—what the fuck? I clear my throat, mind-fucked by her words. "Cade—" My voice cracks and breaks. "Cadence, good lord. I dunno what to say. It was just—"

That hand again, clapping over my mouth. "If you say it was just a kiss, I will be eviscerated. Truly. It was *not* just a kiss. Not for me. It meant something to me." She drops her gaze and removes her hand. "I know it cannot have meant as much to you as it did—"

I silence her with a kiss, lips only, no tongue, and I kiss her until she starts to melt, and then I pull away, destroyed all over again by the stunned, awed look on her face, the wonder in her eyes. "It meant something to me, too, Cadence."

Silence, then, in which Cadence rests her forehead on my chest and just breathes, and I desperately resist the all-consuming temptation to fill my hands with her utterly magnificent ass.

"May I tell you a secret, Riley?" she breathes, finally, looking up at me with her chin on my chest. And my god, is she cute when she does that. Sexy-cute, but cute.

"Anything."

"I quite enjoyed it, shocked though I was, when you put your hands on my…" a long hesitation. "My bottom." This is a whisper so quiet I can barely hear it.

"I shouldn't have," I say. "You're a…a church girl. A good girl. Innocent. Sweet and pure and kind and…and everything I'm not, and I put my hands on you like that?" I shake my head. "I just couldn't help myself. I know church girls believe in waiting for marriage, and all that. And honest, Cadence, I'd never, ever want you to think that I… that all I—"

"I am not a church girl, Riley," she interrupts, softly but firmly.

"Then I'm confused."

"I struggle with organized religion. It is a very complex topic for me. My parents are believers, obviously. But when they felt the call to Africa, it was…deeply personal. It was not about a church. And it has never been about a church for me. My faith is a personal thing, Riley. It is about *faith*, not obligation. I do not speak of it frequently or freely, because I do not see the necessity. I believe my life should illustrate my beliefs. I have rarely attended any church, and I do not see that changing. My fundraising is largely through corporate sponsors from the medical industry who use it for tax purposes, with a few large donations from individuals, like the Crenshaws. It does not come from a church."

"Oh."

"I appreciate your…willingness to respect my beliefs, however."

"So…waiting for marriage…?"

"Is not a belief I ascribe to," she says. "Marriage is a social construct—a human-created ceremony, and a legal status. It is not what defines a relationship. I do believe that the physical expression of love through sexual congress is sacred. I do not believe it is meant to be shared casually or flippantly. This is only *my* belief, however. Others may do as they wish. I just…It is not something *I* will be able to…do…with just anyone. Do you understand?"

"Yeah," I answer, my heart heavy. "I read you loud and clear."

She peers at me. "I wonder if we are understanding this the same. Somehow, I do not think so."

"Cadence, I…" I know I should let her go. I'll never be the man she wants, the man she deserves. The question is if I'm strong enough to make that clear to her without hurting her. "I'm not a man of faith. I don't know if I believe in God, and if I did, I'd have a fuck-ton of questions for the bastard. Sorry, I just…I don't wanna mislead you, or lead you on. I sure as fuck don't wanna hurt you."

"We shared a kiss, Riley." She pats my chest. "You are under no obligation to me. You have done more for me than anyone ever has, in so many ways. You have shown me such wonderful kindness, generosity, and compassion. You have taken care of me in ways I have never known before, and it has been eye-opening. But our kiss, it does not bind you to me. I do not expect anything from you. Now, or ever. It was a lovely, beautiful kiss, and I shall treasure it all my days. You need not worry, however, that I shall be waiting for you to…oh, I do not know. Convert for me.

Or ask my father for my hand. I am well aware that this is not that, for you."

"Cadence…shit. It wasn't just a kiss, though. I meant that. Truth is, I don't know *what* the fuck it was, but it…I…" I pull away entirely, turn around, and cover my face, letting out a sigh. "I don't know what I'm trying to say."

I'm panicking. Hard.

This shit is too damn much, too damn fast—for *me*. The shit this girl makes me feel is…honestly, fucking outright terrifying.

She opens her mouth to say something, but my phone jangles in my back pocket just then, startling us both.

I slide it from my pocket, pathetically grateful for the out. I glance at the screen before answering. "Yo, bro." I fake a breezy tone I don't feel. "How's married life, Fee?"

"Same as before, but married." He laughs. "Nah, it's great. She's just two seconds from popping, and she can't wait to get this baby outta her belly."

"Yeah, I can't even begin to imagine, man."

"Me either." He pauses. "So, you ditched me at my wedding."

"I just bounced a little early, that's all."

"Heard you didn't even have one drink."

"Wasn't in the drinking mood."

"Nuptial bliss too real for you?" He quips, needling what he knows is a sore spot for me.

"Fuck off," I groan. "Why are you bothering me right now? I'm busy."

"No, you're not. I just heard from Cole. Ember and I want to meet this hot doctor you've been parading around town, holding hands with and setting up a fundraiser for… without calling me, your brother, or your new sister-in-law."

"Fee," I start.

"No. You're bringing her over, right now. And then we're meeting the rest of the gang at The Cellar."

"Fee—"

"Try to say no, Rye. I fucking double-dog dare you."

I laugh ruefully. "Fuck." I pull the phone away from my face and look at Cadence. "You up to meeting my brother and his wife?"

She positively lights up. "Yes! I would enjoy that."

Shit.

"We're in," I say to Felix. "Be there in a minute."

"Cool. See ya soon, loser."

Ah, Felix. He used to always be so serious. And then he met Ember, and she changed him for the better. Now, he's light-hearted and goofy, and down to playfully insult each other like old times.

I can't help wondering if I could have that. Someday.

My gaze goes to Cadence, for some reason, when that thought barrels through my brain.

She's grinning like a fool, bouncing on the balls of her feet. "Should I change?" She looks down at herself and then frowns. "I do not have any other clothing, unfortunately. I was not anticipating a stay in Three Rivers beyond a single night at the Crenshaws."

I can't stop myself from chuckling as I tuck a flyaway curl behind her ear. "You're perfect just like that, Gorgeous."

She blushes. "Riley…" her gaze flits to mine, uncertain and hopeful. "Do you really think I'm…gorgeous?"

"I could spend the whole fuckin' night tryin' to show you how unbearably sexy you are and still not get close to the truth of it."

Her mouth forms a round *O*. "Riley, are you—are you implying—"

I run my thumb over her red-again cheek. "Yeah, babe."

Her head lolls forward to thunk against my chest, and she groans. "You should not say such things to me, Riley."

"I know. I'm a bad, bad boy."

"You jest, I know. But I…" she exhales sharply. "I know what lies beyond kissing, of course. My difficulty with being touched by others has long rendered that an impossibility for me…in my own mind, at least. But with you, I—"

"Whoa, hold up. Sorry to cut you off, but…you don't like being touched?" I'm incredulous and horrified. "I've been…fuck me, Cadence, I've been *pawing* at you this whole time and you don't like—" I turn away, furious at myself. "Jesus. Why didn't you say anything?"

She steps into me, erasing the distance I'd put between us. "Because, as I was about to say, with you, it is different. I do not know why or how. But I…" she blushes again. "I like it. Rather more than I should, maybe. When other people touch me—and I mean *any* kind of physical contact—it makes me uncomfortable, at best. The intensity of my reaction varies based on my impression of the person. My parents, whom I love, I can hug. But everyone else, until I met you, I…I cannot. It makes my skin crawl. I cannot tolerate it. It is even worse than denim."

I laugh. "You *really* hate jeans, huh?"

She shudders. "Ugh! It is the worst texture on earth. It feels like wearing sandpaper against my skin, and in truth, I'd rather the sandpaper."

I look down at my jeans. "I've worn this pair most of this week. I live in denim."

She frowns. "Is that not unhygienic?"

"Nope." I grin and rub my hands together. "Wait! Do I know something scientific that you don't?"

She seems truly stunned by this development. "That remains to be seen, does it not?"

"This dude, I think it was a dude, I dunno, but he was a science major, right? And he wore his jeans, like, over and over again, and his peers were giving him shit about it being gross. So he did a study. He wore the same pair of jeans for, like, fifteen months without washing them."

Her stunned expression morphs into disgust. "That is…barbarous."

"I'd agree, except for what science boy discovered," I say.

She frowns. "I hesitate to ask, but…what did he discover?"

"Well, after the fifteen months or whatever it was, he tested the bacteria level in the jeans, washed them, wore them for two weeks, and then tested them again." I pause for dramatic effect. "The difference in bacteria levels was negligible."

She looks away, visibly turning the information over in her brain. "Hmmmm. That is an interesting and unexpected result. Bacterial levels do not equate to hygiene and odor, however, nor how visibly soiled the item might be. After fifteen months without being washed, I cannot imagine those jeans smelled very good, regardless of the presence or absence of bacteria."

I laugh. "That did occur to me. But my point is that you don't need to wash jeans after every wear, or even after a few, unless they're visibly dirty, stained, or smelly. And to be clear, I *do* wash my jeans regularly. Just not, like, frequently. These don't *look* or *smell* dirty, do they?"

She shrugs and shakes her head. "No, they do not."

She indicates the jeans I'm wearing with a flick of her finger. "You will still never catch me in denim."

I cup her arm, sliding my hand from elbow to shoulder. "So, when I do that? How does it make you feel, or react?"

She shudders. "I enjoy it." She frowns, thinking. "It is…a frisson."

"Don't know what that means."

"A brief, intense physical reaction to an emotional stimulus," she says, again sounding like she's quoting from memory. "When you listen to music and it strikes an intense emotional chord within you and experience a piloerective response, often accompanied by a shiver or shudder."

"Pee-loh-what?" I ask.

"Piloerective response. Goosebumps."

"So you're saying you have an intense physical response to me touching you?" I ask.

She nods. "Yes. I do."

"But a good one?"

Another nod. "Yes. Most unusually, I might add. It is…somewhat disconcerting, I must say. My whole life, I have been largely disconnected from my body, primarily as a defensive response to my sensory issues."

"I guess I don't totally understand what you mean by sensory issues."

She sighs. "It is an aspect of autism and ADHD. It manifests in a variety of ways from person to person, and can be just about anything. For some, it's bright lights and loud noises—these things bother everyone to a degree, but for someone with ASD or ADHD, it is markedly more intense. A decibel level that is normal and acceptable to you might be overwhelming to the point of physical pain to the neurodivergent individual. A bright sunny day may be wonderful to you, but that same sunny day might be agony to the autistic person. It can be specific things, such as crunchy foods or slimy things, or the scent of diesel exhaust, or the flavor of mint. For me, it is rough textures, generally. Denim against my skin, in particular. The scratchy type of wool is another personal example, although I do quite like merino wool and cashmere. I dislike constrictive clothing—cuffed sweatpants, tight skirts or dresses, tight leggings."

"So you don't wear yoga pants?" I ask.

"No. The material is soft, but they are too tight. It feels like my lower half is suffocating." She sniffs a laugh. "Why do you look...disappointed?"

I laugh out loud. "Because that fine ass of yours would look pretty fuckin' stunning in a pair of yoga pants."

She blushes, averts her gaze from mine. "Riley, my goodness. You seem to have a fixation with my backside."

"Yup."

"I am sorry to disappoint you, then, because that is something you will never see." Her smile is...teasing.

"Your ass, or your ass in yoga pants?" I ask. "Just clarifying...for a friend."

"You refer to yourself, I believe?" she says.

"Yeah, babe."

"I was jesting," she says, arching an eyebrow and smiling at me. "I left the statement intentionally vague."

"Are you teasin' me, Cadence Creswell?" I demand, sidling closer to her, smoothing my hands down over her hips.

"That was the intent, yes," she murmurs. "The truth of the matter, however, is that you will never see me in a pair of yoga pants. I do not own any, and will not."

I hear myself speaking and can't stop the wildly

inappropriate question from tumbling out. "And what are my chances of seeing you *out* of yoga pants?" She squeaks, a soft, shrill exhale, and buries her face in my chest, and I laugh, stroking the back of her head. "Joking, honey, joking. Mostly."

"Riley, I…"

I groan, head tipped back, and look down at her and lift her chin up so I've got her attention. "Cadence, I'm sorry. I'm not…I'm not trying to….shit, what am I even trying to say? Fuck!" I drop my forehead to hers. "I'm a dirty-minded old hound dog, okay? I say inappropriate shit, like all the time. I'm not trying to…like…push you into anything you're not ready for or don't want. I'd never pressure you into anything."

"But your inference—that you wish to see me naked…" she drops her voice to a whisper, and if I were looking, I'd see her cheeks flame-red again. "That was at least partially truthful, was it not?"

"How honest am I supposed to be, here, Cadence?" I ask.

"Completely."

"It'll make you uncomfortable."

She sighs, nodding. "I am aware. But…one must face things head-on. Often, with me, I fear things prematurely. I am afraid of the idea of something more than the reality warrants. I am afraid of and uncomfortable with… well, to be as honest with you as I wish you to be with me—I am afraid of and uncomfortable with everything to do with you, Riley. You are completely outside my experience, and thus well beyond the bounds of my comfort zone. Which, admittedly, is somewhat microscopic." She holds my eyes for a moment, fingertips trailing over my cheekbone, following the line of my stubble to the corner of my mouth. "You frighten me. You do things and say things that I…that have never been directed at me. I have never been the object of anyone's desire before, Riley. And you…your seemingly genuine displays of attraction to and desire for me…it is hard for me to reconcile that with my understanding of the way of things. Of who I am in relation to the world. It is confusing. Scary. Not because you are scary, but because I am so unfamiliar with the aspect of life which your interest represents."

"I can understand what you mean," I say. "I don't want you to be afraid of me. Of—of what I'd do. I won't do anything you don't want."

"That is just the issue, Riley—I am finding that I *do* want…" she closes her eyes and tries again. "I want to *experience* things, Riley. It is thrilling beyond explanation when you kiss me. When you…ahhhh, when you put your hands on my body in places no one has ever touched me before. I am often shocked or scandalized by the wicked things you say, but…I also like it. It makes me feel…." she trails off, frowning. "I am uncertain how to phrase it."

"Bluntly."

"Very well." She looks up at me. "Adult. I have lived in the adult world my whole life. I am an only child. Beyond the age of two or so, I was never interested in dolls or toys or children's books. I have always been more concerned with knowledge. With learning. With adult things. I related more to adults than to my peers. I conversed more freely with my teacher, in the years I attended public schools, than with my schoolmates. I attended a university hundreds of miles from my parents, alone, at sixteen—I was legally emancipated so I could make decisions for myself.

I attended classes and lectures with students five and ten years my senior. But yet, even after graduation, even as an intern and resident, I never felt fully *adult*. Because of my social naïveté, especially as regards romance and…and the things that go with it." She looks at me again, intently yet briefly. "To return to your inference regarding seeing me unclothed…"

My gut flips, and my heart hammers. "Cadence, I…"

"I will not be offended, no matter what you may say. I will not be angry. Or disgusted. I will not think less of you. I may not always be able to understand what you are thinking or what the truth is beneath the obvious of what you say, but I can tell when you are lying or omitting the truth. And to me, dishonesty, whether through lies or omission, is…far more offensive than a blunt, bold, inappropriate, or vulgar truth."

"In that case," I say, brushing my fingers over her temples and behind her ears. "If I wasn't scared to fuckin' death of rushing you into something or pressuring you to do something you're not really ready for, I'd have you naked right now."

She whines in her throat, averting her gaze and blushing furiously. "Riley, my goodness."

"I'd kiss you until you can't breathe, Cadence. I'd show you all the amazing things your body is capable of feeling."

Her fingers knot in my shirt until she's fisting the front of it with shaky hands. "You tempt me, Riley." She glances at me, curiosity on her face. "The things you would show me…are they all as delightful and intoxicating and…and addictive as kissing?"

"Addictive?" I echo.

She looks at my mouth, unblinking, eyes wide. "Yes.

Since that first kiss, I find myself quite unable to think of nearly anything else." She bites her lower lip, hard. "I confess to being in a similar state as regards the placement of your hands. I was shocked at first when you touched my bottom, but now, I…" red cheeks go redder, and she squeezes her eyes shut and bites her lip again. "I have not stopped thinking of it. Most especially, I cannot stop thinking about how it felt when you paired the two together."

I claim her mouth, part her lips with my tongue and taste her, feel her tongue slide hesitantly against mine, and then I let my hands ghost down her back…and fill my hands with her ass.

Fuck—so tight, so plump, so round. My god, I need this woman naked.

I need her screaming my name.

FUCK.

Of all the women in the world for me to develop feelings like this for, it has to be *her*? The sweetest, most adorable, most innocent, lily-white, pure-as-the-driven-snow virgin on the entire planet.

She whimpers at my touch, arching into me, pressing her tits against me—and yeah, those babies are definitely gonna be as glorious as this ass. I'm not about to push my luck, though. I genuinely care about her. I genuinely do not want to scare her or pressure her or traumatize her.

Her hands flatten over my shoulders, and she lifts up on her toes, deepening the kiss, opening her mouth wide for me. My god, she's incredible. The way she melts into me, pressing every soft curve against my body as if she craves me…although I highly doubt she knows what it is she really wants, what she's asking for when she melts against me like that.

Her hands slide around my neck, and she's pressed against me completely—hips to hips, thighs to thighs, belly to belly, tits squashed between us. She *has* to feel my hard-on—there's no way she can't.

She pulls back enough to whisper. "When you kiss me like that, I forget to be nervous or afraid. My mind slows down in way I have never experienced except when I am attending a patient or performing surgery."

"Is that a good thing?" I ask.

"*YES!*" Her exclamation is unexpectedly intense, exuberant, loud. "It is a relief I cannot express. My mind is an internet browser with ten thousand windows open at once, each of them processing gigabytes of data at all times."

"No wonder you get overwhelmed," I say. "That much mental noise and activity all the time?"

"Precisely," she breathes. "Even asleep, I feel it. My dreams are that way, too, quite often. The only respite I get is when I enter the focused state of work…and now, most unexpectedly, with you….when you do…physical things…to me."

I squeeze her ass, cup the weight of each taut, plump, round cheek, relishing the privilege of this to a degree I can honestly say I've never experienced.

When I do, she exhales raggedly, burying her face in my chest. "Riley…"

"Fuck, honey."

"What?" she breathes, looking up at me.

"I'm greedy," I answer in a gruff murmur. "I want more."

"More?" she squeaks, her shrill whisper breaking. "Oh my. More how?"

"Should I show or tell?"

"Tell," she whispers. "And then show. If I know what to anticipate, I can more easily adapt to what is happening."

"In that case," I growl, gathering the material of her skirt in my fists, handful after handful, so the hem drifts inexorably upward; I feel her tensing with each upward inch of the hem. "I'm gonna lift your skirt up and put my hands on your ass over your underwear."

"Over?" she gulps.

"Yeah. Unless you give me permission to go under them."

"Maybe…" panting, she pauses. "Maybe start with over."

"You want me to stop, just say the word."

"Stop." It's a breath, a whispered syllable.

I immediately release the bunched fabric and move my hands to her waist. "See? You're in control, sweetheart. If it helps, I can tell you what I'm doing before I do it."

"That would help." She gazes up at me, eyes wide and shimmering with concern. "But I…I do not want to disappoint you, Riley."

This gets a bark of disbelieving laughter out of me. "Disappoint me? How on earth would you do that?"

"By asking you to stop."

"God, you sweet, sweet thing. You couldn't. You couldn't possibly disappoint me."

"But…what if you are enjoying something and I become uncomfortable and need to stop? Would you not be…at least a little disappointed? Or…perhaps frustrated is the better word."

I cup her face and look at her intently, shaking my head without breaking eye contact—until her eyes dance inevitably away. "No. Never." I kiss her, a soft but brief touch of lips. "Listen to me, okay? This? Getting to be with you like this? To kiss you? To touch you at all? In any way at all? It's a gift you're giving me, honey. I mean that. It's a privilege. An honor. I'm not gonna take it for granted, and I'll sure as fuck try not to push you to go further. And if you need to stop, that's what happens. No questions asked. No explanations needed. And I swear to you, sweetheart, I will *not* be upset."

My cock might disagree, but that greedy motherfucker can be insatiable, and with this girl, at least, I know I need to keep him on a tight leash. I'm gonna have to learn to tell that bastard to shut up and wait.

"I was only testing you, just now," she murmurs.

"I know."

She rests her chin on my chest, soft, small hands loosely cupping the sides of my neck, and gazes up at me, searching my face in that way she has—open, honest, curious, nervous, eager, excited, anxious, tender, strong.

She's the most complex human I have ever known. A guy could spend a lifetime getting to know her depths and never even scratch the damn surface. I've known her for less than twenty-four hours, and one simple fact is starting to scare me shitless:

I might be addicted to her.

She's waiting, I realize.

Waiting for me to resume what I was doing before she asked me to stop.

Far be it from me to keep her waiting.

9

Cadence

ANTICIPATION THRUMS WITHIN ME, SETTING MY nerves afire and my stomach aflutter.

I have never considered myself an object of desire. Why should I? No man has expressed interest. Well, except Joel, but that hardly counts, does it? My gut twists at the thought of the male who caused me such inexpressible heartache, disappointment, and confusion. I endeavor to set that experience aside. Riley is not Joel. Looking back, there was clear evidence of Joel's true intent at every stage of the process; I was merely blinded to it in my naive excitement to think a boy might like me as a boy likes a girl. Or, well, as one person feels romantic interest toward another, regardless of gender or sexual orientation, because, as Lin-Manuel Miranda once said, "Love is love is love is love is love is love, cannot be killed or swept aside."

I have, ever since, kept those indicators of his ulterior motives front of mind when dealing with men, and thus far, Riley has shown none of them.

He has stated his physical attraction to me. This in itself is new. Joel did not do that. His interest was not in *me*, neither my mind, my body, nor least of all my emotions. His interest was in the cruel entertainment I would provide him and his cronies.

I shudder, and Riley feels it. "What was that?" he asks. "I do something? That didn't seem like an 'I like it' shudder, especially since I haven't done anything yet."

I shake my head. "No, it was…I was remembering something."

"Care to share?"

I tense. "I…no. Not at this juncture." But then I consider the situation and opt for honesty—which I would want from him. "In truth, I was…" I trail off, struggling to know how to begin discussing that event.

"You don't have to tell me anything."

"I certainly must. It concerns you, at least indirectly. You see, when I first began at Harvard, I was sixteen. But, obviously, I had never had a boyfriend. As is common, I would imagine, I began university somewhat excited at the possibilities that come with attending a large university in a new place. I hoped, naively, it turns out, that I would meet someone, and …" I shrug. "Experience romantic interest from a boy."

He groans. "I don't like how this is starting out."

His comment requires no response, so I continue my story. "I did meet a boy. Joel. He was in several of my classes. At first, he seemed merely curious about me—not uncommon, since I am rather…unique. But as I answered questions and the nature of my uniqueness became apparent, he began showing what I, again naively, interpreted as interest. He accompanied me from one class to another. Jested with me. Smiled at me. Drew close to me. I have studied people, and I know the signs of flirtation. He demonstrated them with me. The smiles, the seemingly innocent touches. I…I did not react to his touch the way I do yours. I could not bear it when he touched any part of me, but I…I *wanted* to. I *wanted* his attention to be genuine, and tried to endure his affections, innocent as they seemed."

Riley growls. "Fuck me, Cadence. This is gonna piss me off, isn't it?"

I shrug. "I do not know how it will make you feel. I certainly did not appreciate the way events unfolded. He invited me to a party. I was underage and did not drink. He…I suppose he intended to use my innocence to get me inebriated and unable to ward off his advances. When I declined his offers of alcohol, he became incensed."

"Fucking fuck. I really hope you left."

"I did not. I was at my first university party, Riley. I thought I was supposed to enjoy it, even though I did not. I felt I was supposed to enjoy Joel's attentions, even though I did not. I wanted to leave. I wish I had left." I gather what courage I have for the telling. "He came to me after perhaps thirty minutes elsewhere and apologized for getting upset. He led me away from the busiest area of the party to a quieter alcove. Even though the thought of him touching me at all left me revolted, I could tell he was preparing to kiss me. At last, I thought to myself. A boy likes me.

A boy wants to kiss me." I'm breathing hard, still angry and embarrassed. "In the instant before his lips met mine, he pulled away and began laughing at me. He said…well, I shall not repeat his words. He called me names. Said I was…the R-word. He mocked me for thinking he liked me. As he laughed, a crowd appeared. His friends. They surrounded me and laughed at me and mocked me." I shudder again, fighting the burn behind my eyes. "Darn. I very much dislike speaking of this, but you must know, because I…I think of Joel often, should a male deign to show interest in me. I reviewed our interactions and saw signs that he was not genuine. He often would look behind and smile strangely as we walked together—which I later realized was him sharing the inside joke with his cronies—mockery, me laboring under the delusion that he could like me. It was…it was just so *juvenile*, Riley. Childish. The games one would expect in high school, but not at a university. He was young, too, I suppose. Not even eighteen, I believe, but I was only a few weeks past my sixteenth birthday when this occurred. It hurt, Riley. It hurt badly, and I have not forgotten it. So I shuddered because I thought of him. Of his pretend interest."

"Little fucker oughta have his dick kicked up into his throat," Riley mutters, his tone savage. "Teenage boys are fucking cruel little assholes, sometimes."

"I forgave him," I say. "But I have not forgotten."

"Cadence, I know you have no reason to believe me, but—"

I cover his lips with my fingers, which for some reason I cannot fathom seems to cause his brain to short-circuit, not merely silencing him but making him forget what he was saying—or so it seems. "I *know*, Riley. You are not him. I believe you to be genuine."

"Even in high school, when I was my worst self, I would never have done that shit. I'm an asshole in a lot of ways, but I'd like to believe I've never been cruel." He caresses my jawline with a thumb. "I'm so sorry that jackass did that to you, Cadence."

I smile at him. "I appreciate that, Riley." I cannot maintain the smile, however. "I wish I could say time has dimmed the pain of the memory, but it has not. That was the first time anyone showed interest in me in that manner, and until you, it was also the last."

"I can see how you'd avoid guys after that," he says.

I blink. "You can?"

He nods. "Sure. Absolutely. Pain is a damn effective teacher."

"You are certainly correct there," I say, and then sigh. "I believe I have effectively ended the moment we had. I am sorry."

He shakes his head. "Don't apologize. I'm glad you shared that with me."

"Glad? Why glad?"

"I mean, not glad. I dunno. It's a shitty thing that happened, so I'm not glad it happened. But I *am* happy you chose to trust me enough to tell me about it. Having your trust means a fuckin' lot to me."

"Oh," I whisper. "Trusting you is important to me, as well."

"And you didn't ruin the moment," he murmurs. His hands slip down my spine…and then his phone dings with an incoming message. "Fuck."

He pulls it out and looks at it.

"My brother is wondering where we are."

I swallow the hot lump of nerves in my throat and speak the bold truth on a shaky, uncertain whisper. "Maybe...perhaps we could...resume this interaction later."

He grins at me, and his hands cradle my backside— very gently and very briefly—over my dress, and then he pats me there, once. "I think that could be arranged. For now, let's go hang out with my brother and Ember."

C◦

Riley's brother and sister-in-law live outside town, a few minutes north and a few miles down a dirt road through the forest. Their home is a brand-new build, with lots of windows on all sides, a deep front porch beneath a triplet of dormers, the whole covered by a hunter green metal roof. There is a garage on the right side, with a winding blacktop driveway snaking away through the surrounding forest. Perhaps two acres have been cleared around the house, with verdant green grass still showing the lines where the rolls of sod are joined. The structure itself is a log cabin, but of the magazine-worthy variety. The windows still have stickers on them in places, and there are piles of materials and power tools scattered on the driveway outside the garage, along with a roll-off dumpster piled high with construction debris.

Riley parks his truck behind the dumpster; the garage is open, revealing a gold-colored pickup which is otherwise very similar to Riley's in age and condition, although I know little of such things. Beside the truck is a classic orange Volkswagen Bus covered in stickers. Riley exits his truck and is opening my door before I realize he's parked the vehicle; car rides always put me in a contemplative mindset and I tend to tune the world out until forced to return. In this case, the impetus to shake off my thoughts is Riley leaning into the cab to unbuckle me.

"I know how to do that, Riley," I murmur as he depresses the red button to release the buckle.

He grins at me from very close—kissing close. "I know. I like to. Gets me close to you."

"You…um…you do not need an excuse to draw close to me, you know." I grab his wrist as he steps back down out of the cab.

"No?" He grins at me, and my stomach flips. I wonder, will his smile will always do that?

I shake my head. "No. I would allow, and indeed encourage, your proximity in most circumstances."

"I'll keep that in mind. But unless you want me not to, I think I'll keep helping you out of the truck. Makes me feel like a gentleman."

"You are a gentleman, Riley," I answer.

He snorts his disagreement. "No, I sure as fuck am not."

"With me, you are."

"Does a gentleman grope a girl's ass?"

"If she allows and desires the action, it cannot be considered groping, can it?" I say. "And if the action is both allowed and indeed encouraged, then one can hardly declaim the gentleman's virtue, can one?"

He frowns, puzzling through what I've said. "No?"

"No," I agree, and twist my hand to place my hand in his, and he helps me step down.

I put myself in his space, my other hand on his chest;

I like his chest a lot. I do not know why, but I do. It appeals to me on a visceral level. I like the feel of it under my hand. The firmness juxtaposed against softness, perhaps.

"When we first spoke, I told you I thought there was more to who you are than you give yourself credit for." I trail my index finger from his lower lip to the point of his chin. "The more I come to know you, the more true I believe that to be."

A door opens nearby. "You two gonna hang out on the driveway makin' out all day or fuckin' what?" A male voice—Felix.

I gasp in shock and jump away from Riley as if caught misbehaving, cheeks red.

Riley laughs and tugs me against his side, murmuring in my ear. "Hey, relax. It's alright. He's teasing."

My heart is thundering in my chest. "I was startled."

He chuckles—I have come to learn that he laughs a lot and easily, and now that I believe he is not doing so at my expense, I find his constant, easy laughter refreshing and uplifting. "I'm gettin' that." He pulls me by the hand into the garage, murmuring in my ear again. "So look, there's a better than even chance he might tease us a bit. Me, mainly. It's meant with love, but if he says something that bothers you, let me know, okay?"

I squeeze his hand. "I appreciate the warning, Riley, thank you. I shall."

Felix and Riley resemble each other quite strongly—albeit Felix has dark golden hair, whereas Riley's is jet black. Felix is more heavily muscled, against Riley's leaner physique. But their facial structure and general build are nearly identical. One could not possibly mistake them for anything but brothers.

Felix is dressed very much like Riley—in dirty, faded, ripped pale blue denim and a plain black T-shirt with a well-worn and tattered ball cap on his head, pushed back so a few tendrils of golden hair sprout beneath the bill. His eyes are the twin of Riley's—palest blue and intense and piercing.

He precedes us back through the garage, between the truck and van, and into the house. Inside is bathed in natural light from every direction, even the mudroom in which we find ourselves. Felix leads and we follow him out of the mudroom and directly into the kitchen, which features a gargantuan island topped by a mammoth butcher's block; the rest of the counters are white marble shot through with gold streaks. There's a deep, hammered copper farm sink, an eight-burner range with a matching stainless steel refrigerator.

Felix leans against the island, watching our reactions. "So, Rye. You haven't been in here since we moved in, ya bum. What do you think?"

Riley is looking around with a critical eye, nodding. "It's fuckin' killer, Fee. You really outdid yourself on this one. The butcher block to match the floor, the dark cabinets, and white counters?"

Felix is grinning. "Wanna know somethin' about the interior design? Jess did it."

Riley blinks. "*Jess?* Office Jess? Has carried a torch for your ass for literally years? *That* Jess?"

Felix shrugs, nodding. "The one and the same. We talked about the crush actually, and obviously she knows it's never been and never gonna be returned. I think she's dating someone now. A finish carpenter with Jimmy McKay's outfit. Turns out Jess has had an interior design bug for years. She redid the office, too. Not sure if you noticed or not."

Riley nods, eyes wide. "No shit! *She* did that? It looks great. Been in need of an overhaul since the Reagan administration at least."

"Exactly my words, matter of fact. She's been working with Eric for months, and she's honestly been a godsend. Sped up the design process immensely, and as great as Eric is, there's just nothing like a woman's touch, especially when it comes to staging." He grins my way. "Speaking of women who're a godsend. Introduce us, you mannerless barbarian."

"Fuck off, cockwaffle," Riley says, his tone playful. "You're the one babbling about Jess's designs."

Felix frowns. "I do *not* babble." He arches an eyebrow. "And would you prefer me to return to how I was before Ember?"

Riley cackles, holding up his hands in surrender. "Fine, fine, you win. Babble on, bro. Happy Fee is the best Fee." He gestures at me. "Cadence Creswell, MD, this is my brother, Felix."

I lean close to him, murmuring. 'You don't need to announce the MD part to *everyone*, you know."

He seems confused. "But…why wouldn't you? That's something to be proud as fuck about. You oughta tell everyone that shit."

Felix chuckles. "Don't mind him, he's an idiot. He means well, though." He extends a hand to me; his grip is firm but gentle, not overpowering nor limp. "It's great to meet you, Cadence. Glad you could make it."

I scan the home—the cozy den beyond the kitchen is bathed in more light from floor-to-ceiling windows along the back wall, with cream carpet and a tan leather sectional around a coffee table made from a single section of wood, with live edges around the rim, the top lacquered and polished and adorned with a three-wick candle giving off a pleasant vanilla scent and scattered with pregnancy magazines and a stack of neatly-folded infant onesies.

"Your home is lovely," I tell Felix. "I take it you built it yourself?"

He nods, visibly proud. "Guilty as charged."

"You are a very talented builder, then. Thank you for having me, Felix." I look around. "I heard you are recently wed. Is your bride in attendance?"

I can see Felix's gears turning, metaphorically speaking, as he begins to notice my oddities. "Uh, yeah. Yeah. She just had to visit her favorite place."

I frown. "I do not know what that would be."

He laughs. "She's roughly six hundred and forty weeks pregnant, so…the bathroom. I think she's peed ten times in the last hour."

A female voice carries from a nearby hallway. "I heard that!" The owner of the voice is a short, beautiful woman a few years older than me with white-blond hair in a thick braid down her back; she is, as announced, extremely pregnant, although six-hundred-and-forty weeks is obviously a massive exaggeration. "Your daughter is sitting on my bladder, Felix. I'd love to spend less time peeing, believe me."

She hustles over to me, rubbing lotion onto her hands. "My god, you're beautiful." She leans and embraces me, mercifully releasing me almost immediately. "What are you doing slumming it with this goober?" She jerks a thumb at Riley

I hardly know how to respond—to the unexpected

hug, to her compliment, and most of all to her teasing assessment of Riley as a "goober," whatever that may be.

"I...um. I thank you for your kind words, Ember. It is wonderful to meet you." I hesitate. "You are lovely as well."

She grins at me, winking conspiratorially. "Riley is the younger brother I never had. I like to tease him. Just...you know, so *you* know *I* know he's not *actually* a goober." She drops her voice to a stage whisper—why, I am uncertain. "He's actually a great guy. Just don't tell anyone."

"I do not know what a goober is, I must confess, and I also cannot fathom why I should keep Riley's excellent nature a secret."

She does a slow blink, glances at Felix, Riley, and then me. "Oh. Um. It's not...it's not a secret. I was joking."

"Ah. I see." I am quite nervous to meet Riley's family—this is all beginning to feel rather formal, which is concerning, seeing as I have known the man less than forty-eight hours; when I am nervous, I am less adept at recognizing humor, especially the teasing kind.

The ensuing silence is awkward, even to me. Clearly, Felix and Ember are not sure how to process my strangeness, especially without context or explanation. I am not given to explaining myself to people; I decided when I was quite young that if I went around explaining myself to everyone who did not understand why I am so strange, I would never say or do anything but in self-explanation. And while Riley seems quite taken with me, which is marvelous and wonderful and gratifying and exciting, I have only just met him and see no need to burden Felix and Ember with all that is me and my strange ways.

Felix breaks the silence. "Well, I've got steaks on the grill out back, so I hope you're hungry." He glances at me.

"You vegetarian? Ember hasn't been able to eat meat for most of her pregnancy, so I've got bean burgers if you want that instead of a steak. I could also toss a regular burger on, or some dogs."

I stop myself from asking the obvious question, since a moment's reflection makes it clear he does not mean actual dogs, but frankfurters—hot dogs. My brain goes extra literal when I am nervous.

"I would welcome a bean burger, if it is not too much additional trouble for you. Red meat is hard on my digestive system." I smile at him. "Thank you for providing options. It is most thoughtful of you."

He shares Riley's propensity for dazzling grins, although his does not make my heart flutter. "Ember can get you a drink while I toss that on for you. Bro, you want a beer?"

Riley glances at me, for some reason. "I gotta drive, man. Better not."

I touch his arm. "Have a beer with your brother, Riley. I believe I can operate your vehicle, should the need arise. I shall abstain in solidarity with Ember."

He looks at me for a moment, and I cannot read his emotions on his face. "You sure? It's not a big deal."

"Nor for me," I say. It occurs to me that he may feel self-conscious about alcohol intake and vehicle operation, considering his recent revelation; I lean close and murmur for his ears only. "I feel comfortable trusting your judgment in this matter."

He ducks his head, and I hear him swallow hard. "You sayin' that means a lot." To Felix, then: "Maybe one. Thanks."

I notice neither Felix nor Ember bothers to hide their

intense curiosity regarding our aside. It is his story to tell, however, not mine, so I opt to ignore their curiosity.

Felix twists the top off a bottle of beer, hands it to Riley, and claps him on the back. "Come see the backyard, man. You girls good in here?"

Ember smiles at me. "Oh, I think we'll get along alright."

Riley bumps my hip with his. "You okay with that? Me going outside while you stay in here and talk to Ember?"

"Yes. As she said, we will get along just fine." I give his shoulder a gentle nudge. "Go."

He follows his brother through a sliding glass door to an expansive deck overlooking a gently sloping yard leading to the dense, shadowed woods. A large doe ambles along the edge of the yard, ears alert.

Ember waddles into the kitchen. "Iced tea? Soda? Still water? Sparkling water?"

"Sparkling would be delightful, Ember, thank you very much."

She produces two cans of flavored, sparkling water. But rather than merely handing me the can, she rummages in a cabinet and comes out with a pair of wine goblets. She adds ice, pours in the water, and then adds a small palmful of frozen berries, plunking a stainless steel straw into each and giving them a swirl.

Handing me one with a smile, she gestures for me to follow her into the kitchen, where there is a cozy breakfast nook built into a corner, complete with a padded bench seat and bumped-out windows. "Life is too short to drink boring shit."

I take a sip and hum my approval. "This is delicious

and most refreshing," I tell her. "And I quite agree. A beverage need not contain alcohol to be interesting."

"Cheers," she says, extending her goblet toward mine.

"Afya!" I say in response, clinking my goblet against hers.

"What's that?"

"Oh, it is Swahili. It means 'health.'"

"Swahili, hmm?"

"I spent many years of my youth in Kenya with my parents, who were medical missionaries."

"Are you following in their footsteps, then? I thought I heard something about a fundraiser."

"In a manner of speaking, yes. My parents built clinics, staffed them, and taught the staff basic, essential medical care practices. Each Sunday, there was an open house during which the locals could come and receive free care. At the end of each open house, there was a church service."

"That's pretty cool."

I nod, smiling. "It was. I learned a lot in those years, and their work across the decades of their service changed many, many lives for the better. But I have a different calling."

"And that would be what?"

"To use my skills, talents, and experience in places where the need for medical care is most dire. Namely, conflict zones."

Ember's eyes go wide. "Like, combat zones?"

"Yes. Although I do not operate on the front lines. I am not a combat medic."

"Still, that has to be crazy dangerous."

I shrug, nodding. "I suppose so. But there is risk wherever one goes. We do not live in a safe world, after all."

"No, we do not." She regards me thoughtfully. "You're pretty young-looking to be a doctor already."

"I was academically advanced."

"Why that mission?" she asks. "Adrenaline junkie?"

I shake my head. "No, not at all. Growing up as I did, I saw things which most children from this country cannot fathom—adults, either. I saw the suffering. I saw the results of war. And I saw firsthand the catastrophic results when proper medical expertise and care are not available. People die needlessly. They suffer needlessly. As someone who specializes in emergency medicine and mass casualty triage, I can be of service. I am a child of individuals who spent their lives in service. How can I do anything less?"

"And why Africa?"

I shrug. "It is familiar. I have spent more of my life there than in the United States. I am familiar with some of the dialects and customs." I pose a question of my own, to direct conversation away from myself; I am my least favorite topic. "And you, Ember? You are about to be a mother, but is there a career you intend to return to after your maternal leave?"

"That's a work in progress. I'm studying to be a veterinarian. It's a remote study thing, mostly online with a few in-person classes at a satellite campus downtown. I'll work on it from here while taking care of this little nugget," she rubs her belly, here, "and eventually I'll start working once she's in school."

I find myself asking a question which is likely too forward. "May I ask you a somewhat personal question?"

She grins. "Sure."

"Are you…frightened? Of being a mother?"

She looks away, her smile fading. "No one's asked me that before."

"I apologize if it is an inappropriate question, Ember. I hope I have not caused you offense."

She shakes her head. "No, not at all. I...I appreciate the question, honestly." She stares away, thinking; I remain silent to allow her the time to consider the answer. "Everyone just sort of assumes that you're gonna be *so* excited to be a mommy, right? Like, oh, you're married and about to have a baby with the man you love, that must be so exciting. And I mean, yeah, it is. I love the absolute shit out of Fee. He's the most amazing man I've ever known. I *am* excited. I'm happy. I'm as ready as I can be." She shakes her head, swallowing hard, her voice dropping to a murmur. "But I'm absolutely fucking terrified, Cadence. No one really talks about that. I mean, you hear about the reality of having a baby. They tell you that yes, the pain is the worst thing you'll ever feel, but you'll forget all about it the second you have your baby in your arms. They tell you about not sleeping. Chapped, chafed nipples. Weight that won't come off. Stretch marks. Loss of sex drive. But what I haven't heard anyone talking about is this part right here. I'm like, less than a week from my due date. My water could break any time. She's doing somersaults and kicking me and dancing on my bladder, and it's just...it's *real*. She's real. She's a person, growing inside me. She's gonna come out and everything about who I am and my life is going to change, totally and permanently. And...I'm scared out of my mind." She shudders, and her shoulders shake. "God, it's good to be able to say this. Even Fee, I can't...I don't know how to admit to him that I'm shitting my pants, over here. It's not that I'm not happy and excited. It's not that

I don't want this—I do. I just…I'm scared. What if…"
she trails off, laughing and shaking her head. "There are
so many what ifs."

"For example?"

"My god. *Everything*. I lay awake at night while she's
having a dance party and going nuts in there, and I just…
spiral. What if I fall asleep while holding her and I drop
her? What if she gets sick and I can't do anything? What
if I'm a bad mom? I've read about new moms who can't
emotionally connect to their babies. What if I don't love
her enough? What if I mess her up? I mean, fuck, my own
mom was…she loved me, but I did *not* grow up normally,
and while I can't say I regret anything, it has definitely left
its mark on me."

"It seems to me that one would have to lack sense,
were you not afraid. Procreation is the most natural part
of life. All species rear children. But that does not mean it
is easy or that it comes naturally."

She frowns my way, but then turns away, thinking,
and the frown slowly morphs into a smile at me. "Y'know,
I really appreciate the fact that you didn't dismiss my fears.
Like, 'oh, you're being silly, of course you'll be a good mom,
there's nothing to be afraid of.'"

I shake my head. "That would be disingenuous at best,
I think. Fear is necessary. It gives us caution. It teaches us
to think. You have reason to be afraid. But being afraid
does not mean you are not ready or that you will not succeed—and indeed thrive—in motherhood."

She grins, then. "I think I'm already starting to see
what Riley sees in you. You are very wise."

"You are kind to say so."

"How'd you two meet?"

"Oh, well…I was upset and he comforted me. And now he is assisting me in raising the funds I need."

"Can you tell me about that?"

"Certainly."

I explain the situation, Riley's involvement, and the efforts made so far.

"Wait, so…this all happened in the last couple of days?"

"Yes."

"So you met him when he left our wedding?"

I blink. "Your wedding?"

She smiles. 'Yes. Felix and I were just married two days ago. Riley left the reception early."

"Oh. My goodness. Well, please, allow me to offer my most sincere congratulations. You are not embarking on a honeymoon, I take it, so close to your due date?"

"We went on our honeymoon a couple of months ago, when my doctor was still okay with me flying."

"A logical arrangement, to be sure."

She sniffs a laugh. "To be sure."

Riley is visible through the doorwall, standing and talking to his brother while sipping his beer. He glances at me through the glass and smiles at me. And yes, my stomach flutters.

"Honestly, I wasn't sure we'd ever see the day," Ember says.

"What day is that, may I ask?"

"The one where Riley Crowe catches feelings."

My stomach drops away. "I…I am uncertain what you mean."

"Oh, I mean…" she sighs. "Ah, shit. I've stuck my foot in my mouth, haven't I?"

"I…" I consider my answer. "I do not know about catching feelings. It is an unusual situation we have found ourselves in."

She looks at Riley, then at me. "He's never brought anyone around like this. He's had a few girlfriends in the time I've known him, and I've never met one. Never even knew their names, and he's dated a few of them for weeks, if not months. Yet you've known him, what, barely forty-eight hours, and here you are, in our home? That ain't nothin', honey. For that man? Introducing a woman to his friends and family is a big deal."

Panic swells in my chest like an inflating balloon. "I…I…" I suddenly cannot breathe. "Oh. Oh my."

She frowns at me. "Whoa, hey. You okay?"

"I am going to Africa. I will be there for several months, at least. I…he…we…" I go still, staring at nothing and trying to find the calm space within myself.

I hear her talking, but cannot find the mental acuity to tune into her words.

He cannot think that this is…that we could…with *me*? Feelings? It was one thing to kiss him and feel cared for and seen. I know my own feelings for him are complicated and growing by the moment, but I did not consider the future until now.

"Cadence?" I hear his voice low and quite close to my ear.

"I don't know, Rye," I hear Ember saying. "She just… froze up. We were talking about how you guys met and whatever and she just…"

"She's okay," Riley says. "We just gotta give her a minute to come out of it."

"Did I say something wrong? I didn't mean to upset her, I just—"

"No, no. You're good, Ember. She…" he pauses. "Honestly, Em, it's not for me to explain. She's okay, though, I promise."

The panic slowly subsides, and I am able to bring myself out of the freeze. Ember is sitting nearby, looking worried.

She sees me stirring and comes to sit beside me. "Hey. I…I don't know what I said, but…"

I touch her knee. "It is alright, Ember. I am well."

She shakes her head. "I'm sorry. I didn't mean to upset you."

"Of course not," I assure her, and then look around— Riley is in the kitchen assisting Felix with food preparation of some sort. "I am a complicated human being, Ember. This situation I have found myself in with Riley…you have made me aware that I have failed to take his needs into consideration. I…assuming this fund-raising endeavor succeeds, I will depart for Africa and will not return until the holiday season, at best. And he…I…we…" I groan in frustration as my brain spirals furiously, and my ability to speak cogently dissolves.

She touches my hand. "Hey, it's okay. It's okay. breathe."

"I do not know what I am doing, Ember," I whisper. "I have been so caught up in how he makes me feel that I have not paused to consider how *he* feels."

"Maybe just try and talk to him about whatever it is?" She suggests. "Just be honest. Riley is a good guy. He'll understand."

"He does not agree with your assessment of his character."

"Yeah, I honestly don't know him well enough to say. We haven't really had a chance to sit down and have any deep talks, y'know? I know he's dealt with some difficult stuff, but I don't know many of the details. I hesitate to say too much of what I *do* know, though, because his story is his to tell, not mine."

"I believe he would appreciate your tact," I tell her.

She shrugs, hesitates, and then looks at me, her expression serious. "What I will say is this—he's got this persona of a guy who doesn't give a shit, right? Like, he's super happy-go-lucky, he laughs all the time, he's always got a joke, usually an inappropriate one. He comes off as this... player, I guess. But he's got depth, Cadence. I just...I don't think he lets many people see the deep, serious side of him."

"I do not think he allows himself to see it," I answer. "But I do."

She smiles, rubbing my shoulder. "I'm learning that a lot of times in life, the thing we've been wanting and needing often comes when we least expect it, from a direction we could never have predicted. And in my experience, letting yourself accept that thing requires a lot of courage. But it's worth it."

"You are speaking of love," I whisper.

"Yeah." Her gaze goes to Felix. "He came along when I least expected it and turned my whole life upside down. I wouldn't trade it for the world, but letting myself love him was hard. And I know he'd tell you the same thing about me."

I sigh. "I cannot even think of such things, Ember. I barely know him. I have my path in life...and he has his.

How can they merge? Does he want them to? Do I? It seems rather absurd to even be considering any of this when I met him less than forty-eight hours ago. I just…I have formed an attachment to him, which is in itself rather unusual for me, let alone one as intense as this, and so swiftly developed."

"Feelings can happen faster than you'd think, and they're not any less valid or real for having developed quickly. So you may have feelings, and he may have feelings, but the question to be answered is what, if anything, are you guys gonna do about it?"

What, indeed?

Felix announces that the food is done, then, and we eat outside on their deck. The conversation is light and easy. Felix is funny and warm, perhaps a bit more reserved than Riley. Ember is a delight.

Riley watches me carefully throughout the evening, especially when we drive together in Ember's van to a drinking establishment known as The Cellar, where we meet the rest of Riley's social circle: Bear and Noelle, Sheriff Mannix, their friend Cody Nyx—whom everyone calls Nyxie—and the Cartwright sisters from The Alt. We all gather around a long table near the back of the bar. Several pitchers of beer litter the table, and several more of margarita mix.

I sip a glass of beer as much for the sake of appearances and remain mostly aloof from the various conversations, watching Riley interact with his friends.

He is endlessly entertaining, and high-energy. That dazzling smile and easy laugh grace every interaction. When someone is speaking, he listens closely. He teases everyone alike, but the humor and banter between himself, his brother, the sheriff, and Cody Nyx is particularly brutal in the constant parade of insults. The names they call each other become increasingly creative in their vulgarity, yet no one is ever upset. The more creative, off-putting, and vulgar the insult, the more hysterical the laughter.

I nudge Riley at one point later in the evening. "You and your brother and your friends. Why do you insult each other? You clearly do not take offense, yet you say such offensive things. I do not understand."

He chuckles, sighing, and leans back in his chair, stretching his arm around the back of mine. "Just how we are. How we've always been. Fee, Cole, Nyxie, and me've been best buds since, like pre-K. We've been through literally every stage of our lives together. When I got out of prison, Nyxie sold me a car so I could get to work. It was an eighty-eight Oldsmobile, shit-brown, no AC, no radio, and no shocks. It was like driving a fucking aircraft carrier, but he pulled that bitch out of the scrapyard, fixed it up so it'd run, and gave it to me for ten bucks and a six-pack of Coors Banquet. When that thing died, Cole drove me to work and took me home every day for two months while I saved for a new ride, and he was a deputy working midnights at the time. Fee gave me a job when no one else, even folks I'd known since birth, would even interview me."

Conversations have quieted as people tune into what Riley is saying. "We're family, the four of us. We love each other. But we're dudes, y'know? We don't go around sayin' that shit to each other. Guys ain't like that, for the most part. Instead of sayin' 'I love you, man,' I'll call Nyxie an inbred, slack-jawed, mouth-breathing yokel. It's not true, and he knows I'm fuckin' with him. Cole's a straight-laced, Dudley Do-Right, uptight fuck-tard, and I tell him that all the damn time. Cuz' it's funny. Truth is, Cole is hands-down the most truly *good* human being I've ever fuckin' met. But I can't *tell* him that. I gotta call him a brown-nosing bitch-cake."

I blink. "Bitch cake?" I hear snorts of laughter at my question. "What, pray tell, is a bitch-cake?"

"Cole is," he answers immediately.

"That is unhelpful," I grumble.

"And even though Riley is a loyal, hard-working, smart dude with a heart of fuckin' gold, we call him a slut and a man-whore and a slimy cock-ring," Nyxie says. "Cuz it's funny."

"A man-whore?" I repeat.

Riley is glaring at Nyx. "Dude, fuckin' come on."

Nyx seems puzzled. "What'd I say? I call you a slut all the time." He looks at me, understanding dawning on his face. "Ahhhh, wait, I get it. You think you've got Doc Foxy here snowed."

"But it is June," I say, before I can think better of it. "There is no snow."

This makes Nyx laugh. "Girl, you are too funny."

Riley sighs, annoyed. "Ignore him. He's an ass." He leans closer, murmuring. "Snowed means, like, fooled."

I look at him. "What does he think you have me fooled about?"

Nyx has overheard. "Let's just say that our boy Riley is a *very* experienced lover."

Riley, for the first time, seems genuinely upset, now. "Jesus, Cody. Can you fucking *not*?"

"Cody?" Nyx slumps back in his seat. "Wait, you're *actually* pissed about this? You've said as much yourself!" Again, he looks at me. "Whatever, man. It' was a joke. I gotta hit the head." He pushes his chair back and saunters for the bathrooms, belching so loudly someone on the opposite end of the establishment applauds mockingly.

Riley also pushes his chair back and leaves the table, visibly upset.

I go to follow him, but feel a strong hand on my arm. I see Felix reaching around his wife, who is seated beside me.

He leans toward me. "Give him a few to collect himself."

"While I acknowledge that as his brother you must know him far better than I," I say, "it is not in my nature to sit back when someone I care about is distraught. I will go to him."

Felix opens his mouth, but before he can speak, Ember touches his arm with a look that silences him.

I leave my place and follow him out the back door.

10

Riley

I COULD SERIOUSLY KNOCK THAT MOTHERFUCKER'S teeth down his throat. It's one thing to joke between us about shit. But in front of a girl I'm into? Not fuckin' cool.

After the loud, hot, stuffy atmosphere inside, it's blessedly cool and quiet back here in the alley. I pace and try to calm myself down; I know he was just fucking around. He didn't mean anything by it. And I've never been self-conscious about the fact that my relationships have never exactly lasted very long. Now, suddenly, I am.

Doesn't take a rocket scientist to figure out why—Cadence. She's the opposite of me in just about every way there is, but especially in that regard. And I want her to like me. A good, innocent, believes-in-God and goes on mission trips kinda girl like her? Doubtful she'll think it's cool that I've got more than a few notches on my bedpost, so to speak. That's *very* metaphorical—which I hope is obvious.

I hear the door open, but don't turn to look. "Nyx, it's cool. I know—"

Soft, warm, small hands touch my back. "It is me, Riley. Cadence."

I turn, sighing. God, she's gorgeous. There's a stiff breeze swirling down the alley, fluttering her long, curly, loose hair around her face. Her green eyes are wide and search me, full of concern.

"Hey," I mutter. "I just need a second."

"Will you please help me understand why you are upset? He was teasing you, as you yourself were just explaining. Why does he think you are trying to fool me, and about what?"

My heart twists, plummets. "It's hard to explain."

She frowns. "You are not obligated to do so. I have no right to any explanations, certainly."

Fuck. "It's not that, I just…" I groan, raking my palm down my face. "It's actually not hard to explain, I just don't fucking want to."

She touches my chest. "Then do not. You owe me nothing. It is I who owes you."

"You don't owe me jack-shit." I exhale, scrubbing at my hair. "Truth is, I'm just embarrassed. I…you're different from anyone I've met. I don't usually care what people think about me, y'know? My brother, my buddies, my other friends, they know me and they love me anyway, warts and all. Not everyone knows the details of why I went to prison since I don't talk about it pretty much ever, but they know I did. I care about their opinion, and everyone else can get fucked."

I pause, shake my head. Start again.

"But you…?" I shrug, shake my head. "You're different. And I care about what you think."

"I hope it is obvious that I have a high opinion of you, then," I say.

"Yeah, and I don't want that to change."

"Why would it? Why would what Nyx said make me think less of you?"

"Because…" I groan, turn away from her so I don't have to watch her face turn to disgust. "Because what he said is true."

I feel her absorbing and processing this. "I am not certain I understand what a man-whore is. A slut, so far as I am given to understand such colloquialisms, is a woman of loose morals—a woman who has had many sexual partners. This is different than a prostitute, however, in that a prostitute is paid for sex, whereas a slut does so out of personal interest."

"Man-whore is the same thing as a slut, but for guys," I mumble.

"Oh. I see." A long silence. "So…he was teasing you about your sexual history, inferring that you are of loose morals."

I can't help a bitter cackle. "Loose morals. Yeah."

"And it is true? You have had a significant number of casual sexual encounters?"

I nod. "Pretty much. I…I was pretty bad about it in high school. Prison was obviously a nice, long dry spell. When I got out, I…I sort of set about trying to make up for lost time, y'know?"

"I am not certain I do."

"I hooked up a lot."

A long pause. "I see. And this hooking up…it was purely physical?"

I nod. "Yup." I turn to look at her, finally, and see only curiosity. "Last few years, I've been actually sort of dating girls. Like, trying to have something that resembles a meaningful relationship. But it's…I'm not…" I cut off with another frustrated groan. "I'm not cut out for that shit, Cadence. Nothing sticks. Everyone is wrong one way or another, or it just doesn't work."

I see her thinking and stay silent until she arrives at the question she wants to ask. "Are you manipulative? Are you using your partners?"

"No! No." I hate talking about this, but she deserves the truth. "It's always been purely consensual. I've always been clear about it bein' just a hookup."

She rubs her palms on her thighs repeatedly, looking away, thinking. "I confess this is something I cannot fathom. It is beyond my scope of understanding." She looks at me, then. "But it is not my place to judge, nor am I interested in attempting to do so. All I can think of in this case is that as long as the women you have been with did not leave the experience erroneously thinking you had sex with her out of love when you did not, I cannot see what harm has been done. I do not understand how one can share one's body so casually, but that is merely my personal, subjective experience. Yours is different and does not hinge upon my understanding."

My head spins. "Jesus, woman. Where did you come from?"

"Chicago?" Her nose wrinkles adorably as she frowns in confusion.

I laugh. "No, I meant…" I cup her face. "You're just so…understanding and nonjudgmental."

"It is not for us to judge one another, Riley. Why would I think less of you for having a different life experience than I? You have shown understanding and patience with me. How can I do less? I may not understand, but I do not need to, though I would like to and will try to." She caresses my cheek. "If anyone is judging you harshly for your past, Riley Crowe, it is you yourself. Not your friends, not your brother, and not me. It is yourself you must convince."

Her empathy hits me like a goddamn freight train. My fucking eyes sting. "Dammit, Cadence."

"I…I am sorry?"

"No, no, no," I mutter, pulling her against my chest. "You just have this way of cutting straight to the heart of things. And you pull feelings outta me I didn't know I had."

"Nyx did not intend any harm," she says. "You should not be angry with him."

"I know. I'm not." I pull back and look at her. "I guess I just want to be the kinda guy you…" I trail off, finding it nearly impossible to say out loud. "Can be proud of." It's barely a whisper.

"That is…flattering, I suppose, is the only word that feels apropos." She looks at me so tenderly it fucking hurts, like biting into something so sweet your teeth ache. "But Riley, perhaps you should focus instead on being someone *you* can be proud of."

Right to the gut, that comment. "Wisest person I know," I whisper. "Can I kiss you?"

"Oh," she breathes, "please?"

Feel like the luckiest motherfucker on the planet, then, when she looks at me like that, eager, eyes sparking with desire, excited, asking me to kiss her—it's all there on the surface, unhidden, exuberant. She's just so…*open*. So vulnerable. So brave with her emotions. You get used to people hedging their bets, pulling back behind a veil of indifference so they don't risk being hurt. You get used to people playing it cool. Not her, not Cadence.

I slide my lips against hers and sigh in something like relief, something like happiness so deep it feels sharp and impossible. And then she's melting against my body and her fingertips ghost along my cheekbones and her mouth opens and she invites my tongue into her mouth and gasps in delight when I give it to her.

"I could kiss you forever," I breathe.

She pulls away, and I feel a heaviness descend upon her. "Riley, if this fundraising event succeeds—"

"It will," I insist. "I have no doubt at all."

"Then in less than two weeks, I will be departing for Africa." She pauses, her gaze serious, concerned. "I have planned to be gone for up to six months."

I rock back on my heels. "Holy shit—*six months*? I was thinking a few weeks, maybe a month."

"No. In order to accomplish anything meaningful, I must have enough time to establish myself." She searches me, worried. "I had not considered that until earlier. I…I have gotten caught up in…" she trails off, sighing, shaking her head. "You. This. Coming to know you. And it seems I have neglected to factor in the reality that I will be leaving for a long time, very soon. And Three Rivers is…"

"Not home for you," I finish.

"Precisely." She looks upset, shaken, almost. "Riley,

I care for you. More so than I could have ever imagined I could in so short a time. I worry that our parting will be the source of pain for us both."

"I care about you, too, Cadence." I search myself, and give her the truth. "Fact of the matter is, when you leave, it'll suck. I really, *really* fuckin' like you. If you lived here, I'd be beggin' you to give me a chance."

"A chance to what, Riley?" she asks.

The things I find myself explaining to this girl. Honestly, though, it forces me to look at myself and the things I take for granted. I've learned more from her in the two days I've known her than from anyone else in the rest of my life combined.

"Be with you. To date you."

She rocks back on her heels, eyes flying wide. "You... you would want that?"

I laugh in disbelief. "Want it? Babe, yes. With all my heart."

"With me?"

"Yeah, with you."

"But I'm—"

I cut in. "A legit fuckin' super-genius, wise, funny, fascinating, and beautiful. To name just a few of your qualities."

Her eyes go misty. "Riley, my goodness. I hardly know what to say. I..." She wipes at her eyes with her middle fingers. "If I had not spent months planning this trip, I might think about canceling or at least delaying it—"

"Absolutely not," I growl. "I wouldn't let you. This is who you are. I see that. I wouldn't change it for fuckin' *anything*, Cadence. It'll suck a big one having you leave when I'm just gettin' to know you, but I couldn't live with myself if I held you back from what you feel called to do."

Eyes shimmering, she looks up at me, and the expression on her face makes me feel like the only man on the planet, the only thing that matters, and it's a feeling I'll die treasuring, even if I never see this woman again.

"You are a damned good man, Riley Crowe." Her use of a curse word lends immense weight to her statement.

I almost feel like I could believe it.

She lifts up on her toes and kisses my lips. "We should return to your friends."

"Yeah, I gotta talk to Nyx."

C⌒

The night ends up being the most fun I've had in a long, long time. Cadence is everyone's new favorite, with the girls all playing musical chairs so they can get a few minutes of conversation with her and the guys all trying to impress her with jokes and stories.

I'm proud of my crew, too—no one bats an eye at her unique way of talking or asks invasive questions. They just accept her. And she notices it—wearing her emotions on her sleeve the way she does, it's easy to see how much she's enjoying being a part of this evening.

More than once, I see her literally pinch herself on the thigh.

I wish to fuck this could be our life. I put that aside, though. Can't go there.

We close the bar down and spend another half an hour in the parking lot, standing near our cars in a big circle beneath the glittering Three Rivers night sky, talking.

Eventually, we all get in our cars and head for our various homes. As I'm leaving the lot, Cadence glances at me. "I have a request."

"Anything."

She grins at me. "I am a literal girl, Riley. What if my request was for the moon?"

"I'd contact NASA."

She rolls her eyes. "You have an answer for everything." She lowers her window and leans out, looking up at the sky. "Can we get away from the light pollution? I would like to stargaze."

"I've got just the spot," I tell her.

I take her to Grace Point, a little spit of land jutting out into the bay—it's not far north of the spot we locals call Secret Beach. It's not easy to find, as the access road leading to it is hidden from view of the main road. Once you get there, you have to park in a little circle of dirt and hike up a steep path through towering, swaying pines. The trees thin out gradually, and after a quarter of a mile, they end abruptly, and you find yourself on a bluff some twenty or thirty feet over the water, dune grass waving around you with sand underfoot and nothing but sky in almost every direction.

When we reach the point itself, she stops, hands to her mouth, spinning in a slow circle. The beach stretches away to the left and right, endlessly, curving out of sight. The water ripples, a fluttering black blanket strewn with a billion glittering, spilled diamonds. Above, the sky is infinite. The stars are beyond number, and you could almost be swallowed whole by the breadth and depth of it.

Staring up, Cadence is visibly moved. She looks at me with wet eyes. "This is glorious!"

"My favorite place. I come here to think. To get away from…everything, I guess."

"I will find it hard to leave." She sits cross-legged in the sand, and then lies back, smoothing her dress over her stomach, and lets out a deep, contented sigh. "This has been the best day of my life."

I lay beside her, wishing I could pull her onto my chest. "I'm glad."

She takes my hand. "You gave it to me, Riley. You shared your friends with me." Her eyes glitter in the dark. "I shall treasure this day all my life."

It's hard to swallow, dammit. "Cadence…" I trail off with a sigh. "I will too."

We lay in silence together for a long time, just staring at the sky, counting stars, and holding hands.

I can almost forget everything else. I've never been good at living in the moment—I've got way too much fucking baggage for that—but this feels pretty close to what I imagine that's like.

There's a smear of faint gray on the horizon where it meets the water when Cadence rolls to face me, cheek pillowed on her hands like we're snug in bed together. "I have a question."

"Okay. I'll answer as honestly as I can."

Her smile at this is faint, thoughtful. 'I know you will," she says absently. "My question is…difficult for me to verbalize."

"Take all the time you need," I say, tracing her hair behind her ear, marveling at her beauty in the silver light of starshine.

She takes nearly a full minute formulating her question. "In the realm of physical affection, things seem to exist on a gradient…or a spectrum. On one side, you have simple things, like hand-holding and hugs."

"With you so far," I say, trying and failing to anticipate where she might be taking this.

"Then there is snuggling, kissing, holding one another, touching one's face, and things of this nature."

"Yeah…."

"On the opposite end, obviously, is sex."

"Ah." I think I'm starting to see where this is going. Maybe.

"My question, then, is this: what is between kissing and sex?"

"Touching that is sexual in nature but not sex. I dunno how linear it all is, though. I mean, me caressing your ass is a step in that direction. Touching each other under clothing. Taking off clothing and kissing and touching each other while naked. Then, right before sex, you have foreplay. That's touching each other sexually, like…" I trail off, trying to figure out how graphic I should be.

"Like what?" she presses.

"Trying to figure out how to put it. I don't wanna be crude about it."

"I would rather you be crude and honest than circumspect and vague or dishonest."

"Using your hands to make each other come," I blurt.

She blinks slowly. "Oh. I see." She rolls away from me. "I must seem so childish to you. So naïve."

"No," I protest. "Not at all. Innocent, but not childish or naïve."

She's silent awhile, then, and I watch her breathing come faster and faster. "Riley?"

"Yeah, babe?"

"I…" A shaky breath. "What is it like? To share that with someone?"

"Depends on the person, honestly." I can't stop myself—I pull her to me and cradle her against my chest. She cranes her neck to look up at me, chin on my chest, eyes as wide and bright as the moon. "Ask what you really want to ask, Cadence."

"I would like to share…that…with you." Her voice is so soft, so quiet.

My entire being tenses. "Cadence, I…"

I feel her deflate at my hesitation. "Oh. I see."

"No, no, no," I murmur, cupping her cheek. "You always assume the worst reason for what I say or don't say."

"Because that is my experience when it comes to allowing myself to hope," she murmurs.

"What is it you're hoping for?"

"To feel…" she trails off with a sigh. "I could stop there and say 'simply to feel.'" She gnaws on her lower lip, looking up at me with trepidation and hope in equal measure. "My whole life, Riley, I have been…a *mind*." She taps her temple. "This is who I am."

I frown, not quite following. "I mean, yeah. Me too."

"No, Riley. It is different. You are, by and large, one cohesive individual. You are your mind *and* your body. Your body simply works. You do not *feel* your body, you *are* your body. You think and you feel *automatically*. Your mind is…is *part* of your body.:

"Hmmmm. And it's different for you?"

"Yes. Very. The term is dissociation. I feel physical sensations intensely and acutely. With the mental noise I constantly experience, that hypersensitivity causes me to be easily overwhelmed by physical sensations. It is not merely being overly sensitive, like, 'oh, just toughen up,' as I have been told by plenty of physicians and therapists in my life—those who do not understand autism and ADHD, and especially how differently it manifests in women versus men. It is *painful*. Loud noises are excruciating. Rough, gritty texture on my skin is…like nails on a chalkboard or a fork dragging across a plate."

My stomach twists. "Really?"

"Yes. It is not just me being a silly, sensitive girl, Riley."

"That never crossed my mind," I tell her.

She smiles, resting her cheek on my chest and continuing to talk. "In a world of overwhelming noise, visual stimulation, olfactory input, and tactile sensation, with a mind that is already at a metaphorical redline at all times, the only way I can function day-to-day without being in a constant state of fight-or-flight is to dissociate from my body. I learned to do so at a very young age. I did not cry almost ever, I am told. My parents had to learn to check my diapers on a schedule because I simply would not cry if I had soiled myself. Same with hunger, or heat, or cold."

"So you just…taught yourself not to feel what's going on in your body?"

"Correct." A roll of her shoulder. "I have lived my life in my brain, occupied by my thoughts. My body is merely the vessel in which I move through life. It is…sometimes a separate thing from me, myself, the entity that is Cadence Creswell. It is a burden—it requires sustenance, so I must remember to feed it. It requires clothing, so I must remember to clothe it. It requires sunshine and exercise. Hydration. Proper nutrition. That last is tricky for me when I am working, especially. It is common for me to go a shift or two without eating, or subsisting on protein shakes and coffee."

I lead her back to the truck, grab the old, thick, wool ex-military blanket I keep in the back seat, and spread it out in the bed of my truck. I bunch up a hoodie as a pillow and we lay together and stare up at the stars.

I consider what she's telling me. "So, sex, for you is… what, then? Impossible?"

She thinks about my question for a long time. "It is a complicated topic for me. I have understood the mechanics of human sexuality from a very young age, as I studied anatomy, physiology, and other such subjects—as I have told you heretofore—and one cannot help encountering the subject in that context. But I never applied it to myself. I went through puberty, obviously, and the various physical sensations were terribly difficult for me, so I dissociated even more totally during that period of my life. It was not until I began studying at Harvard that I even wondered about dating or sexuality. I was surrounded by it—my roommate had a boyfriend and was not shy about engaging in sexual activity, even when I was in the room."

"Yeah, that's pretty common, from what I understand," I tell her. "Obviously, I never went to college, but I've had friends who did tell me very similar stories."

"She…" Cadence pauses, and I imagine she's blushing, though my eyes are on the sky and not her face. "She seemed to, erm…enjoy it. Very loudly and very exuberantly. It made me curious. About…boys. I began wondering if anyone would ever see fit to take an interest in me…as a human. As a female. And then the situation with Joel occurred, and I went out of my way to avoid attention from males, and never really entertained the notion of my own sexuality again. To be honest, my thoughts were never about sex, per se, but rather merely a curiosity regarding the attention of a boy. For who I am, I mean. Not because I am weird."

"So…what's different about me?" I ask. "Why do you react to me differently? Why is it okay for me to touch you?"

"I wish I knew," she answers.

I laugh. "Nice."

"Oh." She goes tense. "That could be construed as an insult, I now realize."

"I know you didn't mean it that way."

She rolls toward me, angled against me, hands folded on my chest with her chin on her hands. "Indeed I did not. I only meant that I do not know myself why you. You are extraordinarily handsome, of course. But I have encountered other attractive men in my life and not felt about them the way I do you. My reaction to you was instant. The moment I opened my eyes and saw you, I was…struck. I was immediately plunged into my body. I immediately wondered how it would feel to make physical contact with you. If I would hate it, or if…if I might, for once, enjoy it. The curiosity became a need to find out. And I did."

"So, here's a question for you, then." I slide my fingers into her hair behind her ears. "If you couldn't bear the thought of being touched by anyone, why was the idea of a kiss a good thing?"

"An excellent question, Riley." She touches my lower lip with her index finger, idle, curious, affectionate. "To me, a kiss has always been a symbol. I wondered how it would feel, but was incapable of comprehending the reality. It was a symbol of being the subject of desire. I have been mocked by my peers—here in the States, at least. And if not mocked, misunderstood, underestimated, made assumptions of, dismissed, laughed at, and ignored. Boys saw me as a freak, not a girl to be desired. Even after puberty, when my adult physique had finished growing, my strangeness always outweighed any interest there may have been in my physical form. Once I spoke and they heard me sounding, as you so accurately and comedically put it, like a Victorian age automaton, my femaleness vanished and my freakishness prevailed."

My heart breaks for her. "Cadence, that's awful. I'm sorry you experienced that."

She smiles, shrugs. "I have come to accept it."

"And now, you've had your first kiss." I touch her lip, mirroring the path of her finger along my lower lip to my upper in a slow circuit. "And you liked it?"

She doesn't answer immediately. "Yes," she breathes after a moment. "I did. More than I know how to say. I...I haven't stopped thinking about kissing you since the first time your lips touched mine."

"And now you're thinking about what comes after kissing."

"Yes."

"But...you're..." I exhale sharply. "You're going to Africa. I don't know for how long, but you are, and you have no reason to come back here whenever you do return to the States."

"I would be gone at least four months, most likely closer to six."

"Exactly."

She frowns. "But I..." she rolls to her back and stares

up at the sky. "I suppose I thought that you would be okay with that."

"With fooling around with you even though you're leaving soon?"

She nods. "Yes."

It's my turn to puzzle through my complicated reaction to this revelation. "I...I think if it were anyone else, I would be. But you're different." Before she can misinterpret this, I plow forward. "Cadence, you're a virgin, and experiencing sex is a big deal. It's a big deal to anyone, but you're twenty-four. You've waited a long time. And it's an even *bigger* deal to you, I think, because of your sensory issues."

"You're not wrong."

"I just...I *care* about you. I don't want to...fuck, I don't know. Take something from you that's not mine to have. I dunno if that makes any sense. I just...your first time, and your path *to* that first time should be special. It should be magical. Ideally, your first time should be with someone who you can see being the only one for you."

"You think I cannot see that possibility with you?" she asks.

My heart twists and flips. "I mean, I'm, like, your polar opposite. You're inherently good—you're pure-hearted. Crazy smart. Elite education. Bright future ahead of you, saving lives and being a badass."

She rolls her head to look at me. "You are not the opposite of any of those things, except perhaps educated, and education is not an indicator of intelligence but rather of opportunity."

I sigh, roll a shoulder. "I suppose."

She turns into me again, pressing her soft, svelte body against mine. "Riley, what it comes down to is that I choose *you.* I know what I want. I am frightened but ready—although frightened may not be the right word. Nervous? Anxious? Anticipatory? A little afraid, too, it is true. I know even less what to expect from the things you spoke of than I did of kissing." She scratches her fingernails along my jawline from earlobe to chin, and then tugs at my lower lip with her thumb. "I crave you, Riley. Your touch. Your kisses. Your attention. I want to see your body. I want to show you mine. I want to know how to touch you. I want to be touched. I want to know why Krista, my roommate, screamed the way she did."

Arousal and desire rocket through me. "Cadence… *fuck.*"

She presses on. "I trust you, Riley. That is rare for me. Truly, truly rare. I…have never in my life reacted to anyone the way I do to you. I do not know if I ever will again. I do not know what lies ahead for me, especially after my Sudanese mission. But I am here with you, now. I know I would consider it the greatest of errors if I did not allow myself to explore what my body is capable of feeling with the one man I can tolerate being touched by." She wriggles closer, and my cock stiffens at the soft crush of her tits against my chest and the way her thigh drapes over mine and her core snugs against my quad. "It can only be you, Riley. Please. Be with me."

I groan raggedly. "How can I say no? I've been tryin' like hell to be good with you. You deserve someone as good as you, babe, and that ain't me. But…*fuck,* I want you. I want you *so* damn bad, Cadence. Makes me crazy how attracted to you I am." I make sure she's looking at me. "To *you*—to the woman you are, Cadence. To your personality—to your mind as much as your body."

Her eyes go misty. "You truly mean that?"

"God, yes. You're the most amazing woman I've ever met."

"I…" she blinks hard, and then nuzzles her nose against my throat. "I want to kiss you, Riley. I want to kiss you, and this time, I don't want to stop. I don't want *you* to stop. I want you to teach me what my body can do. How it can feel."

"How the fuck are you even real?" I breathe, not intending to say it out loud.

"I do not understand the question," she murmurs.

"I mean you're too good to be true." I brush my thumb over her lips. "I'll go slow, okay? Stop me at any time, for any reason. Ask me anything."

She huffs a laugh. "I have spoken more about myself to you than I have in the rest of my life combined. I do not like speaking of myself. I do not like explaining myself to people. Most do not care to actually understand. You do." She licks her lips, and starshine glitters in her eyes, stains her skin silver. "I am tired of talking, Riley. I would like to *feel*." A quick pause. "Good things, if you please."

This makes me laugh. "Only good things, I promise."

Her eyes are wide. "You must also teach me what to do for you, Riley. All relationships, even physical ones, rely on an equitable cycle of give and take."

I grin at her. "Oh, that won't be a problem."

"You…you want me to touch you?"

"Do bears shit in the woods?" It comes out before I can stop it. "That's rhetorical. It means obviously."

She smiles. "I believe I grasped your meaning."

"Hard to tell with you, sometimes."

"That is fair. You would not be mistaken if you assume

I do not understand colloquialisms and such. Most of the time I do not, but every once in a while—"

I cut her off with a kiss. "Cadence?"

"Yes, Riley?" Breathy, eager.

"I can't kiss you if you're babbling."

"I babble when I am nervous."

"Gettin' that." I kiss her again, soft, quick. "Remember one thing for me, okay? *You* are in control. You can test me. Ask me to stop or slow down or wait."

"Just…be gentle?"

"How could I be anything less with someone so precious?"

11

Cadence

THE EARLY JUNE NIGHT AIR IS WARM AND THE SKY is so full of stars one could lose count in a space no larger than one's palm. Beneath me, the blanket is a thick, if somewhat scratchy, barrier between me and the cold metal of the truck bed.

Riley is a bulky presence above me, beside me. He radiates warmth and exudes desire and patience and strength.

I am nervous—I have no clue what to expect. Kissing is not at all as I had imagined, in the few times I even endeavoured to direct my imagination toward that end. My skin tingles in anticipation of his touch, and my belly flutters and flips.

I want this.

Badly.

What I have not said to Riley, as I am not certain he would not take it the wrong way, is that this is an opportunity I will not squander—not knowing what the future holds, I cannot be certain a chance such as this will ever come to me again. I am aware that that sounds…well… opportunistic, and perhaps it is. But such is my reality. I am here with a man who desires me. Who seems to care for me, at least to some degree. I may never find anyone like Riley again, or anyone who could want me for me, who could see me the way he does.

I push this line of thought out of my mind—it is worrisome and frightening to consider. If I allow myself to continue down that mental vector, I may never leave this place or this man, and I would eventually resent him if that happened. I *must* go to South Sudan. I could not live with myself if I did not.

Yet so much of my heart, when I leave, will remain here. I can see that, even now.

Mercifully, Riley chooses this moment, when my mind is whirling and conflicted, to touch his lips ever so gently to mine. My mind does not go blank—it will take more than that, I fear— but the chaotic maelstrom of conflicting needs and desires quiets enough that I can tune in on him, focus on his lips on mine.

His lips are warm and smooth and slippery. I tilt my head slightly and find a better angle, and the soft, warm slip of his lips on mine is delightful—a barrage of sensations: the wetness, the warmth, the slippery slide of our mouths moving, the hot waft of his breath, the press of his nose alongside mine. His body is large and hard and hot. His tongue creases the seam of my closed mouth, and I open for him, and his tongue drives into my mouth; this is almost overpowering.

The intrusion of his tongue in my mouth is alien, slithering on mine, stuttering past my teeth, grazing over my lips. I feel his kiss in every cell of my body. It warms me from the inside out, creates a bizarre, unfamiliar pressure in my belly. It pushes a hunger through me, but not for food. My mind is asking a dozen questions all at once:

Will he touch me, now?

Does he want to?

Is he only doing this because I asked him to?

Does he really think I am gorgeous as he keeps saying?

Which part of my body will he touch first?

Will I enjoy it as much as I do his kisses?

Are my breasts large enough? Men prefer women with oversized breasts, I believe, and mine are not especially large, though they are not small, either.

Will he attempt to make me orgasm?

Will I be able to?

What will it feel like?

Will I like it?

What if it hurts?

The way my university roommate screamed, cried, groaned, grunted, whimpered, and otherwise carried on when cavorting in bed with her boyfriend, I always got the impression sex must be very painful. When I asked her about this, however, she laughed uproariously and would only say that it does not and should not hurt, and that I would only be able to understand if I were to experience it for myself.

What about Riley's body? I have only seen the male form

nude in clinical settings, never personally. I have never seen an erect penis before.

What would it feel like to touch his penis?

What if I hurt him, somehow?

What if he does not enjoy the way I touch him?

What if I cannot bring him pleasure?

What if I panic and cannot function?

What if my mind will not allow me to enjoy this?

What if I displease him and he wants to stop?

What if he rejects me?

What if I cannot bring myself to touch him intimately?

What if…?

What if…?

What if…?

"Hey," his voice murmurs. "Come back to me."

"I am here," I mumble.

Levered over me, he traces a fingertip from temple to jaw corner to chin. "Nah, babe, you went somewhere else, mentally."

"Oh, Yes. I…" I swallow hard. "I apologize."

"Care to share?"

"What I was thinking?"

"Yeah."

I let out a breath. "Fears. Worries. A mental storm of what-ifs."

"Then I'd better do a better job of distracting that amazing brain of yours, huh?" He kisses the corner of my mouth, and then my jawline, and then the underside of my chin, and then my throat, and with each next kiss, my heart beats a little faster. "The most important thing, Cadence, is that you talk to me. Or, communicate, at least."

He kisses lower on my throat, and his hand cups my

waist between ribcage and hip. My pulse slams harder at
the idea that his hand might drift up…or down.

"Talking *is* communicating," I answer, my voice soft
and breathy, and I find myself tipping my head up so he
has better access for kissing my throat, which, oddly, is
quite arousing—I had not considered one's throat to be
erogenous. "How else would I communicate except by
speaking?"

"You just did it," he answers. "Tipping your head back
like that tells me you like it when I do this…" he kisses my
throat again, above my Adam's apple, and then lower and
lower, until he is kissing my suprasternal notch.

"Yes," I breathe, unable to summon my full voice. "Yes,
I do."

"If I'm doing it right, you won't always be able to talk,"
he says, and kisses lower yet, centimeters above the neckline of my dress. "So just find a way, nonverbal if necessary, to let me know if you like something. If you don't
want me to touch somewhere, push my hand away. If you
do want me to touch somewhere, guide me there. Gasps,
sighs, groans, things like that also tell me you're liking
something."

He brings his mouth back to mine, and this kiss is all
tongue immediately, and the hot pressure behind my navel
pulsates. His hand drifts toward my midline, his palm covering the precise location in which I feel the heat and pressure. His tongue moves on mine, and I dance my tongue
against his. This feels kind of silly at first, like a child's game
of thumb war except with tongues. But then, when I sweep
my tongue through his mouth, he groans low in his throat
like a grumbly grizzly bear, and the hot pressure in my
belly sinks southward, building behind my privates. I do

it again, and receive a similar response from him—I touch his cheek, and then slide my fingers into his hair at his temple, and then above his ear, and then I cup his neck and find myself at war with his tongue, as if we are each seeking some kind of supremacy over the other, though I know not what victory would look like in this case. My belly flutters the more I kiss him in this manner, however, and my mind is mercifully, blessedly quiet—I think my hyperfocus is taking over. There is only this—only Riley, only his body, his tongue, his hands, only the wild, alien barrage of sensations as he kisses me.

His hand carves up over my belly and halts at my sternum. His thumb presses against the underwire of my bra at the center point between the cups. My heart crashes in my chest crazily, anticipating. He pulls away from the kiss, gazes down at me—I open my mouth to say something, I do not know what, and then...

His large hand cups my breast—over the dress and over the bra, but still. Riley is touching my breast. My nipples harden into achy, tender bullets. I am absolutely certain he can feel the hard point of my nipple even through the two layers of material; I am not sure whether I should be embarrassed about this.

He kisses my breastbone, and then along the neckline of my dress. to my shoulder. He kisses the round of my shoulder, and his finger deftly prods the broad, shallow neckline of my dress over the edge of my shoulder. My bra strap shows, now. I restrain myself from tugging my dress in place—I assume he did that on purpose.

I must let him; I want him to.

He kisses me again, now at the juncture where shoulder and arm meet, the tender crease there. Now, the other side, where he does the same, gently slipping my dress's neckline down, and now the upper slopes of my breasts are exposed. My bra is a plain black full coverage one, as I am a practical, utilitarian woman with no interest in or need for lacy, unsupportive, and immodest undergarments which no one will ever see.

He kisses my breastbone from left to right, right to left, subtly lowering my neckline with each kiss. And then he brings his mouth to mine and claims a hot, wet kiss that short-circuits my brain, causing me to gasp into his mouth and lift up and lean into him, ratcheting up the intensity of the kiss.

He tugs my neckline down, exposing my bra cups fully. He guides my arm out of the sleeve, and then the other, and lowers the neckline again so it stretches around my sternum…and then again so it is around my belly. My heart batters against my ribcage as the night air bathes my skin, and I am hyperaware of his eyes on my chest.

"Okay with this?" he mutters, his eyes searching my face.

I can only nod.

"Nervous?"

I nod again.

He smiles at me. Lowers his mouth to mine and kisses me—this one is gentle and soft and sweet rather than hungry. "I can't get enough of kissing you."

"Nor I," I whisper.

I watch his eyes tug away from mine and slip lower, and now he's gazing at my breasts. My nipples are so hard they hurt, and my breasts feel engorged and strangely heavy. My breath lodges in my throat when he passes his hand over my shoulder, brushing my bra strap aside;

without that support, my breast sags to one side; he repeats the action on the other side.

I am struggling to breathe now, panting and searching his face, watching his eyes linger on my chest. The difficulty in catching my breath only worsens when he moves his mouth from mine to my breastbone again, and then kisses lower and lower…his lips skim my skin between my breasts, and now he is hungrily, almost desperately kissing my décolletage.

With each kiss, my nipples harden more and more until I am panting with…I know not what this feeling is.

Need. Desperation. Hunger.

A yawning, aching, empty, hollowness within me… and the heat and pressure behind my sex pulses and thrums, and I become acutely aware of my clitoris, for some reason; whatever medical, anatomical knowledge regarding the mechanics of sex and female arousal I possess have been scattered out of my awareness entirely.

There is no reason, no knowledge in me, now, only sensation.

Kissing as much of the exposed flesh of my breasts as he can, Riley slips a hand under my back between me and the truck bed—seeking the closure of my bra, I realize.

"Wait," I gasp.

He immediately yanks his hand out and stops kissing me. "What, babe?" He breathes, his gaze concerned. "Too fast?"

"N-no," I whisper, blushing furiously and unable to look even in the direction of his face. "I—it…" I grasp his hand and guide it to my chest. "My b-bra…" I stammer, mortified yet excited, "it is a f-f-front c-clasp."

His grin is…devilish. Heated. "Oh."

He touches my chin, lifts my face. "Can you look at me, sweetheart? Just for a second. Please."

I force my eyes to his, squirming at the acute discomfort of direct eye contact—especially when I see such blatant arousal on his face.

Arousal caused by me.

Perhaps he will appreciate my nude form, after all. That would be rather nice.

"So, what you're saying is," he murmurs, focused intently on my eyes and nowhere else, "you want me to do… *this*."

He grips both bra cups in one hand, pulls them together, and somehow manages to undo the clasp one-handed. His eyes stay on my face—I am blushing furiously, my cheeks flaming hot. My heart crashes wildly.

All he must do now is let go and my breasts will be bared for his gaze. He is waiting. Watching me. I cannot breathe—no longer panting, my lungs ache from holding my breath in anticipation.

"Yes or no, honey?" he whispers, his eyes on mine.

"I…" I pause, searching myself—the answer is *yes*, but the word will not leave my lips. Instead, I hear myself blurt the thought that has been top of mind since he began kissing his way down. "My nipples are very hard and very sensitive. I…I am—"

He grins. "Means you're turned on, babe." He lets the tension out a little. "Tell me what you want, Cadence. Yes or no?"

Turned on. Sexually aroused.

Yes.

I search myself once more and find only that answer. "Yes."

"Thank fucking god," he growls. "Been dying to see your tits, Cadence."

"I am afraid you will not like them. I am afraid they are not big enough. Or—or not the right shape."

He laughs at this—I know by now that when he laughs at me, I must remember not to assume ill intent. "I'm not laughing at you, Cadence, I just—"

"I know that now," I whisper.

He keeps hold, still, his eyes on mine. "There's absolutely, positively *zero* chance I won't find your tits as perfect and incredible as the rest of you. I promise."

"But you have not seen them."

"Don't have to."

I swallow hard. "Explain, if you would. Please."

He sniffs a laugh. "Makin' me work for it, huh?" He nuzzles the tip of his nose against mine, grinning at me. "Easy to explain, sweetheart. One, they're part of you, and you're gorgeous. Just objectively, regardless of how I feel about you, you are fucking breathtaking—and even if you had no boobs at all, like mosquito bites or whatever, you'd still be hot as fuck and I'd still be just as desperate to get you topless."

"Desperate?" I breathe.

"Completely."

"Oh." I gnaw on my lip. "And the other reason? You said number one, which implies the presence of a second reason."

He holds my gaze, and I feel him very gradually releasing his hold on the closure. "Number two? I'm lookin' at 'em, sweetheart, and they're fuckin' perfect."

"They are still almost entirely covered."

"And even so, they're fucking epic, Cadence. Absolutely perfect."

"Let go now, please," I breathe. "I cannot bear the suspense any longer."

He spreads his fingers apart, releasing the cups. They fly apart, and my naked breasts spill out. "*Fuck* me," he groans. "See? Perfect." He licks his lips, and his eyes are locked, rapt, on my breasts, which heave with my almost frantic breathing. "God…*damn*, Cadence. Even more gorgeous than I'd imagined."

"You…imagined them?"

"Fuck yes I have. Frequently. And the reality is *way* better than anything I could have fantasized about."

He slides his hand over my belly, covering my navel, and then up and up until the undersides of my breasts touch the upper edge of his hand. My breath catches, then. My nipples are peaked and hard and aching and I am shaking all over, searching his face and waiting for him to touch me there.

"You are the first and only man to see me like this," I whisper.

It feels important to note that, for some reason. I do not know why.

"Thank you for trusting me with this privilege, Cadence." He cups my face, kisses me softly. "Please believe me when I say that I'm not taking this for granted."

His lips move ghostly-soft on mine as he speaks, and I lift up, mate my mouth to his, open my lips, and sweep my tongue in his mouth to elicit that growl.

Yes, there it is—his chest rumbles with the sound, which sends a searing pulse of heat and pressure billowing through my entire body—my fingertips tingle, my scalp tingles, my toes. My nipples stiffen so hard and so tight that I find myself arching my back in a vain attempt to relieve the ache somehow.

His rough palm scrapes my belly as he caresses upward…and this time, he does not stop.

He gathers the weight of my breast into his hand, cupping it. I whimper through clenched teeth at the feel of his hand, where no hand save mine has ever touched. The whimper becomes a shrill gasp when he strums my peaked, throbbing nipple with his thumb—a sensation like a bolt of electricity sizzles through me, rocketing in a hot line from my nipple to my privates. I arch again, this time pressing my breast into his hand. The ache is not relieved, however; rather, it worsens.

As does the pressure behind my sex—the throb and pulse of blood rushing and pooling and pounding in my clitoris is all-consuming.

This is arousal.

It is utterly maddening. It is a need I cannot meet. A hunger I cannot sate, a thirst I cannot quench.

"Riley…" I breathe.

"Yeah, Beautiful? You okay with this?"

I open my eyes and look up at him; he is staring at my breasts as if memorizing them. Perhaps he is. "I feel…"

"How?"

"It is difficult to put into words." I arch again, and he bends over me, kisses the upper slope of the breast he holds in his hand, and I gasp. "Ohhh…my goodness. I feel…"

He kisses down the swell, and now he cups the underside of my breast, presenting it to himself, offering my breast to his mouth. I cannot even manage a gasp when he covers my nipple with his mouth and suckles it gently, softly—his mouth is scorching hot and wet, and his tongue flattens my aching nipple against the roof of his mouth, and the electric heat shivers through me and makes my clitoris pulse crazily, throbbing so intensely I have to press my thighs together in yet another vain attempt to alleviate the ache.

"Oh! Oh my...Riley—"

He groans. "Fuck, woman. You're so goddamn sensitive. Fucking incredible."

"That I am sensitive?" I ask, confused.

"Yeah, honey," he murmurs. "It's hot. You make the hottest fucking sounds every time I touch you."

"I cannot help the sounds."

"Good. *Don't.* Don't *ever* hold back those sounds. Okay?" he cups my jaw and makes me look at him. "No restraint. No control. I want you *wild*, Cadence."

He returns his attention to my breasts, now caressing the other, cupping it, squeezing it, testing the weight of it, and then offering it up to his mouth—yanking another shrill gasp from me.

I ache everywhere, now, and my dress suddenly feels too tight and too hot and too restrictive. My panties, too. I writhe under his touch and groan, and now I finally understand my roommate's claim that I cannot understand unless I experience it.

His touch on my breasts is driving me wild. My clitoris throbs every time he touches me, more and more, and when he takes my nipple in his mouth and suckles on it and tongues it and worries it with his teeth, I feel like some part of me might explode like an overfilled water balloon—the part of me at the apex of my thighs.

I clasp my hand against his head as he kisses and licks

and sucks on my nipples, feather my fingers in his hair, and clutch him to me—communicating, I hope, how much I enjoy his attentions.

My sex aches so badly it qualifies as pain. I press my thighs together but this does nothing to alleviate the ache, the pressure.

Riley rolls toward me and moves his mouth to mine and kisses my lips, demands my tongue, and rolls my nipple between finger and thumb—the combination of his kiss and the pinching of my nipple is almost the catalyst for my combustion—it feels as if I am teetering on the brink of some abyssal precipice. It frightens me, this feeling. It is intense, wild, and all-consuming.

My dress tangles up my legs, frustrating me. I growl my frustration, unable to otherwise verbalize it.

Cupping my breast, lips whispering against my saliva-slick nipple: "What's wrong, sweetheart?"

"Dress," I gasp. "Too hot. In the way."

I feel his lips curve against my breast in a grin. "Is that so?"

"Yes," I answer.

"Then please, my lady, allow me to endeavor a solution."

I laugh, amused and touched. "Are you...talking like...like *me*?"

His cheeks tinge pink beneath his beard; the man is *blushing*. "That's the idea, at least."

Why this simple, silly thing means so much to me, I cannot say—the answer is obvious and too utterly terrifying and worrisome to even look at in the privacy of my own mind.

In fact, I hardly know how to respond. I have to,

however; I worry he will take a prolonged silence as criticism. "Riley," I whisper, cupping his chin with one hand and stroking his hair with the other. "That you would even…" I shake my head, eyes misty and hot. "I hardly know what to…"

"Might sound like an idiot compared to you," he murmurs, but I just wanted to show you that I—"

A kind of lecherous greed swells within me, or some extraordinarily complex set of multi-layered feelings both physical and emotional tied to my physical desire and my emotional vulnerability, the whole predicated upon Riley's unending sweetness and patience and consideration, and now fueled into an inferno by this latest act of venturing beyond his comfort zone and into mine.

My heart clatters against my ribs and pounds in my throat. I clutch the front of his shirt in shaky fingers, gazing at him as I summon the courage to let myself perform the action my desire and greed is compelling me toward. I lift his shirt, slowly. His grin spreads slowly as he realizes what I am about, and he shifts his weight to allow me to tug the garment over his head.

A shirtless Riley Crowe is a wonderful specimen to behold. In truth, a ridiculous part of me has long suspected, simply through an absence of objectively confirmable evidence, that a body like Riley's does not actually exist. One sees physiques like his only through the suspect barrier of a screen, whether television, cinema, or a cell phone. One does not see such a body in real life. With the advent of photograph retouching, digital alteration, filters, and now AI, it seems all too feasible that bulging pectoral muscles, veiny, sinewy biceps and forearms, and rippling, block-like, sculpted-from-marble abdominal muscles revealed through single-digit body fat is fake, or at very least exaggerated.

I am faced with a living, breathing, and, indeed, rippling proof that my theory is false.

Riley really does look like that.

Shirtless, he rests on an elbow and simply allows me to gaze at him. I press my hand to the firm, hot bulge of his pectoral muscle, to the small, flat, partially-inverted nub of his nipple—he sucks in a sharp inhale when I touch him there, and his nostrils flare.

"Sensitive?" I ask, my voice a hesitant whisper.

"Yeah," he growls.

"You are so absurdly handsome, Riley," I whisper. "It is difficult for me to convince myself that I am allowed to touch your perfectly sculpted body."

"*Allowed*?" he grumbles, his tone one of disbelief. "I could beg you to touch me, if that would help."

My breath catches in my throat again, and the too-hot, too-constricted sensation roars back through me. I let my hand roam his torso, explore the thick, firm swell of his chest, the ridges and grooves of his abs. His jeans sit low on his waist, exposing the waistband of his underwear, beneath which the tempting grooves of his iliac furrows vanish.

I feel my legs writhing, and the folds of my dress gather and tangle and bind until my legs are knotted up like an octopus in a fisherman's net. In my mind's eye, I see Riley in the basement of his home, shirtless and sweaty in those tiny, revealing shorts.

In my mind's eye, I am bold enough to hook my fingers inside those shorts and help him out of them, baring those infuriating, beguiling furrows which lead like twin highways to his manhood. The thought of which makes my heart palpitate most worryingly, and which makes my hands shake and my palms sweat and now my breath comes short and that hot, pulsing pressure behind my privates becomes maddeningly insistent to the point of insanity.

"The solution you mentioned," I whisper. "May I know what it is?"

"You may," he murmurs in answer, bending over me to kiss my chest between my breasts, and then my sternum, and then my diaphragm, and then my navel. "May I please demonstrate my proposed solution, Cadence?"

I grin, huff a breathless laugh. "I should be most pleased if you did."

He rises on his hands and knees and moves over me, his gaze raking over my breasts as eagerly, greedily, and blatantly as the first moment he saw my exposed chest. He bends again, kissing my belly, navel, my sides. His hands rest on my waist, and he looks up at me, hesitating. Watching. He curls his fingers in the material of my dress and slowly tugs it downward, giving me every opportunity to stop him. I stroke his hair and search his face, memorizing the way he looks in this moment—eyes wide and deep and pale blue and fiery with desire and yet concerned for me and ready to stop should I give him the slightest indication I wish him to.

He tugs my dress down to my hips, and then pauses. My only response is to lift my backside up half an inch. He slips the dress past my backside, and I lower myself to the blanket as he slides it down my legs and off.

I am nearly naked now, clad only in a pair of plain black briefs. "Fuck, Cadence," he snarls, his voice low and rough. "So goddamned sexy."

Even the roughness of his voice arouses me. His gaze raking over my body from face to chest to privates to legs and back up—that arouses me.

His hands skimming up my hips and then over my waist and then cupping my breasts, both of them at once—this arouses me.

The wild, frenetic heat building behind my sex is now a crushing, pulsating pressure that I can only attempt to alleviate through the utterly useless yet absolutely involuntary action of rubbing my thighs together. And the more he gazes at me with such obvious desire, the more the pressure of arousal increases.

And then he bends over me again, and I bury my fingers in his soft, cool, thick black hair and stroke and caress his scalp and temples and nape as he kisses my belly and my breasts...and then my belly again...and then my hipbone. Except, in order to kiss my hipbone, he has to tug my underwear down a bit. He repeats this on the other side, and my heart begins to pound harder than ever as I realize what he's doing: the same subtle method of easing me out of my clothing as he used earlier.

Am I prepared to allow him to succeed?

"Riley?" I breathe.

Fingers hooked in my panties at either hip, he freezes in place and looks up at me. "Too fast?"

I shake my head. "No, I...no." I swallow hard. "I know what you are doing. And I...I would like you to know how much I appreciate the care you are taking to ensure my comfort in this process."

He slides the elastic lower, kissing downward in a line from my navel, lower and lower, until he is not longer kissing belly but the delicate curve of my mons pubis, which has my breath caught, hot and thick and pulsing in the frantic rhythm of my heartbeat, in my throat. "This oughta be fun, Cadence. Enjoyable. I know you're nervous, and that's totally normal."

"I am nervous," I admit, "but no longer afraid. I trust you."

He drops his head, and I hear him clear his throat. "Cadence, I…you don't know what it means to hear that."

The emotion is vulnerability on his part—it is him extending his trust to me.

His lips touch my flesh, and he exhales shakily. "Wish to fuck I could express how hard it is for me to not just rip these fucking things off you."

The ragged need in his voice is jet fuel on the pyre of my desire. Arousal blazes through me hotter than ever, and I feel a pulsing rush in my privates, so potent and so hot it makes my sex slippery and so wet my panties stick to my skin. Mortified, I cross one thigh over the other and turn away from him.

He frowns up at me. "What is it? You okay?"

"Yes, I…well, no." Face hot, cheeks hotter, I cover my face with both hands. "Something…happened. Down… there."

Riley growls wordlessly, grins up at me, and then presses his lips to my thigh, high up, inches blow the gusset of my panties where it angles in from my hip toward my sex. Another kiss to my thigh, now closer to the gusset. "Is that so?" he murmurs. "What happened, Cadence?"

"I cannot say it out loud, Riley. It is too embarrassing."

He nuzzles my thigh, kisses, and then nuzzles again, and his nose and cheek and jaw brush my privates; the wet rush happens again, and now my panties are not just damp but quite literally soaked. "I give you my word, Cadence, that no matter what happened, it's not anything to be embarrassed about."

"But it is," I whisper. "I am...ahhhh....aroused."

"Good," he growls, now kissing my other thigh, now nuzzling and kissing so he in no way accidentally brushes my sex with his cheek and jaw and nose. I am quite certain he can smell my...me, down there. I am a fastidious person and I take hygiene very seriously, and I take care to keep my pH down there, well-balanced. So while I am as certain as I can be that I will not smell unpleasant, I am aware that even clean and well-cared for, I will have a scent. And it is mortifying in the extreme to know his nose is *right there*—smelling me.

I squirm, intensely uncomfortable.

"*Supposed* to be aroused, honey. That's the whole point." He looks up at me, grinning. "I can take the pressure off you, though. I bet I can guess what happened that has you all...twitterpated."

"Oh," I breathe. "Do tell."

I am assuredly not as casual and unaffected as I endeavor to sound.

He nuzzles the inside of my thigh—despite my multi-layered mortification, his lips kissing the inside of my thigh has me easing my thighs apart—just slightly. Another kiss, to the inside of my other thigh; another subtle easing of the tension in my thighs. Again and again he kisses and nuzzles my thighs, and again and again I feel myself involuntarily letting my legs sag open farther and farther. Which only serves to expose the source of my embarrassment: my sex, and the way my panties stick to my skin.

He moves further down my body, now on his belly

between my knees, and his hands carve up over my belly and cup my breasts and knead them and twist my nipples until I gasp, until another blast of wet heat sears through me, culminating in another gush of wetness between my thighs.

"Riley!" I gasp.

"Look at me, babe," he murmurs, and I force my eyes to open and to meet his; he drags a finger down the seam of my vagina, the outlines of which I know must be visible, being adhered to my flesh. "Fuck yeah," he snarls, "You're wet as hell for me, sweetheart."

I squeal a groan, covering my face. "I know!" I hiss. "I cannot help it. The arousal your attentions causes in me—"

"Cadence, honey?" Something in his tone catches my attention and rips the words out of my mouth. "You're fuckin' *soaked*." He—and I can hardly believe my eyes—nuzzles his nose and mouth against me, exactly where I am the wettest, inhaling sharply, greedily, eagerly.

"RILEY!" I protest.

He grins. "Sexy as fuck, knowing you're so fucking wet for me."

"But is that not..." I begin, only to lose my train of thought when he nuzzles me again, and then presses his mouth over my vagina and blows a hot breath against me through the cotton of my panties.

I gasp at the heat of his breath, and feel myself pulse, another rush of arousal hitting me like a freight train.

"The more turned on you get, the wetter your pussy gets." When I gasp in shock at his dirty word, he grins at me. "That scandalize you, sweetest girl?" His ice-blue eyes sear me to the bone, slice me to ribbons with their razor-sharp arousal. "Me talking about how wet your pussy is?"

I can only whimper. Shake all over. His shoulders are wedged between my thighs, so now I cannot even hide my arousal by pressing my thighs together; there is no alleviation of the maddening, mind-twisting, body-contorting need for...*something*...that has utterly taken control of my mind and body.

"Riley, *please*," I whisper, my voice breathless; I do not know what I am asking him for.

"What do you want, babe? What do you need?"

"I do not know!" I wail, arching my spine as he seizes my nipple in his mouth and suckles on it until it flattens in his mouth. "Oh! Oh my goodness, I...I do not know *what* I need, Riley. But I need...*something*. Please help me, Riley. Please. I am going mad."

"Going mad, you say?" He covers my seam with his mouth and huffs on me again. "Feeling...needy? Desperate?"

"Yes!"

"I know what you need, Cadence."

I flick my eyes to his and hold his gaze. "Tell me! Please tell me. I cannot bear this any longer."

He does not comply immediately, as I had expected. Instead, he spends several more moments kissing and licking and sucking on my nipples—which only worsens the crazed desperation I feel for any kind of deliverance from this wild, primal, out-of-control need.

And then he kisses down my body again, from breasts to navel to mons pubis. He hooks his fingers in my panties again and tugs them lower in front—the uppermost hint of my cleft is exposed, now.

"What do I need, Riley?" I demand. "Please tell me?"

"You need to come, sweetheart." He grins up at me, releasing my underwear so they snap back against me again. "You need an orgasm."

"How…" I begin in a raw whisper, lose my voice, my courage, and try again. "How do I…How do I acquire one?"

He stares up at me, eyes heated and wild, and tugs the gusset of my panties to one side, partially exposing my sex. I gasp, shrill and shocked—only to gasp again, more shocked yet, when he trails a fingertip down the lips of my sex. I jerk at this touch, every muscle tensing. "You let me make you come." He does it again, and I hunch forward, doing a crunch at his touch. "You ask me to make you come."

"Oh," I breathe. "I see."

I focus on the stars for a moment, then, momentarily overwhelmed by sensation and by need and by awe that I am here, experiencing this—it is real. It is happening. He wants me—Riley Crowe desires me.

Just forty-eight hours ago, I was lost and lonely and sad. I had never been kissed. I had no hope that anyone would ever *want* to kiss me. And now I am in the bed of a pickup truck, wearing nothing but my panties, and the most attractive man I have ever seen wants to give me an orgasm.

And I am going to let him.

Let him? No, no. *Plead* with him to have mercy upon me—that is what I shall do.

"Riley?" I breathe. Run my fingers through his hair. "Please, Riley."

"Please what?" he asks.

"Help me."

"Help you what?"

"You know."

"Yeah. But I need to hear you say the words."

"I do not know if I can."

He releases the gusset, and I am covered again…but then he grasps my panties at my hips and looks at me. "Tell me to take 'em off you," he commands.

"Riley, will you please remove my panties?" My voice is a tiny, embarrassed whisper.

"Louder."

I clear my throat. "Riley, will you please remove my panties?" I say it firmly, cheeks so hot one could almost fry an egg on them.

"Butt up, honey," he says.

I lift my backside. Hold my breath. Watch as Riley tugs my panties down past my hips, and then over the swell of my backside, and then my sex is exposed and he is tossing my panties aside with my dress and I am naked in front of a man for the first time in my life.

Embarrassed and aroused, I want for one desperate moment to curl into a ball and hide from his hungry eyes. But I do not—I cannot.

I *will* not.

Tears stain my eyes—I hate them, but I cannot stop them.

He sees.

"Hey, hey, hey, what's this?" he whispers, rising up the length of my body, leaning on an elbow to smear the tears away. "Cadence, if I—"

I cover his mouth. "No," I whisper over him. "I am not upset. I'm…"

"Overwhelmed?" he guesses.

"Yes."

"Need to stop? Or just take a minute?"

I nod.

He slides one thick, burly arm under my neck, and now he's curled over me on his side, sheltering me from the ever-watchful gaze of the stars, and his eyes are on mine and nowhere else. "I got you, honey. Long as you need. We can get dressed and go, if you want."

"No!" I exclaim, more forcefully than I had intended; it is almost a shout. "No. No. Please, I do not want to stop, or to leave. I am just…I feel so many things, and…"

"This help at all?" he breathes, and his mouth slants against mine, and I whimper at the heat of his mouth.

"Yes," I gasp between kisses. "Yes, it does."

It more than helps, in fact.

It emboldens me.

I explore the broad hard field of his back and shoulders, my sensitive fingertips identifying each muscle—levator scapulae, trapezius, latissimus dorsi, rhomboids major and minor…

Lower.

Lower.

I run into the barrier of his jeans.

I turn my fingertips to face his toes as I explore his abdomen, lower and lower, until I find the beginning of his iliac furrow. When I fit my middle finger into the groove of the furrow and slide my touch toward his waistband, his stomach curls inward.

An invitation?

I believe so.

He, meanwhile, kisses me as if we face execution on

the morrow—with utter desperation, with complete hunger. His tongue demands mine—and I give him what he demands, most eagerly. The kiss erases my overwhelm, and I lose myself in his mouth, his tongue, his hunger. I lose myself in my own desire. I feel my need pooling at the juncture of my thighs, making my sex slippery and so, so wet, so hot. The pressure within is titanic and impossible and maddening.

And with it, now that I am touching his marvelous, masculine body, my own desire for him is a new thing, a hunger to know more of him, a need to feel his muscle, his heat, his hardness, his flesh, his arousal.

I find the cold roundness of the button of his jeans. Flip it through the loop.

Riley growls into the kiss. "It's like that, is it?"

"If you will allow it, yes," I whisper.

"You don't need to ask, honey." He cups my cheek as he kisses me, and then pulls away and we look at each other for a moment. "Listen to me, okay? I'm here for *you*. Whatever you want, whatever you need." Another kiss, hot, all tongue, quick. "My body is yours, Cadence. Explore. Do whatever you want." Heart pounding in my ears, I find the tab of his zipper and tug it down. I am panting with anxiousness and nerves and need and anticipation. Riley's hand smooths over my belly and soars down one bare hip. His mouth covers mine and I whimper and lift up and open my mouth to his, and I offer him my tongue, and he takes it with a growl in his chest. With his jeans loose and open, I let my touch roam his back once more, from shoulders to the elastic of his underwear.

I bury my face in the side of his throat, too embarrassed to look at him as I hesitate...slip my hand beneath the elastic of his underwear…and cup the hot, taut bubble of his buttock. Which is, unsurprisingly, hard as rock, yet the skin is so soft and so hot. I squeeze, whimpering in shocked delight at how much I enjoy the feel of him in my hand. I palm his other buttock, and then worm my other hand around his waist and fill both hands with his buttocks.

He simply lets me touch him. His palm rests on my hip, in the intimate, tender juncture where hip, thigh, and sex meet.

The constriction of his jeans and underwear is abruptly infuriating, and I growl my annoyance—shove them both down out of the way so I may play with the wonderfulness that is his backside unrestricted.

He laughs at my impatience, his body shaking. "Hey, easy. No rush."

"You are clothed and I am not," I point out. "This feels inequitable."

"Whaddya gonna do about it?" he murmurs, his voice rough and amused.

I feel his feet working, moving—toeing off his shoes and socks. I push at his jeans and underwear, but they catch at his belly. Or, rather…near there. A bit lower, perhaps.

"Careful, there," he whispers. "Certain parts of me don't exactly bend in their current state."

I squeak as I realize what he means—his…um…manhood…is erect, and his underwear is catching on it. "Did I…hurt you?"

"No, honey. No. You didn't hurt me."

Relief is a sweet rush of breath in my frozen lungs. "You are…um…aroused."

"Yeah, babe."

"I have not touched you…there."

"No." He pulls his face away to look into my eyes. "You turn me on, Cadence. Just looking at you turns me on—you letting me play with these?" He scoops my breast in his hand, lowers his mouth to it, suckles softly. "Hard as a fuckin' rock, sweetheart."

"Oh," I breathe. "My breasts are an acceptable size and shape to you, then?"

"Fishin' for compliments, are you?" he growls. "Cadence, honey, you have perfect tits."

"You insist on perfection as your favored descriptor, Riley," I murmur. "But surely perfection is a myth."

"Subjective, not a myth." He growls, palming both of my breasts and bringing them together and then burying his face between them. His stubble is scratchy and rough… and inordinately titillating. Pun very much intended.

See? I have jokes.

"I think you're perfect," he says, letting go and returning to lay beside me, half-above me. "Every part of you."

His hand soars down my belly and rests dangerously close to my privates. At the proximity of his hand, arousal pulses in me all over again, and the only way I can bear it is to clasp him by the nape and pull his mouth to mine and kiss him until I moan my desire. He growls an answering sound of need, and his hand slips lower, covering my mons pubis again. I gasp into his mouth and stop breathing when his drifting hand does not stop, but moves lower yet. I squeeze my thighs together helplessly against the pressure within me and the billowing heat of arousal and the slow seep of arousal's wetness.

Another shrill gasp seethes past my teeth when he turns his hand to point toward my feet; my thighs squeeze together tighter than ever, blocking him from going any further.

Except…that is not what I wish to happen.

I open my eyes and look at him, frantic with need yet in an agony of uncertainty and anticipation. "Riley, I…"

"Cadence, honey, if you're not ready, that's okay. It's perfectly alright. You can change your mind about anything at any time."

I grip his nape with trembling fingers. "I have not changed my mind."

"I don't want you to be scared."

I squeeze my eyes shut, press my forehead to his, panting raggedly. I focus my will on my legs, force them to unclench. "I *am* afraid, Riley. And I am allowed to be. This is new for me. I have never been naked with a man. I have never kissed a man until you. I have never been touched by a man with any amount of intimacy." I exhale shakily. "I am afraid, and it is okay. I am not afraid of *you*; I am not afraid of *this*. I *want* this. I want *you*. My fear is of the unknown, the anticipated."

"Brave girl," he whispers. "Just tell me what you need."

"Only a bit of patience." I open my eyes and meet his gaze. "And maybe…more kisses?"

"More kisses?" he echoes. "As you wish, sweetest girl."

I turn my mouth up to his, gasping with desire, open-mouthed and greedy for his kiss. He slashes his mouth against mine and slides his tongue against mine, and now I throw myself into the kiss, whimpering in my throat as our kiss deepens, soars, expands, and my arousal billows and pulses.

My thighs relax by degrees, and his hand remains where it is, covering my mons with a single long middle finger millimeters above my sex, where the hood of my labia guards my clitoris—that aching, throbbing bundle of nerves.

He parts, panting, and then goes in for more, and he twists my nipple until I gasp, a sudden shot of arousal spasming through me, making me gasp and twitch. My thighs fall open, then, and I open my eyes and find his and stare into his wild pale blue eyes and I slide my legs further apart until the night air bathes my wet, exposed sex.

I cannot hold eye contact any longer, but I can continue searching his face and letting him see me, my expression, my need. I part my legs until they are splayed open for him. I cannot give him any clearer an invitation.

His eyes scan and search my face, my eyes—and then flick down, stuttering and lingering at my breasts before tripping down to my sex. His expression shifts into wonder and awe and male appreciation as he gazes down at my sex.

He trails one fingertip up my seam. "Look at this perfect, pretty, pink little pussy."

I can only whimper wordlessly.

Another ghostly soft touch, that same finger sliding up my skin, smearing through the wetness. "Soaked for me, aren't you?"

"Yes," I gasp, and then whine at a third trailing touch.

"You ever touch yourself, Cadence?"

I shake my head.

"No?" Another hot line of scorching touch, and now, perhaps, his fingertip presses in ever so slightly. "Never touched yourself? Not even once?"

I whimper. "Once. I did...once."

"Tell me. Please."

My cheeks flame. "I finished an exam early and went

home to my dorm room. I was alone. I read a book…a modern Regency romance which contained, unbeknownst to me when I purchased it, some rather graphic…erm… scenes. which…ahhhh…caused me to feel…discomfited. I…" I cover my face with my hands. "I touched myself… there. It sent a sensation through me that was far too intense, and I…I panicked and stopped. I returned the book unfinished."

"So you've never had an orgasm?"

"No. Certainly not."

"You want one?"

"Yes," I whisper. "I do. I…I believe it is the only way to assuage the intense feelings your attentions have engendered within me."

"Intense feelings, huh? Like what?"

"Desire. Arousal."

"Desire for what?"

"I…I do not know how to put it. Um?" I swallow hard as he covers my sex with his hand. "Desire for…relief. Desire for…for intimacy with you. Desire to be touched." I gulp. "Desire to touch."

He traces his finger over my seam again. "How's that feel?"

"Good," I breathe.

He does it again, but this time his fingertip presses in a bit, and now when he traces his finger up my seam, it is between my labia. "And that?"

I can only gasp. "Yes," I manage.

A chuckle. "Yes?"

"Again," I breathe; he complies, and his finger slips a little more inside me. "Oh…oh *my*!"

He nips my lower lip between his teeth, and then

kisses me until I lose my breath and whimper and feel my-self rush with arousal yet again—this time with his finger inside me.

He growls. "Fuck, honey, I felt that."

I whine in mortification—and then watch in some-thing like horror when he brings the finger that was inside me to his mouth…

And licks it clean as if he'd dipped it in brownie batter.

"RILEY!" I hiss.

"Sweet as sugar, darlin'," he murmurs, and traces my seam again and again, and now his finger is between my labia again and I cannot breathe from the sensation—his touch is *inside* me.

I shake all over as he slides that finger up, up…and brushes against my clit. A jolting, searing rush of intense sensation makes me shudder and shriek, and my spine arches.

"So fucking sensitive," he growls. "So fucking sexy." He nips my earlobe. Whispers hot words I feel as much as hear. "Ready, sweetheart?"

Panting, I can only nod.

He slowly, carefully, gently plunges his finger inside me, deep inside my vaginal channel, which pulses around his finger. I try to gasp, to whimper, but no sound emerg-es—I am arched, my whole body taut as a violin string.

I feel a slight twinge of something—a slight discom-fort, and then the sensation is gone as if it never was, and he is sliding his finger out of me and then back in, and it is the only sensation in the world, in the universe. Him. His touch. I am more vulnerable now than I have ever been in my entire life—by an exponential amount. I am shaking, but not with fear. His touch inside me causes waves of sensation: a shuddering, a shifting, a billowing of heat and a throbbing of pressure. I am shaking from the intensity.

I am wild with it.

I feel a drive…a need; I need to…I do not know. *Do* something.

I need more.

I just do not know what.

"Riley," I breathe. "I need…"

"What, baby?"

"I do not know."

"I think I do." He rolls toward me and now he is almost above me, and he lifts my breast to his descending mouth, and a sharp bolt of arousal strikes like lightning as he flicks my nipple with his tongue, causing me to shriek, shrill and breathless. His finger moves upward, slipping almost out of me, and I feel the absence acutely.

There is no warning.

He presses his finger to my clitoris, and the bolt of lightning that strikes me then is blinding and all-consuming and white-hot. My whole body spasms, arching off the bed, and I scream.

"Jesus, honey," he growls, and claims my mouth in a hot, fast kiss. "*So* goddamn responsive. Hot as fuck."

And then he nuzzles my breast and suckles on my nipple and swirls his finger in a circle around my clitoris and the lightning strikes and strikes and strikes and strikes each time his finger swirls, with each movement and each shift of pressure and speed, and he seems to know how to read my every slightest, subtlest response to his touch.

"Riley…" I whimper. "Oh…oh my."

His lips curve against my breast. "Oh yeah?"

"Yes."

"More?"

I nod. "Yes. More. Please."

"You're gonna come for me, aren't you?" he demands, and his finger circles—faster and faster.

My hips feel as if they are tied to his movements—each swirl, each circle, each swipe and flick, my hips move. They buck, shift, push. Seeking. Needing.

"Tell me you're gonna come for me, honey."

"I…" a rippling, shearing wave of intense pleasure grips me, then, seizes me with unrelenting ferocity, and I cannot manage words.

He touches me, and I can only arch and buck my hips into his touch and cry out loud in a gasping half-scream. "So fucking sexy, Cadence," he growls. "Come for me, sweetheart. Let me watch you shatter for me. Scream for me. Scream so loud the fucking stars hear you."

That abyssal precipice nears. I shudder at its edge, and his touch pushes me nearer and nearer, and now I do not fear the oblivion awaiting in that unknown space but welcome it. I seek it. Strive for it.

I give in to instinct. Abandon all control, all thought, all need.

There is only what my body craves:

Him.

This.

More.

I grip his wrist with one hand and cover his hand with the other, press his hand against my sex, begging him in the only way I can to never, ever stop.

I grind myself against his touch. My hips buck and fly against him, and his finger swirls and circles and swipes faster and faster…

The edge crashes over me all at once.

A scream rips out of my throat as a battering ram of ecstasy I never knew could exist leaves me shaking and sweating, driving wild, desperate hips against his finger, pushing my sex against his touch to beg for more. I am weeping, but it is with ecstasy, screaming but with desire vanquished, overcome but blessedly so.

Wave after wave smashes through me, and then he slips his finger inside me and moves it in and out through my channel and the waves dissolve and commingle and merge and shatter into something new, and another scream shudders out of me and that becomes a whimper and then a sob.

This is not merely pleasure or bliss or ecstasy or anything I have words for in any of the languages with which I am familiar.

It consumes me.

Time ceases to have meaning.

He plunges his finger inside me, and then circles my clitoris, and then plunges it back inside me.

And then, when I think it will finally end, he kisses my mouth and then my breasts and then my belly and then his shoulders are between my thighs and his stubble scratches the insides of my thighs and—

"RILEY!" I scream as his tongue slides, wet and hot, up my seam.

"Keep coming for me, honey," he growls. "Scream my name." Another hot lick. "Tell the stars who's making you come, baby."

"Y-you!" I gasp, arching and bucking helplessly against his hungry mouth.

"Me what?"

"You…you are…oh! Oh my! Oh—ohmygosh—oh goodness me oh my…" I clutch his head as he seems to be attempting to devour me whole.

Or, at least, my clitoris.

Despite the ferocity of his hunger, though, his mouth is exquisitely gentle upon my tender flesh. His lips are soft and wet, and his tongue hot and insistent. His finger penetrates my sex, and his mouth plunders my clitoris, and the world spins around me and my whole body bucks and clenches and spasms in time with his moving finger and driving tongue.

And then, just when I thought I could not come again, or come any harder—I do.

My orgasm seems to break apart, and from the shards and shrapnel of it emerges something new, something more.

I grasp his head in my hands and brace my feet against the truck bed and buck against his mouth, screaming shrill and loud.

He does not relent.

The ecstasy seems to overlap, waves crashing in on themselves and ripping and expanding, and I lose even the ability to control what my hips do, what my hands do, what my mouth does.

"Riley! Oh! Oh! Oh!" My feet dig against my backside and I grab his hand and guide it to my breast—he pinches my nipples and I scream again.

I clutch his head to my vagina and hand to my breast, and shake uncontrollably, no longer screaming but weeping.

Sobbing.

Wave after waver after wave of shredding, dissolving

ecstasy rolls through, until I cannot tolerate it anymore. "I cannot—I…please, I—please—no more. I cannot take any more."

He listens to me.

His finger leaves me and his mouth too, and his hands cradle me to his chest. I smell myself on his breath when he kisses me.

It is not unpleasant. Strange, familiar, and unfamiliar at once. But not unpleasant.

I feel…wrung out.

Shaken.

Almost broken—but beautifully so.

Abruptly exhausted, I rest my cheek against his chest and listen to his heartbeat.

"Riley?" I murmur.

"Yeah, sweetheart?"

"I believe you have given me my first orgasm."

He chuckles. "Yeah, babe, I think so," he whispers in my ear. "You had multiple, you know. Three, maybe four."

He sounds…pleased.

Aroused.

"Thank you," I whisper.

He just laughs again. "Believe me when I say the pleasure was all mine."

"My eyes," I mumble. "They will not stay open."

"So close 'em, sweetheart," he murmurs. "I got you." He kisses the top of my head.

"But what about—"

He touches my lips—I smell myself on them. Again, not unpleasant, only strange. "Hush, baby. Plenty of time for that later. I've got you."

I let my eyes slide closed.

I drift off to sleep with the feel of Riley's hands roaming my naked body. Not to arouse, now, but to soothe. To calm.

The thought which percolates at the edges of my mind as I drift off to sleep is a worrying one:

Now how will I leave?

Now that I know such incredible joy exists, how can I leave him?

12

Riley

THE AWE THAT I FEEL, THE PRIDE AT BEING THE man she chose to give this gift to, is overwhelming. I gaze at Cadence, and I know I am ruined.

Any woman I have ever known, ever touched, ever kissed, ever felt anything for is utterly forgotten.

There is only Cadence.

She's passed out. Her head lolls against my chest, one hand curled under her chin. She shivers and cuddles closer to me—best get her home, I suppose, even if the last thing I want to do is leave this place, this moment.

I refasten my jeans, shrug into my tee, slide the blanket out from beneath me, and wrap Cadence up in it, discarded clothing and all. I hop out of the truck bed, open the passenger door, lift Cadence out of the bed, and set her in the cab, shutting her door gently. She blinks blearily, mumbling something incoherent. I shut the tailgate and hustle around to the driver's side, slide in, start the truck, and then let Cadence slide sideways until she's laying across my lap; the nice thing about this older truck is that the center console lifts up out of the way to create a three-across bench.

The ride home is quick and silent—Cadence is down for the count, I think. I try not to feel smug, or at least self-satisfied, but…I made the girl come so hard she passed out. Hard not to feel pretty damn good about that. I'm fighting a motherfucker of a hard-on, but that's a small price to pay for the privilege of what I just got to do. Hard-ons will fade. Maybe I'll have a case of blue balls later, whatever. I can deal with that. Cadence is what matters.

She's so smart, so wise, so unique and interesting. I've never met anyone even remotely like her, and I know I never will. The combination of sexy, cute, smart, beautiful, and fascinating is damned addictive.

Two days. I've known her for two days.

She's under my skin. Inside my brain. Buried in my heart.

And she's leaving.

Soon.

She may never come back.

The thought of never seeing her again makes my entire being recoil in horror, but that's something I'm just going to have to live with. This crazy, possibly suicidal mission to Sudan is her calling. I can't stand in the way of that—I won't.

I also know there won't be any other girls…not for a long, long time.

By the time I'm pulling into my driveway, I'm a weird combination of turned on, proud of myself, sad as fuck, and exhausted.

I prop open my side door and then carry Cadence inside, still wrapped in the blanket. I settle her into my bed, trading bed covers for the scratchy wool blanket, and then go back and close doors. Back in my room, I peel off my clothes and put on a pair of workout shorts to sleep in.

I pause in the doorway of my bedroom, glancing back at her; she stirs, one eye cracking open. "Riley?" Her voice is barely audible, muzzy with sleep.

I cross back to the bed and perch on the edge. "Yeah, sweetheart? I'm here."

One eye, a drowsy slit of green, fixes on me. "Stay." She worms a hand out from beneath the covers and grabs my thigh. "Do not leave. Please."

"Uh, yeah," I whisper. "I'll stay, if you want."

"Mmmm."

I go around to the other side and slide under the covers behind her. I hesitate—how close do I get? I'm not a cuddler. I don't have girls stay the night, and I don't stay. I sidle close enough that I can rest my hand on her waist in what seems like no-man's land, but far enough away that I'm not shoving my will-not-go-away erection into her ass, as much as I want to.

I feel myself drowsing, lulling, drifting…

And then she rolls over. Making a soft, delicate mewling noise, she shimmies into me, closer and then closer again until she's pressing every inch of her glorious, warm, smooth, soft, naked body against me. Her bare tit drapes onto my chest, the other smashed against my ribcage.

She's spooning my thigh and hip, rubbing her naked pussy against my bare thigh.

Fuck.

My cock stiffens into an aching iron rod, and my pulse pounds. I ignore all that, curling my arm around her shoulders and trying to find sleepiness again.

It's a long, long time in coming.

C⦿

Erotic dreams riddle my sleep. Cadence, unsurprisingly, is the star of all of them. I dream of what happened—getting to kiss her, to see those big, round, juicy, lush tits, getting to touch them and kiss them and have their beauty all for me…her eagerness, her desperation. Her pussy wreathed in a fine cloud of strawberry blonde fuzz, with plump lips and so fucking tight I could barely fit my fingers inside her, weeping and glistening with her arousal.

The way she arched off the blanket, screaming, whimpering, pleading.

Fuck.

I jolt awake all at once, my eyes flying open. The first thing I see is huge pair of moss-green eyes.

"Good morning, Riley Crowe of Three Rivers." She's hiding a smile behind the blanket she has clutched in one hand, but the glittering twinkle in her eye is so bright it dims the dawn glow streaming in through my bedroom window.

"Mornin' beautiful girl." I caress her cheek. "Sleep well?"

"That was the most refreshing sleep of my life." She

searches my face, her cheeks going red. "Riley, I…last night."

"Cadence, I can't explain how honored I feel to that you trusted me like that." I lean in and kiss her forehead.

She shakes her head. "I should be the one saying that, Riley. I had all but given up on ever getting to experience that. You…" she blushes harder, eyes screwing shut. "I am so grateful. So amazed. You…you made me feel beautiful. Womanly."

"Cadence, you *are* beautiful. So fuckin' sexy, I swear to god. You are all woman. You should feel beautiful all the time."

"There is only one thing that I might wish to change, were that possible."

My heart skips a beat, starts to sink. "Oh. Ah…okay. Hit me with it, honey."

"It was unequal. You did not…or rather, I should say that *I* did not have a chance to…to do anything for *you* before I fell asleep." She looks genuinely displeased about this.

I smile at her, shake my head. "Don't even think about that, Gorgeous. I wanted that to be all about you. Not me. Not what I wanted or what I got. It was about *you*. It was about you hopefully having a chance to feel…wanted. I guess. Desired. To feel beautiful. To know how sexy you are. To be shown that you're, a sexy, beautiful, amazing, desirable woman. I'm the luckiest man in the world that you trusted *me*, with all my bullshit, to give that experience to you."

"You are so sweet and so selfless, Riley," she whispers.

I snort. "I'm really not, but I'm tryin'. It's what you deserve."

She shimmies closer and my heart starts to pound

when I feel her soft, squishy breasts settle against me. Fuck, I want her. Need her. My jaw clenches and I have to squeeze my hands into shaking fists to keep from pulling her on top of me and devouring her all over again until she's cross-eyed and boneless.

She furrows her brow. "You are very tense, Riley. Why, please?"

I swallow hard, mutter through gritted molars, knotting my fingers in the sheet. "Hard to explain, babe."

"Try. Please? I am confused. Did I upset you?" Her hand flutters over my chest beneath the blanket, comes to rest on my belly.

Not fucking helping.

She deserves the truth, at least. "I…fuck. You're naked, Cadence. And if you really wanna know, I'm all tense because all I can think about is how fuckin' bad I want to eat your sweet, tight, wet little pussy again."

She whines, a tight, small, shocked sound from her throat. "Riley!" Softer, quieter, then. "Eat out my…my…?"

"Yeah, babe." I growl in frustration as need overtakes caution, and I roll into her, gaze down at her, knowing my face is giving away the savagery of my need for her. "Got a taste of heaven last night, sweet girl. Now it's all I can fuckin' think about."

"You…you would…" she bites her lip. "You would want to do that again? With me?"

Fuck.

So soft, so shy, so unassuming—she has not a single fucking clue how hot she is, how bad I want her. She sure as fuck doesn't have the first clue what I would do to her, given the chance. I'd shock her silly. Scare her, more than likely.

Yet I can't control myself. It's a victory of self-control that I'm not buried balls-deep inside her right now. I'd throw myself through plate glass, naked, before I did that, though. Before she's ready, at least. I sure as fuck won't be the one pressuring her.

"Riley?"

I've spaced out, I guess. Lost in my efforts to hold back my insatiable need for all things Cadence Creswell, MD.

She gazes up at me, waiting, expectant. Her hand, beneath the blanket, searches across my stomach and finds my hand. Guides it to her belly. Eyes widening, cheeks flaming red, I feel her slide her thighs apart, one pressing against mine.

That's as clear as you can get, I think.

Still. I run my palm over her belly, pausing before I reach the promised land. "You want me to touch you again, Cadence?"

"Yes, please," she breathes, eyes shining eagerly, radiant with desire and anticipation. "If you...that is to say... if you want to."

I whip the blanket away, baring her body in its nude glory.

My good god.

She was incredibly beautiful in the delicate silver light of the moon and stars, but now, like this, in the golden light of the sun?

I am literally breathless. Speechless. My mouth goes dry, and my hands shake.

"*Jesus*," I breathe. "Fuckin' *look* at you, Cadence. So... goddamned...*beautiful*."

She's drawn up, arm barred over her chest, knee over

her thigh—an instinctive reaction to the covers being torn away so unexpectedly. At my words, she blushes and slowly, with visible intention, unfolds. Her full, heavy, creamy breasts pull to either side of her torso, pert, pink, tight little nipples standing straight up. Flat belly, wide hips.

And that pussy.

Fuck.

I rise to my hands and knees over her and claim her mouth. And my fucking god, she's so responsive. The instant my lips touch hers, she's pushing up to deepen the kiss, making a soft sound in her throat. She parts her mouth for me, arching her tits against me, and swipes her tongue through my mouth.

God, she learns fast.

My cock aches, it's so fucking hard.

I cup her breast, groaning at the soft weight of it in my hand, the silky soft skin tightening with arousal around her nipples. She flinches and whimpers when I flick it with my thumb. I slide my finger over her seam, and she rewards me with another of those soft, delicate little sounds of raw, aching, feminine need. When I plunge my finger inside her, she gasps against my mouth.

"Riley!" she breathes, arching her back and then thrusting against my finger in a sinuous, erotic writhing movement.

Fuck, I want to be above her, driving into her, making her cry my name as we move in perfect synch—

"Fuck," I snarl.

"Wh-what?" She breathes. "What is it? What's wrong?"

I shake my head. "Nothing."

"Tell me. Please."

"I just fuckin'…" I latch onto her nipple and make her quake and whimper. "I need you."

"I am here."

"Not what I meant."

"Then what *did* you mean?"

She's not ready to hear the truth. If I told her, she'd freak.

"Riley, the truth." She withes, arches, whimpers as I finger her tight, wet, hot channel, and then palms my cheek. "I know you are thinking something you do not think I am ready to hear. That you will frighten me or shock me."

"Not wrong, sweetheart," I whisper, and move my kisses down her belly, too hungry to taste her sweet honey again to go any slower; I flick my tongue against her clit, and she wails, loudly, arching and already seconds from orgasm.

"I would…I would like to…to know," she gasps between groans of pleasure.

"Cadence—"

She grabs my face in both hands before I can lick her again. "Riley. I want to know. I think perhaps you would be shocked at what I am thinking."

I grin, swipe my tongue against her clit again. She cries out, fingers knotting in my hair and helplessly yanking me against her pussy. "Greedy girl. Come for me, and then I'll tell you."

"You—you—ohhh, oh my…oh good heavens, that feels—*oh*!" She arches her tits to the ceiling as I devour her clit, and her pussy gushes arousal, bathing my lips and tongue with her honey. Fuck, this girl is pure sex, and she doesn't have a goddamn clue. "You have a deal!"

I laugh and give her my tongue, stabbing it inside her just to get a better taste of her, and then swirl it against her clit, and I don't stop this time.

Within seconds, she's coming. "OH! RILEY! OHMYGOD!" She slaps her hands into the bed and grips the sheet as she fucks my mouth.

I keep her coming, sliding my finger inside her and hunting for her G-spot—there it is; she screams, unabashed and uncontrolled, and the most arousing, erotic, stunning, breathtaking vision I've ever beheld.

She spasms, contorts, and writhes. Slowly, she subsides from the peak.

Her eyes snap open. "Now, Riley Crowe. The truth of your thoughts."

"When I said I wanted you," I growl, "I meant…" I slide up her body and lean over her. "I want to do a lot of very, very, *very* sinful things to this…" I kiss the corner of her mouth, "maddeningly…" and then her breast, "perfectly…" I curl my finger inside her and then find her clit, getting her spasming and jerking all over again, "fucking gorgeous body of yours."

"I cannot believe that anything so beautiful as sharing this with you can be sinful," she whispers.

"Not gonna argue with that. I don't think so, that's for fucking sure." I kiss her lips and make her quake with my finger. "What shocking things are you thinking?"

Arched and orgasming, she doesn't answer right away. When I let her back down, shaking and panting and sheened with sweat, she grabs my wrist and her eyes meet mine. "How my disappointment that I did not get to touch you last night was not entirely a…um…selfless feeling." She guides my hand away from her pussy. "No more, please. For...for now."

"Cadence," I start.

She touches my lips. "I want to touch you because of my own selfish desire to..." she shuts her eyes. "To know how it feels. How it...what a man's flesh is like." Her eyes fly open and find mine. "I wish most strongly to know how it feels to touch *you*. To know how it feels to be the one *giving* pleasure, not just receiving."

I cup her cheek. Kiss her softly. "I can give you that, Cadence. But only if you want it for *you*. I don't want you worryin' about me."

"But that is..." She frowns, shaking her head. "That is not correct. I do not believe any relationship should be one-sided. *You* worry about *me*. *You* are concerned with *my* comfort and safety. You have taken the greatest care to see that I am willing, consenting, and in control as I explore my sexuality with you." Her eyes are wet, shimmering. "That is a gift, Riley. A very precious one. My desire to touch you is...complex, because I want to for the reasons I have previously stated, but also because I wish to give you pleasure, as you have given it to me. I do not feel obligated. I know you would not put that burden on me."

"Never."

"Then..." she swallows hard. "Then may I..." She pushes her palm into my chest, encouraging me to lie back.

I do so, gingerly, slowly, and uncertainly. Her fingers trail over my chest, down my abs, and stop at the waistband of my shorts.

"Riley, may I...." she slips her fingertips under the elastic. "May I...explore your body?"

"Yeah, honey," I whisper. "You can do anything you want. I'm here for you."

She grins, shy and eager at the same time. "I have been awake for some time, trying to determine how to communicate this desire I feel."

"Well, you have." I grin at her, but it's wobbly and nervous, and my heart is hammering. "Can't say I'm exactly mad about it, either."

"That is humor through hyperbolic understatement, yes?"

I laugh, caressing her cheek, tracing hair out of her eyes. "Yeah, babe."

"The reverse then being true means you are…eager to be touched?"

I take her hands and kiss each palm. "Yeah, darlin', I am. Very. But only what you feel comfortable with. No pressure and stop at any time. Ask me anything. This is all you, okay? You're in control."

"I believe the first order of business, then," she bites her lower lip, eyes raking down my body to linger at the obvious bulge in the front of my shorts, "is the removal of your shorts."

"You want me to? Or you want to?" I ask.

"May I? Please?"

I roll into her, cup her jaw in both hands, and kiss her. "Yeah, honey. You may."

I roll to my back, tuck my hands behind my head, fingers laced, and try to look casual, unaffected.

The opposite is true. I'm more nervous now than I was before my first time fooling around with a girl. Weird, but true.

This means something to me, though. Not that that

didn't way back when I was fifteen and convinced Heather Marshall to make out with me behind the bleachers after school. That meant something to me, and everything in between has.

It's just this...*her*?

Means way, way more than...fuck. I don't know how to put it into words, even in my own mind.

I clench my jaw and wait as Cadence slowly sits up. My god, those tits. Fuck me. Goddamned glorious. She inhales shakily, deeply, and they tremble. She shifts her weight to sit facing me, and they sway heavily. Lush, pale, high and proud and round, with wide pale pink areolae graced with those tiny little bumps that drive me wild for reasons I can't even begin to explain, with small pink nipples.

I can't stop myself from grabbing them, toying with them as she stares down at me. "Have I mentioned that I'm fucking *obsessed* with your tits, Cadence?"

"Not in so many words, no," she murmurs, gaze hooked and frozen on my bulge. "But the frequency with which you touch them and the way you stare at them even now that you have seen them makes your attraction rather unmistakable."

"You okay with that?"

This gets her eyes flicking to mine for a second. "More than okay. I...it is flattering. And...gratifying. I am a modest woman and do not reveal them to anyone, so I...I was not sure what your opinion of my..." she bites her lip. "My...*tits*...would be." She whispers what she clearly considers a bad word. "Goodness, I feel...naughty, saying that word."

"Naughty, naughty girl," I murmur, gently smacking the side of her ass.

"You call me naughty," she whispers, "but your tone and actions imply approval."

"*All* the approval, sweetheart. You can be as naughty as you dare, with me." I tug on her lower lip. "To me, naughty ain't bad, okay? This isn't bad or wrong or sinful. It's two consenting adults sharing their bodies with each other. Callin' it naughty is just a way to make it fun."

"Thank you for explaining," she whispers.

She sucks in a deep breath, holds it, and then hooks her fingers in the elastic of my shorts. My stomach curls in on itself automatically, and my cock jerks. I'm not breathing. My pulse is erratic and fast. Exhaling slowly, shakily, Cadence lifts the waistband away from my body and pulls the shorts down; I lift my ass up so she can pull them down past my knees, and I toe them off and toss them aside.

She giggles, hands covering her face, eyes wide and…god, so many things. Eager, shy, amazed, aroused? Fuck, she's showing more feelings than I have words for. Normally, if a girl took one look at my dick and laughed, I'd be gone faster than you can blink.

But this is Cadence—and it's not that kind of laughter.

"*Oh.*" This is soft, breathy. "My goodness." Her eyes flit to mine. "I…it…it is…*much* larger than I had expected."

I grin. "That's a damn good thing to hear."

Her eyes go back to my dick, still wide, still full of too many emotions to track or name. I hold absolutely still, hands behind my head again; I can't touch her. Can't make this about me. No leading, no hinting. My role is to let her explore, nothing more.

Fuck, this is gonna be difficult.

Cadence extends a hand toward me, reaching, reaching…and then withdrawing. Gnawing on her lower lip, she glances at me. "I…oh my. Oh *my*."

I gently grasp her hand and place it on my stomach. "It's okay, Cadence. Take your time. Whatever you want is okay."

"But are you not…" she searches me, and then her gaze drifts back to my aching dick. "Is it uncomfortable? Or…perhaps the better question is how *does* it feel?"

"Like being turned on," I answer.

"Riley," she murmurs, gently scolding. "You prevaricate."

"Dunno what that means."

"Lying or avoiding the truth."

"Oh." I sigh. "Fine. I am, a bit, I guess." I shrug, thinking. "It's not…uncomfortable, exactly. Feels like…gah, it's hard to explain. Like…sort of an ache, I suppose. Not pain, just…tension? Nah, that's not right either. Um…I'm turned on. Aroused. Getting to see you naked makes me hard. Getting to touch you makes me even harder. Getting to taste your sweet little pussy? Fuck, woman. The way you look, the way you feel, the way you sound when you're coming? Sinfully fucking sexy. Hot as fuck."

She's red as a tomato. "Riley, you make me sound…" she trails off.

"Like the sexiest woman I've ever met?" I fill in. "Cuz you are. Not even a contest."

She tilts her head. "Have you known many women? To a degree that you can make such a comparison?" She bites her lip. "Intimately, I mean. Naked…um, women."

I lever up, cup her nape, and kiss her. Whisper against

her lips. "Not thinking about anyone else, Cadence. There's only you."

"Oh—okay." She whispers even more quietly then. "I want to, but I am scared."

"Scared of what? Tell me what you're afraid of."

"I…I am not sure. It is…a generalized anxiety rather than true fear. Anticipation, perhaps, is the best word. Nervous. I never, ever, *ever* imagined I could have this, and certainly not with a man like you."

I frown at her. "Man like me?"

Her smile is soft, tender. "Yes, Riley. A man like you. Charming. Cool. Interesting. Rugged. Masculine. Handsome." A blush. "*Hot.*" This is whispered. "Other girls, normal, neurotypical girls dream and fantasize about their first foray into sexual intimacy being with a man like you, Riley. I never dared. Such things are not for me, I have always felt."

"Breaks my goddamn heart to hear you say that, honey." I kiss her again, as gently as I possibly can. "That shit just ain't true. It's fuckin' bullshit. Fuck normal, and fuck everyone else. This is about you and me, okay? Just you and me. Here. Now."

Her eyes water. "I like that. Fuh—*gah*. I cannot say it."

"Sure, you can." I grin at her, tug on her lower lip with my thumb. "Try it. *Fuck* normal and *fuck* everyone else."

She shakes her head. "It is very difficult to break a lifelong habit."

"But you can do it. Just you and me here, sweetheart. No one to judge. Fuck normal. Right?"

"F-f-f…" A hiss of frustration. "Fuck normal!" It comes out loud and forceful, shocking even her. "*Fuck normal*!" She giggles, clapping her hands over her mouth. "That felt good. Fuck normal!"

"Fuck normal!" I laugh with her. "Fuck normal. Fuck normies. Fuck anyone who's ever made you feel anything less than the magical fucking goddess you are."

I lean into her and take her to her back and kiss her, and soon we're lost in the kiss and her tongue seeks mine and her breast is soft and heavy in my hand and her nipple is hard under my thumb. She whimpers, gasps, and then lifts up to crush her mouth against mine and thrusts her tongue into my mouth—the woman kisses with a ferocity and hunger unlike anything I've ever felt. My cock throbs, and, despite my assurance earlier, it is uncomfortable. Painful, even. I growl as I kiss her, pawing her tit and tweaking her nipple until she's gasping and panting, and then I slide my hand to her belly, wanting that gasp of hers, that moan, that whimper, the way she arches when she comes—

She rips away from the kiss and pushes me, as roughly as she's ever done anything, away. "No, no, no!" She leans over me, tits draped and swaying against my chest, hair a wild, sunlit-copper cloud of pale golden-red curls. Her mossy eyes are huge and, frankly, horny. So fucking turned on. Her cheeks are pink and flushed, and she's panting softly. "I think if I let you, all we would do is you…um… giving me…ahhhh…orgasms."

"True. Would that be so bad?"

She giggles, and how the fuck can a giggle be cute yet wickedly arousing at the same time? "No, it would not. For me, at least. But I have other desires than for orgasms."

"Y'do, huh?" I murmur. "Sorry. I'll be a good boy."

She sits up again, this time with her feet tucked

sideways against her butt, weight braced on her left hand, angled toward my feet. Gazing at me for a moment, she gnaws on her lower lip again, worrying it, eyes wide, brows furrowed—that expression on her face is fucking intoxicating: the arousal and the shyness mingling into unconscious coyness, tantalizing innocence at war with naughty need.

Her hand rests on my belly. She traces the outlines of my abs, starting at the top and snaking back and forth on the way down, following the grooves until she reaches my V-cut. I know it's a function of genetics I have no control over, plus hard work and careful nutrition, so it's only partly due to my own efforts, but I can't help feeling a little proud of those grooves. Especially when her expression becomes openly aroused, flicking to mine with a wide, pleased, heated grin.

"I am rather inordinately aroused by these iliac furrows," she says, tracing her finger down the groove, stopping just short of my junk.

"Is that what they're called?"

"What do you call them?"

I shrug. "V-cut."

She wrinkles her nose. "No. Iliac furrows."

She traces her finger down the other one, daring a little closer to my cock, this time. Which, at the proximity of her hand, twitches in anticipation. Cadence jumps.

"Oh! It…it *moved*!" She blushes. "Intellectually, I am aware that you have a degree of muscular control over it. It just…took me by surprise."

I grin, shake my head. "Don't need to explain anything to me, honey."

She licks her lips, looks at my face. "I am sorry to be so…so…"

"Nope," I growl. "None of that. No apologizing. Told you, honey. Take all the time in the world. Not in a rush. Nowhere to go. This is all about you. What you want."

"Okay," she huffs. "Okay. I want to touch you, I just…" she shakes her head. "It hardly seems real."

"Think about what you want to do," I tell her. "Picture it. See yourself doing it…and then do it."

"Visualization and manifestation," she murmurs. "Yes. An excellent suggestion, Riley. Thank you."

She closes her eyes for a moment or two, and her breathing slows, and the tension on her face fades. Her eyes snap open and she fixes her gaze on my cock. Bites her lip—I want to kiss her so damn bad, but I don't dare move. I'm barely breathing. She inhales deeply, holds her breath, extends her hand toward me…

She trails the pad of her index finger down the length of my cock from tip to root, excruciatingly slowly. I hiss an inhale, and she jerks her hand away. "Did I hurt you?"

I laugh. "No, no. Sorry. Just the opposite. You're touchin' me, Cadence. I'm just trying to hold still and let you do what you want."

"If you gave into your desires and urges, what would you do?"

"Something you ain't ready for."

"Oh."

I take her hand and guide it back to my thigh. "It's okay. I won't do anything. You're not gonna hurt me. You touching me, in any way at all, is gonna feel fuckin' amazing."

"You promise?"

"Cross my heart," I murmur. "Did it feel good when I touched you?"

"My goodness, yes. *So* good."

"Then try again. Don't be shy."

She grins at me. "Yes. I shall try again."

She repeats her previous action, trailing one finger down my length—I hiss and jerk again. This time, while she is startled, she jolts and giggles, but doesn't remove her hand. She presses the pad of her finger to the very tip. Looks at her finger—at the smear of wetness. Looks at me, curious.

"Precum," I explain.

"Ah. Of course." This is a quiet murmur, absent-minded, focused on me once more.

She circles my cock with forefinger and thumb, just beneath my glans, then wraps the rest of her fingers around my girth—her grip is exquisitely gentle, barely making contact. And then she squeezes, just a little. I jerk involuntarily, and she glances at me, concerned. I smile reassuringly.

She slides her hand down my length, and fucking hell, she takes a long, *long* time to do so, and my whole body tenses at the wonder of her touch.

I fight the urge to push into her touch.

She reaches the base of my cock, pauses, looks at me, opens her mouth as if to say something, and then thinks better of it.

"Go ahead," I murmur. "Ask anything. Say anything."

"Will I hurt you if I touch your…ummm…testicles?"

"No, sweetheart. They *are* sensitive, but as long as you don't, like, try to twist 'em off or squeeze 'em like a stress ball, you're good. It feels almost as good as it does when you touch my cock."

"Your…" she grins shyly at me, "cock." She whispers it, and then giggles, blushing.

Ah, Jesus, dirty talk outta her sweet innocent mouth? Fuck me, I'm done.

Eyes wide and following the path of her hand, she glides her touch down my length again, just as slowly as before, and this time when she reaches my base, she slips her hand down to cup my balls. And fuck, fuck, *fuck*, that feels like heaven. Her hands are so small, so soft, so clever, and so warm. So gentle.

She toys with me and caresses my balls for a moment and then strokes my length again, once more sliding her hand all the way from tip to root to balls, cupping them and caressing them so tenderly and affectionately it…god, how do I even feel? Sexually on edge, obviously, but… awed. Full of wonder. Amazed. My heart feels hot and full. Never been touched the way she touches me. The emotion she puts into it…

This isn't just a hookup for her. Not just sex. Not fooling around. This is, possibly, one of the most important moments of her life. It's not about me, but…fuck, I don't know.

I'm just trying not to blow my load like a teenager.

She bites her lip and looks at me, hard, searching, nervous. "Will you teach me how to give you an orgasm?"

I look back at her, torn. "You don't need to. It's okay.

"I want to. Please?"

I laugh. "Then just keep doing what you're doing."

"Riley." It's a scold.

I reach up and cup her cheek. "No, really. Just…hold onto it like you were and rub it up and down, just like you were doing."

"That…is that what will make it feel best?"

"Anything you do will be amazing."

"I suppose, but…" She leans the other way, stretching her legs out and resting her cheek on my sternum, near my belly, and grasps my cock around the head. "I want to not just give you an orgasm. I want to…oh my, I am struggling with saying what I really intend."

"Cadence—"

"I want to make you feel such pleasure that you… you *remember* me…always. I want to give you such intense pleasure as you have never known. I want to return to you even a tiny portion of the joy you have given me, Riley. So please. You know what I am asking."

"Being with you at all *is* that, Cadence," I say and speak over her protest. "But I know what you mean. So…don't be in a hurry. That's the first thing. For both men and women, a quick orgasm is a good thing, but a truly *great* orgasm takes a while to build up. So it's not just like this…" I mime jerking off hard and fast. "Harder and faster isn't better. So when I said do *exactly* what you were doing, I meant it. Just touch me. Play with me. Explore. Try things. It will all feel fucking incredible. I promise, you'll give me an orgasm I'll never, ever forget." I brush her lips. "Mainly because it's you giving it to me."

13

Cadence

I TRULY, GENUINELY CANNOT BELIEVE THIS IS happening. This is my life.

    I am doing this.

I am touching Riley's…I said it—out loud:

His *cock*.

Even thinking it makes me grin and giggle.

"What's funny?" he murmurs.

I shake my head. "Not funny. Just…" I shrug. "Surreal."

He does not answer. His eyes are hooded, his lids heavy, his jaw hard and tight. He appears angry but I know he is not. He breathes raggedly, roughly. His magnificent abdomen heaves, curls in, tightens, the thick, hard blocks of muscle hardening and relaxing. I slide my loose, soft grip around the hot, silky-soft skin, down and down to the very bottom, and he tips his hips up, pushing into my hand.

A sign of enjoyment, I believe—a signal that he wants me to do it again. Like when my hips buck into his touch. He went faster and faster until I was mad with need, and then slowed down—it only made me more desperate for the release, but oh, the result.

I shall try that.

I sit up cross-legged, facing him. Watch him with hawklike intensity for any facial expression that might be a clue as to his feelings. I grasp his...I must move past this silly hesitation over mere words; it is childish, and I am a grown woman. If I can touch it, I can say or think the word.

I grasp his cock in one hand—I like that word, I think. I decide to try it out loud again. "I like touching your cock, Riley."

He groans when I say this. "Fuck, honey. Not as much as I like you doing it."

"I think we can each enjoy it without it being a competition," I say.

He laughs. "Sure can. All I mean is it feels fuckin'—" Right then, I caress his testicles, and he breaks off with a moan, head throwing back, eyes closing.

Yes, he likes that—a lot.

I do it again and receive the same intense reaction. "You like it very much when I do...this," I caress his testicles again, "in particular."

"Yeah, babe," he says, his voice tight and raw. "The way you do that? Touchin' my balls like that? Gonna make me come *so* fuckin' hard."

"Balls," I say. "Your cock...and your balls."

He huffs a laugh. "Yeah."

I decide to heed his advice and try new things. If giving him an orgasm is a function of friction and rhythm over time…and if extending the duration by variance of those parameters increases the intensity of the orgasm… then I should be able to maximize his enjoyment of my ministrations by constant and random adjustment of the application of rhythmic strokes to his cock.

What kinds of variances are there, however? Let us find out.

I try a simple, fast stroke, first, one hand traveling swiftly from the plump, round head down to the base. A few of these, and Riley is growling and his abs are contracting—yes, that would be the swift and efficient method. Not what I am after, in this case. I want this to last for as long as possible—for both of us.

So now I try short, shallow, swift pumping movements at the top. Then a long stroke down to the base, and then the short, shallow, swift pumps again down there. He bucks into my hand again, grumbling in his chest.

"Fuck, Cadence…" he breathes. "So fucking good. Never felt so good in my life. Please, *please* don't stop."

I lean over him and kiss him while applying slow strokes like before, long ones from top to bottom, kissing him to show him my desire, my joy, my appreciation, my affection. "I will not stop, Riley. I promise."

"You're learning fast," he growls.

Pride bubbles. "I have always been a quick learner. I am applying the methods you employed to heighten my pleasure."

He wraps his hand around mine which is around him and guides my movement, showing me a new stroke— twisting around the top and then plunging down to the base. I try that on my own a few times, and his eyes flutter and roll back in his head. When I do it again, paired with caressing the soft, hot weight of his balls, he arches off the bed and grinds into my touch.

The best reaction yet.

"What else can I do to make this better?" I whisper.

"With just your hands? You can't. This is…fuck, Cadence. I…ah, *fuck*. So good."

"Just my hands?" I repeat.

He tenses. "Never mind. "

"No, what?"

"You're not there yet, sweetheart."

"Where?" I cup his cheek. "Tell me. I shall decide what I am ready for, if you please."

"Mouth," he murmurs.

"Oh," I whisper. "I see."

"You don't—"

I kiss him quiet. "Hush, Riley. You said *I* am in control."

"Yeah," he growls. "You are. I just—"

"I asked a question, and you answered. What I do with that information is up to me. Yes?"

"Yeah."

"Then let me enjoy myself. Because I am."

He groans when I give him a slow, twisting stroke and caress his balls.

I like his balls. They are quite strange, if you consider them objectively, but this is not the time for objectivity. It is the time for exploration, experimentation, and enjoyment. I like their softness. The wrinkled skin, the veins. The soft ticklish black fuzz all over them.

I like his cock. I like how it feels in my hand.

When I touch him, there is nothing else. Just like when he touches me.

My mind is soothed, blanked. My only thoughts are of him; I can see how people can become obsessed with sex.

I imagine myself kissing his cock. If you had asked me seventy-two hours ago if I would consider putting my mouth anywhere near the privates of a man I've just met, I would have fainted at the mere suggestion. Not literally. I would not have believed you, however.

Yet here I am.

Considering it.

In the meantime, I ply him with my hands. Caress the length of his cock. Twist. Pump. Stroke. Both hands plunging, both hands twisting.

"There are so many possible combinations of ways to touch you," I murmur.

He laughs. "I guess so." His voice is tight, and his laugh had a sharp edge.

"Are you…alright?" I ask.

"More than." He thrusts into my hands as I do what he seems to like best—the twisting stroke and caressing his balls. "Ohhhh fuck. *Fuck.* Too good, babe. Gonna—ahhh fuck—gonna come soon."

"You are?" I ask, unable and unwilling to even attempt to hide my excitement. "Do not hold back."

"No—no chance of-of-of…of that. FUCK!" He arches off the bed, every perfect, hard muscle tensed and straining.

And now he bucks into my hand, not just once, but in a rhythm. Meeting my strokes by thrusting into my hand. Yes, he will soon release. I am very, *very* excited. I have received my first orgasm—several of them!—and now I am about to *give* my first orgasm. Glee and eagerness and joy ripple through me, and I do not attempt to restrain my emotions. I let myself smile and laugh and giggle as he moves, thrusts, grunts.

"You are *so* hot, Riley," I murmur. "So sexy. I cannot believe I get to do this with you."

"Ah fuck, baby," he growls. "Sayin' sweet shit while you're making me come? Jesus. Goddamned goddess, honey. That's what you are."

He likes that? Then I shall do it again. I lean over him and kiss him while I slowly repeat the twisting strokes of his long, thick, hard, straight cock. And all the while, I caress his balls, cup them, and stroke them with my fingernails and fingertips and massage them with the gentlest of touches.

"You have shown me such amazing joy," I whisper in his ear, and he shudders. "You are the sexiest man I've ever seen. And you…" He groans, eyes squeezing shut as he arches and thrusts, making me lose track of what I was going to say, and so I start over. "I wish this could last forever, I wish I could caress your cock forever. I want to make you orgasm like you never have before."

He laughs, but it's a groaned, ragged laugh. "Jesus! Oh god, fuck. You—" he breaks off, gasping, bucking. "You are!"

"Will my mouth make it better?" I breathe.

"Fuck yes," is his immediate answer.

I shift down so I am lying on his legs and pull his cock away from his body toward me.

Oh gosh, am I *really* going to do this?

"Cadie—Cadence, you don't—"

"I know I do not *have* to do anything, Riley. But you

did this for me several times now. You do not seem to find it gross."

"I…it's not. I fuckin'…" he trails off, panting, watching as I taste his flesh with a swipe of my tongue, laving over the groove of his glans and over the weeping tip. "Jesus. I *love* going down on you. Love the way you taste. Love watchin' you lose your shit, hear you scream my name while I make you come. It's not gross, it's beautiful."

"Then why should I feel any differently?" I ask.

I shift forward a bit further and lick my lips, clear my throat, swallow…and then just do it. Carefully keeping my teeth from scraping his delicate, tender flesh, I accept his cock into my mouth, slide it between my lips and against my tongue. It is a strange sensation at first, both in taste and…mouth-feel, I suppose one might say. His precum is rather more flavorful than I had expected. I taste the salt of flesh and the musk of his precum, and my lips stutter against his skin, and then I feel him at the back of my throat—I am quite well aware that some women will use their throats as well as their mouths, but I do not believe I could do that without my gag reflex being an issue.

I slide my lips back up, watching his reaction. His mouth is open wide, working in a silent scream, and his hands are buried in the sheet and knotted, and his abs are tensed.

"Mmmm," I say, "I find that an eminently enjoyable act to perform. Is it enjoyable for you, Riley?"

He only looks at me, but the expression speaks volumes—if only because I am already learning what his expressions mean. This one is disbelief that I could ask such a thing, as if my question is a statement of the glaringly obvious.

"Shall I continue?"

"I'll beg, if that'll help," he growls.

"Tell me what to do?" I murmur.

"Just…" he breaks off with a groan when I wrap my lips around the head of his cock. "Oh, fuck, *fuck*! Now—now swirl your tongue around me and…and—ohhhhmy-fuckinggod—" his eyes cross when I do as he instructed; he bobs his head up and down a few times. "Like that. Not far, just around the head. And use your hands like you have been."

I obey his instructions faithfully, swirling my tongue and bobbing up and down on him so he slides through my lips and against my tongue. All the while, I pump one hand around the thick base of him and caress his balls the way he likes so much.

He enters a state of paroxysm, then, not breathing, seeming unable to so much as groan, his whole body arched and tensed. After a moment like that, he sags back to the mattress, gasping a ragged breath. His hands go to my head, stabbing his fingers into my hair, gathering it into a mass on the top of my head.

I watch him as I perform oral sex on him, and find myself entranced by the faces he makes, the way he contorts his body. And then he starts to groan and grunt and his hips flex and push, and his grip on my hair tightens until my scalp tugs.

Yes—oh yes, he likes this very, *very* much. The feel of him in my mouth, now that I am growing accustomed to the strange sensation, is not unpleasant at all. Not in the least. In fact, I believe I might even come to enjoy this act, were I to have the opportunity to do so again. I find his silly, mindless, desperate reactions endearing, arousing, and strangely adorable.

He is lost to this world, and to everything save me, and my mouth, and my hands. To the pleasure I am giving him.

It is intoxicating.

Addictive.

He must surely be ready to orgasm soon. This is the event I want to see, to feel, to experience. But he said not to hurry. The longer I make this last for him, the better it will be.

And in truth, I am in no hurry. I can breathe quite well through my nose, obviously. I slow the rhythm of my hands and go lower with my mouth…and then fast and shallow, and then fast and deep, playing with depth and rhythm the way I did with my hands. Now, however, there is the added variable of my tongue, and how I use it. Not to mention my hands.

My goodness, this is rather complex, is it not? A fun kind of challenge, one might say.

I taste a rush of the clear fluid he called precum—pre-ejaculate, my memory informs me. Soon, then. I hope. I want it to happen; I am very eager for his orgasm.

He is grunting now, and his hips are moving, flexing—thrusting him into my mouth. I adjust for his movements, allowing him to provide the movement he seems to need, now that he is near to release.

"Cadence!" he gasps. "I'm…oh fuck, oh fuck! Fuck!"

"What, Riley? You are what? Tell me."

"So close. Fuck, your mouth is so good. Oh fuck, it's good. So fucking good." He tightens his grip on my hair, subtly holding my head in place while he thrusts. I trust him to release me if I so indicated.

"Oh fuck, I'm gonna come, Cadence. Oh fuck…yeah baby, just like that. Don't stop!" I find myself unable to stop from going faster the closer he is to orgasm. I pump him with both hands now while using my mouth around the head of his thrusting cock, and I taste him leaking, feel him throbbing against my lips, feel the heat of him and taste the salt of his skin, and I let him thrust into my mouth until he is frantic and grunting.

"I—ohhhhh god, oh god—ohfuckohgod." He tugs on my hair twice—why I am not sure. "Oh fuck, I'm gonna come—now, Cadence, I'm—shit!" The last is not a sound of release or pleasure but a sudden realization.

He pulls me away so his cock slides out of my mouth, and he pushes my face to the side. I still have my hands on him, and while I cannot claim to know why he removed me from his cock when I know without a doubt how good my mouth made him feel, I know he must have his reasons, and I trust them, so I stroke him with both hands as fast as I can.

With a wordless, guttural shout, Riley thrusts once into my fists, arched off the bed, and then…gasps, breathless. His eyes fly open and find mine, and then we both turn our attention to his cock.

A stream of viscous white fluid erupts out of him and splashes in a stripe up his belly. And again—he grunts and gasps, and ribbon after ribbon of semen shoots out of him, and it seems the more I stroke him through his orgasm, the more crazed he becomes, his whole body jerking helplessly, spasming as he groans and thrusts into my hands.

I see now why he pulled away. Had he not, I would

have been surprised by the eruption of his orgasm. Once again, I know the medical, anatomical explanation of human intercourse. I have witnessed it both in person in various circumstances—my roommate, for example—and in informational videos. But nothing can prepare one for the real, live, in-person experience of a man's ejaculation.

After several long seconds of orgasm, the flood of semen ceases, becoming a dribble and then nothing. There is quite a voluminous puddle of the stuff on his belly.

Curiosity convinces me to swipe my index finger over his tip, catching a smear of the fluid on my finger, which I lick away. It tastes like precum, only more intensely flavored.

I meet his eyes, and see bemusement in his expression. "What?" I ask. "Why do you look at me so?"

"How's it taste?" he asks.

I shrug. "New, to me. I have no comparison. It is not unpleasant." He is still erect, and a string of the stuff droops from him to his belly; I take him in my mouth and taste it, feel it—the texture is decidedly unique. A little slimy, kind of thick. Very warm; not hot, but almost.

Riley is in a daze, his gaze heavy-lidded and vacant, and he is sweaty and panting.

I feel quite proud of myself.

"That was fun," I tell him, resting my chin on his thigh. "I liked it."

He struggles to focus. "I almost came in your mouth."

"You did not, however, and I must admit I am glad you did not. It would have been a most unexpected event. I think I would not be opposed to the experience in the future, however, now that I know what to expect." I frown up at him. "Why did you pull my hair in the moment before your ejaculation?"

"Oh, uhhh…" he hesitates. "That's a signal. A warning that I'm about to come, so you can decide what you're gonna do when I come."

"Most women…ummm…" I grin, blushing. "Most women swallow it?"

"I dunno about *most*. It's up to you, what you're okay with."

"What is your opinion? Your preference?"

"Don't get one, babe. Not me doing it." He pulls me up his body and cradles me in his arms. "Going down on me will always be your choice, sweetheart. You want to? Please, fuck yes. You don't want to? Don't do it. All I care about is being with you."

I turn my face to his, nuzzle his cheek, kiss his stubble, whisper with my lips against his ear. "I liked it. I want to do it again. And when I do, I will swallow it. It does not taste bad at all. It is strange, in the sense of being a new experience for me, but how much you enjoy it makes it wonderful for me."

He sighs. "I kinda can't believe you went down on me."

"Why not?"

He rolls one shoulder. "I…well…I don't think most girls would choose to go down on a guy like that their first time so much as even *seeing* a dick."

"I am not most girls."

"No, you are not," he agrees. "And that's a *hell* of a good thing."

"Really?" I ask.

"Yes," he huffs, laughing. "And not just because you just gave me the best orgasm of my life."

"Hyperbole is unnecessary," I tell him.

"It's not. It's the truth."

I meet his gaze—I do believe he is telling the truth. I should not doubt him, at this point, but part of me does.

Riley's phone rings, jarring us out of the moment, and he groans. "Fuck off, whoever you are."

"Riley," I scold. "You should answer."

"Fuck, fine." He stretches one long arm out, grabs his cell phone, and answers it, putting it on speaker and resting it on my back between my shoulder blades. This makes me laugh, for some reason. "Yeah? What's up, Fee?"

"You got Cadence near you?" I hear Felix's voice from the phone.

"Yeah," Riley answers. "Both here. You're on speaker."

"Is that so?" I detect amusement in his tone.

"Fee, with respect? Fuck off. What's up?"

"So, I'm calling with news regarding the fundraiser Noelle was putting together."

"*Was*?" I cut in, my voice faint and wobbly. "Did something happen?"

"Sort of, but not like you're thinking—I'm calling with good news, not bad. I just got off the phone with Noelle. The word got out, and Three Rivers has proven yet again why we're the best small town in the state. Local businesses and business owners—such as yours truly—have already cleared your goal by quite a margin."

The breath leaves my lungs in a whoosh, leaving me blinking and flapping my mouth like a fish. "I, um—*what*? You...you are being truthful? This is not a joke?"

"I wouldn't joke about this."

"But…there was no event."

"Nope."

"And they just…*donated*? Just like that?"

"Yep."

I clear my throat. "And when you say my goal has been *cleared*…you mean to say your town has raised *more* than the eighty thousand dollars I need?"

"Looks like…" I hear paper flipping. "A hundred and nine thousand, four hundred and twenty-three dollars."

"But…but…*how*? *Why*? I am not from Three Rivers. I only know Riley, you, your lovely wife, Bear, Noelle, and the Cartwright sisters. And except for Riley, I only met all of you once. How…why…" I feel tears pooling. "I do not know what to say."

"Noelle knows the right people. So does Mrs. Aldis. There was…ohhh, lemme see…about ten grand from private, small-dollar donations. The rest of it came from businesses here in town and the general area. I'll give you the full list later. Just thought you'd like to know."

I cannot breathe. I am so overcome by shocked gratitude that I cannot breathe, cannot function. I hear voices, register nothing. Eventually, I feel Riley's warmth behind me, and his arms wrap around me, and his chin rests on my shoulder. Faster than any other tactic, strategy, or calming technique I have ever used, Riley's mere presence calms me.

My lungs open. My mind slows.

"I cannot believe it," I whisper.

"Told you, sweetheart. This place comes together when there's a need."

"Truly." My mind is whirling. "I need to prepare. With the funding secured, I can book my flight and leave early."

He tenses. "That's good."

I turn my face to his. "Riley—"

"Hey, no. Don't think about me."

"You may as well tell a fish not to swim, Riley. What are *you* feeling?"

"Glad you're gonna get to do this thing that's so important to you."

"And?" I prompt. "I know there is more."

"Sad you gotta leave. And I know…" he clears his throat. "I know there's no real reason for you to come back here."

"But there is." I turn in his embrace, spreading my leg over his thighs. "Not just because I will have to come back to give an account for how their money was used." I cup his cheek. "For you."

"Cadence—"

"Cadie." I feather my hands through his hair. "Call me Cadie."

"Cadie," he echoes. "I like it." A pause. "I…I'd like nothing more than for you to come back just for me. To see me. To be with me. But you've got a bright fuckin' future. A mind like yours? Talent like yours?"

I cover his mouth. "Hush, Riley. Do you not see?"

"See what?"

"How much I have come to care for you. It has happened faster than belief would merit, but I cannot deny the facts. I would not have shared my body with you, otherwise. I know for you, sex is not—"

He cuts over me. "Whoa, *no*. Do *not* do that. Don't assume that. I've had quite a few sexual partners, yes. I've never been in love. I've never dated anyone very long. But…sex has *never* been meaningless to me." He looks hard at me. "And this, with you? Means more than I can put into words. Yes, partly because I know how big a deal this is for you. But for me, it's meaningful. It's deep. It's... more real than...I don't even fuckin' know what to say. I just know I care about you too, and..."

I touch my forehead to his. "I am coming back, Riley Crowe. I am coming back to you. This I swear."

"And I'll be waiting." His voice is low, rough.

"I know I have no right to ask you to wait, but—"

"Six days, six weeks, or six years, Cadie, I'll wait." His eyes drill into mine, and I do not doubt him. "There won't be anyone else. How can there *be* anyone else but you, when there isn't anyone else but you?"

I sniffle, laugh. "For me as well, Riley."

He kisses me. "C'mon. Better get cleaned up and make a plan."

14

Riley

I'M A FUCKING MESS.

I don't sleep for shit anymore. Why? Because I'm thinking about her.

Missing her.

Remembering the few, short, incredible hours I had with her—two and a half days that changed my life. Changed *me*.

I'm not suddenly some pious, Bible-quoting, church-going goody-goody, but I find myself trying to be…better. Kinder. More generous. I try to spend more time reading and learning shit than scrolling and drinking.

I wrote a letter to Ellen Johnson forgiving myself;

I wrote it and burned it in the backyard. Perhaps not so weirdly, I've felt lighter ever since.

Cadence warned me she would not be able to communicate with me regularly, and more than likely not at all or very rarely, and that's been the case. I got one letter from her back in August—the paper had bloodstains on it, and it was more of a note than a letter—*I miss you, I'm thinking about you, I'm fine.*

Better than nothing.

I track the news out of Sudan religiously, even though I don't even know exactly where she's located. Some hospital that is supposedly nowhere near any of the heavy fighting. She wasn't happy about that initially, when the company she hired insisted, for safety reasons, she not be near the hotspots. But it was either accept that placement or not go, so she went.

It's hard not to worry when I hear about a new battle or reports of some heinous new atrocities. Knowing she's there, on the ground, in the country where that awful shit is happening. She's *seeing* it all firsthand.

It was abstract, discussing it when we met: *Oh yeah, you're going to Sudan. You're a doctor.*

It's another thing helping her prepare.

I took a week off work, borrowed Bear from Fee to be in charge, and helped Cadence get ready to leave. I saw the crates of supplies, helped her take inventory. Helped her pack the crates, address them, and ship them off. I saw her bedroom—diplomas, awards, certifications. Books— so many books. No band or movie posters adorned her childhood bedroom walls—instead, she had the periodic table, a line graph of the history of the world that wrapped around three full walls—handmade by her, apparently.

That weird diagram of a man by Leonardo da Vinci. Diagrams of the human body—nervous, skeletal, muscular, organs, et cetera.

I helped her pack her suitcase.

I drove her to the airport.

I kissed her goodbye.

That made it pretty fucking real.

We didn't do anything else, physically. She was fixated on preparations, and there just wasn't time—she was gone within a week of Felix's call, and we were running from dawn to midnight every day in between. We did sleep in each other's arms, though.

And that's another reason I'm not sleeping for shit—I spent a week in heaven, going to sleep every night with Cadence's soft, naked, warm body in my arms. Yeah, she always sleeps naked; it's fucking glorious.

I saw my future in that week with her, and I fucking want it.

I want her.

I want life with her.

The days seem to go by fast, but the weeks slowly.

OCTOBER

The more time that passes without her, the more unhinged I feel at her absence. Which is ridiculous, I know. We spent less than seventy-two hours together, yet I feel like I know her better than anyone except maybe Fee, Cole, and Nyx. There's a distinct "before" and "after" in my life: before Cadence, and after.

I dream about her.

In some of them, she's just looking at me with those deep green eyes full of love and affection and tenderness, and her hair is all in her eyes, and she's smiling at me like I'm the only person in the world.

The rest? I wake up hard as a rock just about every night, having dreamed about Cadence doing all sorts of wicked and delicious things with me, some which we did and some which we haven't…yet.

I'll tell you one thing—my right hand is getting a lot more action than it has since I was a teenager. Even that is tricky, though—I'm conflicted about thinking about her in that context. Using her like that.

She's…fuck, *special* is absolutely the wrong fucking word.

Precious.

Not just some cheap hookup.

Not jerk-off fodder for my horny-as-fuck brain.

Eventually, by the end of October, I swear off masturbation entirely because it's just not worth the release; it never does anything to reduce my tension anyway.

Which means that my newfound goodness is tested frequently, since a sexually frustrated Riley can be a real dick.

C⸰

NOVEMBER 1st

My phone rings at three in the morning, jarring me out of a wildly erotic dream in which Cadence was repeating her truly earth-shattering oral performance.

I peer at the screen, but the ID just shows a bizarrely

long string of numbers. I debate killing the call, but answer on a whim. "H'lo?"

"Riley? It is me—Cadence. Cadie."

My heart stops. I'm suddenly and fully awake. "Whoa, hey! Hi! God, it's good to hear your voice. How are you?"

There's a long pause, and I hear a shaky breath, and a sniffle. "It has been…much more difficult than I anticipated. I…*ugh*! I do not have long—this is a borrowed phone. Mine was destroyed months ago. I just…I miss you, Riley. I simply had to call and tell you that. I could not bear you thinking I'd forgotten."

I'd…

A contraction. I don't call attention to it, though—I just file it away as odd.

"I think about you all day, every day." I sigh. "I dream about you."

"Oh, Riley. I am sorry to call you in this state, I just…I just lost my eighth patient today alone. There are so many…so many. I can't save so many of them. Often, all I can do is make them comfortable and witness their passing."

"Jesus, honey. How are you coping with all that?"

"Some days are better than others." A heavy sigh. "Today is a not so good day. Gosh, I am terrible. The first time I call you in four months, and I am a weeping disaster. I just…I needed to hear your voice."

"Don't be sorry for calling me. I'm here, sweetheart," I whisper. "I'm so sorry it's so hard."

"I knew it would be difficult and emotionally taxing, but I wasn't prepared for exactly how much so. I do not think anyone could be. Not for this."

She sounds different. Not just the occasional

contraction, which is new, but…something I can't pin-point. I set that aside—it's not important right now.

She sniffles. "How is everyone in Three Rivers? I find myself thinking of them often. Not as often as I think of you, of course, but…I grew to like that place very much in the short time I was there."

"Oh, y'know, mostly the same. Noelle gave birth not long after you left. They named her Ella Faye. She's a sweet li'l nugget. Cute as a button, super smiley, and only throws up on me occasionally."

This gets me a laugh. "Oh, that is wonderful to hear. Ember is well?"

"Yeah, she popped that kid out like a champ, to hear Fee tell it. He's biased, but then, Ember is one seriously tough bitch."

"She is *not* a bitch, Riley Crowe."

I laugh. "That's a term of endearment between us. We call each other names out of sibling-in-law love, same as I do with the guys."

I hear a siren, a horn, and shouting. "Damn," she hisses. "I have to go, unfortunately. We just received another truckload of victims."

Truckload? She's not prone to exaggeration like that, and not about this, so she means *literally* a truckload of victims? Fuck that.

"Go, baby, go. Do your thing. Call me any time, for any reason. I luh—" I almost say it. "Cadie, I…"

"I know," she whispers. "As do I. Do not say it, however. Please. Just…just save it, if you will. For when I see you again in person."

"Yeah, yeah." Fuck, I wish I knew what to say. "They're lucky to have you over there, Cadence. I'm proud of you."

For some reason, that last part wrenches a single sob out of her. "Oh, my heart. How I needed to hear that, my sweet Riley. Thank you." A bracing sigh. "Now. I must bid you farewell until we speak again."

Ah, there it is—the formality. Aside from the contractions, she was speaking less…formally. Less archaic. I'm not sure how I feel about it, to be honest.

But it's back again, there at the end. Like putting on armor, almost.

"Bye, honey. Be safe."

"I shall. Goodbye, Riley."

I wait until my phone beeps, indicating the call has ended, and then I toss my phone aside.

My eyes burn.

Fuck, I miss her.

And fuck, I wish I could just give her a hug. She sounded so…not broken, just…exhausted and brutally sad, I guess.

$$C \oslash$$

She doesn't call again. Two weeks later, though, I do get a tattered, bloodstained scrap of prescription pad paper with another quick, scrawled *I miss you, things are hard, but I am making it* sort of note on the back.

$$C \oslash$$

I keep the notes in my truck with me.

When she left, she said her visa expires in December, so I'm counting the days until then.

Not long, now.

15

Cadence

THANKSGIVING

I STRIP MY LATEX GLOVES OFF AND TOSS THEM IN THE receptacle. Same with the plastic apron. I swipe the surgical cap off my head, along with the PPE glasses. Gasping, every muscle aching, I stagger out of the makeshift OR and beeline for the nearest marked exit. I had quite forgotten that it was day, still. I have been in that OR for six hours, trying valiantly but in vain to save the life of a young girl not even old enough to have her menses.

My hands shake. They always do, after. Never before, never during. Only after an operation. That was my third such effort in the last twenty-four hours. I hardly remember the last time I slept more than two hours in a row. A week since, at least.

I find myself in a tiny outdoor space created by the layout of the hospital—it is just barely big enough to host a few native flowers and a bench, but it is fresh air and sunlight.

As I do a dozen times every day, I mourn the loss of my phone—it fell out of my scrubs when I was helping transfer a victim from a truck to a gurney. I did not notice until much later, but by then it had been run over by who knows how many vehicles. There is no way to get a new one, not here. I hardly have the time, anyway.

I just miss him.

I would love nothing more than to be able to call him right now. Hear his voice. Perhaps he would say something amusing. Tell me a crude joke which I would playfully scold him for.

I hear the door open and close, and soft footfalls behind me.

I sigh, knowing I am being summoned. "Yes, I am coming." I start to rise, already reaching for my scrub cap.

A soft hand on my shoulder keeps me in my seat. "No, please, Dr. Creswell. Stay as you are." The speaker has the distinct rhythm of a Sudanese individual—I know the voice, as well: Nurse Duwana.

I sink back down onto the bench and toy with the cap. "Duwana." She comes around the bench and stands facing me. "Is there something I can do for you?"

She smiles, showing even, white teeth. She is a lovely, wonderful soul, Duwana. The very image of compassion. Tireless. Fierce when need be. She is beautiful, with very dark black skin. Tall and slender, always wearing a colorful *toub* and *hijab* pairing. I rely on her—she is my translator here at the hospital as well as my liaison with the other Sudanese nurses, many of whom still do not entirely trust me and certainly do not like me. They recognize my skill, however, and as long as I go through Duwana, they heed me. This hospital would run into ruin without her.

So would I, for that matter.

She sits beside me, hands folded on her lap. I expect her to say something or do something, but she does not. She merely sits in silence with me; her spirit is one of calm, of healing reassurance, despite the violence of her world in which I am merely a visitor.

I feel my weary, aching, troubled soul soaking up her calm, and I realize the subtlety of what she is doing—giving me the few moments of peace and quiet I need, the comfort of companionship without the burden of conversation.

Exactly what I need, without having to ask.

I reach for hands and fold them in mine. "Thank you, Duwana."

She smiles. A hint of mischief glitters in her eyes. "Come, please. I have a thing to show you. A surprise." She rises and gently urges me to my feet as well.

"A surprise? For me?"

Her only answer is to lead me back into the hospital and down crowded, overflowing corridors, past moaning patients and weeping family members and walking wounded with thousand-yard stares. She brings me to the stairwell and we ascend, ascend, all the way to the rooftop. She presses the crash bar delicately, ushers me out into the blinding African sun and oppressive heat. A helicopter thuds in the distance; faintly, so distant as to make you question your hearing, there is the soft chatter of automatic weapons, the occasional crump of an explosion.

We are, supposedly, rather far from the nearest hotspots of fighting, but whenever I come outside, it seems the sounds of war have drawn incrementally closer.

I am assured it will not come here, but I am not sure I believe that claim. The gnawing pit of dread in my gut feels like a premonition, a warning.

I shake my morbid thoughts off as Duwana leads the way across the roof and around the stairwell structure, around the revolving silver domes. I hear voices, an eruption of laughter.

I halt, puzzled: a handful of off-duty nurses, the ones who dislike me the least, are clustered around something, their bodies hiding whatever it is. They look eager—pleased, excited.

I cannot fathom why, or about what. It is not my birthday, so I cannot imagine what surprise they could have for me.

Duwana stops and faces me. "Dr. Creswell," she says, and then gestures at the surrounding nurses, "we have talked for weeks about how we can show you how thankful we are for you. You are here, fighting for the lives of our people, when this is not your war and not your people."

"I feel called to help," I say.

"I know. Few others would risk and sacrifice all that you have to come to a place like this." She takes my hands in hers. "It is not very much, I know, but hopefully this will give you even a small taste of your homeland."

She steps aside, and so do the others. Behind them is a small folding card table laden with dishes of food. I see a whole roasted chicken, rice, sweet potatoes, flatbread, roasted vegetables…

"I…" I shake my head. "This is…*why*? This is so much food, and there is so little to go around as it is. Why, Duwana?"

She frowns in confusion. "Perhaps you are unaware? Today is your country's Thanksgiving holiday. I read a book long ago, before all this began, about your holiday of giving thanks, and I remember the foods it is said you enjoy on that day. We do not have turkey, I am afraid, but I hope a chicken will do."

"Thanksgiving?" My eyes burn, water. "You...you made all this...for *me*?"

"You have done more than anyone could ask, Dr. Creswell." I have tried a dozen times to get her to call me Cadence, but she always seems to forget. "This is but a small gesture of our thanks to you." She guides me to the table, which has but one plate, one tarnished, bent-tined fork, and one butter knife. "Please sit. Enjoy."

I shake my head, fighting back tears. "But...ohhh, Duwana." I look at the others. "My friends. In my country, Thanksgiving is...it isn't really about the food. We are thankful for that, of course, but really, it is a day to be thankful for the *people* in your life. For the good things you have, the good things you have experienced. It would not be a proper Thanksgiving if I did not share this bounty with my friends."

They seem confused.

I set the place settings aside and take Duwana's hand on one side and another nurse's on the other—slowly, the rest join hands in a circle around the table.

"There is precious little to be thankful for, in times like these," I say. "But today, I am thankful for you all. I am touched beyond words at your gesture, which is just so thoughtful. It is my most fervent wish that you join me in this celebration. We are alive, this day. We have breath in our lungs. We are here. We are together. And that, indeed, is something to be thankful for." Duwana translates my words for the others who do not speak English well or at all.

We eat with our hands, and for a few blessed, wonderful minutes, there is feasting and laughter.

My heart is lightened. Sometimes, you just have to take a few minutes and simply be grateful that you are alive.

Sirens howl nearby. Engines roar and brakes squeal, and orderlies shout.

Duty calls.

⁂

DECEMBER 2nd

We are inundated with victims. The fighting has drawn closer by the day: the once-faint chatter and crump is no longer quite so faint.

My friends here at the hospital and the men hired to protect me have tried repeatedly to get me to leave while I can.

But how can I? When they need me the most, I leave to save my own skin? I think not.

Truck after truck full of dying soldiers and civilians arrive, one after the other. The hallways are nearly impassable. We have run out of the best pain medication and are now using old stockpiles of morphine. Old bedsheets are torn into strips to extend our rapidly dwindling stores of bandages.

I have not left the floor in seventy-two hours. There is no time to think, to breathe, to miss home or even Riley. There is only blood and death and the next patient.

An explosion shakes me out of a dead sleep, so close and so loud it rattles the windows and the bones inside me. I sit up, gasping. Another explosion rocks the floor under me, this one even closer.

A barrage of gunfire crackles like Fourth of July firecrackers—this, too, sounds like it is right outside the window. I creep to the window and peer out; I know not the time, but it is night and the shadows are long and the sky is lit by tracers and muzzle-flash and explosions.

It is here.

The war is here at my very doorstep.

For a moment, I am frozen in terror. I cannot breathe. The overwhelm I have suppressed and ignored and buried and refused to give into and fought as ferociously as I can for so many months now threatens to suffocate me.

The door to the closet-sized office which functions as a makeshift place to catch a few hours of sleep slams open. "Dr. Creswell!" Duwana hustles in, *toub* flowing around her. "Come! Come! Quickly!"

She shoves PPE at me—mask, glasses, gloves, gown. I don everything as we jog, and she next hands me a small paper cup sloshing with cold, strong black tea which I drink like a shot of alcohol.

I reach the triage floor—screams, moans, and curses rise like a miasma of agony. The floors are slick with blood, which the few, exhausted, overworked orderlies work frantically to sop up. I scan the scene, my brain clicking into work mode, and I begin snapping orders to Duwana, who passes them on to the others.

And then I recall nothing else as I am swept up in the chaos of lifesaving.

⌒

My eyes burn, feeling as if they are filled with gritty, hot sand. My feet ache and throb. My stomach gnarls and rumbles, empty. My hands hurt—both from so many hours of constant use and from the dryness that comes from wearing rubber gloves for so long.

The fighting is right outside. I still cannot help occasionally ducking when a particularly close explosion rocks the ground under my feet; more than once, a drop tile has shaken loose and fallen on my head. But better a drop tile than an HE shell, I suppose.

I cannot recall when this began. Two days? Three? I have passed beyond exhaustion and into a trance-like state. I have treated more patients than I can count. Enemy soldiers, friendly ones, women, children, old people. Gunshots, machete wounds, shrapnel, missing limbs, evisceration, crush wounds from collapsed buildings.

The fighting does not cease, night and day.

Where do all the bullets come from? Surely they must run out at some point?

It is an errant thought as I try to remember what I was doing.

Oh, right. New gloves. Only the box is empty; there are no more.

Duwana, ever nearby, shoves a handful of clean gloves at me. I put on a pair and stuff the rest in my scrub pockets.

A fresh wave of patients arrives. These are newly

wounded, still in shock, thrashing, spurting, gushing, seeping, weeping.

The trance-state takes over and my hands do their work.

$\mathcal{C}_{\odot}$

"—Well? Dr. Creswell?" Duwana? Yes, Duwana. That is her name. "...Must rest. You cannot continue."

I look at her and see not her but the previous patient. A woman who looked much like her. She had a hole in her gut so large a cantaloupe could have fit in the space. All I could do was ease her suffering, and even that not much, for even the years-old morphine is nearly gone and must be rationed.

It is quieter, now; I do not know why.

Someone screams nearby, and I move toward the sound. A young man—a boy, really, not old enough to shave every day. I scan him—oh. No. He will not survive. I hold his hand as he cries, fades...stills forever.

Duwana pulls me away, then. "Come. You must come, Cadence."

"No...no. I can't."

More hands. They pull, they push. What is happening? I see familiar faces—nurses. Doctors. Orderlies. My companions here, these last six months. Some faces are wet with tears. What is happening? Have I died?

Duwana is beside me, arm around my waist, guiding me down a hallway to an exit. This is a service corridor near the receiving dock. Why are we here? What is going on?

We reach the exit. Bodies cluster around me. Hands reach for me. Squeeze my arms, my shoulders.

Prayers are whispered in Arabic:

Go with God—go with God—go with God.

I see the faces of my protectors: Deng, Malong, and Gorte—three local men who have treated me like a sister, an aunt. They have brought me food, fresh clothing, and tea. The few times I have left the hospital, they accompany me, protect me, translate for me, see that I do not forget a headscarf in public or otherwise run afoul of local customs through ignorance.

They escorted me here from the airport, and when the time comes, they will escort me back.

I see my small suitcase full of my few personal possessions near the exit.

"Duwana?" I ask. "What is happening?"

Duwana frames my face in her strong, gentle hands. Her fingers are so black against my pale skin, a juxtaposition I find lovely. "You must go now, my sister."

I shake my head. "No. No. I cannot. I—I can't. How can I leave, Duwana?"

"You *must*, Cadence." She is weeping. "You *must*. It is time. There is a lull in the fighting. You must go. You have done more than anyone could ask. Allah brought you here, and now Allah calls you home."

"No!" I protest. "Duwana, I—"

Fatima—another nurse to whom I have drawn quite close—squeezes my hand. She is short, stout, quick-tempered, and prefers a plain black hijab. She has a deft, quick touch with IV insertions. "You must go."

Go with god, sister.

"You can do nothing more, here," Duwana says. "Soon this hospital will be overrun. The enemy will come and you cannot be here when that happens. You must go now, Cadence. Please."

My protectors form a wall behind me. I try to push past them, to return to the triage floor.

Duwana's grip is fierce. She shakes me. "*CADENCE!*" She raises her voice to an angry snap for the first time since I met her. "It is time for you to go. You cannot save us all."

"I can try!" I shout. "I won't leave you!"

"I will *not* see you *die*!" She shouts back. "You must go. You *must*. Please. For me, if not for you and if not for your Riley, who waits for you so patiently."

Riley's face fills my mind. His pale blue eyes, his black hair. *You've done all you can, baby girl,* I hear him say. *Time to come home. You dyin' in Sudan ain't the mission.*

I sag, the fight going out of me. "Duwana…"

She sees my capitulation and guides me to the exit. A small, filthy white pickup truck is idling a few feet from the door, a driver with a scarf around his mouth and nose behind the wheel. Two armed men crouch in the truck bed, eyes scanning, scanning. My protectors climb in with them, and Duwana tosses my suitcase in after them. Fatima hustles me to the passenger side and into the seat. Someone shouts—a distant explosion sends vibrations through the ground.

Fatima unwinds the hijab from her own head, despite the presence of men, and puts it on me. "Keep your face hidden. Say nothing."

Another nurse drapes a bloodstained flat sheet over Fatima's head to preserve her honor even as she preserves mine.

Duwana reaches in through the open window and squeezes my hand. "May Allah carry you home, my sister."

I cannot see through the haze of tears. "Du—Duwana, wait, I—"

She presses a kiss to the back of my hand. "Go. Go." She says something to the driver in Juba Arabic, and the driver guns the throttle.

She clings to my hand until momentum tears us apart. I twist in the seat and watch, weeping, as the best friend I have ever had vanishes as we turn a corner.

"Down," the driver snaps at me in heavily accented English. "Down. Hide your face."

I wrap the hijab around my nose and mouth and tuck it so it stays in place, turning my face down and away.

It is a rough, jolting, too-fast drive through the city, then, and I do not dare look out the window. I hear shouts, screams. Weeping and wailing. Gunshots. Once, I hear a scream cut short in a wet thunk. Every few minutes the driver reminds me to hide my face, to keep down.

The truck slows and I feel the driver go tense. "Do not move. Do not speak. Head down."

I hear chatter in a local dialect—Dinka, I think. I do not know for sure. A pidgin of Dinka, English, and Juba Arabic, more likely.

A single gunshot cracks from the truck bed, jolting a scream out of me, and then there is shouting—I cannot stop my eyes from lifting, watching, seeing.

Men with covered faces dart this way and that, AK-47s pointing and firing at the men in the bed behind me, who fire back. A grunt, and a body topples out of the truck, but the attackers are all down. I look back, and Gorte is bleeding from a wound to his shoulder. Gorte had a wife who died a year ago; he was silent and huge and imposing; he once gave me the shirt off his own back when my scrub top was too sodden in blood to wear.

"I have to help Gorte!" I say.

The driver ignores me, gunning the engine and driving over the enemy—*thud-thud*. He grabs the back of my head and shoves me down into the footwell; I am bent double, painfully.

Gunfire—loud, hot, and close—accompanies the tinkle of shells.

Then abrupt silence except for the roar of the engine and the crackle of dirt and rocks against the underside of the vehicle and the skid of tires as they weave this way and that.

I huddle in the footwell, fighting panic, for long minutes. Slowly, I hear the buzz of propellers, which grows steadily louder until it is right outside.

The door opens and a hand reaches in—I take it, and allow myself to be helped out to my feet on shaky, aching legs.

Someone tosses my suitcase into the waiting aircraft, and someone else pushes my purse at me, presses my passport into my hand.

Go with god, sister.

I'm buckled into a seat in a narrow metal tube, which is hot and dusty and smells of oil and fuel and cigarettes.

And then my stomach is in my feet as we lurch skyward.

At one point, we bank over the ruins of a small village and all I can see is patches of blood-stained sand and stacks of corpses.

I remember nothing else after that.

"…Captain speaking…altitude of thirty thousand feet…"

"…She's been just sitting there for four hours, staring at nothing. Won't respond."

"Ma'am? Can you hear me?" A Black male face hovers in my line of sight. "Is there anyone we can call?"

I blink, once. "Call?" My voice hurts to use—it is rusty, hoarse.

"Do you have any family expecting you?"

"Family."

"Ma'am? Ma'am?" His hands shake me gently. "Ma'am, please. We wanna help you get home."

"Home?" My head a maelstrom of images. Emotions are a boiling cauldron. Thoughts are like leaves in a tornado.

"You got a boyfriend, maybe?"

"Riley." It emerges from my mouth unbidden. "Riley Crowe. Three Rivers." It's all I can manage. "Riley Crowe. Three Rivers…Riley Crowe, Three Rivers." I feel myself rocking, arms wrapped around my middle. "Riley Crowe, Three Rivers. Riley Crowe, Three Rivers. Riley Crowe, Three Rivers."

"…See what comes up on Google…oh, yeah, here we go." A woman's voice, quiet and Jamaican-accented. "Riley Crowe, Crowe Demolitions in Three Rivers, which is…way the hell up north. I got a phone number. I'll see if he answers…"

16

Riley

M Y PHONE RINGS AT FOUR IN THE MORNING.

I answer it. "Hello?"

It's not an international number, but a 313
area code: Detroit. Not Cadence, then.

"Riley Crowe?" A woman's voice, unfamiliar, with the
lilt of a Jamaican accent.

"Yeah, who's this?"

"My name is Candace. I'm a security guard at the
Detroit Metro Airport. I have a woman here who seems to
be having some kind of trouble. She won't say anything but
your name and Three Rivers. Her luggage tag says Cadence
Creswell, MD."

I blank for a second. "Cade—*Cadence*? She's there?
Now?"

"Yes, sir. She has been here for a few hours. At first, we thought she was waiting for a transfer, but she's…she's just staring at nothing. Has been for hours. We barely got her to give us your name. Do you know her?"

"Yeah, yes, yes. She's my…yes, I know her. I'm several hours away, but I'll get there as soon as I can. Just… keep an eye on her. Leave her be, just keep an eye on her."

"Okay, I understand."

I throw on yesterday's clothes, cram a hat on my head, nuke leftover coffee and put it in a to-go tumbler, and head south as fast as I can, pushing the envelope of safety and legality. I send Felix and Bear a voice note detailing the situation, and then focus on driving.

I make it to DTW in record time—don't tell Cole, though, or he'll yell at me for speeding. I park like an ass-hole in the pickup line at Arrivals behind a few idling taxis and run inside, dodging and ducking, weaving through the crowd. I make it as far as the luggage carousel, but I'm stopped by a security guard at the door that would take me up to the concourse where Cadence must be.

"A guard named Candace called me," I say, panting. "My…ah, girlfriend is up there—"

"Yeah," the guard says. "You're Riley Crowe from Three Rivers, huh?"

I blink at the interruption. "Oh, uh, yeah, that's me."

"Cmon, man. This way." He does a chin-lift at another guard, who comes to take his place at the door. "Your girl must've been through some kinda shit, bro. She's fucked *up.*"

Fuck.

He senses my urgency—possibly assisted by the fact that I'm clearly about to shove past him and start sprinting.

We reach the concourse, and he points to the left. "Down at the end. Gate A3."

"Thanks," I mumble, and take off running.

I'm a sweaty, gasping, shaky-legged mess by the time I get to the far end of the concourse.

I see her. A gate on the left, sitting in one of the blue seats. She's rocking back and forth, muttering under her breath. Her arms are wrapped around her midsection, and her eyes are fixed on the floor in front of her, seeing nothing. She has one small carry-on suitcase beside her with a small brown leather purse on top of it, and the handle of the suitcase slipped through the handles of the purse.

I skid to a stop, dropping to my knees in front of her. Take her hands—she's been picking at the cuticles of her thumbs with her index fingernails so much that the nail beds on each thumb are bloody.

"Cadie?" I whisper, trying to catch her attention. "Hey. It's me. It's Riley."

"Riley Crowe, Three Rivers. Riley Crowe, Three Rivers." Repeated on a loop, her voice scratchy.

A crowd is gathering, and I glance over my shoulder. "Fuck off!"

An imposing Black woman with pale pink hair hustles over, herding and ushering the onlookers away firmly but kindly.

"You must be Riley Crowe," she says to me once the area is cleared.

"Yeah," I answer, distracted. "Candace?"

She nods. "Yeah, I called you. Poor thing's been there since before my shift started, and I'm about to clock out. Won't respond to anything, not since we got her to say your name, and now that's all she'll say. She sick or something?"

"Or something," I answer. "I've got it from here, Candace. Thanks."

"I'll be around for a few more minutes if you need anything, yah?"

Even through my worry for Cadence, I recognize the compassion this woman is showing, and I smile at her. "I will. You're an angel, Candace. Thank you *so* much."

"I dunno 'bout all that, but anyone can see she is *not* okay."

"She will be." I squeeze Cadence's hands, kiss her knuckles; her hands are dry and cracked, her lips are chapped, and she has heavy black bags under her eyes. "Cadence, hey. It's me. I'm here."

Her eyes flutter, twitch, and she blinks once, focusing on me—not without effort, either. "R-Rye—?"

I sniff a laugh. "Yeah, honey, it's me. Riley. I'm here. I've got you."

She blinks at me. "Real?"

"Yeah, I'm real." I place her palm on my cheek—I quit shaving weeks ago, so I've got a scraggly beard going. "Touch me, honey. I'm real."

Her fingers curl into my beard. "Beard."

"Yeah, I grew a beard."

Her eyes go unfocused again. "Riley Crowe, Three Rivers…."

"Hey, hey, hey—baby, come back." I shimmy closer, so she rocks into me. "Cadence, sweetheart. It's Riley, I'm here."

"Riley—Riley." Her eyes try to focus on me, fail, try again. "Riley?"

"Yeah, right here. Hey, look at me, yeah?" I clutch her hands inside mine. "You wanna go home?"

"Home?"

"With me."

"Three Rivers?"

"Yeah, honey. Home to Three Rivers with me."

"Home to Three Rivers with you."

My heart is in a billion shards, seeing her like this. Fuck me, what did she go through over there?

I slide backward and start to rise to my feet, but she abruptly and violently lurches at me. She hits my chest and we tumble backward together to the floor. "*NO!*" She clings to me with shocking strength. "Don't leave me! Don't leave me!"

"I'm not leaving you, I'm not—" I cradle her against me, but she's shaking and sobbing. "I'll *never* leave you, sweetheart. I've got you."

"Got me," she repeats. "Got me."

"Yeah, honey, I've got you. Just…just hold onto me."

"Hold onto you."

I work to my feet with Cadence clinging to me like a spider monkey baby with its mother. Her legs are around my waist and her arms around my neck, her face buried in my throat. She's shaking, trembling violently, now.

"Riley?" It's a shredded whisper. "I'm thirsty."

I twist around, looking for Candace, catch her gaze; she's a few feet away, watching with concern all over her features. "Can you get her some water?"

She bustles off and returns with a sealed bottle. I crack it open; Cadence is clinging to me so tightly I have both hands free.

"Here," I whisper, perching on the edge of a seat. "Drink."

She turns sideways on my lap and takes the bottle from me in a quaking hand—water sloshes out. "C-can't."

I put it to her lips. "Just a sip at first."

She takes a mouthful and swishes it around; another, just as small. Sip after sip, until her hands stop shaking and she can drink it on her own. When she's finished most of the bottle, she sets it aside and turns back to me, legs around my waist, and rests her cheek on my shoulder. "Home," she whispers. "Home to Three Rivers with you."

I carry her through the concourse like that, Candace trailing behind with the suitcase. I reach my truck, finding the security guard who met me at the stairs guarding it so I don't get ticketed or towed.

I set Cadence in the passenger seat and buckle her in. "I'm not leaving, just going around to the other side."

She reluctantly releases her grip on my wrist, but her eyes don't leave me as I circle the hood. As soon as I'm behind the wheel, she latches onto me again.

Once we're on the freeway heading north, I unbuckle her and slide the console up out of the way and pull her toward me. She curls up against my side.

She doesn't move the rest of the way.

⌒☉

Felix, Ember, Cole, Nyx, Bear, and Noelle are all at my house when we arrive. It's a noisy bustle in my tiny kitchen, and Cadence shrinks against me.

"She's gonna need some time before she's ready for visitors," I say. "An' I don't know any more than any of you."

Bear claps his huge hands once. "Out."

Cadence stirs at the clap, seems to momentarily tune back in. "I am very tired," she whispers. "I am sorry."

Ember, with Ella cradled in the crook of her arm, kisses Cadence on the cheek. "We're all here for you, Cadence. We're all glad you're back safely."

"Safe?" She repeats the word as if unsure of its meaning. "Safe."

Noelle looks at me quizzically, but I shrug—I don't have any answers. Everyone but Fee files out.

"You good, bro?" he asks, his eyes full of concern.

"Me? I'm fine. Just gotta get her settled."

"Want me to wait?" His voice is pitched low.

"Nah," I say. "Just cover me at work for now, yeah? Dunno how long."

"Long as you need," he says. "Long as *she* needs."

"Thanks, brother."

He claps me on the back and heads out, but not without one last worried glance at Cadence, who's clinging to me in a way that suggests she may never let go.

Fine by me.

I bring her into my room, sit on the edge of the bed. Pull her back enough that I can look at her. "Hey—you with me?"

Her eyes focus on me slowly. "With you."

"Do you want to take a bath?"

She frowns. "Bath?"

Dirt and dust cakes her face around her eyes. She's wearing a set of blue surgical scrubs with filthy, once-white Keds sneakers, and, strangely, some kind of black fabric wrapped in a tangle around her neck like an oversized scarf. One of those headwrap-things women over there wear? I dunno. I doubt she's changed those scrubs in days, if not longer. And not that I mind, but she smells like she's gone for who knows how long without a shower.

Her eyelids flutter and her eyes flicker with life, with thought. "A bath. Yes, please." Her green gaze flicks to mine. "Riley, I…"

I kiss the knuckles of one hand. "Hush, baby. I've got you."

She seems to sag at my words, as if whatever strength has kept her intact thus far is fading fast. "So tired."

"Let's get you clean." I brush filthy, tangled hair out of her eyes—the rest is bound up in a tight knot at the top and back of her head, out of the way. "Can I leave you here for a second while I run the bath?"

Panic fills her eyes at the suggestion. "No!"

"Okay, okay, it's okay. I've got you. C'mon." I stand up with her and carry her into the bathroom, sit on the toilet lid, and run the hot water. Once it's running so hot it's steaming, I add some cold water until it's piping hot but tolerable and then sit with her while the tub fills. Once it's nearly full, I stand up and set her on her feet.

"I'm not going anywhere," I assure her. "We're just getting you out of your clothes."

She nods, standing motionless. I unwrap the black scarf-thing from her neck, and she grabs it, clutches it in shaking hands. "Fatima. Duwana." Names, I think.

I let her hold onto it, whatever it is, as I kneel and untie her shoes. She balances with one hand on my back as I tug her shoes and socks off, one foot at a time. Tug her scrub bottoms off. Her top. She lets me unknot her hair from the bun, and it collapses in a cascade of kinked waves. I feel nothing but worry for her as I peel her out of her sports bra and panties—she's lost weight, and she was fairly slender to begin with. She's not emaciated, but it's clear she didn't eat properly over there.

I help her step into the water, and she sets the black thing aside onto the toilet lid and slowly sinks down to her butt, drawing her knees up to her chest. Her eyes go to mine, and she grabs my hand. "Riley. Please." She tugs me toward the tub. "Please."

Fuck, she can't even form sentences.

"Okay, I'll get in with you."

I strip and climb in with her. The water overflows with a splash, but I put down towels just in case. Not that I care right now, anyway. She ducks under, comes up wiping her eyes, hair spreading on the water like ink, then lays back, putting her back to my front, pulls my arms over her chest, and rests her cheek against my arm.

After a while, I use my foot to drain some of the water and then turn the hot water on to refill and warm it up.

We sit like that for a long, long time.

"Can we get out?" she whispers, eventually. "Cold."

"Of course. Let me get towels."

She watches me, never taking her eyes off me, as I climb out and towel myself off, wrap it around my waist, and grab another. Help her to her feet and step out. Scrub her dry, squeeze most of the water out of her hair—it's so thick, though, it'll take hours to dry completely.

She shivers as I help her to the bed. She discards the towel as she climbs under the covers, eyes on me as I circle the foot end and climb in next to her, tossing the towel aside.

As soon as I'm in with her, she surges against me, tangling herself up with me as if she can't get close enough. "Need you."

"You've got me, baby. I'm here. I'm not going anywhere. Not for as long as you need."

Her cheek on my chest, she's already fading. "Forever. Need you forever."

"Then that's exactly what you've got."

A minute of silence, then five. "Riley Crowe, Three Rivers."

"Hey," I whisper. "You're home. You're safe. You're with me."

She startles, cranes her neck to look up at me. "Home."

"Yeah," I murmur, kissing her wet hair. "You're home in Three Rivers with me."

"No," she murmurs, tightening her grip on me in a full-body hug. "*Home*. With you." Again, she squeezes me with her arms and legs. "*You* are home."

My throat goes hot and tight at this. "Fuck, baby."

She palms my cheek. "Eyes, please?" I look at her, blinking hard as hot salt burns behind my eyes. "Will you say it now, please?" She brushes a thumb under my eyes, one and then the other.

I wonder if she realizes what she's asking, that I've never spoken those words aloud to anyone, ever, except an occasional "love you, bro," to Felix over the years. Never to a woman.

The words feel like hot, thick, hard lumps in my esophagus, like partially-chewed bites of overcooked steak.

The shattered desperation in her eyes and her voice overcome the fear and hesitation. "I love you, Cadence Creswell."

She shudders, a soft sob escaping, and she buries her face in my neck. "Riley."

"I'm here," I whisper. "I've got you. You're okay, now."

I feel her fading back down into sleep. "I love you…
Riley Crowe…of Three Rivers…"

The dam breaks, then, and I let the tears fall; there's
no one to see them.

She cannot know what that means. How it feels to
hear that.

The ferocity of my feelings for this woman in my arms
stuns me, then, as if her half-asleep murmured declaration
of love lit some kind of pilot light inside me.

⟳

I wake up; it's late afternoon. I'm stiff from being in one
position for so long, and my right arm is asleep. Cadence
is curled up against my side, more on top of me than not.
I slither carefully out from beneath her, wait to make sure
she stays asleep, and then relieve my screaming bladder.

I return to find her sitting up in bed, bleary-eyed, disoriented. "Hey," I whisper, climbing in beside her. "I'm
here."

She clings to me once more. "I am going to need time,
Riley."

"You have it. Long as you need."

She shakes her head, craning her neck to look up at
me. "No, I mean…I…I am lucid and present, at the moment, for you. So I can…explain." A pause, a hard swallow. "I am going to be out of commission for a while. I may
sleep, I may be awake, but I will not respond to anything.
I will not even know you are there. Just please know that
I am okay. You do not need to worry."

"One of those freeze things?"

A shrug of one shoulder. "Sort of. This is…deeper. I

call it a healing trance. I just…there is too much inside me. I…it is the only way I know how to cope."

"What can I do?"

"Nothing. Just be there. I will need you when I come out of it." She nuzzles under my chin with her nose. "I meant it, you know." She pulls away to meet my eyes in a rare moment of prolonged eye contact. "When I said that I love you. I meant it."

"Me too."

"Oh, I know. " She goes back to nuzzling me. "You have proven it."

"Cadie, what—?"

She covers my mouth with her palm. "Not yet. Please."

"Okay."

"Just hold me. I will tell you as much as I can when I can, but for this moment, I just need you to hold me some more. Once I enter the healing trance, I will be unresponsive. You do not need to be quiet, and you do not need to stay near me. I will come out of it on my own when my mind and body are ready."

"Okay."

Slowly, she settles, drowses, and falls asleep again. I won't be able to sleep anytime soon, though.

Eventually, I become restless and ease her off of me. She curls up away from me, sighing softly. I cover her and tiptoe out.

⚬

She wasn't exaggerating. Over the next three days, she's in and out of sleep. When she's awake, she stares at nothing, only blinking owlishly once every so often. Even if I enter the room and crouch in front of her, she doesn't register my presence.

She doesn't leave the bed. Barely stirs when she's asleep, curled up in a tight, protective ball, covers in her fists, which are balled up under her chin.

If she hadn't warned me, I'd be worried. But having seen her in a similar state before prepared me somewhat. It's how she processes things, I guess. I know she told me I don't have to stay, but I couldn't leave her here alone.

I leave a bottle of water on the table beside her, and though I never see her drink from it, the level drops consistently, so at least she's staying hydrated to some degree.

$$\mathcal{C}$$

On the morning of the fourth day, I wake up to find her sitting up, sipping water, and looking like herself again, to a degree, at least.

"Hey," I mumble, stretching. "How are you?"

"Ravenous."

I smile. "That's a good sign. Let me rustle something up. Any requests?"

"A cheese omelet?" She blushes. "Do you have bacon?"

I snicker. "Do I have bacon? Do bears—"

"Shit in the woods," she finishes with me, grinning. "Riley, I—"

I kiss her lips, a soft, quick peck; I'm not trying to start anything. God knows when she'll be ready for anything like *that*; no time soon, if I had to guess, and that's okay. "Eat first. Talk second. Yeah?"

Her eyes fix on my mouth when I pull away. "We have much to discuss. I have much to tell you."

"And there's time for all of it. But first, you need food. God knows when the last time you ate was."

She shrugs, frowning. "I…I do not know. Before the attack."

"Attack?" I echo, my heart sinking into my stomach.

Her gaze darkens. "I shall tell all, I promise."

I gaze at her, but I see that she's not ready yet. So I leave the bed reluctantly, step into a pair of jeans and shrug into a clean T-shirt, and start up a pair of omelets and a whole package of bacon, along with some toast and fresh fruit—I started keeping my fridge stocked with stuff she likes at some point—not sure why, or when I started doing it.

Despite her obvious hunger, she forces herself to eat slowly, taking tiny bites which she chews thoroughly, and takes time between bites.

When we're done, I set our plates aside and wait.

She gives me one of those slow, thoughtful, owlish blinks. "Do you have any tea?"

I nod. "Yeah, I have green tea, black tea, and a three-mint kind."

"May I have a mug of mint tea? Please?"

"Of course, sweetheart." I stand, clear our plates into the sink, fill the kettle, and get it going. While the water heats, I find the tea bag and a mug.

I lean against the counter by the stove and wait, watching Cadence. She's lost in thought, or memory, or both, her gaze fixed on the middle distance. After what feels like an hour, the kettle whistles, and I pour the boiling water over the tea bag, bringing the mug to the table.

Cadence wraps her hands around it, and I sit and wait, knowing she'll start talking when she's ready.

"I have seen many horrors in my life, Riley," she murmurs. "Starvation. Disease. Rape. Murder. War. Genocide. Accidents of all kinds. From the time I could walk, I accompanied my parents everywhere. Their mission was simpler than mine—provide medical care to those in need, and to spread the love of God wherever they went. They were not missionaries in their own minds. They were simply answering the call. They did not venture too near the more war-torn countries—for my sake, I think, but...it is impossible to avoid, over there. Or the results of it, at least."

I frown. "Not sure how I feel about the decision to let a little girl see shit like that, if I'm honest."

She wrinkles her brow, nods a couple of times. "I understand your position. In theory, for normal people, I agree. But I have never been normal. This is not self-deprecation but mere reality. You must also understand that the vast majority of the cases they allowed me to witness were fairly innocuous. Broken wrists, colds, cuts and abrasions, things of that sort. And in the few rare instances where the patients had suffered violence, they arrived unexpectedly. They did not allow me to be present for the treatment of violence until I was ten or eleven, by which point my capacity for detachment was already well established."

"Capacity for detachment?" I ask.

"Yes. It is...from a medical professional standpoint, somewhat of a superpower, you might say. It is not a lack of care, compassion, or concern, but an objectivity which allows me to view a patient from the perspective of their symptoms alone, which provides my eidetic memory the room to operate unhindered by squeamishness."

"I guess I see that."

"Emergency medicine is…it is a unique beast, Riley. Every second that passes is utterly critical. One must make split-second decisions which often mean life or death, recovery or…not. To an emergency medicine caregiver, be it an ER nurse or doctor or combat medic, pain is a symptom. An indicator."

"I don't follow."

She frowns, blinking. "We do not treat *pain*, we treat the *problem*. If I am in the ER and a patient comes in complaining of pain in his or her lower right side, pain so severe that coughing, walking, or palpitation worsens the pain, I can determine, using the location and presentation of the patient's discomfort, that the problem is appendicitis. The pain is merely a symptom, not the problem."

"Okay, I follow that."

"I cannot allow myself to be distracted by the patient's discomfort—I must treat the problem as swiftly and accurately as possible. Just so, if a patient arrives with an open femur fracture—that patient will be in excruciating pain. Yelling, screaming, howling, grunting, cursing—or, in some cases, unwisely bearing it in silence. It is obvious what the problem is in that case. But I cannot allow the fact that treatment will cause further discomfort to slow me down. I must reduce the break. I must assess whether the patient has a pedal pulse. In that second case, the presence or absence of a pain reaction assists in the determination of a pedal pulse. In emergency medicine, we use pain to triage and treat. We must inure ourselves to the patient's discomfort so that we may treat him or her or them. We cannot be distracted by their discomfort; this is detachment, and I am excellent at it. So much so that many patients find my bedside manner disconcertingly stoic. They mistake it for a lack of care. But I *do* care. I care more than I am able to express. I care so much that I will stop at nothing to treat their problem, even if it means causing them more discomfort in the short term."

"I understand now," I say. "Quick question, though– you said 'unwisely bearing it in silence. Why 'unwisely?'"

"Oh. Studies show that vocalization while experiencing pain releases endorphins and other chemicals which help the body process pain. Studies also show that doing so can even speed the healing process. I always encourage my patients to be as loud as they wish." She sighs. "Anyway. My point in telling you this as an introduction is to provide context. I worked in one of the busiest ERs in the country. I have worked in violent places all over Africa. I have seen horrors, as I have said." Her voice shakes, now. "What I saw in Sudan…" she shakes her head. "I was not ready. I did not know. I…I was unprepared."

"God, Cadence, how…how could you be prepared?"

She shrugs. "I could not. I went knowing, intellectually, that I would be…challenged…by the experience. I did not know how badly it would…" she swallows, sighs, starts over. "My capacity for detachment was strained and then broken, and then shattered completely." A long pause. "I have never required much more than four or five hours of sleep. I have what is known as the P384R mutation to the DEC2 gene, which allows one to function at full capacity on half the amount of sleep as everyone else. Just another way in which I am unique. I am used to extraordinarily long shifts. Twelve, eighteen, and twenty-hour shifts are not unusual for me. I have worked on call in the ER for days at a time, catching only cat naps here and there between rushes. I am used to it. But that? Over there?" A shake of

her head. "I was pushed beyond capacity to the point of…"
she shrugs, trailing off, unable to find the right word.

"I can't even imagine," I say.

"No, I don't suppose you can." She blinks at me. "Oh.
I…I did not mean that as a derogatory statement."

I smile, cover her wrist with mine. "I know it's true—I
can't imagine. Not any of it."

"So much death," she whispers. "So much suffering. The hospital where I was stationed was where people fleeing the fighting went to be treated. It is where the
wounded and dying were brought from miles around.
It was constant. Trucks, vans, cars, buses…they arrived
full of patients all day, every day, without cease. Women,
children, men, old men, and women. Pregnant women.
Babies. Gunshot. Stabbed. Blown up. Hacked apart. Raped.
Brutalized. Beaten. Tortured. I…there was no time to eat,
to sleep, to rest. I worked for days on end without eating
or sleeping. The nurses often had to force me off the floor.
My guards had to force me to leave the hospital for a day
or two of rest. But there was no rest. I found sleep difficult,
knowing what was happening in my absence." She sighs
shakily. "It never, ever ended. There were lulls. Times when
fighting moved farther away, and the injured were slower
in arriving, or in fewer numbers. But it was never none.
We were always short on rooms. I treated more patients
in the hallways than I did in the rooms. I removed bullets
while the dying watched from their gurneys. I lost more
patients than I saved, I think. I do not know how true that
is, but that is how it feels. That I…that I failed. Again and
again and again."

She sniffles.

"You will lose patients," she says. "It is a certainty.

You will make mistakes. You will fail. But I…I received so many patients who were beyond saving. One must still try, however."

Her eyes fill, shimmer, and then tears spill over and trickle down her cheeks unheeded. "I lived a whole lifetime over there, Riley. I fear I…I will never be the same."

My throat is hot and tight again. "Cadie…"

She smiles weakly. "I will be alright. I will seek therapy for the PTSD. And…" She swallows as she gazes at me. "Being here, with you…that will help more than just about anything."

"Anything I can do, Cadie, *anything*."

"I know." She smiles again, brushing tears away with her knuckle. "Understanding and patience and love—that is what you can do, and I know down to my soul that I will receive it from you."

"You will. I promise."

"Now we come to the hardest part to relate." She inhales deeply, filling her lungs and holding her breath, and then letting it out slowly through pursed lips. "In the weeks before my departure, we could hear fighting in the distance. The influx of patients increased by the day, and then as the fighting grew closer, by the hour. The gunfire and explosions came without cease, all day and all night. I often wondered where all the munitions came from that the fighting could carry on for so long without stopping."

She stops, staring at nothing.

"And then…the fighting came to our city. It washed over us like a tsunami. It surrounded the hospital. The wounded came not in vehicles but were merely carried in from the street. We ran out of beds. I treated patients on the floor. On counters. In closets. We ran out of bandages, painkillers, plasma, everything. Day after day…two days, three. I…there was no stopping. I do not really remember much of those days. Just fragments. Faces. Injuries. The floors were swamped with pools of blood the orderlies could not work fast enough to clean away. We slid and tripped like baby deer on an icy lake." My gut clenches at her description; I cannot fathom it. "The fighting came to the hospital itself. The whole building shook with explosions. Stray bullets ricocheted through windows and floors and walls. Everywhere you looked, it was…it was just…dead people. Dying people. People I could not save. I remember a little boy. He was so afraid, and I could do nothing but hold his hand as he died."

"Cadence, my god. My god."

"I was closest to Duwana. Here, we would have called her the charge nurse. She…she wanted me to leave before the whole city was overrun. I couldn't. How could I leave when so many needed help? But I…I think I had been awake and working for something like four days straight by then. I could not think. I couldn't…and Duwana and Fatima and my guards, they…they…they brought me to an exit and put me in a truck. I hardly knew what was happening to me. I…" she swallows hard, seems to realize she has the mug in her hands, and takes a sip. "I heard your voice. In my head. You told me that I'd done all I could, that it was time to come home, that dying in Sudan wasn't my mission." Her eyes go to mine in that rare gift—direct, prolonged eye contact. "I think in some ways, Riley, I came home for you."

My heart squeezes, the hot knot in my throat pulsing in time with my heartbeat. "Glad you did, sweetheart."

"I *left* them, Riley," she whispers.

"You're not God, honey," I murmur, holding her wrists. "You can't save everyone."

"Duwana said the same."

"Sounds like a smart lady."

"I came to love her as a sister."

Silence.

She sips her tea and stares at nothing for a long time, and I just sit with her.

"I thought of you every day," she whispers. "I missed you so much it hurt."

"Been a fuckin' wreck without you," I admit. "Worried about you. Missin' you."

She hesitates. Her eyes flit to mine, drop, and flicker back to mine. "I dreamed of you, also." Her cheeks flame red. "I dreamed of…of what we shared."

I can't help grinning at her. "I did too."

She tenders a small, shy smile. "You did?"

"Of course." I reach for her, and she lets me pull her out of her chair; I lift her onto my lap, legs perpendicular across mine. "C'mere."

Her hands flutter in her lap like restless starlings, and her gaze searches my face, her chest rising and falling in the swift rhythm of nervousness.

I frame her face in my hands. "I did a lot more than just dream about you, Cadence. I missed you like fuckin' crazy and when I tried to fall asleep, some nights what we shared was all I could think about. You, givin' me the gift of your beautiful, perfect body. Lettin' me kiss you. Lettin' me touch you. Lettin' me show you how things should be."

She bites her lip. "I have a confession I must make to you. But I am…afraid. Or, no, not afraid. Only nervous."

I think I have an idea what she's about to say. I tilt

her face up to mine and kiss her, softly, sweetly. "Tell me, sweetheart."

"The longest period I spent away from the hospital was three days. There was a lull in the fighting. I do not know why, only that Duwana convinced me to go so I could try to rest. She assured me she would send word when I was needed. I...at first, I could not sleep. Whenever I tried, I saw...bad things. I showered, and that helped a bit. But still, all I could see when my eyes closed were bad things. So I...I thought of you. Of how you made me feel. I thought of you kissing me. Removing my clothing. Touching me. I thought of you..." her voice drops to a whisper I have to strain to make out, "naked. I thought of you, Riley." Her eyes flit to mine. "And I...I touched myself, the way you did. When you...when you gave me such wonderful, amazing, beautiful orgasms. I touched myself. I gave myself an orgasm while thinking of you, and I was able to sleep. And then...thereafter, it was the only way I could fall asleep. To think of you, and...and...do that."

I grin and then laugh out loud. Before she can say anything, I pull her closer, lips to her ear. "I'm glad, Cadence."

She pulls away to look at me in shock. "You are?"

"Yes. I'm glad that I could help you sleep when you needed to, even if I couldn't be there in person." I swallow, the grin fading. "I did the same thing, but I..."

She catches my hesitation. "What, Riley?"

"I couldn't. I couldn't come. I...I felt like I was using you. It just...I dunno. I couldn't."

She frowns. "But you are glad that I did?"

"Yeah." I shrug. "So?"

"So would you not think I should be glad in the same way?"

I nod. 'Sure. That's logical enough. But I never said what I felt was logical." I brush a thumb under her eyelid, wiping away a stray glimmer of tears caught on her lower lashes.

She searches me again, hard, and for a long time. "So in the time I have been gone, you have not…"

I shake my head. "Nope. Well, not since October. I…I would wake up thinking about you, dreaming about you, and I'd be hard, y'know? And I'd jerk off, but it…it never helped. I'd just feel weird and…guilty, I guess. Because you're…you're special, Cadence. What we shared together, that was precious to me. I've…." I swallow hard. "I've been with a lot of women. Had a lot of…fun. But none of it has ever really…*meant* anything the way it did with you. And I just…I had to stop. Because it just…it wasn't…it didn't feel right."

"Is that a long time for you to go without…that?" she asks.

I nod. "Yeah. It is."

"I wish I could have reassured you that it was alright with me," she says, caressing my jawline.

"Doesn't matter anymore. You're here now." Her mouth opens and I touch a finger to her lips. "You've been through hell, honey. I'm here to help. To do anything I can to be there for you, however you need. I know it may be a while before you're ready for anything physical. I don't want you to waste a single second thinking about that or worrying about it. I'm here whenever you're ready—no matter how long that takes."

She frowns, looks away, thinking. "I am conflicted on that score."

"How so?" I ask.

She shifts on my lap. "I…I do not know how long I…" she sighs, frustrated. "I am struggling to put things into words." Her eyes go to mine, and I see boldness and determination written in her features. "I feel intense desire for you. I need to…to…to share our bodies once more. To feel the comfort of your arms. I want to kiss you. I want to…" her voice drops to a whisper. "I want to forget the last six months. Just for a little while." Her eyes seize mine, fiery and fierce and bold. "I need you, Riley. But part of me feels guilty for that. Duwana and Fatima and the others… they suffer who knows what. I left. I came home. But they have nowhere to go. They suffer while I think of making love with you."

My whole being jolts at her words. My heart manages to leap and sink at the same time. "Cadence, honey, I…I don't know the answer to that. I understand the conflict you're feeling. I don't know your friends, Duwana and Fatima. But they cared enough about you to basically *make* you leave. And if that's true, then I think maybe they wouldn't begrudge you finding comfort after what you've been through." I touch my forehead to hers. "I just don't want you to feel like I'm trying to convince you of anything."

"I don't."

"Can I ask you something?" I say.

"Of course."

"You've used contractions a few times, recently."

She nods. "I wondered if you noticed."

"What's that about?"

"It is hard to explain. The way I speak, as I believe I have already told you, comes from my choice of reading material as a child and how my brain processes information.

It is also, to a degree, a choice. I always felt different. An *other*. An outsider, or outcast. So, especially in the time I attended public schools here in the States, I chose to embrace my uniqueness. I do not know if you can comprehend what I mean when I say this, but speaking formally and using archaic speech devices became a kind of armor. I cannot explain it any better than that. By speaking this way, I... feel protected against my own strangeness. Circular logic, perhaps—using my own odd ways as protection against itself. Said out loud that way, it makes no sense."

I shake my head. "No, I get it, I think. Sort of. It puts space between you and everyone else. They're gonna make fun of you and not understand you anyway, so by setting yourself apart, you sort of...rise above the hurt of it."

Her smile is shimmery. "Yes. Precisely." She cups my jawline again. "You *do* understand me."

I snort. "Not fuckin' hardly, babe. You're complex as hell, and I could spend a fuckin' lifetime trying to understand you and not come close. But the process of trying is its own reward."

"No one, other than my parents, has ever even tried."

"Losers."

She sniffs a laugh. "That is not nice. Not everyone possesses the courage you do."

I frown. "Courage? Getting to know you is a goddamned *privilege*, Cadence. Trying to understand you and learn...*you*, it's...it's not courage. It's selfish."

This time, her laugh is sniffled, wet and emotional. "Oh, Riley. There is truly no one else like you. No man I have ever known is your equal." Her eyes search me, and her fingers tease along my jawline, trace my lips. "And I believe you are correct. Duwana would urge me to find comfort and peace wherever and however I may."

She turns in my arms, straddling me on the couch. My breath hitches, and my heart pounds. The need to kiss her, to fill my hands with her curves, is overwhelming. Debilitating. Excruciating to resist. Yet, until I'm sure of what she wants, I have to let her lead.

"I—"

She cuts me off with a kiss. "I choose to find my comfort in *you*, Riley." Her words are whispered against my lips. "Help me forget. Please."

17

Cadence

GUILT IS A BITTER PILL LODGED IN MY THROAT. My pulse is frantic.

I realize I never finished explaining the contractions issue. "My time in Sudan stripped me of my defenses against the world," I murmur. "There was no me, no judgement, no mockery—there was only the work. I didn't speak the language, so Duwana was my translator, and time was always our most precious commodity, so learning to shorten my phrases was imperative. I had to speak more simply, more swiftly. And also, I think with you, I feel no need to shield myself because I know I am safe with you. I trust you."

"I *like* how you talk," he whispers. "I don't want you to change a single goddamn thing about yourself."

Desire is a deep, dark pool within me, swirling with currents which threaten to suck me down into the depths. I surrender willingly. I give myself to the desire.

For a moment, I see Duwana in my mind's eye. She stands watching me depart in a cloud of dust. Fatima is beside her. I see Duwana raise a hand in farewell—smiling.

I do not know if I will ever see her again, but I know she would be happy that I am back with Riley once more.

Boldness fills me. I know Riley is concerned for me, and not without reason. I know that my road to recovery, mentally and emotionally, will be a long one. I am not suddenly cured of my PTSD merely by spending a few days in a quasi-vegetative state. Being with Riley will not affect a cure either. But both are a start. A place to begin.

He will be hesitant. Reticent to press me into anything I am not ready for. What I do not know how to verbalize is that I *am* ready.

For him.

For us.

I will have to show him what I want. I have dreamed of this for so long—every time I closed my eyes, I saw this.

Now it is real.

He is real.

His body is huge and hard beneath me. His eyes are pale, glittering, piercing blue, steel and ice. His big, strong hands rest on my thighs, low, near my knees, as I sit astride him on the couch. There is so much I want, but to start, I need his kisses.

The rest will follow, I know.

"Riley," I whisper, his bearded jawline in my hands. "Will you kiss me?"

He grins. "Fuck yes."

He slides fingertips along my temples and into my hair, over my scalp. This touch is gentle, soft, tender. My heart flutters at the delicacy of his touch, as if I am made of glass. I cast a quiet breath upon his lips as they near mine— one of long-simmering desire and bated need.

And then he is kissing me. His mouth is wet and hot, his lips strong and soft. He commands my mouth with his, demands and devours, quests and invites. I part my lips for him and accept his tongue, relishing the taste of him, his breath tangling with mine. I dreamed of kissing him for so long that the reality is nearly overpowering in its intensity. I whimper as his tongue sweeps through my mouth, inciting arousal in every fiber of my being. I feel my skin tingle and tighten as his hands skim up my thighs—I am clad in the T-shirt he wore yesterday and left discarded on the floor—and nothing else. I do not have any clean clothes, and putting dirty clothes on—panties in particular—after bathing is something I simply cannot do. Riley's shirt is different—it smells like him, comfortingly so.

I shift closer to him, and the denim of his jeans scrapes roughly against my inner thighs. For some reason, rather than the near-agony I would feel wearing the material myself, in this context it is…arousing. But then, I think in my state of desire, everything would be arousing.

His hands continue their slow, careful journey up my thighs; I pull away from the kiss, panting, as his touch reaches the place where my thighs bend and crease; when I told him I was hungry, he left me in the bed to begin cooking for me. He did not witness me dressing, so I do not believe him to be aware of my state of undress beneath the shirt. I did, however, catch the way he looked at me when

I entered the kitchen in his shirt: approval, attraction, his gaze stuttering and lingering on my bare legs.

It felt very nice to be looked at with desire. To be *seen*.

To feel like a woman once more. Not a doctor. Not an American. Not a white person.

Just…me.

His eyes widen as he carves his hands up to my hips, discovering more bare skin rather than the cotton of underwear.

"Cadie, sweetheart," he murmurs, his thumbs roaming the tender, silken skin where my hips crease. "Forgot somethin'?"

"No, I did not."

"No?"

I shake my head, smiling down at him, curls bouncing. "For one thing, I have nothing clean to put on."

"That's the reason, is it?" he asks, mischief and teasing on his face.

"No," I say. "That is not the only reason."

"Oh no?"

"No." I slip my hands under his shirt at the neck, biting my lip on a grin as I scour the hot skin of his neck and upper back. "I woke up afflicted with the most potent desire."

"Afflicted, were you?"

"Oh yes. Afflicted."

He tugs at the hem of the shirt I wear, freeing it from between my buttocks and his legs. "If it's an affliction, does that mean there's a cure?"

"Yes, certainly," I murmur, removing my hands so I can lift his shirt up and rip it off, toss it aside to the kitchen floor. "You."

"Me?"

"You are the only cure." I kiss him. "*This* is the cure." I roam his broad, hard shoulders, the bulge of his pectoral muscles, his thick arms. "*This* is the cure." Heat flames in my cheeks, but I feel nothing except need, bold and wild and fierce; I cup the hard wedge behind the cold metal of his zipper. "*This* is the cure."

"Fuck, baby," he growls, tearing his shirt off of me, leaving me naked. "You're a goddess."

My heart swells to bursting, and I am afire with desire, with need...with love. In this moment, at least, there is nothing but us. Everything else is out there, beyond these walls. Beyond his arms.

"You make me feel like one," I whisper.

"Good. You *should* feel like one."

He slumps back and gazes at me, letting his eyes roam my naked form. He studies me greedily, taking in my face, my hair, my throat...my breasts, lingering there as if hooked, dipping down to my belly, my thighs, the shadowed space between them.

"So fucking beautiful," he breathes, and I am not certain the words were even meant for my ears, but were torn from his soul by the mere sight of me; my blood sings. "You wet for me, honey?"

"I do not know," I answer, lying through my eager, mischievous smile. "Perhaps you should find out."

"I think I will." He lifts, leans into me.

His hand cups the back of my head and pulls me down into a kiss, and this one is rough with need. The exquisite delicacy of earlier is gone, replaced by ravenous need. His mouth is hungry, and he nips my lower lip hard enough that I squeak in surprise—but the squeak becomes a growl so low and feral it startles even me. I follow it by scraping my nails through the beard along his jaw.

"I like this," I whisper. "Very, very much."

"You do?" he murmurs. "Wasn't sure how it'd go with your sensory issues."

"It is sweet of you to consider that," I answer. "My sensory issues find it delightful." I grip the beard and use it to pull him to me, and I kiss him, scour his mouth with my tongue, giving in to every urge without hesitation. "It makes you look rugged *and* distinguished."

He chuckles. "Distinguished? That's a new one." The laugh fades, and he cups the back of my head and tilts me backward.

I give him my weight, trusting him to hold me. He dips me to a forty-five degree angle and leans over me, supporting me with one hand and cupping my breast with the other, offering it to his greedy mouth. I whimper as his lips brush my erect nipple, and then gasp when he flicks his tongue against it. His beard is rough and scratchy yet still somehow soft against my flesh, creating a maddening juxtaposition of sensations. If I were not wet before, I am now. He suckles my nipple, and heat slams through me, tightening behind my belly and swelling into wetness leaking from my folds.

I arch my back, push my breast against his mouth, clinging to his nape with both hands. He slides his lips to my other breast, worships there with lips and tongue and breath. Riley lifts me upright and then stands, taking me with him. I wrap my legs around his waist, feeling my naked sex smearing my desire against his bare, hot belly, and I cling to his shoulders and bury my face in the side of his neck, taste flesh as I kiss him there greedily, and then kiss his throat, rough stubble below the neckline of his beard like sandpaper on my lips. He groans, tips his head back to offer me access, which I eagerly take, kissing his throat, his jawline, behind his ears, his temples. He grips my bottom with greedy hands, groaning and growling as I kiss his cheekbones, his eyelids, the side of his nose, the tender strip of skin between sideburn and the tragus of his ear.

"Need to taste you, Cadie," he murmurs.

I feel wild, frenzied with desire—need for Riley is a volcanic heat in my core, spreading like wildfire to my extremities, short-circuiting my brain so my need for his body, his touch, his kisses, his heat and muscles and hardness and intoxicating masculine brawn take over all of my higher functions.

"Please," I whisper, my lips moving against the shell of his ear, hissing against his helix. "Taste me. Take me. I need you, Riley Crowe of Three Rivers."

He pivots on his heel and marches toward his bedroom, kicking it closed with a loud slam that makes me jump in his embrace, giggling as he snarls against my cleavage. And then I am airborne, hurled bodily onto the bed. The mattress greets me, bounces me weightless for an instant.

Riley covers me before I can bounce a second time, anchoring me to this world before I float away on clouds of joy, so happy, so eager am I to be reunited with the man I love.

I can hardly believe that to be the truth, that I am so blessed as to have Riley in my life. To be able to call him the man I love. I'd all but given up on ever finding love, and then it finds me—*he* found me—when I least expected it.

I cup Riley's face as he hovers over me. My eyes burn

with unshed tears of pure, overwhelmed emotion. "I am *so* grateful for you, Riley," I whisper. "You have changed my life. You have changed me. You are the greatest blessing I have ever known."

He barks a huffed laugh of disbelief, squeezing his eyes shut and pressing his face against my breastbone. "Fuck, honey. You're killin' me."

I feel something hot and wet on my skin; frowning, I pull his face up so he has to look at me. He tries to pull away, to hide. I refuse to let him.

"Riley, you *may not* hide from me." I cup his face in both hands and kiss his eyes, tasting salt—kiss and kiss and kiss his eyes. "Trust me, Riley. *Show me*. Please."

He opens wet eyes and looks at me. His voice is thick and low. "Fuck." He growls wordlessly, blinking hard. "Fuckin'…sissy shit."

"Stop that!" I snap, and then soften my voice. "There is *nothing* stronger and manlier than a man who can weep when he feels powerful emotions. It is a gift, Riley." I kiss his damp, hot eyes again and again. "Trust me with all of you, as I trust you with all of me. I have given you everything I feel. My worries, my fears, my tears, my silence, my weirdness. Do you love me less for any of that?"

"Fuck no," he growls. "Of course not."

I palm his cheek, brush a thumb under his eye. "Then why should I love you less for the same? Because you are a man? Are men not humans, Riley Crowe? Do you not feel sorrow? Do you not feel joy?"

"Yeah, but—

"Then, if you love me, you will bless me with *all* of your emotions. I do not want only the good ones, or the ones our society has labelled *manly* ones. I want *all* of you. So do not hide your tears. Not from me."

"You wanted to be distracted, not burdened by my dumb shit."

"Nothing about you is dumb shit!" I protest vehemently, cupping his nape in a strong grip. "Nothing! This is what I need. This is what I want. You and me. Together." I cling to his waist with my legs. "Now." I cup his face in both hands and kiss his lips. "Share your heart with me, my love."

He chokes on the last two words. "I never wanted to fall in love," he whispers. "I fought it fuckin tooth and nail my whole life."

"Why?"

"Because I saw what it did to my parents," he answers. He sees the question in my eyes, sighs, starts over. "As a little kid, my parents were in love. They laughed together and were playful. They took Fee and me to the park and whatever. I have a few pretty vivid memories from that time. Mom in the kitchen, laughing like a crazy woman as Dad chased her around the island."

I push at his shoulder, and he topples to his side, tucking me against his waist and chest. "What happened?"

He shrugs. "I don't know. It just…soured." He sighs, and I can feel him thinking. "I'm only guessing, but I think it started when Dad got hurt on the job. Freak, stupid accident. His foot slipped as he was climbing down from a bulldozer. It was a wet, cold, rainy day in October, I think. Maybe November? Hard to remember since I was only, like, seven or eight, maybe. I just remember the house phone ringing and Mom freaking out. Must've been a Saturday, since Fee and I were home. Something happened to Dad, she said." He is quiet a moment, and then resumes. "His foot slipped and he fell. Landed on his back and fucked it up. I'm sure you can guess where it went from there."

I sigh, bitterly aware indeed where this story goes. "He was prescribed an opioid."

"Ding-ding-ding," he mutters. "Got it in one. I'm puttin' this together from hindsight, mind you. Back then, all I knew was Dad got hurt and he wasn't the same. Weird moods, mood swings. Angry one second and way too mellow the next. Then the fighting started. Mom yelling at Dad, Dad yelling back. One of 'em would storm out, usually Dad. It got *really* fuckin' bad. The fights got seriously ugly. Dad would come back stinking of booze and stumbling around. Mom would lay into him. He'd slap her, she'd hit him back. Sometimes Mom hit first—just so you don't think it was all Dad. It wasn't. Mom was…I dunno. Maybe she got into drugs too. I dunno. Maybe it was just Dad fucking with her head. She just…she turned *mean*. Really, really fuckin' mean. To Dad, to Fee, to me. To everyone. She just…soured. Everything soured. I think eventually Dad kicked the pills, but he never kicked the booze. But by the time he got off the pills, it was too late for the marriage, I'm thinkin'. Too much nasty shit had happened between them. And it just…escalated."

"My god, Riley. I'm so sorry."

A sigh, a shrug. "Yeah. My memories after Dad's accident are all centered around them fighting. Dad coming home at three or four in the morning, wasted, and Mom greeting him by hucking plates at him, or mugs, or silverware."

I blink into the silence, stunned. "She threw things at your father?"

"Fuck yes. Anything she could get her hands on. Fortunately for Dad she had shitty aim, but she'd catch him once in a while. They'd just scream and scream and *scream* at each other. Fee and I would huddle under the blankets in Fee's bed and try not to hear. Eventually, Fee got his hands on one of those tiny radios and when they started up he'd turn on the radio and we'd listen to music or a football game instead of the screaming."

"You have not mentioned either of your parents until now," I say. "So what happened?"

I hear him suck in a long, deep breath, hold it, and let it out with a growl. "Mom happened. I don't know what prompted it, other than she'd finally had enough of Dad's shit and decided to do something about it. Dad came home from work one evening. Fee was fourteen and I was twelve, I think. We were at school for football practice, as I recall, so we didn't witness it, but we got the story from neighbors and the cops."

"The police?" I breathe.

"Oh yeah. When I say it got ugly, I mean really fuckin' nasty. Dad came from work at the usual time. A UPS truck was parked on the curb, but that wasn't super unusual, as Mom had a bad spending habit, which was a constant factor in their fights. Point of interest here is that our usual driver was…not a friend of Dad's, exactly, but someone he'd known all his life. He walked in after work, cracked a beer, and headed to their room to change. Found the UPS driver fucking Mom. She calculated that shit, Cadence. It was no accident. He walked in and there was Mom on all fours, facing the door, taking Bert the UPS guy's dick from behind. I mean, he was pounding away like Ramjet the Rookie, to hear Dad tell it."

"My god. How cruel."

"Stupid, is what it was. Bert was five-eight and a buck-thirty soaking wet, nerdy, weak, and soft. And Dad… well, you've met Fee, and obviously you know what I look like. Those genes came from Dad. He was a fuckin' monster. Six-two, two-ten, and even after the accident and the pills and the booze, he was built like a goddamn linebacker. He had this party trick he used to do. He loved walnuts. He'd buy bulk bags of them in the shell, and he'd crack the shells with his bare hands."

"It did not go well for Bert, I imagine," I say.

"No, it certainly did not. Dad hospitalized him. Almost killed him, and that's no exaggeration. Mom had to call 911 and it took four cops to pull Dad off the poor fuck. Bert spent weeks in the hospital and had to have reconstructive surgery on his face and eventually left town. Dad spent two months in jail for aggravated assault and battery. When he got out, he filed for divorce. Started drinking harder than ever." He growls another irritated sigh. "Divorce wasn't the end of it, either. Mom dragged her heels. Fought over every little thing. Custody, alimony, everything, just to be a bitch. Just to fuck with him. Drew it out for years. She got an apartment in town and we'd spend weekdays with her and weekends with Dad, and they'd talk shit about each other to us. Mom would tell us all sorts of shit about Dad. How small his dick was, that he was nothin' but a drunk and pill junkie and wife-beater. And then we'd get to Dad's house on the weekend and he'd do the same thing. His favorite thing to call Mom was a cheating whore. I never once heard him refer to our mother after that as anything other than 'the whore,' or 'that cheating whore bitch.' Shit like that. Wasn't just her, though. All women were all cheating whores. Turned him into a cruel, hateful asshole who belittled any woman he encountered. He'd take us for breakfast on Saturday mornings, and he'd be so mean to the waitress that she'd be crying when we left. Taught Fee and me not to trust women. 'Don't trust anyone,' he'd tell us all the time, 'but especially not women.'" He sighs. "He'd get drunk and make us promise we'd never fall in love, never marry. Women were nothing but cheating, scheming, faithless, loveless whores and sluts who'd only break our hearts and ruin our lives." He sounds so angry, so bitter. But he's also not done.

"Once Mom finally got sick of dragging out the divorce, she took half of his money, forced him to sell the house we'd grown up in for her half of that, signed over custody to him, and fucked off. Never saw her again. Never heard from her again. That *really* fucked with Fee and me." He goes quiet, his hands gently roaming my back and shoulders, scratching and smoothing in alternation—so gentle and loving, at odds with his harsh words. "Fuckin' bitch just took off without a word. We got off the bus after school on Monday, went to her apartment...and she was gone. I was bitter about that for a long, long time."

"You still are," I murmur.

"Yeah, probably. I mean, who the fuck *does* that? What kind of person abandons her boys without a fucking word of goodbye? She just *discarded* us like we were trash." He swallows audibly. "Dad never let up the shit-talking, even after she left. He'd get wasted and just rant and rant and rant about her. About women. About love being a fuckin'...a fuckin' lie. Hard not to absorb that, y'know? I...I can admit now that once I started to get interested in girls, I...I'd internalized Dad's poison. Treated the girls I hooked up with like shit, for the most part. Used 'em, didn't…didn't appreciate them. And then I went to prison, and that sorta… hardened me a bit. Like, after all I'd seen growing up, and then being an ex-con without a high school diploma, the guilt I felt, the shame, pile all that on top of Mom's betrayal of Dad and the shit-talking and then abandoning me? You couldn't have paid me enough to trust a woman. I didn't lie to you, though—I never lied to them or manipulated them, I just…didn't trust 'em."

"Riley," I whisper. "I…I didn't know."

"Course not," he answers. "How could you?"

"So…what changed?"

He shrugs. "Time, to start with. Last couple of years leading up to Bear's release from prison, I'd started to feel…I dunno, discontent. Restless. The girls I dated— well, dated is a loose term, but you know what I mean—"

"I do not, as a matter of fact," I cut in.

A sigh. "I mean it wasn't dating. I wasn't trying to get close to them, emotionally. It was…sex. And companionship. Someone to talk to once in a while. But I never let them anywhere near my heart. Either I dumped them when they started acting like they wanted more from me emotionally, or they got sick of my emotional unavailability, and they dumped me. It was a cycle. Meet, fuck, fight, move on. I got tired of it. And then Bear happened."

I frown into the morning light. "Bear happened? I do not understand."

"Bear spent a decade in prison for a crime he didn't commit. He was part of my work-release program. Two years, he got early release through the program, and I did what I do—got him a place, a spot on my crew, the usual. But he was different. He met this girl named Noelle and she saw something in him, I guess. Saw beneath the giant exterior, the rough shell of who he thought he was. Saw a good man inside him. Wasn't hard, because Bear *is* a good man, even after what he went through. I watched her change him from the inside out. He started to believe in himself. I…"

He chokes again. Shudders.

Starts over. "The way she looked at him, Cadence? The way she touched him. So gentle. With just…so much fucking love, like he was…like was the only human being on the entire planet, like he hung the goddamned moon in the sky. I saw her love him. And I saw him trust her. And she…Noelle, she…she *deserved* it. Earned it. Kept it. I saw the truth, finally—that my dad was just this bitter old fucking bastard who filled me with poison because he was so goddamned miserable and refused to do anything about it. I saw what *they* had, and for the first time in fucking life, *I* wanted it."

I lift onto an elbow and gaze down at him. "Riley." It's a whisper. "It must have taken a lot of courage to admit that to yourself."

He huffs. "To be honest, yeah. It wasn't easy to admit how bitter and closed off I'd been. How much time I'd wasted acting like a fuckboy himbo hound dog asshole. Chasing ass that meant nothing. All because my mom was a bitter, angry woman, and my dad was just as bad or worse. They both poisoned me and Fee. But Fee, he figured it out first. How to let go. How to trust. Ember, she opened him up, and I saw that happen. Watched him change. He was…well, his story is his to tell, not mine, but he went through his own shit while I was in prison. Made him as bitter and closed off as I was. He never smiled, never joked, never laughed. He was just this brooding, angry guy with no more interest in love than me. And then Ember came along, and now he's happy. He's full of joy. He's a fucking Dad!"

I lean over him, relishing the way his eyes seem to gravitate to my breasts; I enjoy his gaze on my body, the obvious desire for me in his eyes, the frank appreciation. It makes me feel beautiful. Desired.

I kiss his sternum, trace his rock-hard abs. "And now?" I ask between kisses. "How do you feel, now?"

He tucks my hair behind my ears. "Lucky as fuck." His voice drops, goes husky. "I've never been in love. Never said that word to literally anyone except Felix on a couple of rare occasions. *Never* a woman."

This makes my eyes sting, my throat tight and hot. "Truly?"

"Never heard it, either."

My heart skitters, flutters. My belly heats. Desire pools hotter than ever in my core, tightens, pulses. "So, when you told me you loved me…"

His voice shakes. "I was scared outta my mind to say that. Big fuckin' step. But I do. I fucking love you, Cadence. I don't think I could have loved anyone else *but* you. You're the only person on the planet who could have reached my heart like you have."

I shimmy closer to him, crush my breasts to his chest, my core to his thigh, and drape my leg over his. Rake my fingers through his hair. "I did not truly believe any man could ever fall in love with me. But you did. You…you made it safe for me to fall in love with you." Cup his cheek. "You own my heart, Riley Crowe. I love you."

His eyes well, spill over, and I kiss them, taste salt and

smile against his cheeks. "Cadie, Jesus, I…fuck." He blinks, but does not hide, this time. "God, I love you."

"Show me," I whisper. "Please."

"You mean…"

I sniffle, touch my forehead to his. Unbutton his jeans, lower the zipper—his manhood bulges into the opening. "Make love with me, Riley? Please?"

He tilts his face to mine, claims my mouth in a soft, slow, questing kiss that takes my breath away and leaves me gasping, shaking. "Cadence, I—"

I cover his mouth with my palm, smile down at him, hoping he sees what I feel: adoration, desire, readiness. "There is no doubt within me," I whisper. "I dreamed of us. Of making love with you. Not just touching, as we did before. I want it all. I have never been more sure of anything in my entire life."

18

Riley

H ER SMALL, WARM, CLEVER FINGERS SLIP beneath the elastic of my underwear; my stomach curls in by itself, and then my breath catches when she wraps her hand around my cock. Her grin as she grips me is eager, playful, hot. She wants this. Wants me. Wants us.

"There is something I believe you should know about me," she murmurs, driving her fist down my shaft in a slow slide.

I arch, groaning, and find her eyes searching mine. "Wha—whazzat?" I mumble, dizzy and delirious at how incredible her touch feels.

"A hallmark of autism is hyperfixation. I believe I have mentioned this."

"Y-yeah," I stammer, arching again as she jacks my length a few times and then slips her hand down to cup my balls. "Fuck, that feels good."

She works my jeans down, her gaze never leaving mine. "In short, it merely means I become...obsessed, some might say. As a child, it was information. Knowledge. Languages, history, anatomy, medical procedures, things like that."

I kick free, and now I'm naked with her. She's caressing my cock, slowly and gently, affectionately, as if reacquainting herself with a long-lost friend. "Fuck, sweetheart, I love the way you touch me."

"As much as I love touching you, I wonder?" She leans down and kisses my mouth, steals my breath with a slow swipe of her tongue, and then shatters me completely with a loose-gripped flutter of strokes around the head of my cock. "I believe, Riley Crowe of Three Rivers, that I am becoming hyperfixated on sex with you—" here her voice hitches, and she pauses, swallows, and continues. "You were all I could think of. That night in your truck bed. Here in this bed. The things you made me feel. The things you taught me."

I groan as she switches from light fluttering touches to long strokes from tip to root, twisting in the way that makes me crazy. "Fuck! Fuck, baby." I grab her wrist and stop her. "Cadie, honey, you keep doing that, and I'm gonna come. Been a while, and that feels fuckin' *amazing*."

She nips my earlobe. "I would be okay with that. You can be ready again in not very long, can you not?" Her grin curves against my cheek. "I want you. I need you."

"You have me, honey. And I...I want you and need

you too. I want to make love with you." I let go of her wrist. "This happens the way you want it to, okay?"

She resumes stroking my length. Kisses me, all tongue from the jump, and I growl into her mouth, rake my hands down her back to snag a rough handful of her plump, taut, perfect ass. This gets me a whimper, a squeeze of her hand around my throbbing cock. My balls boil and ache at her touch, and fuck, it's been over a month since my dick has gotten any attention, even from my own hand.

I'm on the edge and it's been a matter of minutes. Maybe I should just let her—

Whatever thought was in my head is erased when she bites my lower lip harder than expected, drawing a shocked grunt from me—she then licks the offended lip, and draws it into her mouth. Strokes my length. Cups my balls, squeezes gently, massages, kneads, rolls them in her palm until I'm writhing and groaning.

"There was one thing I dreamed of doing *almost* more than anything else," she whispers, her lips against my ear.

"What's that?" I gasp. "Show me."

She hums, a pleased, happy, aroused little sound as she watches herself pump my cock until precum leaks out of me. Without warning, she slides down my body and takes me in her mouth, her eyes locked on my face. Her strawberries-and-cream curls trail around her cheeks, obscure her mouth, and my cock. I gather her hair on top of her head and hold it, growling my arousal.

"I dreamed of doing this to you," she whispers, her eyes on my cock, now. "I dreamed of it again and again. I made myself orgasm thinking of getting to do this again. I dreamed of the way you taste. The feel of you in my mouth. The way you sound when you come for me."

"Oh god…*Cadie!*"

She hums happily again, a tuneless little melody of joy, as if nothing could be better than this. She wraps her lips around my cock again and slides her mouth down my shaft until I reach the back of her throat, and she backs away, only to drive back down again. She shifts her weight to free both hands, and now she's straddling my legs and gripping my cock in both hands and stroking me and pumping me and sucking around the head, eagerly, greedily, vigorously.

She wants me to come—hard…*now*.

I have no choice but to give her what she wants—she draws it out of me. I could no more stop it than I could lasso the sun. One second I'm arched and gasping and writhing under her touch, growling and thrusting as she greedily sucks my cock, pumping my root with both hands. And then the next second my vision goes white and my pulse roars in my ears and I can't even warn her before my orgasm detonates like an atomic bomb. I hear myself roaring and cursing, and I have her head in my hands and I'm holding on for dear life as she sucks and sucks and sucks, swallowing gulp after gulp and pumping me for more and more and more, and I'm helplessly thrusting, or trying to. When I think I can come no more, she lets me pop out of her mouth, but she's not done yet. She keeps stroking me, pumping my length, rubbing her thumb over my tip and twisting and stroking, and another wave crests through me, making me spasm as she milks it out of me with soft caresses, and when the seed dribbles out of me, she licks that away, too, humming as if the taste of my cum is the sweetest of treats.

Even after I can come no more, she toys with me, curling up against my chest and dotting kisses to my chin, my jawline, my cheekbones, caressing my cock all the while, petting and playing with me as I go slack.

When I can function again, I find her eyes. "*Jesus*, Cadie."

She grins at me. "That was even better than I'd dreamed it would be."

I laugh. "For you or me?"

"Both, I would hope."

I kiss her, tasting myself on her breath—it only turns me on even more, and I roll into her, push her to her back, and kiss her and kiss her until she's panting and writhing, and I keep kissing her. As I ravage her mouth with my tongue and steal her breath and nip her lips and suck on her tongue, I caress her breasts and her belly, flick her nipples until she whimpers, pinch them until she shrieks and then caress them with my thumbs. Carve my hand over her belly and cup her pussy.

She arches as my hand covers her mound. "Oh, please, please, *please*, Riley. Please touch me. Please give me an orgasm, my love. Please."

"You don't need to beg, sweet girl," I whisper in her ear. "But I love it when you do."

She clasps the side of my face. "Riley!" It's a gasp, a whimper. "Please—*please* touch me. I beg you. I need to feel your touch. I need you."

I slide a finger inside her and find her absolutely soaked, dripping with need. I explore the hot, wet depths of her pussy with my finger, almost immediately adding a second—she's that ready for me. She gasps as my fingers slick inside her tight, wet pussy, and then her hands rake through my hair, grip my head. And then, with wide mossy eyes drifting to mine, and away, and back to mine again, she none too subtly guides me down. "I need your mouth, my love," she breathes. "I need your tongue."

I growl in anticipation, and then I have her clit in my mouth and she's arched and shrieking already, hands gripping my head and pulling me against her greedily. I taste her, lush and sweet and fragrant and totally her—a flavor all her own, delicate and intoxicating. I lap her seam, swipe my tongue up through her folds. She whimpers, arches, and then her hips spasm with the first precursors of her orgasm. A freshet of desire spurts through her folds, and I lap it away, greedily drinking the cream of her need. She knots her fingers in my hair and grinds her pussy against my face, and I slick my fingers inside her tightness, feeling her channel squeeze me as she comes.

"*RILEY*!" She cries, arched and wracked and spasming. "Ohhh—oh my god oh my god!"

I eat her pussy and finger her through another wailed orgasm, and then she tugs me away. Pulls me up her body and wipes her palm over my face, grinning deliriously. "You have, my—um—"

I withdraw my fingers, slip them back inside her and gather her essence, draw it out and slip my fingers into my mouth and lick them clean while she watches.

"Riley," she murmurs. "I'm ready."

"You're sure?" I can't help asking.

"I told you." She reaches down and finds me hard for her, aroused at the taste of her, hardened at the way she writhes and cries out as I devour her sweetness. "I've never been more sure of anything. Make love to me. Please, Riley." She rolls over astride me, gripping me. Bends over me, lips to my ear. "You said you love it when I beg?"

"Cadie—" It's all I get out.

"I'm begging you, Riley." Her voice is low and soft and sweet and eager. "Please, please make love to me. I do not wish to wait any longer. I cannot. I'll die if you do not make love to me. Please, I beg you."

I yank open my bedside drawer and find the un-opened box of condoms. "I've had these in here since you left, hoping and praying we'd need them at some point when you came back to me. I…I wasn't sure you *would* come back, sometimes. But I…I hoped. And I…I hoped you would want me. that you'd want this. So I got them." I hold her gaze. "I have never been with anyone here. I've never had a woman in my home other than you. Not in my home, not in my bed. Never. There is only you."

She holds my eyes for longer than she ever has. "I be-lieve you. I trust you. I love you." She opens the box, re-moves a string and rips one free, puts the rest in the box and tosses the box onto the table. "Will you allow me to put this on you, please? It is something else I dreamed of quite frequently."

"Anything you want," I breathe, even as my entire body is on fire, and I have to restrain myself with every last iota of willpower I possess.

It takes everything I have to keep still. To not take over. To not flip her to her back and drive inside her.

Instead, I grit my teeth and hold absolutely still as she tears open the condom wrapper and removes the latex ring. She fiddles with it, determining which way it rolls. Fits it to my cock, and then pauses, her eyes on me. And then, grinning lopsidedly, her lower lip caught in her teeth, brows furrowed with wide, awed, innocent eyes, she rolls the condom onto me, hand over hand.

And now…she gnaws on her lip. Searches me.

Hesitant, suddenly shy after such boldness. "Riley, I...I need you to...to show me how. I...I do not know what to do and I..."

I pull her down to me and claim her mouth in a soft kiss. "I've got you, sweetheart."

She slides off of me, rolls to her back beside me, gazing at me expectantly, trembling with anticipation. "I'm not frightened," she whispers. "I am nervous but not afraid."

"I'll be as gentle as I possibly can," I murmur. "I promise."

"I cannot wait to be yours," she breathes as we face each other on our sides. "And I cannot wait for you to be mine."

I slide closer to her, slip my hand beneath her head, curl my arm around her, caressing her shoulders, her back, fill my hand with the lush swell of her ass. At my touch, she presses her hips against mine, and the pulsing iron rod that is my erection nudges her belly. I feel her awareness of it in the way her breath hitches as her mouth finds mine, and then she writhes against me, finding that eager heat once more, that wild aggression, that bold assertiveness. She slings her leg over mine, delves her tongue into my mouth and stabs her hands into my hair. Whimpers as I slip my hand between our bodies and find her slit, draw a fingertip up her seam, and find her clit.

"Riley," she gasps. "Please, please, please. No more teasing. Make love to me. Make me yours. Please, my love."

I angle into her, and she willingly, eagerly tips to her back, taking me with her, hands soaring over my shoulders and back. She welcomes me into the soft cradle of her thighs, my hips wedging them apart. Her eager hands flatten against the small of my back, and then she cups my ass in her hands, grips it, digs her fingers into the fat, muscle, and flesh. Her eyes are open wide, unblinking, fixed on my face.

I brace a hand in the pillow beside her, caress her breast, find her clit again and make her jump, gasp, flinching as her arousal pulses at my touch.

"I love you, Cadence Creswell," I say. "Now and forever."

Her eyes water, spill over, and I know they're tears of love, of joy. "Riley, my love. My love."

"Ready?"

"Yes." Her answer is simple and sure.

It's all I need.

19

Cadence

RILEY IS A HUGE PRESENCE, ALL HARD PLANES and harsh angles and soft skin and rippling muscle. Some part of me still cannot believe a man like him is mine. I've never been more glad to have an eidetic memory than in this moment—I'll be able to relive this forever.

His arm is a pillar beside my ear as he braces above me, and his hips are a hard wedge between my thighs. I grip him with my legs—to hide the way I tremble.

But then I let go. I let him see it. Feel it.

Let him feel the way my thighs shake at his presence.

"You're shaking," he whispers, concern filling his ice-blue eyes.

"Yes. But I am not afraid. I promise."

I have never wanted anything the way I want this. Never been more ready than I am for this. Even so, I am nervous. Shaky with excitement, with anticipation. I do not know what to expect. If it will hurt. I have heard that it does, but I am not afraid of a little pain. Not when I know it will be temporary, and followed by...well, what I can only hope will be pleasure that makes it worthwhile.

He hesitates another moment, reading me. He must see the truth in my eyes—I *am* ready.

He reaches between us, grips his erection, guides himself to me. Despite it all, I feel a frisson of fear as his manhood nudges my sex—this is it. After this, I will no longer be a virgin. I will be a woman. *His* woman. And I only lied a little—there is a tiny bit of fear at the prospect of pain when he enters me.

I am panting, I discover, short, sharp, shallow breaths. Riley is not breathing at all, however, his brow furrowed in concentration, in restraint. I feel his fingers at my sex, stroking my labia. His touch is gentle, soft, reassuring. And then he fits a finger to my clitoris, and I jump, gasping, at the sudden bolt of intense sensation, and the fear subsides as he begins touching me, oh-so-slowly, oh-so-gently, oh-so-softly. Circles, circles, and my hips tighten and my belly heats, and the dregs of fear are burned away in the heat of renewed arousal.

I gasp as pleasure fills me, swelling the ocean of heat behind my navel, the crushing balloon of pressure behind my sex. I feel my orgasm rising, and I close my eyes and go to meet it, fling myself headlong into ecstasy.

As I quake and shake and shudder through my climax, I feel Riley grip himself again, and his thumb presses against my seam, and then he's aligned with my entrance.

"Cadie, my love, eyes on me, sweetheart," Riley commands.

My eyes flick open in immediate obedience, and I focus on him, panting and whimpering as my climax keeps me shuddering and shaking and helplessly gyrating. "Riley," I whisper. "Oh god."

And then it happens.

My eyes fly wide as he enters me. My mouth fixes in a shocked, breathless **O**, and my entire being—the entire universe—shrinks and narrows and tunnels down into the single point where we are joined. His cock—I feel a giggle bubble through me as I think the word, feeling deliciously naughty and wickedly wanton in the best possible way—is notched inside me, splitting open my sex.

"Oh!" I gasp, a soft, high breath.

"Okay?" he murmurs.

I nod. "Yes. yes. I…" I clutch the hard bubble of his bottom, digging my nails in—he doesn't seem to mind, and indeed, it seems to arouse him when I do that. It arouses me, so it suits us both.

He shakes all over, my big, handsome Riley. Trembling in restraint. But I cannot wish this to go faster. I want to relish each second. I memorize the look on his face, the feel of his cock just inside my entrance. The tension in his body—he's quivering, his mighty muscles bunched.

And then he drives a little deeper, and a gasp is torn from me as I am filled that much more. It does hurt a little—his cock is so huge, and I feel stretched beyond my limits, an aching burn as my body struggles to accommodate this new sensation.

A flutter of panic ripples through me:

What if I cannot handle all of him?

What if it hurts too much?

What if my vagina is not big enough for him?

But then, as he holds stone-still following the second push, I understand the process. My body is adjusting. I feel the burn subside as my sex stretches around him, and the ache is all that is left—the ache of need, the ache of an orgasm I must build up to. The ache of an orgasm only Riley can give me. I tighten my grip on his bottom as I feel myself growing used to the feel of him inside me—the alien fullness, the aching burn. It is strange, but so was kissing, at first. So was the way it felt when he touched my sex with his fingers the first time, and made me come for the first time with his mouth. It was strange when I touched his cock for the first time. And all of those things I have come to love—to crave.

So too will I come to crave this, I know.

For now, I must focus on the moment.

He shakes above me, panting, sweating.

"Riley?" I breathe. "Are you…are you okay?"

"Yeah," he growls. "Just—"

"Just what? Tell me."

"Trying like hell to go slow, to be gentle. I know I'm a pretty big guy and I don't wanna hurt you."

I caress his cheek, his beard. "You aren't. I promise." I meet him for a kiss. "Keep going."

With a ragged growl, Riley arches over me, dipping his head to my breasts, pausing for breath. And then he pushes a little deeper—gives me a little more of him, and now the ache of stretching around him is a hot burn of muscles and stretched flesh, and my whole body is shaking and all I know is his cock, the way it feels filling me.

Another nudge, and I whimper—he freezes. I claw

at his backside, pull at him. Words fail me, but *that* he understands.

"Okay?" he breathes.

I can only nod, gasping. "More," I pant. "All."

His mouth fuses to mine and his tongue sweeps against mine, and he cups my face in his free hand, hooks his fingers under my head and lifts me to kiss me deeper, harder, and I give myself to the kiss, lose myself in it, and now the ache of taking him isn't pain any longer but a pleasure unlike anything I've ever known. Riley snarls into the kiss and thrusts deeper, and now his hips bump against mine, and I've taken all of him.

"Cadie," he whispers, his voice shaky. "Fuck. So... so tight." He shakes above me, and I am filled with him.

"Riley!" I breathe. "Ohhh...oh god!"

He rears back to look into my eyes. "Okay, my love?"

I answer him with a kiss, feeling a wildness burgeoning inside me—a kind of fury, but one of love, of need, of desire. I am filled with his cock, and I quake around him, my sex rippling around his thickness. I feel it pulsing inside me, throbbing. I need more. I need him to...I know not what.

But I *do* know; my body knows.

I fuse my mouth to his and devour his breath and give my body free rein. My hips tip, push toward his. This makes him groan, and he shudders, arching.

"*Fuck*!" he snarls. "I need to move."

"Show me, Riley. I'm ready. You feel—"

He nips my lip. "Tell me how I feel inside you, Cadence."

"Perfect," I whisper. "Too good for words. But I need more."

"Ah god, thank fuck," he breathes. "Fucking torture trying to stay still." He adjusts his weight, kisses me, cups my breast…

Tilts his hips away so his cock slides through my stretched-thin lips, pulling out and out and out…I think I am going to lose him, but he stops at the last instant, and now we are back at the beginning again, just the plump head of his beautiful cock inside me.

And this time, when he enters me, it is a slow, smooth stroke. All at once, I take all of him, and now…now I understand.

I understand why people become obsessed with this act. I understand why it is called "making love."

I whimper as Riley drives into me, and I tilt my hips to meet him, gleefully accelerating our union—there is only ecstasy, now, only the wild thrill of oneness. I hook my feet around his backside and use them to pull him to me, lifting my bottom off the bed to crush upward into his thrust, and I cling to him with one arm around the broad cliff-face of his shoulders and plaster my other hand to his nape, clutching tensing tendons.

He withdraws once again, and my entire being seems to clench in protest at the loss of him within me, making me crave desperately the fullness of having him inside me. I wail as he crushes into me without hesitation, arching and driving to take him, and I feel my body clutch around his cock, feel the tight heat swell and surge, expanding from my belly and sex, making my thighs shake around his waist and my arms tingle and my hands tremble.

"Cadie—Cadence," he gasps, sounding shaken, awed, overwhelmed. "You feel…fuck, you feel incredible." He braces both hands beside my face, levered over me, his eyes boring into mine. "You're so goddamned beautiful, Cadence."

I reach up and hold his jaw in my hands and hold his eyes for as long as I can, refusing to look away, to blink, to breathe as he slides into me, withdraws and slides in again, and now I feel him find a rhythm and I pump my hips against him, gasping each time he fills me and whimpering as I lose him—gasp…whimper, gasp…whimper. He groans as he thrusts, and each groan becomes a growl timed to his movements, and our sounds of exertion and ecstasy become a song, a symphony of sighs.

The heat and tightness and pressure and desperation is fire in my veins, and as Riley strokes inside me in slow, deliberate rhythm, I feel a new kind of orgasm rising inside me, this one slow and deep and gripping my body with relentless fury, stoked by Riley's cock sliding inside me, filling me, stretching me, cruising against my clit and sending sparks bursting behind my eyes.

Riley shudders, now, his muscles quavering and quaking as he pulses inside me, pushing deep and thrusting deeper, grunting roughly with each push.

He needs more. He is holding back out of concern for me.

I nibble on his earlobe and then whisper to him. "Let go, Riley."

He shakes his head, snarling softly. "I…I can't. I'll hurt you."

"You will not." I push his face away far enough that he can look at me. I give him my gaze, unflinching and honest. "I want everything you have to give me. You feel incredible inside me, Riley. I want more. I want you to be…I want to feel how badly you crave me, Riley. I don't want your control or your concern. I am strong. I will not break. I can take all of you. Stop holding back, my love. Please. Take me how you need me. *That* is my desire."

He groans, long and low, thrusting slowly and gently, almost teasingly—the way he shakes tells me this is no tease, but torture for him.

This is where my inexperience is a hindrance. A woman with more knowledge of the sexual arts might know how to encourage him to relinquish control.

I lean up and kiss him, give him my tongue and demand he kiss my breath away, and I feel him respond, feel him thrust harder, faster.

How else can I fuel the fires of his desire?

How else can I strip away his control?

I slide my legs down around the back of his thighs and clutch at his backside and pull him against me—he gives a ragged growl, and responds exactly as I'd hoped: with a harder thrust that sends heat boiling through me, swelling the pressure of my nascent orgasm to a shuddering crescendo.

"Riley!" I cry. "Please, my love! More! More!"

I pull at him with my hands and legs and he obeys, thrusting harder, faster, setting a relentless rhythm, now.

"Fuck," he snarls, burying his face in my throat. "Cadie!"

"Riley! *Yes*!" I dig my fingers in his bottom and pull harder, squeezing, gripping, clawing. "More! I need more of you! I need you, Riley. Love me, please love me more."

He shifts his weight, punching one fist into the pillow at my left ear, and holds my eyes. "Sure you know what you're asking for, sweetheart? Cause it sounds like you're askin' me to fuck you harder."

"I am," I gasp, clawing my fingers into his backside. "I *am* asking that."

"Let me hear you say it, baby." He dips to kiss me, nips my lip.

"What shall I say?" I whisper back. "Give me the words and I shall say them."

"'*Fuck me harder, baby,*'" he growls, the words scorching directly into my ear. "'Fuck me, Riley.' That's what I want to hear you say. Beg me to fuck you."

There is no hesitation in me. The words emerge from my lips—I move my mouth against his ear. "*Fuck* me, Riley. Please, *please*, my love. Show me how it feels when you fuck me as hard as you want."

My heart pounds as I say this, thrilled and shocked and ecstatic—and free.

My soul is wide open, my heart wrapped around his. Fucking is dirty, I'd always thought—crass and crude and bad.

Now I know better: he can fuck me with love, and it is beautiful.

Riley shifts his weight again, leaning back to sit on his heels. He lifts my left leg and drapes it over his shoulder, and then my right, and I feel so vulnerable like this, helpless to his will. At first, he moves as slowly and gently as he has been this whole time, thrusting into me with exquisite gentility. And at this angle, I feel him inside me differently, feel his cock in a new and exciting way. I clutch the sheets at my sides and gaze up at him with my mouth hanging open, so fraught at the new and wild fullness, the way he strokes into me, sliding against my sex in ways that stoke my orgasm hotter and hotter.

I need to touch him—I grab at his forearms and cling

to them as he thrusts faster, now. He hunches over me and bends down to kiss me as I am curled up almost double beneath him, my knees crushing against my breasts as he drives into me. I happen to glance down the length of our joined bodies, and cry out as I see his thick, hard cock glistening with my essence disappearing inside me, and for some reason, watching my sex swallow his cock is so arousing I nearly orgasm.

"Oh *god*, Cadie," he rumbles, breathless and ragged. "So fucking hot—you're so fucking sexy I can't stand it. Tell me I can fuck you, sweetheart. Please *fuck* tell me you want it harder."

I reach around the back of my thigh and find the slick, hot shaft of his cock with my fingers, find the taut, soft weight of his balls and caress him, stroke him as he slides inside me, cup his balls when he fills me to the hilt, and then trail my fingers along his shaft as he pulls out. "Harder, my love," I whimper, "please, please, please, Riley, I need you. I want it harder. I want you to fuck me harder."

He kneels tall, then, and my bottom is lifted off the mattress, and he fills me, withdraws, fills me, harder and faster. He grips my bottom and squeezes, hard, and thrusts even harder. He drives into me and our bodies meet with a loud slap of flesh cracking against flesh, his hips and belly smacking into my thighs and bottom.

"That feel good, sweetheart?" Riley demands.

"Oh yes, my love," I answer. "It feels perfect. Please, please don't stop."

"You gonna come for me?"

"I…I think so."

He shifts closer to me and now my bottom meets the bed again, but he is pressed hard against my thighs and he leans over me, into me, against me, stretched out on the bed with his hands in the pillow and he thrusts faster and faster.

"Wrong answer," he growls. "Touch yourself, honey. Let me see those fingers on your pussy."

"My—" I gasp, even as I do as he commands, pressing my fingertips to my clit.

"Your sweet, hot, wet, tight, pretty little pussy," he whispers. "Can't get enough of this pussy."

"You say such dirty things, Riley," I breathe.

"Makes you hot, doesn't it?"

"Yes," I whimper. "I like it when you say those things to me."

"You want me to talk dirty to you, baby?"

"Please, yes."

"Then you gotta talk dirty back to me."

"I…I'll try."

"You love my cock, don't you?"

"Yes!" I gasp, as he thrusts harder, faster, slapping into my thighs with a sound like applause and my fingers swirl around my clit and send heat billowing through me, ratcheting the pressure behind my sex to unbearable new heights.

"Say it, baby. Tell me how much you love my cock."

"I love it, Riley. I love your cock."

He growls when I say this. "Fuck, that's hot. Your pretty little mouth, so sweet and so innocent, saying that shit—so fucking hot." He grunts as he thrusts, rough masculine greedy sounds, and now I hear a wet squelching as he drives into me. "I know you love my cock. You want it, don't you?"

"*YES!*" I cry. "I need it. I need more of your cock."

"You sucked my cock so fuckin' good, baby," he murmurs. "You like doin' that, too, don't you?"

"Oh god...*yes*!" I whimper. "I love sucking your cock so much! I...oh god, that feels *so* good, my love. Don't stop, please don't stop."

"You love having my cock in your mouth, don't you?"

"Yes!" I wail. "I do, I really, really do."

"You love swallowing my cum, don't you?"

"Yes!"

"You love taking it all like a good girl, don't you?"

With each new demand from Riley, arousal pulses hotter inside me, swelling and surging until I do not know how much more I can take, and yet I am still touching my clitoris and I am shaking and quaking and wailing as he pounds into me, and his powerful abs contract with each thrust, and I watch my pussy swallow his cock with greedy delight.

"Yes," I answer, when I have caught my breath. "I love how your semen tastes."

He huffs a laugh. "Cum, honey. Call it cum."

I blush at this, which I realize is ridiculous, after all the other filthy things I've said. "I love the taste of your cum, Riley Crowe."

He seems to lose himself, then, head hanging as he thrusts faster and faster. "*Fuck*, baby. Your pussy is so tight, Cadie—so fucking wet for me."

"It's you," I answer. "*You* make my pussy wet. It's wet for you, my love."

He feels me spasming, then, as my flying fingers stutter on my clitoris. I feel my walls clench around him, and I know he feels it—he grunts as I squeeze him. I exert control over my vaginal muscles, squeezing as hard as I can, and he bucks when I do so, fucking into me helplessly. "I've never felt anything like this. It's never, *ever* been as good as this. Never."

I lose control as my orgasm detonates at long last. It is a nuclear explosion in my core, white-hot and furious, and there are no words for the intensity of it. I can only scream a hoarse, ragged cry as he pounds into me, and I feel my pussy pulsing around him so tightly he growls, slowing his pace. "Fuck, the way your pussy squeezes, baby. It's so good, so damn good."

I clench. "Like this?" I gasp.

He arches with a brutally hard thrust that smashes the breath from my lungs and sends my orgasm to shattering new levels of ecstasy. "*FUCK!*"

I do it again, with the same response—I feel a new wave of orgasm break open in my belly as he thrusts into me, and then again, and again, and Riley is frantic, now, frenzied and wild and I cannot look away, dare not breathe or blink so as to not miss a single second of watching Riley finally relinquishing the last of his self-control.

My orgasm wrenches me to helplessness, and now all I can do is give myself to him, holding on to his forearms as he fucks me with absolute abandon, and it is the most beautiful thing I have ever felt, ever seen, ever known. I cry out in shrill screams as he fucks me, a scream for each wild thrust, and now I feel his cock pulse inside me, and his massive, powerful muscles are sheened with a coat of sweat.

"RILEY!" I shriek.

His jaw drops open, and his eyes lock with mine and I refuse to look away, knowing his release is here. "Cadie! Cade—Cadence, oh god, oh fuck, ohgodohgod, baby, I… oh god. I love you, Cadence, fuck I love you!"

I reach between our bodies and find his balls as he pushes deep and I caress them as he thrusts deeper, lifting up and pushes closer so his thighs crush into my ass and he pushes deeper, grunting and groaning and growling and shaking all over, and then he throws his head back and shouts wordlessly, slamming deeper yet until he is as deep as my body will allow.

"Riley, look at me, my love. Look at me when you come."

His eyes snap open and he is on another plane of existence, utterly lost to his ecstasy, and I am still coming, or perhaps coming again as he finds his release inside me. "Cadence…my love, my love."

He withdraws, gasping, only to thrust into me again with a ragged, shaky exhale, his whole body trembling and sweating.

I slip my legs off of his shoulders and wrap them around his waist again, hugging him with my thighs, and pull his face to mine and kiss him until we're both panting and dizzied.

His arms shake as if he cannot support his weight any longer. His eyes are fraught, shimmering with emotion so intense words could not begin to express it all. "Cadie, I—I…"

"Come here," I whisper, pulling him down to my chest. "I know, my love. Me too."

He resists for a moment and then collapses onto me. I accept his weight eagerly, cradling him against my breasts, and I caress his scalp, his neck, his shoulders, his back, his bottom, everywhere my hands can reach as he lays upon me, gasping for breath.

"I'm crushing you," he murmurs. "But I can't move."

"You are not crushing me," I whisper. "I don't wish for you to go anywhere."

He lays in the cradle of my thighs, face pillowed on my breasts, his breathing slowing as I caress his beautiful, hard, powerful body. "I didn't know it could be like that," he whispers, after a time I do not even attempt to measure.

Hours, minutes? Who cares?

"Was that..." I trail off and try again to express the question on my mind. "For me, that was as close to heaven as one can get without dying, I think. I have never known such joy, Riley. I...I just...I can only hope I was able to please you as well as you have me."

"I'm fuckin' *shattered*, honey," he mumbles. "Can't even move."

And then, rousing himself with obvious effort, he rises to his elbows and gazes at me, tucking flyaway curls behind my ears. "I don't know the right words, Cadence. Saying that was the best sex of my life falls *way* fuckin' short. I swear I saw God."

I find a grin spreading across my face. "Truly?"

His eyes shimmer again. "You're...I...I didn't know it could be like that," he repeats. "I really didn't. I didn't know I could feel so..." he shakes his head. "I dunno— one. With you. With anyone."

"'Therefore a man shall leave his father and his mother and hold fast to his wife, and they shall become one flesh.'" I quote. "I never understood what that meant until now. Not really."

He rolls to his back and wraps me in his arms; I lose him from inside me in the process, whimpering at the loss. I cling to him, tangle myself as tightly around him as I can, legs twined with his, arm across his waist, breasts against his ribs, cheek on his chest, hearing his heart pounding, still.

We drowse, then. I feel Riley drifting into sleep, and though I am wrenched utterly limp by our lovemaking, I cannot seem to join him in sleep.

I look out the window and see heavy gray clouds drifting across the sky, and then I watch fat, thick flakes of snow swirl, a few at first, and then more and more, until the air occludes with snow, wind driven and wild.

Already, I crave Riley again. Now that I know what it is to be loved by him, to be his, to have him inside me, I crave him. Yet when I twist to look up at him, I see his face cast into innocence by sleep, and I can only smile to myself, filled with a love beyond words.

A love I can only express with my body.

It seems I shall have to wait for him to wake up.

I do so impatiently, yet contentedly—aching and sore yet needing more.

Eager to learn.

Eager to take him inside me again.

I wonder if he understands what my being hyperfixated on lovemaking with him is going to mean.

Good thing he is a powerful, virile man. He will need every ounce of stamina he has to satiate the ravenous hunger for him I feel.

20

Riley

I WAKE GRADUALLY AND THEN ALL AT ONCE— gradually drifting up from a deep, content sleep, and then all at once as I become aware of Cadence's soft, hot, naked body tangled up with mine.

I'm still shaken to the core by how intense that was. It wasn't just sex. It was making love—seems obvious, but to a guy like me, it's a *big* motherfucking deal.

I feel her eyes, crack mine open and glance down at her. She's smiling up at me, her face radiant with happiness. "Hi," I murmur.

"Hi." Her voice is soft, quiet, shy. "I have never felt so happy in my life. Thank you for giving that to me, Riley Crowe of Three Rivers."

My heart swells to bursting, as if I can contain no

more love, no more joy—so full it hurts. And yet, when she passes her palm over my belly and cranes her neck to press a kiss to my cheekbone, I am filled further yet.

"Never been this happy, either," I say. I shift and feel the condom drooping heavily. "Gotta get cleaned up."

Cadence pushes on my chest. "Stay. Please. I would like to do it."

"Um…okay?" I relax against the pillows, pile them higher behind me so I'm reclined rather than lying. "If you really want to."

"I do."

I sure as fuck don't mind the view as she wriggles away and rolls out of bed, her lush curves swaying as she moves. I feel my cock stirring at the mere sight of her as she wets a washcloth in warm water, wrings it out, and then comes back to me—her tits bounce and jiggle and sway heavily with each step, and her thighs brush around her pussy, and fuck, that pussy is so goddamned tight and wet and I want to be inside her again.

Now.

Cadence crawls onto the bed and kneels beside me, tugs the blankets off of me. She has a folded length of toilet paper in her hand, and she lays it across her thigh, slowly easing the used condom off of me and wrapping it up in the TP. And then she has my cock in her soft, small hand and she's wiping me clean with it, her touch so tender and gentle and loving it takes my breath away. She lifts it this way and that, dabbing and wiping until I'm clean. But she seems to want nothing more than to just play with me, using the washcloth to caress me.

"You do know what's gonna happen if you keep doing that, don't you?" I murmur.

Her answering smile is all the confirmation I need—she knows exactly what she's doing. "Yes, darling," she whispers. "I am quite well aware." She tosses the washcloth under-handed into the bathroom, sets the neatly folded square of toilet paper containing the used condom on the bed-side table. "One might even venture to say that I not only know what will happen, but that that is my aim."

"You, uh, sore at all?" I ask.

She smiles, shrugs. "A bit, perhaps. Not enough to hinder my need for more."

She gathers my cock in her palm, brushing the tip with her thumb, watching me as I grow in her hand.

"That so?"

"Yes. It is." She looks down at me, meeting my gaze. "There is one thing I feel you should know."

"Okay."

My cock is hard, now, and she caresses my length in her soft little hand. She gnaws on her lip as she watches her hand slide down my cock, twist up around the head, and then her eyes go to mine again. "One of the precautions I took, medically, leading up to my departure for Sudan was to go on birth control. Not…ahhh…not because I had any anticipation of having sex, obviously, but as a means of re-ducing the frequency, duration, and intensity of my periods. I took a shot which prevents pregnancy for up to a year."

I blink as I absorb this information. "Oh. Okay."

Her eyes fix on mine, frank and open and honest. "There were other reasons. In case of…well…in case anything untoward were to happen. I do not wish to think of such things at the moment—and indeed, nothing of the sort happened, please be assured of that. I just…I wanted you to know."

I hiss as she cups my balls in one hand and strokes my length with the other, arching up into her touch. "Fuck, baby. Feels so fuckin' good, the way you touch me."

This makes her grin. "Your pleasure brings me joy. Feeling you orgasm inside me…" she bites her lip. "It was nearly as powerfully pleasurable as my own orgasm."

I pull out of her grip and flip her to her back, burying my face in the sweet honey of her pussy and devouring her greedily. I have her wailing in seconds, and she crushes her thighs around my ears and grinds against my mouth, arched and bucking into my mouth as she comes.

"Riley," she pants, after her second wave of climax. "Please—please. I need you, my love."

I slide up her body; she wipes her juices off my beard and then kisses me.

"You have me," I say.

She stops me when I reach for the box of condoms. "I have a question, first."

I pause. "Yeah?"

"Are you…you are…you have only been with me… right? Since, um…?"

My heart flutters in my chest as I realize where she's going with this. "Yeah, honey. I'm clean. After the last time I…um…was with anyone, I got tested. Just to be sure. But I…I've always used protection. *Always*. But I know I'm clean. I can show you the results.

She shakes her head. "Unnecessary. I trust your word."

"Why…um, why do you ask, honey?"

She swallows hard. "Because I want…" she bites her lip, eyes shining as she looks up at me. "I don't want you to wear a condom."

"Baby, even though you're on the shot, there's still—"

She covers my mouth. "I know." She squirms, restless hands roaming my shoulders. "I know," she repeats. "Do... do you love me?"

"With all that I am."

"Would you abandon me, should...*that*...happen?"

My heart turns to stone at the mere suggestion. "*Fuck* no," I snap, angrily. I soften. "No. Never. I'll never, *ever* abandon you. No matter fucking what." I swallow hard now. "Why, though? Can you tell me why you don't want to use protection?"

"I want to be one with you—totally. I want nothing between us. I..." she frowns. "I think perhaps it is also a sensory issue. I could feel it. The latex, I mean. I didn't...I did not like the way it felt. I want your skin and nothing else."

"It's a risk, honey."

"I accept the risk, if you do."

"I..." I feel rattled. Shaken. Scared. "I've never had sex without one. I couldn't ever handle the idea of..." I shrug, fighting for the right words—trusting her with the absolute truth. "I never wanted to risk a pregnancy. I'm not—I'm not a guy who should be a father. Risk of disease was a distant second for me. I'm not that guy, babe. I've never been that guy. No one in their right mind would pick me for that."

Her eyes shine with tears. "I do."

I convulse at her words, a gutted sob wrenched out of me. "*Don't*," I whisper, turning away. "Fuck—*fuck*. You can't say that shit to me." I sit on the edge of the bed, facing away from her.

She moves behind me, breasts soft against my back, and her arms slide over my shoulders and cross over my chest, and her cheek is silk against my ear, her words soft whispers. "I do say it to you, Riley Crowe of Three Rivers."

Why am I so gutted by this? I'm fucking wrecked. Crying like a bitch. She wipes at my face. Kisses my tears.

"*Stop*!" I hiss. "You can't mean that."

"I do. I mean it down to my soul." She wraps herself around me from behind. "I choose you. I choose to love you. I know your secrets, Riley. Do I not?"

"Yes," I breathe.

"Are there any other secrets?"

"No."

"So I know your secrets. I know your guilt. I know your fears. You fear you are not enough. You fear your own inadequacy. You fear that your parents' toxic relationship ruined you."

"It did."

"Wrong." She presses her mouth to my ear. "Do you love me?"

"*Fuck* yes," I growl. "I love you so fucking much it scares the shit outta me."

"Will you hit me?"

"*Fuck* no. I'd murder anyone who hurt you."

"Would you curse at me? Call me names?"

"Never."

"Would you cheat on me?"

"I'd cut off my own dick first."

She tightens her embrace. "Do you think I would cheat on you? Hit you? Throw things at you?"

"No," I whisper. "Never."

"I love you, Riley. I choose you as you are *right now*. I love the man that you are—*right now*. I am not afraid of your past and I am eager to be a part of your future." She palms my cheek, turns my face to the side so I'm looking at her over my shoulder. Her lips meet mine at an angle. "I am fully cognizant of the risks involved in making love to you without protection. I am not ready for a child at this time in my life, either. I have my own reservations about that, to be honest."

"What reservations?"

"Passing on my autism."

"The world would be a better place if there were more people in it like you," I say.

She exhales shakily. "You truly believe that?"

"Absolutely."

She hugs me so tightly I grunt. "Every time I think I could not possibly love you more, you do something or say something and…somehow, I do."

This melts me. "Ah, god, Cadence. Same."

She leans around me, fingers trailing gently down my cheek, and nuzzles my mouth with hers. "Then show me, darling. Please."

I feel that inexorable swelling of my heart again, and I think, absurdly, of that line from *The Grinch* about a heart growing three sizes that day, and I sorta get it. What that story doesn't mention is that it kind of hurts, having your heart grow a few sizes real quick. It's a good hurt, though, like sore muscles after a killer workout.

She's hungry for me, my Cadie. Her mouth is eager on mine as I twist toward her, and she leans into me, angles across me; I scoop her up by the ass and lift her onto my lap. She whimpers as my erection glides against her seam, the shaft pressing lengthwise into the groove of her pussy.

I grind against her, and she whimpers, leans into me to rub herself on my cock. Fuck, she's eager.

"You didn't sleep when I did, did you?" I ask.

She shakes her head. "No," she huffs, and takes my

mouth again, grinds against me, gasping and shaking as my cock slides against her clit. "I lay awake as you slept, waiting for you to wake up so I could have you again."

"Jesus," I growl. "How the fuck are you real?"

She pulls back. "That is not the first time you have said that, Riley. Please explain." She moves against me. "Quickly. Or I shall have need of your mouth for other purposes again."

I laugh. "Don't threaten me with a good time."

She cups my jaw. "Why, Riley? Why do you keep asking if I am real? Do you not feel me?" She lifts my hand to her breast. "I am real."

I roll us to my back so she's straddling me, and I grip her hips, caress her ass, and then find her clit, flick it with my thumb, and circle it as I answer. "It's rhetorical. It means…" I pause, thinking. "It means you're too good to be true. You trust me. You love me. You…you heal me. You gave me the most precious gift I could ever receive."

"That being…oh, oh, oh god! That being what?"

"Your virginity. Your body. *You.*" I hold her gaze as I circle her clit, get her hips moving. "And yet, despite your innocence, you…you learn *really* fuckin' fast what you like. You're not afraid to take what you want and ask for what you need. You…" I pause, lift up to kiss her as she comes, softly quaking, gently gasping. "You show me how much you want me. You sucked me off the first time you touched me."

She rocks on her hands and knees above me, tits swaying as she shakes and shudders, and when she settles down from the peak, her eyes find mine. "Is that…oh god, is that unusual?"

"For me, yeah. I mean, I've never been with another virgin so I don't know about, like, *everybody.* I just…I didn't expect you to want to try that so soon. But you did, and you fuckin' rocked my *world*. Everything you do, you're amazing at it." I keep her coming, keep her rocking against my hand, and now I fit a finger inside her channel, and then two, still using my other hand on her clit. "I've never in my life felt so…so *wanted*. I've never felt as treasured as you make me feel. You make me feel like a god, Cadence. I could spend the rest of my life trying to deserve everything you are and never come close."

She wails breathlessly as she comes a third time, and fuck me, the girl has a hair trigger and a seemingly endless capacity for climax. Which, needless to say, is fucking hot. My cock is aching I'm so hard, yet all I want is her pleasure. I plunge my fingers inside her, curl them and fuck her with them as she rocks into my touch, her eyes squeezed shut as she gasps and shudders.

Her eyes fly open and meet mine. "Riley! Oh god, I'm— oh god! I feel like something is going to…like I have to—"

I slash my mouth across hers, whispering before I kiss her. "Let go, baby. Give it to me. Let me have it."

She shakes helplessly, rearing back as I work her pussy with both hands, relentlessly seeking her release.

"Oh…*FUCK*!" This is from Cadence.

She erupts, her curse drawn out into a whimper, and then a scream as she dissolves into full-body trembling, and her walls clench my fingers and she shakes and shakes and shakes, and then goes still, tensing…

A rush of wetness spurts out of her, dripping down my hand and wrist, coating my fingers and sluicing down to my elbow, and she screams out loud, rocking into my hand.

As she shudders through her climax, I slide my fingers out of her. She whimpers, fingers clawing into my chest as she braces on my body. "Rye—Riley! Oh my god oh my god, I—oh god, what did I—?"

I palm her ass, pull her up my body, pull her against me, nudge the tip of my cock against her seam. "You squirted, baby."

"I *peed*," she hisses. "I *peed* on you!"

I nip her earlobe. "You came so hard you squirted. It's not gross, it's hot as fuck." I guide one of her hands down to my shaft. "Feel how hard I am for you?"

She grips me, squeezes, caresses, groaning. "I need you, Riley. Please."

"So take me."

Her eyes fly open. "With me…up here?"

I grin. "Hell yes. Ride me, sweetheart. Take my cock and ride me."

Her eyes spark with frenzied arousal, and she bites her lip in anticipation, gripping my cock. She presses me to her entrance, slowly sliding me between her lips, feeding me inside her centimeter by centimeter, and her mouth drops open wider as I slowly fill her.

"Ohhhh…" she whimpers, as she settles her ass onto my thighs. "Oh…oh my *god*."

I cup her face and kiss her. "You're in control." I grab her ass and pry her cheeks apart and drive up deeper, getting a whimper out of her. "Feel me?"

She nods sloppily, rocking backward onto me, testing. "I feel you, Riley." Her eyes find mine. "So good. So, so, *so* fucking good. You feel *incredible* like this."

She lifts up, hovers, and then sinks down to take me in a single smooth, fast drop of her hips. And I'm now at a loss for words, overwrought and overcome at the feel of her bare around me. I thought she felt like heaven before, but *now*? Bare? Nothing between us? I feel each ripple of her pussy around me, the wetness of her need slick and hot.

"Love hearing you curse," I mutter. "Love hearing dirty words from those sweet, innocent lips."

"Not…so innocent…anymore…" she gasps.

Rocking against me, ass slapping against my thighs, she moans, drives harder onto me, taking me as deep as I can go, and then she rises, slips me almost out of her, hesitates, eyes on mine. "I like to watch," she whispers.

"Watch what?"

She braces on me with one hand, splays the fingers of her other hand around her pussy, and now as she impales herself on me, my cock slides between her fingers, and she's watching, rapt, aroused, as I slide inside her. "This." Again, a long slide up, pause, and then she sinks onto me. "Your big…hard…beautiful cock…"

I almost come, then. "*Jesus*, honey. So fucking hot."

She grins, bites her lip, cups my nape and bends over me, kisses me, and as my tongue sweeps her mouth, she sinks onto me again, ripping a hot groan from us both in unison. Again. Again. Faster, and faster.

She rocks on me, now, finds her rhythm. Her big, round, perfect tits sway and bounce with her movements, hypnotizing me, and I cup them, lift up and kiss them, palm one and find her clit with my other hand. When I find it and circle it, she shrieks, and I feel her spasm around me.

"Oh…*fuck*," I snarl as her pussy ripples around my cock. "Fuck!"

She's relentless and greedy, now, confident and proud. Her eyes stay on mine, flick down to our joining and then back to mine as she rides me, rocks on me, sinks down until I'm buried in her sweet pussy to the hilt, and she bounces on me like that, buried deep and rocking hard to take me deeper. I feel her spasms again, rippling around me, squeezing my cock until I can barely move inside her, she's so tight.

"Riley!" she cries. "I'm coming!"

She screams, and her movements become spastic and uncontrolled, sinking down on me and trying to get more of me, writhing on me, and then she screams again and hangs her head and braces her hands on my chest and rocks her hips with fast, relentless, sinuous, erotic need, fast and hard and wild, and she cries out in gasps and shrieks and screams as she comes around my cock.

Her mouth finds mine, shuddering. "Please, my love. Come with me. Come with me, Riley."

My body obeys her without hesitation, as if her words were a trigger. I wrap an arm around her shoulders and the other around her hips, pin her against me, flattened on me, and I take over, driving into her as hard as I can, fucking her as my orgasm blasts through me.

She cries out when she feels me cut loose, her eyes flying open wide to fix on mine as my cum floods through her in wave after wave, and she finds her rhythm again, moving with me as she screams through her ecstasy.

I've never felt this, either. The usual hot rush of climax is always good, but without a condom? Nothing between us? It's hotter than ever, wetter, more intense. I feel her rippling and clenching, feel her spasm with her own release, feel her juices mingle with mine, and we move together in perfect synchronicity, gasping in unison, chanting each other's names as a song.

We come together for an eternity.

When we finally descend from the peak, Cadence

collapses on me, panting. Draws her knees up and wriggles down to keep me buried inside her, still hard but slackening.

Our sweat mingles, our breath merges as she finds my mouth in a kiss soft and sweet and slow that my heart seems to shatter and break and swell all over again. "Fuck, I love you," I whisper against her lips. "I fucking love you, Cadence."

"I fucking love you too," she whispers, giggling. "I like saying bad words in bed with you."

"They're not bad words, they're just words," I tell her. "Someone else decided they're bad. I don't agree."

She blinks at this, frowning. "Oh. I…oh. "That is an interesting take." A long, thoughtful pause. "I approve."

I chuckle. "Well, that's a relief."

She goes serious. "I do not say this from a place of judgment, but I simply cannot fathom the notion of casual sex."

I look away from her, up at the ceiling. "I…I don't know how to explain it, babe. Now, having experienced *that* with you? I agree. But I…it's…" I sigh, shaking my head. "I dunno. Now that I'm with you, I don't even want to try to remember what it was like with anyone else."

She shakes her head. "Your body was *inside* mine, Riley. We are naked together. There is no greater vulnerability than this. I simply *could not* share it with anyone else. I could not have shared it with you at all if I did not love you. I just simply cannot understand having sex with someone you do not know and do not love. It does not compute in my brain."

My eyes burn. "I know. Believe me when I say that I fully understand what a precious gift you are, Cadence. What a precious gift you've given me in yourself."

This melts her. "Riley, my love. I do not think you

understand that I feel that *I* have been given a gift as well. You are a gift to me. You have shown me a whole new world. I know joy because of you. I know what it is to love and be loved. I know the freedom of trusting you."

"Freedom?" I echo.

"Yes," she says. "Certainly. Trust is freedom. True, real trust, like I share with you, means I am free to be absolutely and utterly myself. I am free to show you my worst self and know that I will be accepted anyway. I can be weak with you, when I have had to be strong for so long—because you know me and you accept me. I am not alone. I am seen." Her eyes water, spill. "That is a gift most precious indeed, Riley, and you have given it to me. So yes. I am free because you love me."

I blink back my own emotion. "Fuck, Cadie. You have a way of making me emotional like no one else."

She wriggles up my body, groaning and going still as she loses me. "Oh…oh, that is…oh *my*." she sounds unsure.

I chuckle. "What's up?"

She makes a face. "I am…um…leaking." She shakes her head. "Not important at the moment. Riley, you honor me with your emotions. I know you are not a man who displays such emotions easily. I am proud that you feel safe enough to give them to me."

Fuck, that guts me to the core. "I feel things I didn't know were in there. Things I didn't know I *could* feel."

"I know how that feels." She bites her lip. "I would really, really like to clean up, now."

"I've got you."

I roll so she's on her back and then pull away, get a fresh washcloth from the bathroom and wet it in warm water, bring it to her. "I, um…I've never done this part before."

She splays her thighs open, and I see my seed trickling down her seam. This makes me feel a bizarre range of emotions—pride for some stupid reason, arousal, and above all, possessiveness. I use as gentle a touch as I possibly can, swiping down her seam. I know she feels awkward, allowing me to do this—I see it in her eyes, on her face. But she lets me, watching me, blinking at me with wide eyes as I clean her folds.

When I'm done, I climb back in bed with her, pull her into my arms. "I'd like nothing more than to just stay in this bed with you for, like, at least a week."

She giggles. "I would like that as well. Although we may need snacks."

I cackle. "Yeah, snacks would be good."

She goes serious. "When I told you I was becoming hyperfixated, I was not joking, Riley." She looks up at me. "The intensity of my obsession with you is starting to worry me."

"Why would it worry you?"

"What if you get tired of me?" She bites her lip. "I am already thinking about you again. I want you again."

I boggle at her. "For real?"

She blushes. "Yes."

I laugh, pull her fully on top of me. "Sweetheart, that's the best news I've ever heard."

"Really? You…you aren't too tired?"

I flip her to her back and prowl above her. "Too tired? Babe, where you're concerned…" I slide down her body, kissing as I go. "I'll never, ever, fucking *ever* be too tired, or get tired of you."

She catches at me. "But I…you…won't you taste—?"

I swipe my tongue up her seam. "Yup."

"Is that not—?"

"Nope."

I look up at her. "Please consider this my formal invitation to attack me whenever you feel the desire. Use me, Cadence. Test me. See if can ever get enough of you."

"I am not sure you know what you're asking for, darling. Hyperfixation is no joke."

I grin. "I'm eager to find out, then."

She isn't fucking kidding.

Over the next seventy-two hours, we barely leave my bed. I bring food and we eat it in my bed together. Watch movies on my laptop. Sleep.

And make love…

Frantically.

I lose count of the number of times we have sex over those three days.

She is, quite literally, insatiable.

I've always had a sex drive so high that no one I've ever been with could keep up. I was always left wanting more and knowing that whoever I was with wasn't ready for me yet. I've literally had girls tap out and go home because I've left them—well, never mind.

Cadence?

By the end of three days of near-constant fucking, *I'm* the one worn out and barely able to walk. My balls are so drained they feel empty and shriveled.

It's glorious.

C⁀

We find a rhythm, then. I eventually have to go back to work, which sucks. But Cadence has to figure out her life and she says she needs time alone to do so, which means she encourages me to go back to work and leave her to think.

Which I do. And I discover aspects of joy in life that I didn't know existed. I see things that are beautiful and I FaceTime her just to share them. I have a spare moment or two and I call her just to talk. To hear her voice.

Within a week and a half, I come to the not exactly shocking conclusion that she is my best friend, even more so than my boys. I mean, it's different, but still. I get Fee and Bear, now. How they choose their women over the crew more often than not.

C⁀

It's less than two weeks to Christmas—a holiday I've never had a lot of time or patience for. Growing up, it was never a big deal. It's not like Mom ever put forth the effort to make it special. If we got gifts at all, it was shitty stuff— one year, I got a GI Joe, but a dollar-store knock-off version that broke that same day. So yeah, Christmas has always been whatever for me.

But I realize that to Cadence, Christmas is vitally important.

Her parents, she tells me, always made Christmas special, even in Africa where they didn't have the stuff to make it look like Christmas as we'd know it. To her, Christmas is the most important season of the year.

And fuck me if I know how to do that for her.

I figure a nice date downtown is a good place to start.

I find her on the phone when I come home from work, discussing with her folks the logistics of getting her stuff shipped up her. She greets me with a bright smile. "Hold on, please, Mother." She mutes the phone and kisses me, soft and sweet. "I missed you."

I pinch her chin playfully. "I'm gonna shower real quick. And then we're going on a date."

Her eyes go wide, big and bright. "A…date?"

I laugh at how eager and excited she sounds. "Yeah. I realized today that I'm a terrible, horrible, awful, shitty boyfriend. We've been together for almost a month, not including the time we spent together when we met, and I've never even taken you on a real date."

She shoots to her feet, vibrating with excitement. "A date! With my boyfriend!" She unmutes the phone. "Mother, I am afraid I must end the call. I am going on a *date*."

I hear her mom laughing happily on the other end, and wait as she says her goodbyes and ends the call.

"What should I wear?"

"Somethin' warm. I figured we'd walk around downtown. It's all lit up with Christmas lights. Looks pretty and, like, festive or whatever."

She's about to pop with excitement, bouncing on her feet and clapping her hands. "Is there a Santa Claus?"

I laugh, and kiss her. "Yes, there is."

"Caroling?" Her voice is up an entire octave.

I frown. "I, uhhhh…maybe?" I blink, thinking. "Yeah, come to think of it, I think there's a whole choir thing that happens."

"I have always wanted to go caroling. We were always in Africa during Christmas growing up, and then I was in college or working or overseas, so I have never gotten to do any of the usual Christmas things."

An idea forms—a crazy, wild, utterly batshit idea forms. I don't show it on my face, though. I kiss her again. "Get dressed in warm clothes. I'll be showered and changed in a few minutes, and we'll go, yeah?"

She hops up and down, clapping, laughing. "*YES!* I am so, *so, SO* excited!"

It's that easy to make her happy? Jesus, I'm lucky.

I shower in record time, not wanting to make her wait any longer than necessary. I do shoot off one quick text first, though. By the time I'm dressed in flannel-lined jeans, a thermal long-sleeve shirt, and my thick Carhartt jacket, she's ready to go, similarly clad—Noelle and Ember took her to the mall earlier in the week so she could get some better winter clothing.

I'm only a few blocks from downtown, so we cram winter hats on our heads, put on gloves, and walk.

It's after six, and dark, so the glow of downtown Three Rivers at night in Christmas is visible as we approach, a soft, warm sepia staining of the skyline. A gentle snowfall starts as we reach Main Street near the north end of town, the sky filling with small, hard, swirling flakes. The roads are freshly plowed, the sidewalks shoveled and salted. Most businesses are dark and shuttered, but a few are still open. The downtown development authority hires a company every year to drape the entirety of Main Street in white Christmas lights, decking the streetlights with holly and mistletoe.

As Cadence and I make the left turn onto Main Street, I hear Cadence's breath catch. She turns to face me, hands over her mouth, eyes wide. "It is glorious! Just like a Hallmark movie!"

I chuckle. "C'mon, let's head downtown, see what's what."

We stroll slowly, the cold winter air nipping our noses. Her eyes stay wide and awed, full of joy at the lights and the holly and the decorations. Small speakers hidden in the trees lining the sidewalk play traditional Christmas songs, and couples stroll together, just like us. A ten-foot-high mound of snow in the back of the municipal complex parking lot is swarmed with laughing, squealing children.

We wander to the far end of Main Street, cross, and head up the other way until we reach Benji's Cafe—it's a new place that popped up in the last six months, replacing an overpriced clothing boutique that went under. Benji's is a coffee shop during the day and serves beer and wine in the evenings, offering prepackaged salads and sandwiches and such during the day and limited made-to-order meals later in the day. It also offers free Wi-Fi and community workspaces.

I lead Cadence in and we order some drinks and a snack—light beer and hummus with pretzels, flatbread, carrot sticks, and celery slices.

We sip and eat and talk about nothing in particular.

Eventually, Cadence sets her pint glass down and gives me a look that says she has something to say. "I wanted to thank you, Riley."

I frown, shake my head. "For what?"

"Giving me the space I need, these last few weeks. It's no secret that I've struggled a bit since coming back, and I think if it wasn't for you, I would be in a much worse place, mentally and emotionally." She clears her throat; she's begun dropping the formality and archaic speech patterns with me more and more, but when nervous or upset, falls back into it. "Your love, patience, and support have been invaluable. I am not sure if you are aware, but I have been seeing a therapist via Zoom while you are at work. She has helped me process a lot of what I went through."

"You mentioned you were planning on it, but I'm glad you're getting that help, baby."

She hesitates. "I am faced with decisions, now, however. What do I want to do next? Where do I belong? I... my parents' home in Chicago has been my home, or at least my home base, my whole life. But I am increasingly dissatisfied with that arrangement."

My heart pounds. "I...um...what are you...?"

"I love being with you, Riley. But I feel like I am taking advantage of your generosity. I have lived with you for weeks now and contribute nothing."

"I...it's not generosity, Cadie. It's love. It's support. You went through hell, and if you need a few weeks or months to heal and figure out what you want in your life, I am absolutely fucking thrilled to be able to give you the time and space you need. I make more than enough money to take care of us."

She shrugs, shakes her head, eyes on the table instead of me. "I used all my savings to get to Sudan."

"That's okay."

She shakes her head again. "It's not." She sighs. "I feel dumb, I suppose. I went over there knowing it was dangerous, knowing that I would see and experience things that were...difficult. I just...I did not understand the scope of it. And now I feel adrift in my life because of my choices. I am relying on you and that does not sit well."

"You felt called, and you worked your ass off to answer that call, sweetheart. You sacrificed to help people. You should be proud of what you did. And yeah, you're gonna need therapy and such to help you process it all, and that's okay. You're not broken." I lean across the low table between our chairs. "I'm glad you're relying on me. I'm glad you're here. I'm glad I can take care of you. I *want* to. But I also get the need to work, to contribute. So I support whatever you need to do as your next step."

She swallows hard. "I think what I am really asking, Riley, is about us. If...if I am overstaying my welcome in your everyday life. You did not sign up to have me move in one day and never leave. We did not discuss it. You just... you showed up at the airport and brought me to your home and—" she trails off, sniffling. "I love you, and I know you love me. But is this...are we in a relationship? Am I what you want for your life?" She shakes her head again, tips it back and sniffles. "You bring me on a sweet, romantic, beautiful Christmas date, and this is my response? I am sorry, Riley. You deserve better."

I stand up and offer her my hand. "C'mon. Somethin' I wanna show you."

She takes my hand and lets me pull her to her feet. "Oh—okay."

I lead her back out in the sepia-and-gold lighting, "White Christmas" floating in the air, the strains of the song all tangled up with the swirling snow. There's a small courtyard, more of a tiny park, between the bookstore and the movie theater, and it's Three Rivers's Christmas hub. There's a twenty-foot-tall spruce tree garbed in lights and ornaments, with gift-wrapped boxes beneath it, and benches surrounding it. There's a tiny hut made to look like a gingerbread house with Santa Claus inside—a jovial, white-bearded local named Jimmy Kazinski—dandling kids on his lap and listening to requests and taking photos every night from Thanksgiving to the week of Christmas, from five to eight. Once his time slot is up, he rides away on a sleigh pulled by giant draft horses wearing fake reindeer antlers—weather permitting, obviously. It's a fun spectacle, and Cadence watches with obvious glee as kid after kid approaches Santa and climbs on his lap while Mom and Dad snap photos. And then he's trundling away through the snowfall, ho-ho-ho-ing out of sight…behind the municipal complex, but the kids don't need to know that.

Now comes the part I wanted her to see: a church choir from St. Michael's, dressed in red velvet robes and hats, carrying candles and singing "O Holy Night" as they fill the square. The candles flicker in the cold and the dark, and their harmonizing voices soar, and beside me, Cadence is quietly crying, squeezing my hand, alternating looking at me with that adoration I have a hard time feeling like I deserve, and watching the choir sing. They finish "O Holy Night" and start in on "Silent Night," and one by one, more voices join in as locals and tourists and shopkeepers and shoppers and diners fill the square until we're packed in shoulder to shoulder.

Cadence presses into me, rests her head on my shoulder, and we sing. I keep my voice low, because I've been told the sound of my singing is so offensive it's a violation of the Geneva Convention, but Cadence, at least, has a high, soft, lovely voice.

The choir leads us through a couple more songs, and then they file out. I feel a hand press something into mine—Felix, coming through with the request I texted him earlier.

Cadence doesn't see him, thank goodness—she's too fixated on the scene around us.

The square empties until she and I are the only ones left.

When silence reigns once more, Cadence turns to me. "Riley, that was—" she gasps, hands flying to cover her mouth.

My heart is crashing in my chest as I kneel in front of her. My mouth is dry, my stomach flip-flopping, my hands clammy as I clutch the small red velvet box—a family keepsake Felix has held onto for years.

"Riley?"

I've had this moment in the back of my mind since I saw her in that airport lounge, all but catatonic. I've put it aside. Tried to dismiss it as premature.

Too soon.

But it's all I can think of.

All I want.

Her.

Mine.

Forever.

And yet, now that the moment is here, the speech I've crafted in my brain is totally gone and my mouth is glued shut.

"I…"

21

Cadence

I AM FROZEN WITH SHOCK, AND NO SMALL AMOUNT of panic. I cannot breathe, cannot make my legs stop shaking, cannot make my mouth form sentences. Riley, for his part, looks like he is feeling nearly as panicked as I am. The box in his palm is a red velvet ring box, but it's old, the velvet worn by decades. From Main Street, I can barely make out Nat King Cole's voice. Snowflakes swirl thickly, now, settling on Riley's broad shoulders and clinging to his beard.a

His mouth opens and shuts, but no sound comes out; he clears his throat and tries again. "I…this is…shit. I'm already making a mess of this." He squeezes his eyes shut, inhales, holds it, exhales, and then looks up at me, opening the box; my heart skips not one but several beats.

"Cadence, I love you. I can honestly say I never thought I'd hear myself say those words. I avoided relationships because I…I've never felt like I'm worthy of being anyone's…anything. You showed me otherwise. You make me feel like…" his eyes water and he blinks hard, clears his throat again. "Like someone you're proud of being with."

"Because I am," I whisper. "I *am* proud to be with you, Riley."

"What you said back at Benji's? Baby, you're *home*." He licks his lips. "At least, that's what I want you to feel. You *can't* overstay your welcome because you're *home*— with me. I've never had a real girlfriend before. Not really. I just…" he squeezes his eyes shut. "Fuck, I'm really messing this up."

I shake my head, sniffling. "Not at all."

He laughs softly. "Feels like it. I had a speech, but it flew out of my head. I just…I love you. So fucking much I don't know what to do with it, sometimes. You've changed my life—you've changed *me*. I never want to go back because the months you were gone were the hardest of my life. I missed you so fucking bad, and…now you're here. And these last few weeks? You living with me? It's what I want out of life. I want *you*, Cadence."

He opens the box, and my heart stops completely for a brief, medically inadvisable moment. The ring is very old, and very simple. A gold band with a tiny round diamond solitaire. "This was my great-grandmother's, and then my grandmother's, and then my mother's. She…I guess she took it off and gave it back to Dad at some point—I don't know, to be honest. If she did, it's the one good thing the bitch ever did. I just know that after Dad had his heart attack, we found it in his stuff. I…I remember my grandmother wearing it. She told me once that it was meant for me to give to my wife someday. Why me and not Felix, I don't know and she wouldn't say but since I never intended to get married, I…" he halts, shakes his head. "I'm babbling, I'm so fucking nervous."

I cannot help but laugh a little. "Riley, my love—"

"Marry me, Cadence," he blurts, shoving the box up toward me. "Please. I love you. I want you in my life forever. Be mine. Be my wife. Be my forever."

The tears I've been fighting back tumble out as he utters the question I truly never thought I would ever hear. I can barely see through the haze of tears, and my heart is pounding, palpitating in my chest, and my hands shake and there is only one possible answer.

"Yes," I breathe, the word shaky, a nearly inaudible syllable. "*YES!*" Louder, then. "Yes, yes, yes!"

Riley surges to his feet, wraps his arms around me and swings me in circles, laughing. "Yes?" He sets me down and pulls the ring from the box. "I've got no clue if it'll fit or not." He stops, looks down at me. "You mean it?"

I laugh. "Do *you*?" I hold up my left hand, and he slides the ring on—it fits, which seems wildly improbable. "Riley, you really…you *really* want this? With *me*?"

He stares at my finger. "More than I've ever wanted anything, Cadie. It's all I've thought about since I saw you in the airport."

I frown at this. "Truly?"

He nods. "I saw you and I knew. I just…I knew I never wanted to be apart from you for that long again. I…while you were gone, I felt…incomplete. And these last few weeks with you, I've felt the opposite—like…like I finally have the thing I've been missing my whole life. You.

You, Cadence. You're what my life has always needed, I just…I didn't know it until I met you. Now I know, and I can't imagine a day without you."

"Oh, my Riley." I bury my face in his shirt between the edges of his jacket. "I never dared dream of a proposal, you know. I have long felt as if such things are for others, not me. But then you…you made me feel…I don't know. Not normal. I'll never be normal."

"And thank god for that."

I frown up at him. "You…you accept me as I am, and you have proven your love for me—not just in spite of all the strange and unusual and difficult things about me, but even *because* of them. You said I changed your life, and changed you—but Riley, you have done the same for me. I love you so, so much, and I never want to be apart from you, either."

"Good thing you're gettin' married, then, huh?" comes a voice from nearby—Nyx.

I turn, startled and see the whole gang of Riley's friends and family gathered in a huddle, watching; Noelle is snapping photos of us with an expensive camera.

Felix and Ember are arm in arm, with baby Ella bundled in a fluffy pink snow suit, only her nose and eyes showing. Bear towers behind Noelle, grinning at us. Cole in his Sheriff's uniform, a knit cap with the Sheriff logo on it on his head and a wistful look in his eyes. Nyx is beside Cole, wearing dirty gray mechanics coveralls, heavy boots, and a thick, battered Carhartt jacket, his head bare, snow dusting his black hair. The Cartwright sisters are there, too, along with Noelle's friend Raina.

I look at Riley. "Did you know they'd be here?"

He seems stunned, too. "No, no idea. The only person I told was Fee."

Felix is smirking. "Think *any of us* would miss this one, bro? You? Proposing? To a fuckin' hot ass doctor?"

Ember whacks his chest. "Felix Crowe!"

He rolls his eyes. "What? She's gorgeous. Way outta his league. I'm happy for his ass."

Nyx cackles. "Still time to run, Cadence! It's not too late!"

Ember and Noelle both give him a dirty look. "Don't listen to Nyx, honey-buns," Ember says. "He's an idiot."

They both come toward me and sweep me up in a three-way hug. Noelle peers at me, tearful. "The Three Rivers Girl gang just gained a member. You're one of us, now, girlie."

I look around at the gathered crew—friends, family... found family. "I have never belonged anywhere. Never belonged with or to anyone."

The Cartwrights and Raina gather around the three of us, and then suddenly I am being crushed as everyone surges in to join the hug.

"Alright, alright," Riley says, pushing everyone away. "Give the girl some space."

I shake my head. "No. I do not want space. I want this. I want *this* life. With you all." I look at Riley. "With you. Could we...do we have to wait a long time? To get married?"

He laughs, shakes his head. "What are you doing tomorrow?"

I sniffle. "Maybe not tomorrow."

He laughs again. "Teasin', babe. Although I would, if you said the word."

"Spring," I whisper. "In the cherry blossoms."

"Perfect."

Noelle takes my hands. "By the way, my older sister Natasha is a pediatric resident at the hospital."

"I see," I say, unsure where she is going with the statement.

"She told me the other day that the Emergency Department is severely short-staffed, and that the department chief is transferring downstate. So...you know, if you were to, say, submit your resumé, there's a pretty good chance you'd have your pick of positions."

My heart lifts higher than ever—I am soaring on the winds of joy so expansive and all-consuming I could fly away, and this only adds to it. "Truly?"

Noelle nods, smiling. "She also told me she spoke to the big dude in charge at the hospital and I guess he's looking to change things up, so an ER chief who's a little...out of the box, shall we say, might be exactly what he's looking for."

"A whole department?" I breathe. "I've barely dared dream of such a thing."

"I'm just passing along the info," Noelle says. "But I think you should apply. I'm being selfish, by the way. Since you showed up, Riley has been...a whole new man. When you were gone, he was miserable. Unbearable, almost. And since you've been back, he's been on cloud nine. We all love you for him. And we love you for you. We want you around. You're ours, now, sweetie."

Riley kisses my knuckles. "You're where you belong."

I sling my arms around his neck, gaze up at his face, bathed in the glow of the Christmas lights. His hands clutch my waist, and his smile is bright, contented, full of love as he stares down at me.

"*Now* I am where I belong," I say. "With you."

"Jesus fucking Christ, Riley, kiss the woman already!" Nyx shouts.

I laugh, but then the laughter is stolen as his mouth slants across mine, and I barely hear the wolf-whistles and the cheering from his—from *our*—friends and family.

When we part, I keep my hands tangled together behind his neck. "I am going to have to thank the Crenshaws for denying me that funding," I murmur. "They changed the course of my life in doing so."

"I'm gonna buy them the biggest fruit basket there is," he says. "Or maybe one of those giant wreaths."

I laugh. "I think a thank you would suffice."

Whatever response Riley was about to offer is lost when Nyx reappears from somewhere with two bottles of champagne and a stack of red plastic cups, and there's laughter as Nyx fires the cork at Riley, the two playfully wrestling and spilling champagne, until Ember snags the bottle from Nyx and starts pouring, and then somehow it's a party in the little square. Children appear from the street, and someone has a thermos of hot cocoa, and people I don't know are congratulating me. My plastic cup of champagne never seems to empty no matter how much I drink, and I find myself tipsy and clinging to Riley for balance.

Riley kisses me until I'm breathless, and now that everyone around us is occupied, no one notices. "You said yes," he whispers.

"I did say yes." I gaze up at him. "Did you fear I would not?"

He shrugs. "I…yeah, a little. I was scared out of my

mind. You're the most amazing woman I've ever known, and I just…fuck, I love you."

"Did you plan it?" I ask.

He tilts his head to the side in a noncommittal gesture. "I texted Fee before I jumped in the shower. He passed me the ring while the choir was singing. I had no idea he brought everyone." He hesitates. "I hadn't planned on it being a group thing."

I touch his lips. "They are your family. Your joy is theirs. And this is…" I look around. "The best day of my life. The best Christmas. I could not be happier, Riley."

"I just…when you asked if this was the life I wanted, with you, that clinched it, because I knew the answer and I couldn't wait another second to ask."

I lift on my toes and nuzzle his ear. "When can we go home and…celebrate?"

He grins, chuckles, dips to kiss me, and then murmurs in my ear. "Why, Cadence Creswell, are you propositioning me?"

"Yes I am, Riley Crowe of Three Rivers." I nip his earlobe. "I am excited to be Cadence Crowe, MD, wife of Riley Crowe. Your wife." I trace the shell of his ear with my tongue. "Take me home and make me yours, my love. Please?"

"As you wish," he murmurs.

We slip away, trudging through the snow-hushed streets. The glow of Three Rivers fades behind us into a dim yellow smear, the sounds of laughter and music distant now.

The lightness in my heart is here to stay, I think. Riley put it there. This place put it there. These people—his brother, his friends. His love. His acceptance of me exactly as I am—stimming, hyperfixations, strange habits, odd speech patterns, freezes, freak-outs, panic attacks, all of it. He just accepts me.

I always wondered how I would ever find someone to love all that I am. How I would find someone who could love me despite all that.

It turns out that I was thinking about it wrong. He doesn't love me *despite* my ASD—he loves me *because* of it.

It *is* me. It is not *all* that I am, but it is part of me. I need not change it, hide it, or think I need to be fixed.

It is a blessing so great I cannot express the joy it brings me.

We walk through the swirl of snow, and for the first time in my life, I indulge in something I never thought I'd get to do:

Daydream about my wedding day.

Epilogue

Lacey

W HAT AM I DOING? Why in God's name did I think coming back to Three Rivers was a good idea?

I sit in my car, everything I own packed into the seats. I'm parked downtown, on Main Street near the bookstore. The stores are draped in vertical strings of white lights from one end of the strip to the other, on both sides, with holly and mistletoe on the streetlamps and merry Christmas tunes playing from hidden speakers.

I hate Christmas. I used to love it, but Eddie ruined it for me. I'd spend literal weeks decking our house in the finest decorations. I spent thousands of dollars and hundreds of hours. I handmade wreaths from live holly branches, complete with battery-operated light strings. I could have sold them on Etsy for a fortune. I handmade garland. I put up trees in every room of that fucking mansion and decorated each one to a room-specific theme. I bought festive candles. Little scenes with hat-clad penguins that danced and sang Jingle Bells. Pillows. Blankets. It was never enough. Never good enough.

I threw epic holiday parties for his fancy-ass friends. As in live bands, catering, full bar with bartenders, and cocktail waitresses. I flirted with his asshole boss and dealt with the bastard's fat, sweaty, wandering hands.

I was faithful.

I even sucked him off regularly, on top of regular sex, just to try and keep him happy.

I cooked. I cleaned. I gave up my *career* for the fuck-ing *bastard*.

I gingerly touch the black eye that is my Christmas present. That and the string of sexts I found on his iPad between him and his PA. Who, by the way, is nineteen. Eddie is forty-fucking-seven.

I didn't go snooping, by the way. He left it unlocked and open while he answered a phone call from his boss—oops. I didn't go looking. I just happened to be wiping the counter when a message popped up. *DING*! The no-tification slid down from the top of the screen, showing a thumbnail of a photograph.

Of a teenager—a literal *child*. Legal? I suppose, tech-nically. But it's vile, if you ask me.

She was topless. Pinching her silly little child's nip-ples with a vapid, open-mouthed expression which I as-sume was meant to be, like, saucy, or erotic or something. She just looked dumb. Wrong number, maybe? Nope. She followed it with a long message detailing all the things she wanted to do to him. Lots of typos and grammatical errors. No punctuation. Used his name a few times. No question it was for him.

Eddie is a silver fox, it's true. Damn good looking. But he's *almost fifty*. Why would a hot, nubile nineteen-year-old want his old ass? He's thirty years older than her, for fucks sake.

Money? Is that really all it is?

I did a reverse image search and found her socials. She's all over IG, obviously. And wouldn't you know it? She got hired four months ago. I remember him telling me about it. Well, four months ago, her feed started to reveal fancy new things. New athleisure clothing. A new Coach purse. New Louboutins. Diamond-dripping tennis brace-lets and sapphire pendant necklaces.

And about four months ago, Eddie started acting... less interested in me.

I tried harder.

Bought lingerie. Seduced him. Surprised him with lunch dates to his favorite place in Detroit.

So when I saw the proof, I went a little crazy. Sue me. I'm a hot-tempered woman; he knows this.

I yelled, I screamed, I called him names. Dialed up my friend Susan, a man-eating divorce lawyer who would, in another time period, be the type to wear men's testicles as trophies. I told her, in front of him, that I wanted her to draw up divorce papers.

He slapped me.

I grew up watching my dad hit my mom. He never hit me, but I swore to myself that I would never, fucking *ever* allow that to happen to me.

I waited until he left for work this morning, packed

my shit, left the signed divorce papers on his desk at home, and took off.

I left my cell phone.

I left my rings—not the jewelry he bought me as apologies for forgetting anniversaries and birthdays; that stuff I took with me because fuck being broke.

And now, here I am, back in Three fucking Rivers.

Why?

What's here for me?

Mom and Dad are gone, living in a retirement community down in Palm Beach. I know no one here, anymore.

Yet this is where I came.

I just don't know what to do next.

I need to eat. I need to stretch my legs—I ran into seriously bad traffic on the way up, and the four-hour drive turned into six.

My bladder is on fire and I'm so hungry I could eat a horse.

I spy a cute little coffee shop across the street—Benji's. As I watch and contemplate getting out and going in, a tall, black-haired figure steps out, followed by a smaller individual with curly reddish-blond hair.

My attention is on the man, though. He looks familiar in silhouette. He turns, and I'm stunned—it's Riley Crowe. Good god, he got hotter. Look at those cheekbones! Like every girl in Three Rivers, I had a crush on him at one point, and then on Felix. But it was Cole Mannix who ended up stealing my heart.

Fuck. No, no, no.

Not going there.

Not thinking about *him*—about *that*.

I realize my hand has gone to my belly, and I snatch it away as if burned.

My eyes prickle.

Dammit, dammit, dammit.

I fight the prickles for a while, the tight throat, the ache of memory.

I should have told him.

He deserves to know.

I just…I *couldn't* tell him, back then. I didn't know how.

And then a month passed, and then a year, and then five, and then a decade and I was a wife and a business owner, and it was painful history.

I hear singing—"O Holy Night." The St. Michael's choir files out of the church, carrying those candles with the little paper discs, singing in angelic harmony.

God, it's beautiful.

I can't seem to stop my feet from carrying me out of my car and into the cold. Snow stings my nose, cold nips my ears. I fish my wool hat out of my coat and put it on, and then my matching mittens. Hood up, face hidden. I stay back as a crowd gathers, singing.

My heart wants to lift at the bucolic, cozy, Hallmark-worthy scene. If only I didn't have Eddie's voice in my ear, bitching and complaining and criticizing.

I press up against the side of the cinema's brick wall as the crowd files away once the choir is done with their performance.

I'm about to walk away and find something to eat and a bathroom when I see Riley and his girlfriend still in the square, huddled close. I have to muffle a gasp when he goes to his knee. Good for him, truly. I heard what happened all those years ago, and while I've avoided any information about you-know-who, I've kept tabs on the Crowe brothers. I know Felix got married and has a baby, now, but I'd thought Riley would be a lifelong bachelor.

The woman claps her hands to her mouth as he makes a pretty long-winded proposal. She accepts, and god, they look happy.

I thought that was gonna be me. Eddie swept me off my feet. He was wealthy, successful, handsome. Funny. He seemed to like me. And then love me. I had no reservations about accepting his proposal, which was on a boat on the Detroit River as part of a Valentine's Day date. Yeah, should've seen the truth then. Didn't see the warning signs—how he treated servers or anyone he thought was beneath him…which, spoiler alert, is everyone. The way he spoke to his mother—rude, often mean. I didn't see the possessiveness as a problem until I realized he was tracking my movements with spyware. I didn't see the way he'd hide his phone whenever I was around as a problem until I realized why—that he was a serial cheater.

Yeah, I knew he was cheating on me. It was the fact that his latest side piece was fucking *nineteen* that was the last straw.

That, and the slap.

No sir.

You only hit *this* bitch once.

I watch the happy couple whisper and kiss and cry together. Oh, god. Fuck me, so sappy. He's crying?

Deep down, though, I admire that.

Up top, it's easier to let myself feel bitchy and cynical, because I'm angry at him and myself and the whole world, and I feel like a fool.

And then there's a crowd of people I recognize—
the Cartwright twins, who have aged very, very well, indeed. Cody Nyx, the silly fuck, who doesn't seem to have
changed a bit. A giant red-haired guy I don't know with
Noelle…something—I didn't know her well—who seems
to be with the ginger giant. A blond woman who must be
Felix's wife, since Felix is behind her with his hands on
her hips. There's another woman who I don't know, too.

And *him*.

Cole Mannix.

All six feet two inches of him, in a Sheriff's uniform,
wearing a knit cap.

My heart stops.

Cole.

My Cole.

I whimper as my heart drops out of my chest. I can't
be here. I can't be near him. I can't see him. And god fucking forbid he sees me.

I whirl and flee—or at least, that's the intent.

Instead, I slip on a patch of ice hidden under a layer
of snow and face-plant.

Nose? Definitely broken.

I groan and push to my knees—which are bruised and
aching and now getting wet as I kneel in the snow.

"Fuck me," I mutter. "Fuck my *entire* life."

Eddie hates my cursing. It's not 'demure,'" he says.
Yeah. Demure and mindful I am not—ha fucking-ha.

Fuck you, Eddie.

I try to get to my feet, but I slip again, and I would
hit the ground again if not for a strong, hard hand steadying me.

"Hey, whoa. You okay, ma'am?"

No, no, no, no, no, no, no.

His voice is *not* gravelly and rough and deep like that. Not warm and concerned and friendly.

"Yeah," I rasp, my voice hoarse and tight. "All good. Thanks." I keep my hood up and turn away from him.

His hand is bare, despite the cold. He has my arm. "You took a pretty bad spill, there. Sure, you're not hurt?"

My nose is sluicing blood all down my mouth, chin, neck, and chest. "Yup. I'm good."

He hears the lie, though. He always could. "Hey, you're bleeding. Ma'am, let me help you, please."

"I don't need your goddamned *help*, Cole!" I snap, yanking my arm out of his grip.

And then I realize what I'd just said.

His name. Out loud.

Fuck me.

The silence is thick and freighted. "How…how do you know my name?" He knows. I can hear it.

He moves around in front of me, and suddenly I'm face-to-face with Cole Mannix again for the first time in fifteen years.

He's more handsome than ever. His face is lined, weathered, and hard-bitten. Rugged. He's got a beard, short and thick and neatly-trimmed. His eyes are as liquid brown as ever, and so deep, so expressive. The kind of eyes you get lost in. He's got a new scar bisecting his left eyebrow. His mouth is…

Jesus, that mouth.

The things he could do with it, my god. I've dreamed of those lips off and on my whole life.

The patch on his jacket and the gold star say he's not just another deputy, he's the big deal himself. Figures. He always said he'd be sheriff one day, just like his dad, God rest the old man.

"L-Lay…" he blinks, swallows hard, stumbles back a step, literally staggering in shock. "Lacey?" his voice is utterly stunned.

I sigh, ignoring the blood still bathing my front. "Hello, Cole."

ALSO BY
Jasinda Wilder

Visit me at my website: **www.jasindawilder.com**
Email me: **jasindawilder@gmail.com**

If you enjoyed this book, you can help others enjoy it as well by recommending it to friends and family, or by mentioning it in reading and discussion groups and online forums. You can also review it on the site from which you purchased it. But, whether you recommend it to anyone else or not, thank you *so much* for taking the time to read my book! Your support means the world to me!

My other titles:

Forbidden Fruit

Wild Ride: Biker Billionaire

Delilah's Diary

Big Girls Do It:
Big Girls Do It
Married
On Christmas
Pregnant
Rock Stars Do It
Big Love Abroad

The Falling Series:
Falling Into You
Falling Into Us
Falling Under
Falling Away
Falling for Colton

The Ever Trilogy:
Forever & Always
After Forever
Saving Forever

From the world of *Wounded:*
Wounded
Captured

From the world of *Stripped:*
Stripped
Trashed

From the world of *Alpha:*
Alpha
Beta
Omega
Harris
Thresh
Duke
Puck
Lear
Anselm
Sigma
Gamma
Delta

The Houri Legends:
Jack and Djinn
Djinn and Tonic

The Madame X Series:
Madame X
Exposed
Exiled

The Black Room (With Jade London)

The One Series
The Long Way Home
Where the Heart Is
There's No Place Like Home

Badd Brothers:
*Badd Motherf*cker*
Badd Ass
Badd to the Bone
Good Girl Gone Badd
Badd Luck
Badd Mojo
Big Badd Wolf
Badd Boy
Badd Kitty
Badd Business
Badd Medicine
Badd Daddy
For a Goode Time Call…
Not So Goode
Goode To Be Bad

A Real Goode Time
Goode Vibrations
A Very Badd Christmas
Badd Apple
Badd Baby

Dad Bod Contracting:
Hammered
Drilled
Nailed
Screwed

Fifty States of Love:
Pregnant in Pennsylvania
Cowboy in Colorado
Married in Michigan
Christmas in Connecticut

Billionaire Baby Club:
Lizzy Goes Brains Over Braun
Autumn Rolls a Seven
Laurel's Bright Idea

Club Sin:
Rev
Kane
Chance
Silas
Saxon
Solomon
Lash
Inez

Blood Heir
Blood Heir
Blood Rising
Blood Bonds
Blood Reign

Three Rivers:
Into the Light
Light in the Dark

The Cabin:
The Cabin
Christmas at the Cabin

Standalone titles:
Yours
The Parent Trap
Wish Upon A Star
Big Hose

Non-Fiction titles:
You Can Do It
You Can Do It: Strength
You Can Do It: Fasting

Jack Wilder Titles:
The Missionary

JJ Wilder Titles:
Ark

To be informed of new releases, special offers, and other Jasinda news, sign up for Jasinda's email newsletter.